The Secrets of

Hickory Hill

John Anthony Miller

his chin.

Dr. Jones frowned. "Some sort of heart failure, perhaps."

Burton eyed a glass that lay on the floor, a puddle of whiskey beside it. He examined it briefly, withdrawing a white handkerchief from his pocket. He dabbed the edge of the puddle and lifted the cloth to his nose, sniffing for a scent he didn't detect. "You don't think he was poisoned, do you?"

Jones shrugged. "I suppose it's possible. I'll conduct some tests and make a determination."

"Poison would suggest murder," Burton offered, glancing at Naomi Jackson.

"He wasn't murdered," she replied a bit too quickly. "No one came in the house."

"No one that you heard," Burton said delicately, perhaps implying more.

"His death should be investigated," Dr. Jones said. "Regardless of the cause."

Inspector Burton glanced at the corpse. "How old was your husband, Mrs. Jackson?"

Naomi wiped her eyes with a lace handkerchief. "He's thirty-nine, Inspector."

Burton turned to the doctor. "Quite young for heart failure, isn't it?"

Jones nodded. "Yes, it is. Although his size could have contributed." He knelt, collecting the puddled whiskey on the floor with a business card, directing it into the glass. "I'm not familiar with his health."

"He had no ailment or illness," Naomi offered.

Burton eyed her closely, lips pursed. "How old are you, Mrs. Jackson, if I may ask?"

"Almost twenty," she replied.

"Quite a bit younger than your husband," he noted, sharing a guarded glance with the doctor.

She nodded as a faint smile poked through tears. "A

perfect match nonetheless, Inspector. I've never regretted a minute."

Burton looked at her curiously. "What was the attraction, Mrs. Jackson?"

Naomi wiped away more tears. "He had so many good qualities," she said, her voice distant, as if recalling a world that no longer existed. "He was persuasive—could charm the devil himself." She paused, chuckling softly. "And he certainly charmed me. He was the most successful man in St. Lucia, if not the whole Caribbean. When he decided to marry, eligible women from around the world waited in line—all social classes and walks of life."

"Yet he chose you," Burton said.

She nodded. "Yes, he did. Only God knows why, I suppose."

"Were you aware of his financial difficulties?" Burton asked softly. "Potential bankruptcy?"

"He mentioned some challenges. But it wasn't the first time. He always found solutions."

Burton eyed her cautiously as if hesitant to speak. "I'm sure you've heard rumors," he said delicately. "About other women."

She shrugged. "I hear rumors all the time. But that's all they are—rumors."

Burton eyed the corpse, his thoughts fixed on a potential cause of death. "Was his financial situation dire enough to warrant drastic action?"

It took Naomi a moment to understand the question, but when she did, she moved her hand to her mouth. "Oh, Inspector, I would hate to think so. He was such a strong man."

"Strong men take their own lives, too," Dr. Jones muttered as he dripped whiskey from the glass into a vial with a cork stopper. He looked up at Burton when he'd finished. "I should have test results by morning."

Burton took a thin blanket from the back of a sofa

and draped it over the corpse. "The mortician arrives tomorrow."

Naomi stood, not sure what to do. She stared at them as they studied her, and then shifted her gaze to her husband's body. She closed her eyes, trying to will the image away.

"Come along, Mrs. Jackson," Dr. Jones said softly, lightly taking her arm.

They left the study and entered the foyer, Burton closing the door behind them. "Try to get some rest," he said. "We'll return with the mortician."

"Can I get you anything before I go?" Dr. Jones asked.

She numbly shook her head. "No, thank you, Doctor."

Burton opened the front door but then paused. "Mrs. Jackson, please don't go anywhere," he said gently. "I'll want to talk to you again in the morning."

"Yes, of course," she said, her face pale, her eyes glassy.

She stood by the door while they climbed into a waiting carriage. A moment later, the driver urged the horses forward, and they trotted down the cobblestone lane that led down a hill to the town of Soufriere.

Naomi waited, listening as the horse's hooves grow fainter, the carriage fading in the moonlight. After several minutes of silence, she walked out to the lane and peered down the hill. The street was deserted, bathed in darkness.

She went back inside, closed the door, and locked it. "Phoebe," she called.

A black woman came into the foyer, slight but strong. Only a year older than her mistress, Rufus Jackson had bought her a few years before. She had come cheap. Claiming her mother was a voodoo queen, she had threatened her owner with a hideous spell. He was anxious to get rid of her, no matter the price. But most laughed when they heard the story, suspecting she was harmless and her owner was a fool.

"Yes, ma'am?" she asked.

"It's time," Naomi said. "Take the luggage down to the dock."

"Right away, ma'am." Phoebe started for the stairs but paused, turning to her mistress. "Did it work as planned?"

Naomi smiled faintly. "It worked perfectly. You were marvelous."

Phoebe chuckled. "I knew it would. Some plants kill anything."

"He never guessed his fate, I'm sure," Naomi said as she entered the study.

She paused at a bookshelf, opening the cabinet doors at the bottom. Removing a sturdy leather satchel, she crossed the room, stepping over her husband's body, to the wall behind his desk. A landscape of Soufriere harbor hung between two bookshelves, tall ships sailing the seas. She grabbed the left side of the frame and tugged. It opened, hinged on the right, exposing a wall safe. Delicately she dialed the combination.

Tucked inside were stacks of American currency in high denominations and leather pouches filled with silver and gold. She transferred the safe's contents to the satchel, taking all of the money her husband had hidden. When the safe was empty, she closed it, and returned the painting to its original position.

Naomi hurried out the back door. Stone steps carved in the hill led to a secluded cove away from the road. A dock jutted from shore, a small boat at the end bobbing in the waves. As she walked down the wooden wharf, she glanced over her shoulder. No one followed.

Phoebe waited by the boat. "We all ready, ma'am. Our bags are on the boat."

A man emerged from the shadows, a boy about

twelve with russet hair beside him. "I'll take that for you, ma'am," he said, reaching for her satchel.

"No, it's all right," Naomi said, pulling it away. "I'll keep it with me."

"Of course, ma'am," the man said, taking her elbow as she climbed aboard. "A clipper waits in the channel. We'll be there in a few minutes."

"Where's our destination?" Naomi asked.

"Baltimore, Maryland," he replied. "Is that acceptable?"

Naomi didn't know much about Maryland. But she knew it was far away from St. Lucia. "Yes, that works perfectly," she said. She paused, her gaze fixed on his, and handed him a few gold coins. "No one must ever know where I went."

He eyed the money, more than he made in months. "Yes, ma'am. You can trust me. I promise."

Minutes later the boat left the cove.

Chapter One

Twenty-five years later, May 25, 1857

Hickory Hill Plantation on Maryland's Eastern Shore

Hickory Hill seemed like it sat at the end of the world. A four-thousand-acre plantation owned by Gideon Banks, it sprawled along the Chesapeake, tucked between coves, and wandered inland. Founded a hundred years before, it was serviced by eighty slaves, eight of whom acted as household servants. A three-story mansion sat by the water, broad balconies wrapping each elevation, tall windows stealing breezes to cool rooms of wealth and grandeur. Hidden between groves of trees, it rivaled Europe's finest estates and offered a peek at the world of a privileged few. It would never be known to the masses, those who worked from dawn to dusk, toiling to put food on the table, seeking shelter from the storm.

Naomi Banks, nee Jackson, admired a lavender dress crafted by her seamstress, an older slave named Venus. She laid it over a bedroom chair, fingering the lace around the neck, marveling at the artistry. She was interrupted by a knock on the door.

"Mr. Banks asked to see you, Miz Naomi," Phoebe said, looking in. She had been with her mistress since St. Lucia. More than master and slave, they were friends and confidants—at least in private. They shared secrets, the sting of failure and joy of success, birthed babies—

although Phoebe's two sons had died young—and together had gradually begun to grow old.

Naomi cast one last glance at the dress. "Do you know what he wants?"

Phoebe shook her head. "He didn't say much. But he's waiting in his study."

Naomi went down a sweeping staircase that spilled into the foyer and through the hall to her husband's study. She had met Gideon Banks in Baltimore shortly after her departure from St. Lucia. A wealthy widow in search of a suitable husband, Gideon had captured her heart—witty, handsome, and the owner of Hickory Hill. They had married three months later.

She knocked on the paneled door.

"Come in," her husband called.

He sat at his desk, turned to a chessboard on a table behind him. Tall and slender, his black hair showing signs of gray, his blue eyes were as bright as the day she first saw them.

"Phoebe said you wanted to see me," she said, sitting in front of the desk. The room fit a man's taste—dark green with walnut molding. Windows flanked the desk, bookcases lined the far wall. Two plush chairs, an oval table between them, sat in front of a marble fireplace, a portrait of Naomi hanging above it.

"I did," he mumbled, referencing a paper on his desk and glancing back to the chessboard.

She leaned closer, looking at the letter. "From Benjamin?" she asked, referring to their son. A West Point graduate, he was now a captain stationed in New Orleans. They also had two daughters: Emma, married to a New York City financier, and Annabelle, still at the plantation, a replica of her mother with a mind no one could change.

"Yes." he muttered as he wrote down his chess move. "I think he has me cornered. I do enjoy these long-distance matches, although I'd prefer to play in person. I'm hoping he's transferred closer. He writes that it does look promising."

"I'll temper my excitement until we know for sure."

Gideon looked up from his desk. "You've yet to meet the new overseer,"

"Not by intention, I assure you," she said. "Although I suspect Jack Dunn will be difficult to replace."

Gideon nodded. "He was a good man who managed Hickory Hill for fifty years, God rest his soul." He paused, reflecting. "But I think you'll like the man I hired."

"Our paths will cross, I'm sure," she said, not caring much for work in the fields.

"He thinks you're avoiding him," he teased.

She laughed lightly. "I don't even know who he is. How can I avoid him?"

Gideon glanced at his pocket watch. "I asked him to come by. If you wait a few minutes, I'll introduce you."

"Where did you find him?"

"At a slave auction in Annapolis. At the time, he was working in Virginia."

She cocked her head. "Why would he come here if he already had employment?"

Gideon shrugged. "I'm not sure. I told him about Hickory Hill and all we had built together. He seemed impressed."

Naomi pursed her lips. "I hope you didn't tell our life story to a stranger."

"No, of course not," he said, but chuckled. "Maybe the highlights—how we met, expanding the plantation over the years."

Naomi was leery. "Why come here sight unseen, even if he was dissatisfied where he was?"

"More acreage, more money, I suppose. He's ambitious—like anyone else."

She sighed, still not convinced. "Did he have references?"

Gideon hesitated. "I didn't ask. It seemed a delicate situation, leaving his prior employer with little notice."

Naomi sat back in the chair, briefly distracted by a bird fluttering past the window.

"He is highly qualified," Gideon continued, as if he needed to defend an impulsive decision. "He worked a sugar plantation before coming to Virginia."

"Seems a good fit," she muttered, no longer caring. "But I would have preferred references."

"A man at the auction claimed he's loyal and hard-working."

They were interrupted by a knock on the door.

"Yes?" Gideon called.

The door opened and a stately black servant named Caesar entered. More educated than other slaves, he wore black trousers and coat with a white ruffled shirt. Tall and dignified, he took a single step into the room, nodding respectfully. "Mr. Payne wishes to see you, sir."

"Send him in," Gideon replied.

A man came in from the hallway, a broad-brimmed hat in his hands. He wore boots and brown trousers, his white shirt unbuttoned at the neck. Devilishly handsome with an impish grin that stole women's hearts, his russet hair was a bit too long, his blue eyes bright and twinkling. "You wanted to see me, sir?"

"Yes, I did," Gideon said. "Zeb Payne, I want you to meet my wife, Naomi."

Zeb's eyes widened, a flash of recognition crossing his face.

Naomi gasped. Had a ghost from her past come back to haunt her?

Chapter Two

An eerie stillness stole the day as swollen clouds consumed the heavens, pregnant with moisture to bathe the bay. Lightning snapped, golden snakes whipping across the sky. The Chesapeake, fed by rivers, streams, and creeks that cut wrinkles in the landscape, surged from the wind, white waves kicking the shore and splashing wooden wharfs. Much rain had already fallen, with a promise for more, drenching tobacco, corn, and wheat fields sprawling in the distance and turning the road into mud.

Annabelle Banks studied the lane by the bay, wind blowing her blonde hair about her face. Youngest of Naomi's children, she was attractive, slender with blue eyes, an exact replica of her mother.

"Should I walk back?" she asked her coachman.

"No, ma'am," he replied. He examined the carriage wheel mired in mud. "I'll get her out. It'll just take a minute."

Annabelle warily eyed the sky. The rain would come—in minutes maybe, not much more, unless the wind blew the storm out to sea before it spilled on land. She stepped away, sparing her shoes and hem of her dress from the mud. The road was rimmed with reeds, the bay just beyond in the distance.

The coachman grunted, quietly cursed, breaking branches and gathering reeds. He shoved them under the wheel for traction so the horse could pull it free. Annabelle walked a few feet farther where the reeds were not as high.

Seventeen shacks sprawled across a clearing. Carelessly constructed, some crooked and leaning, most were built of planks, gaps between them inviting the wind to wander inside. Weathered front porches held benches and chairs, a few dolls, balls and children's toys. Brick chimneys poked through rippling roofs, mortar cracked and crumbling. Home to the plantation's slaves, they now were empty, all hands working in the fields—at least until the storm arrived.

The closest hut trembled with each gust of wind, the windows gently rattling. Gaps between planks were plugged with mud, paper or branches from pine trees—anything to block the wind. The cedar roof was patched with pitch, rotting shingles sealed to last a few years more. A hint of smoke drifted from the chimney, the fire only embers while the occupants worked the fields.

The shacks were wrapped in groves of trees, screened from the rest of the plantation. Annabelle had passed them many times, visited when babies were born, played with children, attended weddings and funerals—a graveyard off in the distance, wooden crosses marking homes of the dead. But now as she studied them, she realized she had never really seen them at all. Not like she did today, cold and empty like the lives they contained. She eyed the tiny village, wondering what it was like to work the fields from dawn to dusk. Sunday was their only day of rest, when the adults gathered on weathered porches and children played in the clearing. From the main house, she could sometimes hear their music, improvised and emotional, so different than the structured sonatas she meticulously played on piano. And in that instant, spurred by this memory, she saw the life they lived, the people they loved, the dreams they shared.

The front door to the nearest shack abruptly swung open. Zeb Payne, the new overseer, stepped out, putting a wide-brimmed hat on his head. With barely a glance in any direction, not seeming to care who might be watching, he hurried to a horse hitched at the edge of the trees.

Annabelle cocked her head, intrigued. The slaves were spread throughout the fields, watching the approaching storm. Why had Payne been in a slave's shanty?

"Almost through here, Miss Annabelle," the coachman called.

She turned, eyeing his progress. Branches and reeds had stiffened the mud. The horse had almost yanked the carriage free.

"Wait there, ma'am," he said. "I'll bring the carriage to you."

She nodded but didn't reply. She looked back at the shack, now a mystery that had to be solved. The door again swung open.

A female slave named Coffey Green walked out. Petite and quiet, her skin a flawless mocha, she had been bought at auction when only a child. Barely twenty, she lived with another slave named Molly and her two daughters, sometimes joined by Phoebe Yates.

Coffey turned, her angry eyes speaking shame and desperation, a private moment not meant to be shared. Her gaze met Annabelle's, and the two merged in mutual understanding as a sordid secret collided with an unexpected revelation.

Chapter Three

Coffey Green stared back at Annabelle Banks. An awkward moment passed, neither flinching, as they subtly acknowledged a wrong that couldn't be righted.

"Come along, Miss Annabelle," the coachman called as the carriage moved forward.

Coffey and Annabelle remained transfixed as their wordless communication continued. A stray tear dripped down Coffey's cheek. She quickly wiped it away. Compassion was etched on Anabelle's face, mirrored in her eyes. Each showed a helpless desperation but for different reasons. Neither moved, neither averted her gaze, and as seconds passed Coffey saw an Annabelle she had never seen before. Not a mistress to be obeyed, but a woman with a heart who sometimes couldn't show it. She also realized that Annabelle understood her desperation, how her days were defined. Both of their worlds had changed in just a matter of seconds.

The coachman braked and climbed down from the driver's seat. He opened the carriage door and waited, standing erect and proper. A moment passed.

"Miss Annabelle?" he asked, looking at her curiously.

The women stared a moment more. Coffey nodded subtly, grateful for words that hadn't been spoken, revelations that weren't revealed.

Annabelle nodded, too—a sign she understood. She turned abruptly and climbed in the carriage. The coachman closed the door and got back in his seat, released the wooden handle that served as a brake, and scooted the horse forward.

Coffey watched the carriage pull away. Just as she stepped off the porch, Annabelle lowered the window. She leaned out, looking back.

When she was sure Coffey was watching, she waved. "Goodbye, Coffey."

Coffey forced a faint smile. "Thank you, Miss Annabelle," she said, waving to a friend who had appeared when she'd needed one most. "You take care."

She had known Anabelle for ten years, ever since Gideon Banks bought her at a Baltimore auction. Coffey's family had been sold individually, yanked from each other's arms amid screams and tears, their pleas to stay together ignored by all. She had been stranded, a ten-year-old girl alone, her loved ones sold first and gone forever. Her chest had heaved as she'd sobbed, her heart had raced, her eyes wide with fear of the unknown. She had been terrified. How would she eat, find shelter, stay warm? But Gideon Banks had watched, compassion etched on his face. He had offered the winning bid, took her home, and she had been at Hickory Hill ever since.

It had been hard to lose her loved ones, even harder to survive in a world so unfair, especially for people like her. But she had been fortunate, finding a flower among thorns, an angel in a hell she hadn't created. Phoebe Yates took her in as soon as she'd arrived, acting as the mother she no longer had. It had been good for both of them; they each had lost loved ones—Phoebe to death, Coffey to an evil that much of the world condoned. As the years passed, she'd taught Coffey all she knew about people, the plantation and plants—those that healed and those that harmed. Phoebe became Coffey's mentor and closest friend, and she would always be grateful.

Coffey watched the carriage fade in the distance. Black clouds still hung on the horizon, thunder rumbling across the sky. Zeb Payne had gone, telling her to tend the vegetable garden near the kitchen. The others would come back in the wagons they had taken to the fields that morning.

She walked toward the garden tucked behind the outdoor kitchen and smokehouse, just beyond the trees. She doubted Annabelle Banks would do anything about what she had seen. She would be forced to ignore it, regardless of any compassion housed in her heart. Coffey understood why. Who would ever believe her? And who would care if they did? It wasn't just and it never would be. But that was the world they lived in. What made Annabelle Banks mistress of the manor and Coffey Green a poor soul whom everyone assumed had no feelings, intelligence, hopes, or dreams? Someday it would change. It had to. Not today or tomorrow, or next week or next month, but eventually it would. Wrongs had to be righted. A merciful Lord said they did. She just had to be patient.

Zeb Payne was a bad man, the devil's seed. Every inch of his frame was drenched in a wicked stench; those who were good and just could smell it. His warm smile and bright eyes hid the savage that lived inside; those who were good and just could see it. The words he spoke, slick and beguiling, masked insults thrown that slit and sliced; those who were good and just could hear them. But he would get what he deserved.

Coffey Green would make sure that he did.

Chapter Four

Coffey tended the vegetable garden the rest of the day, interrupted by the storm that blew in from the bay. She dreamed of a life she didn't live—anything to distract her from what had happened—and suffered alone, hiding her pain, doing what had to be done. She doubted she was the only woman who suffered the same humiliation, and she wondered who else, among the slaves now at Hickory Hill, also silently endured. The last overseer, Jack Dunn, was a cruel man who had gotten satisfaction from whipping slaves—men, women, and children. But he had been an old man. She doubted he bothered anyone—at least not in the same way that Zeb Payne did—although she didn't know for sure. Zeb Payne was different. He liked to prove he was master—in more ways than one. No one could claim he wasn't.

The wagons returned from the fields, and as the slaves got out and went to their shacks, Coffey didn't say a word to anyone. They couldn't help her. Each had their own scars. Some had welts from the whip, some had endured pain that seared their soul. After she ate supper, sharing dinner with Molly and her two young daughters, she went outside and sat on a weathered bench on the porch.

A man was perched on a rocking chair at the neighboring shanty, nodding as she came out. "Hey, Coffey Green," he called.

She smiled. "Hi, Billy Giles," she said and looked up at the sky. "Seems like the storm done broke the heat."

"It did," he agreed. "Right pleasant, now."

Billy Giles lived next to Coffey with his mother

Venus and daughter Betsy, who did all the sewing for the Banks family, from dresses to drapes. Betsy's momma had been sold a few years before, torn from her family's grasp, never to be seen again. Billy and Venus did their best to fill the void for Betsy. The overseers liked Billy. He was perfect for field work, strong and obedient. As black as a bear's claws but as gentle as a newborn babe, he was a hard-working man who dreamed, someone who saw what others could not and wished he could see even more.

Coffey knew Billy had taken an interest in her. But she wasn't sure what to do about it. She suspected he would figure that out, if he really wanted to pursue her, and it sure seemed like he did. In the meantime, they were friendly, talking on their porches every evening, sometimes holding hands, stealing kisses when no one was watching. The others left them alone, suspecting something was blooming and not wanting to interfere.

Billy walked over from his porch and sat beside her, gently taking her hand in his. "Sometimes I wonder what's over there," he said, pointing to the bay.

Coffey chuckled. "Same thing that's over here. Just more of it. There's a big city. Lots of people. Baltimore, it's called."

"How do you know about that?"

"It's where I got sold to Mr. Banks," she said. "I used to belong to Mr. Green. That's why I'm Coffey Green."

"A man named Giles sold my mamma," he said. "So I'm Billy Giles." He paused, familiar with Coffey's story. "Is that where you lost your family—in the big city?"

"Yes, sir, it is," she said, the pain still sharp. "Saddest day of my life." She looked at him, eyes misty. "A body just don't get past a hurt like that."

"No, it don't," he agreed. "And each time you think about it, it hurts just as bad."

Coffey was quiet for a moment. "I knew something

real bad was gonna happen. They washed us all up first, put on new clothes."

"So you'd fetch more money."

"Yessir," she said, shaking her head. "They sold my mamma first. We was all cryin' and screamin,' beggin' someone to buy us all, our whole family."

"A man with a heart would have."

"They ain't got no hearts," she muttered. "None of 'em. My daddy went next, and then my brothers, one at a time."

"And they left you all alone," he said, shaking his head.

"I suppose I'm blessed Mr. Banks bought me," she said, sighing, "Could have been worse."

He grimaced, and gently caressed her hand. "I don't know how."

"I ain't sure where they went. All of us split up and took away separate. I'll never see them again."

"Ain't right," Billy said, shaking his head. "Just ain't right."

"Nothin' is right," Coffey said, her thoughts wandering to Zeb Payne. "And it ain't never gonna be."

Billy wrapped his arm around her and pulled her close. He kissed her, his lips lingering.

She pulled away, embarrassed. "Billy, half the plantation is watching us."

He looked at the other shacks, children playing, folks visiting, an older man playing a banjo. "They minding their business."

Coffey chuckled. "They can't mind their business. We're all too close together."

"It'd be nice to have some space, wouldn't it?"

"Yes, it would," she agreed. "But it ain't ever gonna happen."

"Did you ever wanna do something about it?" he asked, his voice lower.

She looked at him, head cocked. "Like what?"

"Run," he said simply.

She shrugged. Billy talked about running a lot. More lately than usual. "I don't know where to go. Nobody else does, either."

"Does it matter?"

"It sure does," she said. "What if you end up somewhere worse?"

"Being free ain't so bad," he said, his eyes wide. "No matter where you are."

She smiled. "No, it wouldn't be bad at all. But I can't even dream about it. At least, not like you."

"Why not?" Billy asked as if shocked she couldn't see what he did.

"Because I don't know what to dream."

He started laughing. "You're a good woman, Coffey Green."

"You ain't so bad yourself, Billy Giles. At least as far as men go."

He shook his head. "Ornery," he said. "You ornery as sin sometime."

She smiled. He liked teasing—and flirting, too.

"You gotta dream, Coffey Green," he continued. "Everybody does."

"Billy, you do enough dreamin' for both of us."

He laughed. "I suspect I do. I dream about everything. Like what's at the end of a rainbow."

Coffey grinned. "A pot of gold, the old folks say. But I suspect we'll never know."

"No? What's over there, where the sun comes up?" he asked, pointing east. "And where it goes down?"

"The same as we got here, I suspect," she said, chuckling. "You ain't never gonna find out, no way. So why you gotta dream all the time?"

"It's all we got," he said. "They may own my body, but they don't own my mind."

"No, they don't," Coffey agreed. "They don't own my soul, neither." She was quiet for a moment. Billy was a smart man. She could learn a lot from him.

"If I ever find out where to go, I'm gonna do it," he said. "Just so you know."

"Some folks say you follow the North Star," she said.

"But what if I follow it, and it takes me someplace like this?" he asked, pointing to the sprawling bay.

"You gotta figure out how to get across," she said.

"I just want a little land of my own, that's all. Ain't much to ask."

She followed his gaze, sweeping northward. He would run as soon as he could, she sensed it. But she didn't want him to. "What about your momma and little Betsy? What are they gonna do if you run?"

"They already know I might. I told them. But I'd come back and get 'em, if I do. As soon as I got somewhere safe."

Coffey smiled. "That's nice, Billy. You're a good man." His family was all he had. But at least he had family. She had no one. Except for Phoebe. And Molly and her daughters.

"And you know what, Coffey Green?"

"No, what, Billy Giles?"

"I'm gonna come back and get you, too. And then I'm gonna marry you."

Chapter Five

The following morning, Coffey and Billy tended rows of tobacco at the far end of Hickory Hill. A dirt road bordered the fields, dusty and deserted, winding into the distance. Across the lane, wheat waved in the wind, the edge of a neighboring plantation.

Billy pulled ripened tobacco leaves from the base of the plant. Largest and heaviest, splattered with mud from rain, they were the most difficult to handle. Coffey collected them, bundled them together, and stacked them at the end of the row to load on the wagon.

Billy glanced over his shoulder. Zeb Payne stood in the distance, watching the slaves work. "I don't much like Mr. Payne," Billy called to Coffey, who was two rows over, collecting harvested leaves. "He knows his business. I'll give him that. And he ain't whipped nobody like Jack Dunn use to. But he got something evil in his eyes."

Coffey scowled and turned away. "He is evil," she muttered. "It's more than his eyes, too."

"But he can't be no nastier than Mr. Dunn. Nobody can. God rest his soul."

"I ain't so sure about that," Coffey said. "Nasty comes in a whole lot of ways."

Billy looked at her, head cocked. "What you talking about, Coffey?"

She shrugged, head down, tending the tobacco. "I'm guessing he likes makin' everybody do what he says. Ain't because it's his job, neither. He just a mean soul."

They kept working, a half dozen other slaves spread along the rows around them. Billy eyed the road. Every time he worked beside it, or traveled upon it, he wondered where it would take him. He had seen some places: Chestertown where they bought supplies, Rock Hall, the harbor where they shipped their crops, the forest owned by Adrian Reed, one of Miss Annabelle's suitors. But he knew it went out past Chestertown somewhere. Maybe it went to the end of the world. He didn't know for sure.

"Why do folks live in a big city like Baltimore, all clumped together?" he asked Coffey.

"I don't know," she said. "But they must have a reason. Maybe they got family livin' there."

"I suppose," he said, not convinced. "Folks in Chestertown is different. Not a whole lot of 'em and farms and such nearby."

"People buy stuff in towns, too. At the feed store and places like that."

"Did you ever see the free black folk in Chestertown?"

"Just the preacher," she said. "But sometime he come here to preach, too."

"The man who run the feed store is free. And the girl who minds the white women's children."

"I ain't never seen them," Coffey said.

"Why they free and we're not?"

Coffey shrugged. "Maybe you can ask them. They might tell you."

"Maybe," he said, sighing. "But it don't seem right."

Although his mind wandered as he chatted, his hands moved quickly, pulling ripened leaves, his back bent and aching. They had planted in a fallow field at the end of winter. Wood ash and powdered horse manure were laid over top of the plants and then covered with branches to protect from frost. But they had removed it all in spring, the plants had sprouted, and now they were picking leaves, getting them ready to cure.

As he came to the last row of plants beside the road, a wagon loaded with wooden crates approached. One of the back wheels wobbled, making a thumping sound, but no one paid any attention. A white man with a broad-brimmed hat guided the horses, a slave sat in the back, his legs dangling over the edge. The wagon came to a halt not far from Billy. The white man set the brake and got down.

"You stay where you are, boy," he said to the slave. "I won't be long." He left the wagon and walked across the tobacco field.

Zeb Payne was a hundred feet away. He saw the man approach, the overseer at the neighboring plantation, and went to greet him. They met in the field, sixty feet from the road.

Billy eyed them for a moment, wondering what they were talking about, but he never stopped working.

"Hey, Billy," hissed the slave in the wagon, a man named Jim.

"Don't be gettin' me in trouble," Billy said, keeping a wary eye on Zeb Payne.

"I almost got away," Jim continued. "I got as far as a place called Wilmington 'fore a man named Amos Quigg caught me."

Billy bent over the plants. "I know Amos Quigg. Caught a man here at Hickory Hill last summer. Whipped him somethin' awful. Where'd you run?"

"Through the forest at the edge of the field," Jim said, pointing. "Then there's marsh and a stream."

"I ain't never seen it," Billy said.

"Across the stream is a farm owned by young folks—Jacob and Ruth Yoder."

"That's a funny name."

"They called Amish. Come from a place called Pencil Vaney."

"I don't know no Amish."

"They different from the rich folk," Jim continued.

"They work the land themselves. I was hid at their barn for a few days."

Billy listened closely. It was good information. "Do they help everybody?"

"Yeah, I think so. They strange, though. Men have funny beards. But they good people."

"Hush," Billy said. The overseer had left Zeb Payne and was heading back to the wagon.

"You can do it," Jim urged. "It ain't hard."

Billy wasn't convinced. "If it ain't hard, how come you got caught?"

"I was hiding in a woodshed, a good man looking out for me. But some lady came snooping and she saw me. Called the sheriff."

"What happened to the man who helped you?"

"Nothin'," Jim said. "He said he didn't know I was there."

Billy glanced across the neighboring field to the edge of the forest. It was tempting, the chance to be free. But it wasn't easy, either. Maybe he just wasn't brave enough. "I'll just get in trouble if I go."

"Not if you don't get caught," Jim said, laughing. "You can make it, Billy. I know you can."

"I ain't so sure."

"Just find Jacob Yoder. He'll help you get away. Ain't nobody gonna catch you."

Chapter Six

Naomi Banks hadn't been prepared for Zeb Payne—if that was his real name. He wasn't local, but he obviously knew who she was. And even though he looked familiar, she couldn't quite place him. But twenty-five years was a long time, and she was consumed by a few nagging doubts. Was he from St. Lucia, or was he someone she knew from Baltimore? Had fate brought him to Hickory Hill? Or had he planned it? She didn't know for sure, although she hoped he mistook her for someone else. But she doubted it.

Phoebe Yates was helping her get ready for dinner. "I think the light blue dress is best for this weekend's dinner party."

"Really?" Naomi asked. "I had planned to wear green."

"No, this one matches your eyes," Phoebe said, pointing to a dress hanging in the wardrobe. "Such a beautiful blue."

Naomi smiled. Phoebe had no agenda. She gave compliments because she meant them. And she gave good advice because she didn't fear retribution for saying something wrong.

"You look good in anything," Phoebe continued. "You always have. Built like a long, cool drink of water. Any man with eyes is thirsty for you."

Naomi laughed. "I'm not sure I'd agree."

"It's easy to see—for me, anyway. And Mr. Banks, too. He still look at you like a dog in heat."

Naomi smiled while Phoebe fussed with her sleeve. "Have you met the new overseer?"

"I have, but I'm not sure I like him,"

"Why not?"

Phoebe shrugged. "I don't know what it is. He sure know his business, I'll tell you that. He was tellin' Mr. Banks about curing tobacco ahead of time and what he was gonna do in fall and winter to make things better. And Mr. Banks just nodding' his head, wonderin' why he hadn't found Zeb Payne a whole lot sooner. Ole Jack Dunn was a good man as far as the fields and such but horrible cruel through the years. He'd just as soon take a child from their momma and sell 'em as he would whip the daddy. But near the end he was so old I suspect he was nappin' most of the time."

Naomi chuckled, always amused by Phoebe. But she needed information, and Phoebe might have it. "Does he look familiar?"

Phoebe sighed and looked away, thinking. "I didn't give it no thought. Why, should he?"

Naomi paused. Maybe she was mistaken. But her instinct told her she wasn't. "He seemed to recognize me."

"Where does he come from?"

"Virginia, most recently," Naomi said. "But I don't know anything more."

"He a handsome man, I'll give him that. With those blue eyes and that rust-colored hair. I bet ladies like him."

"Yes, I bet they do," Naomi muttered, clouded memories still unclear.

Phoebe paused, looking at Naomi with head cocked. "Should I know him? Seems like you think I should."

Naomi held a finger to her lips. She went to the bedroom door, quietly opened it, peered into an empty hallway, and then returned. "Could we have known him a long time ago? Before we came here?"

Phoebe hesitated, her hands on her hips. "Maybe," she said, thinking of days she had tried to forget. "It's hard to tell twenty-five years later. Lotta time between."

"I'm not sure, either," Naomi said. "But I'm

positive he knows me. I could tell by his expression."

Phoebe shrugged. "Well, if I ain't sure, and you ain't sure, then he ain't, neither."

"He had a spark of recognition in his eyes," Naomi continued. "And he was clearly surprised. He either hadn't expected to see me or he'd finally found what he'd been looking for, I'm not sure which."

Phoebe pursed her lips as if trying to place him. "I ain't never seen him around here. That's for sure."

"What about that night in St. Lucia?"

Phoebe hesitated. "Just the doctor and inspector. And they both dead by now."

"How about the boat, the one that took us out to the ship?"

Phoebe drew a deep breath. "We didn't bother much with the crew. It was such a short ride. Just the captain."

"How old do you think Zeb Payne is?"

Phoebe shrugged. "Not much younger than us. Seven, eight years maybe."

Naomi was quiet. Images from her past drifted through her mind like pages in a book. "The only other person who saw us was the boy."

Phoebe looked at her strangely. "What boy you talking about?"

"When we got on the boat, and I paid the captain, a boy was standing in the shadows."

Phoebe sighed. "I just don't know, Miz Naomi. Maybe he is, maybe he isn't. I don't remember much."

"What do you think I should do?"

"You kept a secret all these years. He don't know any different. You play the game you been playing. It don't matter if he thinks he knows you or not."

Naomi thought for a moment. "Good advice," she said. "Even if it is him, he can't prove anything."

"No, ma'am, he can't. That trail done gone cold."

Chapter Seven

The dining room at Hickory Hill rivalled that of an English manor. White molded panels dressed lower walls, floral wallpaper above them. A serving buffet with lion-paw feet sat next to the door while a long oak table dominated the room, seating sixteen. A crystal chandelier hung above it, holding half-burned candles. Consistent with the rest of the manor, tall windows let the breeze blow in, cooling the room.

When Naomi came down for dinner, Gideon was seated at the head of the table, Annabelle beside him. They lowered their voices as she entered.

Naomi was concerned about Annabelle, who resisted any and all attempts to play mistress of the manor. They had never been close, not like Naomi was with her daughter Emma. Annabelle had an independent streak which bordered on defiance and was sometimes too intelligent for her own good. She had no fear, a foolish trait the young possess, which had thankfully caused no issues. Sometimes, Naomi saw herself in Annabelle—both good and bad. She suspected that might be why they didn't always get along; they were too much alike. They so closely resembled each other that they could almost pass for sisters. Emma was more like her father, with black hair and blue eyes as well as a head for business. She would go far in a world that seemed about to change, but Naomi wasn't so sure about Annabelle.

"My lovely bride," Gideon said. He rose to seat her, lightly kissing her cheek.

"Am I interrupting anything?" she asked, glancing

at Annabelle.

"No, of course not," he said. "We were discussing Snowflake."

"She's a beautiful filly," Naomi said, referring to a recent gift she and Gideon had given Annabelle. "Such a beautiful white horse, barely a marking on her."

Annabelle continued the discussion she had been having with her father. "I'm sure she could race, if trained," she said. "But I prefer to ride for my own enjoyment."

"She'd do well in competition," Gideon said. "Why don't you enter her in the equestrian events in Annapolis?"

Annabelle paused, pensive. "Maybe I will. That might be fun. But I don't have much time to train her."

"I would think she'll learn quickly," Naomi said, trying to engage in the conversation.

"It'll be challenging," Gideon added. "Many good riders compete."

"I'll have the finest horse, regardless of the rider," Annabelle said, smiling. "She's the best present I ever got. Thank you, Father."

Naomi frowned. "And mother," she said, miffed she'd been omitted.

"I'm going to ride her every morning," Annabelle continued, ignoring her.

"She's meant for you to enjoy," Gideon said. He smiled at Naomi, lightly caressed her hand, and looked at the buffet. "That smells absolutely delicious."

"Thank you, sir," Phoebe said. "Got a little bit of everything this evenin'. Turkey, corn, beans, rice, and cornbread. And some sweet puddings for dessert."

"Fabulous, as always," Gideon said. "My compliments to the cook."

Phoebe smiled and started serving, placing ample portions on each of their plates.

Gideon turned to Naomi. "Have we received responses for this weekend's party?"

"Yes, of course," Naomi said, leaning back in her chair while Phoebe put food on her plate. "Most replied last week."

"Eighteen? With the guests we discussed?" Gideon asked.

Naomi nodded slyly, glancing at Annabelle. "Actually twenty."

Annabelle caught her gaze. "We have dinner guests all the time. What's so special this time?"

"We've added someone to the usual guest list," Gideon said.

Annabelle hesitated. "And who might that be?"

Naomi glanced at Gideon; a plan they'd prepared was finally coming to fruition. "I invited Artemis Wentworth."

Gideon leaned toward Annabelle. "A successful attorney who recently argued a case before the Supreme Court. And he's about to run for senator."

"He'll likely win, too," Naomi added, hoping to encourage a daughter who didn't seem interested. "He's very popular."

"I know Artemis," Annabelle said, poking at her turkey with a fork. "He's been here several times."

"I'm told he's not yet spoken for," Naomi said slyly.

Annabelle rolled her eyes and didn't reply as she sipped her cider.

"He has such a promising future," Gideon continued. "He'll be a powerful man one day—someone the Eastern Shore will be proud of."

Naomi took a bite of cornbread. "I suspect he'll want to marry soon."

"I agree," Gideon said, discreetly winking at his wife. "A family man with good values is attractive to constituents. Don't you think so, Annabelle?"

She shrugged. "He seems like a good man. I hope

all goes well for him."

"Rumor has it that he's expressed an interest in a certain young lady," Naomi said coyly. "I intend to discuss it with him at the dinner party."

Gideon waited for Annabelle to react. When she didn't, he did. He looked at his wife, head cocked. "Who might that be?"

"Our Annabelle," Naomi said sweetly. "What a wonderful match they would make."

Annabelle frowned. "I'm not attracted to power and prestige."

"Don't be ridiculous," Naomi scoffed. "He would make a perfect husband."

"Yes, he would," Annabelle agreed. "But for someone else. I prefer to find my own husband. Although your efforts haven't gone unnoticed."

Naomi couldn't resist a sarcastic reply. "I failed to notice a line of suitors at the door."

Annabelle pursed her lips. "I don't need a line of suitors. I already know who I want to marry."

Naomi gave Gideon a guarded glance. "Who might that be?"

Annabelle eyed her parents triumphantly. "Adrian Reed."

Chapter Eight

Adrian Reed was a successful businessman. One of two suitors who would seek the hand of Annabelle Banks, he was handsome with brown hair and dark inquisitive eyes. He worked hard, chasing the American dream and all that came with it. He had recently built his own home, tucked in a cove and sheltered from the wind that blew off the bay, preparing for the day he married and raised a family.

He had known Annabelle since they were toddlers. They had shared the same private tutor—with a handful of other children—played by the bay at Hickory Hill or rode horses, another of Annabelle's loves. Gideon Banks was a close friend of Adrian's father—their properties were adjacent in several locations. At some point in his late teenage years, Adrian found much more than a friend in Annabelle Banks. Now that she was ready to court and had shown that she felt the same, they'd begun spending more time together. He had decided to move slowly, perhaps ask for her hand at the end of the year, even though Annabelle was willing to move much faster. But he wanted to respect tradition, which was important to both his family and hers.

Unlike the farms and plantations that sprawled across the peninsula, growing tobacco and grains, the family business—Reed and Sons—harvested timber and built ships. The operation was managed by Adrian's father, Thaddeus, who was assisted by his three sons. Adrian was youngest, and sometimes he wondered how he fit in the family. His brothers were a year apart, eight and nine years older than he was, and stern, like their father. Adrian took after his mother.

He trotted up to the family sawmill and climbed off

his horse, tethering it to a post. Three harbor slots revealed ships under construction, the wharf alive with workers. Product and produce were handled at nearby docks, the ferry from Annapolis approaching from across the bay. He was about to enter the mill when his father came toward him.

"Have you secured any additional labor?" Thaddeus Reed asked. A stern man with white hair and blue eyes, he wore distinctive muttonchop sideburns, meticulously groomed.

Adrian shook his head. "I've added all the men that I can. No others seem interested." The Reeds owned large tracts of woodland. Adrian harvested timber, protecting their investment and ensuring mature trees were always available for logging.

Thaddeus frowned. "Most prefer work less physical and more lucrative." He tugged at his sideburns. "We're adding a new saw, much more efficient than what we have."

Adrian understood the implication. "And more logs will be needed."

Thaddeus nodded. "It has multiple blades, cuts several boards from a log at the same time. We can expand production once it's installed."

Adrian watched a steamboat chug up to the dock. "Sails will only propel pleasure craft in the future," he said, pointing to the ferry, smoke drifting from its stack.

Thaddeus frowned. "Your brothers don't agree, and neither do I."

Adrian shrugged. "I do think we should expand," he said, hesitant to speak. "But I suggest a different direction—steel hulls and steam engines."

"You're tasked with finding additional labor," Thaddeus said, not interested in the discussion. "I suggest you approach neighboring plantations and ask for slaves to rent."

Adrian nodded, lips pursed. It was a common practice, but one he detested. "I'll ask Gideon at the dinner party."

"And I'll talk to Lucas Crane when I see him," Thaddeus said as he walked toward a two-story office building. "He has sizable slave holdings. He may have someone to offer."

Adrian wrestled with his conscience. How could he turn a practice he abhorred into a situation acceptable to all? He wanted to try something bold, innovative but controversial, typical of suggestions he often made regarding the family business. It seemed he could see what his family could not, his eyes on the future, theirs on the past.

He would reward the slaves he rented. It was a simple process. He only had to track their work and the profit they generated. After he deducted expenses—the cost to hire, clothe, and feed the men—he would assess the profit they'd made and share a portion with the slaves, a form of compensation for their services.

He debated discussing it with his father and brothers. They wouldn't understand, and he doubted he could convince them no matter what the justification. To Adrian, it seemed simple: the slaves would work harder if they had a personal stake in the outcome of their efforts. But his family would never see the reward, only the risks. His plan would be unpopular as well as unconventional. Some would attack him personally, knowing he threatened a financial system that rewarded those who least deserved it. But he was willing to shoulder the criticism his decision created.

It was the only way he could live with himself.

Chapter Nine

Coffey Green worked the fields every day except Wednesday, when she managed the vegetable garden that flanked the trees beside the main house. Tending the garden had always been her favorite task. She was allowed to do what she wanted, as long as she produced, without anyone watching over her. Sometimes Phoebe Yates or one of the other house servants came to visit, and she would chat with them, catching up on household gossip. But now every Wednesday posed a problem. It was the most convenient time for Zeb Payne to demand what he had no right to have.

Coffey spent the morning picking vegetables and filling baskets with potatoes, onions, beets and cucumbers—all crops which weren't grown in the fields. Watermelon grew in the far end of the garden, some apple and peach trees scattered along the lawn that led to the bay. A flower garden sat on the edge, not part of the formal landscaping, with iris, lilies, hibiscus, and mistflower that she picked for vases and centerpieces in bedrooms, parlors, and the dining room table.

"You busy out here this morning, ain't you?" Phoebe Yates called as she approached.

"I picked a little bit of everything," Coffey said, pointing to the baskets.

"I'll send one of the boys to come get 'em," Phoebe said, referring to the children who assisted the house servants. She bent over to look at the last row of beets, pulling a stray weed.

"Flowers blooming, too, if you need some for the dining room table."

"I'll get a bunch on my way in," Phoebe said. She looked up at the rising sun. "Be another hot day."

"Yes, ma'am, it will," Coffey replied. She looked back at the house. "Do you have what you need for the dinner party?"

Phoebe glanced at the baskets, a watermelon on the ground beside them. "I think so, with what you picked. Maybe a little more in a day or two."

"How many folks are coming?"

"Should be twenty," Phoebe said. "We gotta add another table to the dining room to fit everybody." She leaned closer as if sharing a secret. "Some suitors startin' to call on Miss Annabelle."

"Is that right?" Coffey asked, pausing to look up.

"Artemis Wentworth," Phoebe said. "Miz Naomi spitting that name out all day long."

Coffey looked at her, head cocked. "I don't know who that is."

"He a rich lawyer, I think. Live across the bay in Annapolis. Miz Naomi say he gonna be president someday."

"President?" Coffey asked, eyes wide. "I bet Miz Naomi real happy about that."

Phoebe looked back at the house, made sure no one approached, and continued. "Miz Naomi is, but Miss Annabelle sure ain't."

"Who does Miss Annabelle want?"

"She like Adrian Reed, the man who built the house on the edge of the cove."

"I know him," Coffey said. "Seem like a good man. His folks build ships."

"It don't matter what they build," Phoebe said. "Miz Naomi want Annabelle to marry Mr. Wentworth. And Lord willing, she gonna make sure of it."

Coffey chuckled. "Miz Naomi forget that Miss Annabelle has a mind of her own. She don't care much what anybody else want."

Phoebe laughed. "No, she don't. I can promise you that. But you know how Miz Naomi get when she want something. Ain't nothing else in the whole world that matters."

"Oughtta be fun to watch," Coffey said. "Miss Annabelle is too much like her momma. She don't mind no one. And she ain't about to start."

"No, she ain't," Phoebe agreed. "I'm gonna be real interested in this dinner."

"How long will suitors be calling?"

"All summer, most likely. But Miz Naomi wants Miss Annabelle married off to Mr. Wentworth quick."

"Yeah, before somebody else gets him," Coffey joked.

Phoebe laughed. "You right about that." She turned, looking toward the trees and frowned.

"What's the matter?" Coffey asked, watching her.

"That man has an evil bone somewhere in his body, I can feel it."

Coffey followed her gaze. Zeb Payne sat on his horse at the edge of the clearing, watching them.

"I know I told you my mamma knew voodoo," Phoebe said, still staring at Payne.

Coffey rolled her eyes. She had heard about Phoebe's momma a thousand times. But other than knowing about plants, Phoebe didn't seem to know much about voodoo.

"I told you all about that, didn't I?" Phoebe prodded.

Coffey smiled faintly. "Yes, you did. Ain't never gonna forget it, neither."

"Well, I can see things other folks can't," Phoebe said. "You know that 'cause I told you. And I can feel things, too. You know what I mean?"

"Yes, ma'am, I do," Coffey confirmed, although

she wasn't sure if Phoebe was any different than anyone else. But she must have learned something from her momma. And Coffey suspected that when it came to Zeb Payne, Phoebe felt the same way she did—without even knowing why.

"He up to no good, I can tell you that," Phoebe declared. "What do he want, staring at the two of us like that?"

Coffey didn't reply. She knew exactly what he wanted—even if Phoebe didn't.

Chapter Ten

Billy Giles knew all about Amos Quigg. A slave had escaped from Hickory Hill the summer before, a young man who was strong and defiant. He had only been gone a few days before Amos Quigg brought him back, whipped and tied and meek as a kitten. The poor man never resisted again. He minded his business, worked hard, and just wanted to be left alone. But it wasn't long before Miz Naomi sold him off. She didn't tolerate any nonsense.

Billy couldn't stop thinking about Jim, the slave from the neighboring plantation. He had gotten far, to a place called Wilmington—wherever that was. He came close to living free. Billy kept dreaming, wondering what it was like to do what he pleased and go anywhere he wanted.

Masters controlled slaves by keeping them scared. They feared a whipping when they didn't do enough, act fast enough, or work hard enough. They feared sickness—even if the doctor from town came to look in on them—although Phoebe Yates mostly took care of them using plants and herbs. She had taught Billy early on that some plants could cure and some could kill.

Older slaves were sometimes granted freedom when they reached their forty-fifth year, mainly because their bodies began to break, and they couldn't work like younger folks. But it didn't matter to most because they had nowhere to go. Billy wasn't surprised when most chose to stay on the plantation like Caesar, the house servant. It was the only life he'd ever known. He stayed because he was afraid. And maybe the rest did, too.

A few days after he had talked to Jim, Billy was

working the same field of tobacco next to the road. Across the way, wheat fields wandered into the distance, the forest just beyond. The trees ended at a marsh that drained into a stream that led to a farm where friendly people named Jacob and Ruth Yoder would help him—if he ever found the courage to run away.

Billy eyed the road, wondering where it went. He knew it ended down at the harbor. And it twisted and turned the other way, crossing roads he'd never been down, to get to Chestertown. He had been to both places many times. But what was past Chestertown? Is that where Wilmington was? And if so, how much farther? Did he have to get past Wilmington to be free? He didn't know. Maybe he would never know. But he realized if he waited to learn much more, he would waste his whole life picking tobacco.

He stood up and rubbed his back. His muscles tightened near the end of the day and, no matter how much he stretched, the pain wouldn't go away. The sun was sinking in the horizon, so twenty minutes more and they would be done for the day. He glanced across the field. Zeb Payne was several acres away, not paying much attention. He was watching something, looking off toward the main house, the chimneys poking over the trees that screened it.

Billy glanced at the slaves nearby, bent at the waist, pulling leaves that were ripe and adding ash and manure to the soil of plants that weren't. They worked hard, all of them. They always had. He watched them a moment more, their heads down, focused on what they were doing. Some sang songs or hummed to themselves; a few chatted. No one paid him any attention. They had no reason to.

He looked across the road. It didn't seem hard. He only had to get past the wheat fields and through the forest, cross the marsh, and ford the stream. Somewhere on the other side lay the farm of Jacob Yoder—at least that's what Jim had told him. And Jacob Yoder would take him to a place where all his dreams could come true.

"Billy Giles, don't you do it," Coffey Green hissed. She was bent over a row of tobacco plants, looking back at him.

"I may never have the chance again."

"You don't even know where to go, Billy. Don't be no fool."

"I may never know," he said. "But I got to do something."

"Mind your business," she scolded. "That's what you oughtta do. Your momma and daughter are waitin' for you."

He hesitated. "They know I'll come back to get 'em as soon as I'm settled. I'll be back for you, too."

"You ain't even gonna say goodbye?"

"I can't," he said. "I gotta find Jacob Yoder, like Jim told me. And he gonna help me."

"Stop dreamin' for one minute, Billy," she said sharply. "You ain't got no chance. They come after you with dogs. You hear me? Dogs! Don't be stupid."

Billy took one last lingering look at Zeb Payne at the end of the field, facing the other way. "Bye, Coffey. I love you."

He scampered across the lane and into the wheat fields, destined for Jacob Yoder's farm—wherever that might be.

Chapter Eleven

Jacob Yoder was the youngest of eight children, born to an Amish family who lived just over the Maryland border in Pennsylvania. The Amish were known as the Pennsylvania Dutch even though they were Swiss and German. They valued the rural life they created—devotion to family, hard work, humility and a strong belief in God. Content to forego advances that helped society prosper, they shunned anything ostentatious. Women wore simple frocks with aprons and bonnets; men wore dark trousers, suspenders, and white shirts. Married men grew beards but not moustaches, which they believed had military connotations. They left much of their face shaved, leaving only whiskers along the jawbone. Quiet, hard-working people, they revered their lifestyle and supported their community, not interested in the influences of an outside world.

With little family land available to Jacob and no nearby properties to purchase, he worried for his family's future—his wife Ruth, their four-year old daughter Elizabeth and two-year old son Eli. But when a traveler purchasing goods at a nearby store offered five hundred acres of prime farm land for sale on the Eastern Shore, Jacob had packed up his young family and left, splitting the purchase with four other Amish families: the Zooks, Stutzmans, Bachmans and Boehms. They'd made the journey together, found the soil rich and ready to plow and bought the land, splitting it into hundred-acre farms, the most a single family could handle.

Jacob settled along a wide stream six miles from the Chesapeake, a few miles from Chestertown. He grew vegetables and grains, finding ready markets locally and afar. His product shipped from Rock Hall, a nearby port where seafood, crops, and tobacco were dispatched around the world. He quickly prospered with the rest of the small Amish community, and they added to their holdings whenever the opportunity arose.

He and his family lived in a modest two-story dwelling, functional and clean with a broad front porch. He'd built a barn with the assistance of the other Amish, much larger than the residence, with a chicken coop and smokehouse beside it. Fields of wheat, corn and hay sprawled to the horizon, a tract for fruit and vegetables between the house and barn.

Shortly after they'd arrived in Maryland, a runaway slave had stumbled onto Jacob's farm. Frightened and disoriented, starving and dehydrated, he was battered and bruised from a journey he hadn't been prepared to make. When he begged for help, Jacob couldn't refuse. Even though he understood the risk his family faced, he hid the man in a livestock stable and gave him food, water, and clothing. He confided in his closest friend, a fellow Amish named Samuel Zook, and they formed a pact, enlisting in a network that helped escaped slaves reach freedom.

The danger was significant from local law enforcement should any suspicions be aroused, and from slave catchers who received a bounty for slaves they captured and returned to their owners. He had confided in his wife, Ruth, a quiet, strong woman who loved her family above all else, when she'd noticed a pair of trousers missing and, a jug of milk gone from the kitchen. She'd agreed to help those in need, but on one condition: if the family was ever impacted, or the risks exceeded the reward, they would stop. Jacob had agreed.

On a hot day in mid-June, Jacob returned from the fields, the plow blade lifted, his horse in a gentle trot. Ruth, now expecting her third child, churned butter while Eli and

Elizabeth played nearby. He went into the barn, unhitched the horse, stowed the harness and plow, and threw hay for the horses.

"Lunch is ready," Ruth said as he approached. A frugal woman with brown hair and bright eyes, she wore a gray frock with white apron and bonnet. "Whenever you're ready to eat."

Jacob gently moved her away from the butter churn and wrapped his arms around her. He kissed her lightly, gently rubbed her swollen belly, and took her place at the churn. "I'm expecting Samuel Zook."

"I have his produce packed in crates," Ruth said. Samuel Zook bought fruits and vegetables and sold them to nearby businesses—inns, taverns, and Reed & Sons shipping.

Jacob finished churning the butter. He couldn't imagine a better partner than Ruth, a devoted wife and wonderful mother. She worked hard, helped on the farm, raised their children, and he loved her more than life itself. "Samuel will take the runaway," he said simply.

Ruth nodded. "I will assist, husband, should you need me to do so."

He shook his head. "We'll hide him on the wagon, the crates stacked around him."

"And then where?" she asked.

He shrugged. "Better that we know less, should we ever be asked."

Hidden in the Yoder barn, accessed from the back of a stall and buried in the side of a short knoll, was a secret cave that housed the runaway, desperate to reach Philadelphia where his brother had gone the summer before.

A moment later, Samuel Zook's wagon came down the trail that led from the road to the house. He tipped his hat to Ruth as he approached.

"Would you like lunch, Samuel?' she asked.

"I have deliveries to make," he replied. "Even though I hate to decline."

She smiled. "If you change your mind, I'll prepare a plate."

He guided his wagon to the barn where crates of vegetables lay on the ground in the shade cast by the building. He came to a stop and climbed down from the seat.

"Everything is ready," Jacob said. He picked up a rectangular crate of peppers, put it in the wagon, and set another beside it, along the edge.

"Let's get everything loaded first," Samuel said as he picked up a crate of lettuce. He put it and another crate along the opposite side, leaving a slender cavity in the center of the bed, starting at the headboard behind the back of the bench seat.

Jacob got more crates, filling the wagon's length.

Samuel did the same on the opposite side. "Go and get him," he said. "I'll load the rest of the crates."

Jacob went in the barn. The foundation was made of stone, the walls resting upon it. Attached to the wall in the first stall was a rectangular board, rope and reins hanging on it. Jacob unhooked a clasp and pulled the board forward. It swung on hinges, exposing a narrow doorway, a cavity dug in the little hill behind it.

"Come on out," Jacob said. "But wait in the barn while your eyes get used to the light."

The young runaway emerged, using his arm to shield his eyes. "Is it safe, sir?"

"Yes, it's time to go," Jacob said. "You'll lay in the back of a wagon, hidden by crates of vegetables. Not for long, six or seven miles."

"And then where?"

Jacob shrugged. "Good people will help you make your way to Philadelphia."

The runaway smiled. "I'll see my brother again

after more than a year. I don't know how to thank you."

Jacob smiled. "There's no need for thanks. Just live the life you've always dreamed."

"I will, sir," the young man said. "And I'll never forget you and your missus."

Jacob led him to the wagon. "Lie in the back," he said, eyeing the landscape to ensure no one watched.

The young man did as directed, crawling into the open space. Samuel and Jacob climbed up on the wagon and stacked the next set of crates horizontally, covering him. They then put more along the side so the wagon appeared fully loaded.

"It's time I was going," Samuel said, tipping his hat. "I'll be back for more next week."

The wagon bounced down the dirt lane. Just as it approached the road, the sheriff appeared on horseback, two men with him.

"Hold on there," the sheriff called, ordering the wagon to halt.

Chapter Twelve

Gideon Banks sat in his study early the next afternoon. He eyed the chessboard, trying to predict the next move his son Benjamin might make via their frequent correspondence, then reviewed receipts for purchases and sales. Managing the plantation was time consuming. Massive amounts of tobacco and grain were harvested and sold, bills had to be paid, profits collected. As slaves grew older, they had to be replaced, either by their children or others purchased, usually at auction. He suspected slavery had a dim future, just one more issue that was tearing a nation apart, like tariffs and state's rights. But he knew of no alternative.

He was interrupted by a knock on the door. "What is it?" he called.

Caesar stepped in. "Mr. Payne is here to see you, sir."

"Thank you, Caesar. Show him in."

The butler exited, and Zeb Payne came in. "Sorry to interrupt, sir."

"Not an interruption at all," Gideon said, motioning to a chair in front of the desk. "It's an opportune time to tell you how impressed I am with your performance. I'm reviewing the books now, and I'm astonished by the positive impact you've had in so short a time."

"Thank you, sir," Zeb said, nodding humbly. "It's a privilege to work at Hickory Hill."

"Your efforts are greatly appreciated. If there's anything at all you want or need, please let me know, and I'll ensure that you get it."

"I appreciate that, sir," Zeb said, shifting in the

chair.

Gideon eyed him curiously, suspecting something was wrong. "What is it that you wanted?"

Zeb sighed, hat in his lap, and ran his hand through his russet hair. "I'm afraid we've got a runaway, sir. Left yesterday, end of day. We looked a little last night, couldn't find him, and checked again this morning. He's gone, no doubt about it."

"Who is it?" Gideon asked, eyebrows arched. "I thought Naomi sold off our troublemakers."

"Billy Giles, sir."

Gideon frowned. "I'm surprised. He seems mild-mannered, never been in trouble before."

"No, sir, he hasn't," Zeb said. "Most of the field hands speak highly of him."

Gideon sighed, fretting over the expected expense. "We had a runaway a while back," he recalled. "His return was costly."

"I suspect this will be, too, sir."

"Who do you recommend?"

"I'm told Amos Quigg is the best slave catcher around."

"Yes, he is," Gideon muttered. "The most expensive, too. We used him last year."

Zeb nodded. "If we get him quick, before Billy gets too far, it'll cost less."

"I don't remember his fee," Gideon muttered. "I wasn't involved. Jack Dunn took care of it."

"Regardless of the cost, he's worth it."

Gideon pursed his lips. "Yes, I suppose he is. He has a stellar reputation, although I've never met the man. How much will he want?"

"I've got it all written up," Zeb said, handing him the paper.

Gideon scanned the page and then read it aloud. "Billy Giles, aged twenty-six years, is of black color, about five feet eight inches tall and strong. Pleasant disposition, never caused trouble. He's bright and handsome, speaks rather deep. $150 if caught in Maryland, $300 if out of state."

"I think that's fair, sir," Zeb said.

Gideon eyed the paper. It was a step he was reluctant to take. But he had no other way to recover his property. He gave it back to Zeb. "Nicely written."

"Thank you, sir."

"How soon can you engage Mr. Quigg?"

"I already did, sir," Zeb said. "Negotiated the price a little lower, too."

Gideon was surprised. "You are very efficient. Thank you, I appreciate that."

"He's waiting in the hall," Zeb said. "I took the liberty of bringing him with me."

Gideon eyes widened. "Excellent," he said. "We won't waste any time. Bring him in."

Zeb went to the door and opened it. "Come on in, Amos. Mr. Banks wants to talk to you."

A man entered a moment later. About forty, he wore brown trousers and a leather vest with a white shirt, a broad-brimmed hat on a head of wild brown hair. He was scruffy, a two- or three-day growth of beard accented by a half-smoked cigar, unlit, clenched in his teeth.

"May I present Amos Quigg, slavecatcher," Zeb said.

"Mr. Quigg, please sit down," Gideon offered, motioning to the chairs in front of his desk.

"Pleased to make your acquaintance, Mr. Banks," Quigg said as he sat. "Got a bad one, I'm told."

"Yes, we do," Gideon said, assessing the man before him. He seemed crude, not that you needed sophistication to catch runaways. He handed Quigg the paper. "A good worker, though. Are these terms acceptable?"

Quigg read over the notice and stuck it in his pocket, having already agreed to terms with Payne. "Yes, sir, it is. This should work just fine."

"Billy left end of day yesterday," Zeb said. "I suspect he went straight across the wheat fields and into the forest, probably headed for the marsh."

Quigg pulled the cigar from his mouth. "Ain't no bother, believe me," he said and then chuckled. "My dogs will get him."

Chapter Thirteen

Adrian Reed came down the lane to Hickory Hill, empty carriages lined in a row to his left, his father's closest to the house. Two men chatted by the horses, a field hand and someone Adrian didn't recognize. As he brought his carriage to a halt, the field hand tethered his horse to a hitching post. The stranger came over to greet him.

"I'm Zeb Payne," he said, hand outstretched. "The new overseer."

Adrian climbed from his carriage and shook hands. "Adrian Reed. Nice to meet you."

"You're one of the shipbuilders?" Zeb asked.

Adrian nodded. "Our facilities are just south, in Rock Hall. And my property is adjacent to yours along the cove."

"It's nice to meet you, Mr. Reed," Zeb said. "I met your parents a few minutes ago. They were the first to arrive."

Adrian smiled. Of course, his parents were first to arrive. They had to be early, no matter what the occasion. "My father and Gideon are close friends," he said as if he needed to explain. "And my mother has known Naomi since they married."

"They're all good people," Zeb said. "I'm sure you'll enjoy the party. We'll take care of your horse."

"Thank you," Adrian said as he turned to go. "I appreciate that."

The Banks family liked to entertain. Gideon was popular—sociable, jovial, and with no agenda. Naomi was absolutely stunning—age hadn't hindered her beauty—

sophisticated and graceful. But she was often distant and most never really got to know her—if any did at all. But Adrian most looked forward to Annabelle—beautiful, intelligent, available, a bit spoiled as he was the first to admit, and rarely far from his thoughts.

He never failed to admire Hickory Hill, one of the grandest mansions on the Eastern Shore. A prime example of neoclassical architecture, broad balconies supported by Corinthian columns wrapped each elevation. Dual, curving steps led to the entrance, the left for ladies and the right for gentlemen, identified by a boot scraper at the bottom. Separate staircases kept men from eyeing women's ankles as they poked from underneath their skirts while climbing the steps, which was considered a breach of etiquette.

"Good evening, Mr. Reed," Caesar, the butler, said as he opened the door.

"Caesar, how are you?" Adrian asked as he entered.

"Fine, sir," Caesar said with a respectful nod. "Thank you for asking. You'll find the other guests scattered, some in the library, others in the parlors."

Adrian entered a spacious foyer accented by a broad staircase with marble balusters that led to the second floor. Parlors sat to the left and right. Cigar smoke drifted from the right where the men had gathered, piano music from the left where the women entertained. A library behind the sitting room on the left was across the hall from Mr. Banks's office. And the back of the house contained a small ballroom and large dining room.

He turned into the parlor on the right. Phoebe met him at the entrance with a tray of drinks, and he accepted a glass of rum. A half dozen men wore tailored jackets and ruffled shirts, standing in pairs, engaged in conversation. His father talked to Lucas Crane by a bookcase, Gideon Banks stood by the fireplace with an attorney named Artemis Wentworth, a man many on the Eastern Shore were talking about. Wentworth was a talented attorney, a compassionate man with an intellect few could match, who would likely enter politics. Adrian remained near the entrance, watching those in the room. He had hoped to speak privately to Gideon about renting slaves, but it didn't seem the time. Maybe after dinner.

The piano music stopped, the last few notes lingering. Whoever had been playing had paused, perhaps searching sheet music for their next piece.

"Adrian. It's so nice to see you."

He turned to find Anabelle leaving the women's parlor. He brightened, the smile on his face mirroring hers. "Annabelle, radiant as always."

She glanced back in the sitting room, ensuring they couldn't be overheard. "Perhaps a walk after dinner," she suggested. "I can show you Snowflake, my new filly."

"I would like that," he said, anxious for time alone with her.

"Or we could walk down to the bay. It's more private."

He smiled, preferring the second option. "Whichever you like."

She leaned close to whisper in his ear. "As soon as we can slip away unnoticed."

He smelled her perfume, a cinnamon scent, and saw the swell of her bosom peeking from her dress as she leaned forward. His face flushed. "I would enjoy that very much."

She lingered, teasing, smiling coyly. "So would I," she said and slowly moved away.

He glanced back in the gentlemen's parlor. "I do have to speak to your father. It's business. I hope it won't interfere."

She looked at him oddly. "I won't let it interfere. I'll call him now."

"No, that's all right," Gideon protested, lightly touching her arm. "I hate to impose. I can talk to him later."

"Nonsense," she said and smiled sweetly. "He'll interrupt whatever he's doing if I ask him to. Just watch."

Adrian grimaced. "No, it's all right. I have all evening. Why interrupt him? He's engaged in a rather animated discussion."

"Father," she called, ignoring Adrian. "Can you come here for a minute?"

Gideon disengaged from his conversation with a last nod and chuckle and came toward them.

"See?" Annabelle whispered slyly. "I told you."

Gideon crossed the parlor, nodding to Thaddeus Reed and Lucas Crane as he passed. "Adrian, how are you?" he asked as they shook hands. "I'm glad you could come."

"I wouldn't miss it," Adrian said, furtively glancing at Annabelle. "I greatly appreciate the invitation."

"Adrian has something to ask you," Annabelle said, intervening.

Gideon looked at them curiously, wondering why Annabelle spoke for him. "What is it?"

Adrian hesitated, glancing at Annabelle, but realized she had no intention of leaving. It was rare for women to engage in business discussions—but Annabelle wasn't like most women. She never would be. "I was hoping to rent one or two of your slaves. Our business is expanding rapidly, and the shortage of workers hampers our growth."

Gideon frowned. "I'm sorry, Adrian. I can't really spare anyone."

"It would be short-term, through summer and early fall."

Gideon shrugged. "I can't. I'm sorry. It's my peak season. And I have problems myself. One of my best workers ran off."

Adrian pursed his lips. "I'm sorry to hear that."

"Maybe if he's caught and returned, I'll reconsider.

But unfortunately, there's nothing I can do right now."

Adrian hesitated, not wanting to offend. "If there's anyone you can spare, anyone at all, I would be hugely indebted."

Gideon slowly shook his head. "No, I can't think of anyone."

"I can," Annabelle interjected.

Both men faced her with surprise. "Who?" Gideon asked.

"Coffey Green."

Chapter Fourteen

When dinner was finished, Annabelle left the dining room and followed the women to the parlor for music and conversation. But she stopped in the hallway before she got there, waiting for the men.

"Annabelle, why don't you play the piano for us?" Naomi asked.

"In a minute, Mother. You go ahead."

Naomi paused, glancing down the hallway. "Who are you waiting for?"

Annabelle didn't reply. A moment later the men filtered down the hall, Adrian Reed among them, destined for their parlor.

Naomi frowned. "Annabelle, your father and I are about to give Artemis Wentworth permission to court you."

"Yes, I know," Annabelle said, not very interested. "You already told me."

"I think you should make yourself available to Artemis. He'll want to spend time with you."

Annabelle smiled as Adrian came closer. "I'm sorry, Mother, but I told Adrian we could go for a walk after dinner. I want to show him Snowflake. She's such a beautiful horse."

"Annabelle, do not destroy this opportunity," Naomi scolded.

"I won't," she replied as innocently as she could. "But I promised Adrian."

"Ten minutes," Naomi hissed. "No more. Or I will come get you and drag you back. And I'm sure you won't like that."

Annabelle ignored her. "Adrian, you promised me a walk," she said as he approached.

Naomi grabbed her arm tightly. "Ten minutes," she repeated sternly. "I mean it."

"Yes, I did promise you," Adrian said. "And I keep my promises." He turned to Naomi and nodded.

"Please don't be long, Adrian," Naomi said sweetly. "We wouldn't want Annabelle to ignore our other guests."

"No, of course not," he said as they stepped out the door.

When they reached the bottom of the stairs, Zeb Payne came across the lawn. "Annabelle," he called. "May I speak to you for a moment?"

"Yes, of course," she said, waiting until he reached them. "What is it?" She hid her disdain, given what she had seen—Coffey's eyes consumed by terror and shame.

"Mr. Reed," Zeb said with a nod and turned to Annabelle. "Your father told me you've agreed to hire out Coffey Green to Mr. Reed."

"Yes, I did," she said. She wondered when her father had told him. It must have been right after they'd discussed it. "Mr. Reed is desperate for labor, and it seemed Coffey would have a minimal impact on your efforts."

"But that's not true, ma'am," Zeb informed her politely. "I already have a runaway to address. I'm short as it is."

"I can't imagine Coffey making much of a difference," Annabelle said, lips pursed. "She's such a tiny little thing."

"But she does," Zeb assured her. "She bundles tobacco leaves as the others pull them. Then they get loaded on the wagon for curing."

"Can't it be done by someone else?" Annabelle asked. "It doesn't seem difficult."

"No, it isn't," Zeb said. "But if someone has to

replace her, it's one less person working the fields. Production will suffer."

"I understand your concerns," Adrian interjected. "Why don't I use her as a trial, maybe for a month? If it hampers your efforts, we can revisit the agreement."

Annabelle hid a smile. Adrian's compromise was difficult to decline. "Is that acceptable, Zeb?" she asked innocently. "I'm sure the runaway will be back by then."

Zeb shifted his glance between the two. He didn't seem satisfied, but he also didn't want to offend. "Yes, I suppose," he said reluctantly. "A month at most, though. I would prefer two weeks. It is our busiest time."

"Yes, of course," Adrian said. "Whatever you deem appropriate. I do appreciate the help. I'll send a wagon for Coffey on Monday morning."

"Can you have her come see me before she leaves?" Annabelle asked. "Around breakfast should be fine."

"Yes, of course, ma'am," Zeb said. He tipped his hat and left, not among the party guests.

Adrian and Annabelle walked around the house toward the rear of the property. "He seems upset," Adrian whispered.

Annabelle put her hand in his arm and led him along. "I enjoyed making him upset," she admitted with a wry grin. She had been successful on two fronts. She'd provided some protection to Coffey Green, and she'd angered Zeb Payne.

Adrian chuckled. "Why would you want to upset him? He seems like a good man. And he's obviously devoted to Hickory Hill."

Annabelle considered telling him. But she couldn't. It was a secret only she and Coffey shared. "Someday I'll tell you, but not now."

Adrian didn't reply, and they kept walking. "I am grateful for Coffey, but I had hoped for a strong male, someone to fell trees and help transport them to the mill."

"She won't disappoint you," Annabelle assured him. "She's a good worker. A tiny lady, but don't underestimate her."

"I'll find work for her. It'll just be less physical. Tasks that don't require brute strength."

"Let's sit," Annabelle suggested. She led him to a bench, sheltered by trees and shrubs, with a view of the bay and setting sun. It was secluded, not visible from the house. That's why she chose it.

Adrian looked nervously back at the mansion. "Are you sure it's all right to sit here?" he asked. "It's a bit isolated. You mother may not like it."

Annabelle chuckled. "It's fine. Don't worry about my mother. I never do."

They had spent five or six weeks delicately expressing their romantic interests. It was awkward at first, having known each other most of their lives, former childhood playmates. It seemed natural to move slowly, their relationship blossoming into so much more. But now that Artemis Wentworth was part of the equation, there was a sense of urgency. Annabelle realized Adrian was too shy and polite, tied to tradition, and unwilling to move much faster. She had to steer him in the right direction, especially if she hoped to avoid an unwanted engagement to Artemis.

She snuggled up against him and took his hand in hers. If he wouldn't make advances, she would.

Chapter Fifteen

"I told you ten minutes," Naomi snapped, eyes blazing. She waited on the porch as Annabelle and Adrian climbed the stairs. "I was about to come find you."

Annabelle rolled her eyes. "We weren't gone that long."

"It's my fault, Mrs. Banks," Adrian said. "I kept Annabelle longer than planned."

Naomi forced a faint smile. "It's inconsiderate, Adrian. She has other guests who deserve her attention."

"Yes, of course," he muttered, nodding meekly. "My apologies."

Naomi opened the door and led them inside. "Come with me, Annabelle. Artemis is waiting."

Adrian went in the gentleman's parlor while Annabelle followed her mother down the hallway. "I don't know why you're so upset," she mumbled.

"Because I told Artemis to meet us in your father's study. Do you deliberately disobey me? You seem to enjoy this constant combat."

"You're being dramatic, Mother," Annabelle droned. "As always."

"You're being inconsiderate, as always."

"*I* promised Adrian," Annabelle stressed. "*You* promised Artemis."

Naomi was about to reply but decided not to. If she did, the argument would continue until one of them stomped away. She stopped in the hallway and took a deep breath, calming herself.

"We want to make a good impression," she

whispered to Annabelle, pointing to the study.

The door was open, and Naomi breezed in, Annabelle behind her. Artemis Wentworth stood on the far side of the room, his fingers trailing the spines of leather-bound books that lined the shelves.

"We're so sorry to keep you waiting," Naomi said, smiling sweetly. "Annabelle wandered off, and I had to go find her."

Artemis turned and bowed slightly. "Not an inconvenience at all, I assure you."

Naomi lightly urged Annabelle forward. Artemis would make a perfect politician—tall and slender with a thick head of blond hair, blue eyes that twinkled invitingly, and a perfect smile. Actually, everything about him seemed perfect, causing most to inspect him closely, searching for a flaw.

"I've been admiring your husband's books," he continued. "It's an interesting assortment."

"Gideon is quite proud of them," Naomi said. She sat in one of the chairs by the desk, forcing Annabelle and Artemis to sit together on the small sofa.

"You look radiant this evening, Annabelle," Artemis said.

Annabelle blushed. "Thank you, that's very kind."

"As radiant as your mother, I might add," he said, turning to Naomi. "The resemblance is uncanny. You could pass for sisters."

Naomi chuckled. "Mr. Wentworth, I do appreciate your compliment, but I'm afraid it strays from the truth."

"Not at all," he said, looking at each in turn. "And please, call me Artemis. We're past formalities, don't you think?"

"Yes, of course," Naomi replied, glancing at Annabelle. "We only want to give you the respect you deserve."

"Are you really running for senator, Artemis?"

Annabelle asked.

"Yes, most likely," he said. "Although I find several offices attractive."

Naomi was already plotting Annabelle's future. "Would you move to Washington?"

He shrugged. "I don't think so. I can always rent a room when my presence is required. My primary residence will always be in Annapolis."

"Would you still maintain your office in Chestertown?" Naomi asked, knowing it kept him close to Hickory Hill.

"Yes, I suppose," he said, as if he hadn't given it much thought. "Although I'm only there a day or two each week."

"Isn't that your father's residence?" Annabelle asked.

"My sister's, actually," he replied. "And it's not an inconvenience to her, should I still use it, assuming my schedule permits."

"Washington isn't too distant," Annabelle said. "Especially from Annapolis."

"Or from Hickory Hill," Naomi interjected, hinting that any location was favorable to their relationship. She needed to ensure no obstacles surfaced, location or otherwise. "Just across the bay and upriver. Or overland, I suppose. It seems easily done."

"Yes, I would think so," he said, "If I do run for federal office. And if I am elected."

"I'm sure you'll be successful, regardless of what you choose to do," Naomi said. "You're a man of many talents."

He nodded politely. "Thank you, Mrs. Banks. That's very kind."

"We do anxiously await your announcement," Naomi continued. "Don't we, Annabelle?"

"Yes, of course," she said. "All of Maryland does,

I'm sure."

Artemis paused, as if hesitant to reveal too much. "I should reach a decision shortly. Although I have a few details to address, campaign financing for one. But I do expect to run for senate."

"I'm thrilled to hear that," Naomi said. She then frowned, feigning a problem, part of the charade. She intended to steer the courtship, ensuring it didn't run aground. "Although it does offer an unexpected challenge."

"And what is that, Mrs. Banks?" Artemis asked, head cocked.

Naomi sighed audibly. "It's difficult enough for a bachelor to maintain one household, let alone two."

Artemis chuckled and glanced at Annabelle, understanding her implication. "Yes, I suspect you're right. And to be quite honest, Mrs. Banks, I accepted your dinner invitation tonight with an ulterior motive."

"What is that?" Naomi asked, although she knew quite well what it was.

He hesitated as if he didn't want to seem abrupt. "It's always been my intention to ask permission to court Annabelle. I'm so pleased that you and Mr. Banks have granted it."

Naomi feigned surprise and glanced at her daughter. "How wonderful! Annabelle, you must be thrilled."

Annabelle offered a taut smile. "It promises to be an interesting summer."

Chapter Sixteen

Billy Giles' escape hadn't gone like he'd thought it would. No one came to look for him at first, but he knew they would. As soon as the slave wagons got back to the shacks and they realized he was missing.

He had crawled across the neighboring wheat field, close to the trees, and lay in a ditch, waiting for darkness. He was afraid to go farther. A few slaves worked the field, an overseer watching. He couldn't get to the trees, not yet. They would see him.

It was almost dark when the slaves left. He heard horses and risked raising his head. Zeb Payne and two of the field hands wandered up the road. As soon as they moved past him, Billy panicked. He ran blindly across the open field and into the forest. When someone shouted, he scrambled through foliage, his heart racing, his body trembling. And when the voices got louder, he kept running, changing direction.

The forest wasn't friendly. Bigger than expected, it was so dense he could barely pass through it. He eluded Zeb Payne that first night, running in different directions, hiding when he had to. Even after he no longer heard them, he kept stumbling through bushes and shrubs, totally confused. By dawn he was lost. For all he knew, he had wandered around in circles all night.

He covered himself with branches and slept during the day. He wasn't sure if Zeb Payne still pursued him; he couldn't hear anyone. But he knew a whipping waited if he got caught. Afraid to move after he woke, he lay quietly, waiting for dusk. Sometimes he ventured a few feet to scrounge hickory nuts or wood sorrel to eat. He did know plants, those you could eat and those you couldn't. Phoebe Yates had taught him. He never had much use for it on the plantation, but now it kept him alive.

The forest was quiet. Birds sang, an owl asked if anyone approached, branches and leaves rustled in the wind. The towering trees—hickory, pine and oak—only let weak streams of sunshine wash the moss carpet. Ferns, shrubs, and brambles competed for any available space. But it all looked the same, especially to Billy, who had spent his life tending farm fields. And maybe it was all the same. Maybe he'd gone nowhere.

He spent a second night stumbling through darkness, a moonless sky making it hard to see. He was exhausted, constantly peeking through foliage, expecting to see Zeb Payne or Amos Quigg in hot pursuit. The terrain was unfamiliar, and he had only a vague sense of where to go. He was confused, continually changing direction, convinced he was going the wrong way.

By dawn on Sunday, he was forced to admit he was lost. He suspected he hadn't gone far from Hickory Hill even though he doubted he could find his way back. Plodding through darkness, he'd likely made little progress. His escape was failing, and he knew it. He couldn't continue at night; he had to travel during the day, fix the sun's position and use it to guide him. Coffey had said to follow the North Star, but he wasn't sure where that would take him—maybe to the marsh or maybe not. But it would get him to freedom eventually. He finally decided that his destination didn't matter as long as he was free. When he stumbled upon a narrow brook, turning and twisting, he followed it, hoping it trickled into the marsh that fed the stream. After walking for an hour, he heard voices. He crept forward, hiding so he wouldn't be seen.

Seven men, one on horseback, were a hundred feet away. Two were cutting a hickory tree starved for sunlight, crowded by stronger trees. They sawed through the trunk, one on each end of a long heavy blade, sliding it back and forth. The others stood by, chains and prongs stacked on the ground. Horses neighed in the distance, used to transport the tree once it was cut. Billy was surprised. He hadn't expected to find anyone in the forest on the Sabbath.

He couldn't identify the man on horseback. He shifted through the undergrowth to get a better view. But after a few moments, the rider led his horse away so it wouldn't be frightened when the tree came down. Billy watched him as he made his way through the trees, moving in the opposite direction, disappearing and then reappearing as he traveled through the brush.

With an explosive crack, the tree swooped through its neighbors and fell. The ground shook, dirt and dust swelled upward in a plume that hung on the branches, blocking the sun. The loggers began coughing, covering their mouths with their arms, breathing into their sleeves.

While they were distracted, Billy crept forward. Hidden in the underbrush, he circled the loggers and eyed the sun when it peeked through trees. Once he was sure they hadn't seen him, he raced northward.

He tore through brambles, skirting the massive trunks of trees, and stumbled upon a dirt trail. Twelve feet wide, it was marked by trampled reeds, broken twigs and branches—the path the loggers used to drag felled trees from the forest. It had to lead to the stream, river, or even a road. Each could be used to transport logs to the mill. Billy kept running, hoping to find out by nightfall. A quarter mile later, the path veered to the left, hidden by trees and shrubs. As Billy rounded the corner, he stopped abruptly.

Adrian Reed blocked his path, sitting astride his chestnut steed.

Billy gasped, mouth open, eyes wide. He was totally defeated—lost, tired, hungry—and now caught trying to escape. Why did he ever run away, leaving his daughter, momma and Coffey Green, with some naïve notion he would come back to get them?

Adrian Reed didn't speak. He watched Billy fidgeting, frightened and confused.

"Just don't hurt me, Mr. Reed," Billy said, eyes lowered. "I'll go back real peaceful."

Adrian studied him curiously. "Billy Giles."

"Yes, sir," Billy said, eyeing the man who controlled his destiny. He had known him his entire life—a close friend of Miss Annabelle. And he knew what the law said Adrian Reed had to do with a runaway slave.

"The Banks had a dinner party last night. They told me you had escaped."

"I didn't really escape, sir. I don't know where I am or where I'm going. I been wandering around these woods for two days now."

"You didn't get very far," Adrian said. "Only a few miles."

Billy sighed. "Just chasing dreams, is all. But it looks like they gonna get away from me."

"What dreams are you chasing, Billy?"

He rubbed his eyes with his hands, making the weariness go away. "I just want somethin' to call my own. A little land to farm, a place I can raise my daughter, take care of my momma, have a family." He paused, looking back toward the loggers. "Didn't expect to see nobody on the Lord's Day."

"Production is falling behind. A few asked to earn extra money, so I let them work."

"I won't do nobody no harm," Billy pleaded. "I'm just trying to get to the stream."

Adrian was quiet, seeing a man who only wanted what most already had. He hesitated, knowing what was expected, but also knowing what was right and just. After a tense pause, he turned, pointing northeast. "That way," he said softly.

Billy stared, head cocked. He nodded slightly, out of respect, aware of the risk Adrian was taking. "Thank you, sir. I won't tell a soul. And I'll never forget what you did for me."

Adrian nodded. He nudged his horse around the frightened man with pleading eyes and continued down the trail. He didn't look back.

Chapter Seventeen

Jacob Yoder hurried down the lane that ran from his house to the road. The sheriff and his two deputies had stopped Samuel Zook just as he was about to leave the farm. The sheriff despised the Amish—he was the original bidder for the land they occupied, but he wouldn't pay what the Amish did. His deputies hated the Amish, too, their animosity fueled by the sheriff. Any visit came with confrontation. But with a runaway slave stowed under the crates on the wagon, their untimely arrival could be disastrous. The penalties for harboring runaways were severe—prison time and stiff fines—and Jacob realized the tremendous risk his family faced.

"Hold up, Zook," the sheriff called. He was a lithe, older man around fifty with gray hair poking from his broad-brimmed hat. His younger deputies flanked him, three men on chestnut horses blocking the road.

"What's wrong, Sheriff Dodd?" Samuel asked with apprehension.

Dodd scanned the wagon. "We're looking for a runaway. He's been missing for two weeks from a plantation farther south. Where are you off to?"

"I'm delivering these vegetables to my customers," Samuel replied.

"I don't know anything about a runaway, Sheriff," Jacob called as he approached. He had to keep Dodd and his deputies away from the wagon. He just wasn't sure how to do it.

"I can't help you, either," Samuel said with a shrug. "If we'd seen any runaways, we would have contacted you."

Dodd paused, eyeing each in turn. "I don't believe either one of you."

"Why would you not believe us?" Jacob asked, feigning indignation. His heart was racing. The runaway, tucked under crates, could easily be discovered.

Dodd didn't answer, his gaze scanning the farm. "The runaway was seen a few days ago, a mile or so upstream."

Jacob shrugged. "If he came this way, I would have seen him."

"Maybe," Dodd said. "Or you could be hiding him."

"I'm not hiding anyone," Jacob insisted.

Dodd eyed him closely, face firm. "I don't like your kind, Yoder. Never have, never will. And you know why,"

"Yes, I know why, Sheriff," Jacob said, his gaze meeting Dodd's. "And I wonder if someone else had bought the land, if you would despise them, too?"

"You stole the land," Dodd muttered.

Jacob chuckled and glanced at Samuel Zook. "Paying a man the price he wanted is hardly theft."

"I still don't trust you."

"I've given you no reason not to," Jacob said. "And neither has Samuel."

"It's more than the land," Dodd growled. "Everything was fine around here until you people showed up. Now we got runaway slaves and cheap produce flooding the market."

"Farmers up and down the bay been complaining," one of the deputies added. "They can't make any money."

Jacob refused to be bullied by the sheriff or his deputies, regardless of the precarious situation. "Is that it—cheap produce? Maybe if your friends worked harder, they would be more successful."

"You people think you know everything, don't you?" the deputy retorted.

"Easy, Jake," Dodd said to his deputy. "We came to find the runaway. We'll work on getting rid of these folks some other time."

"Won't be soon enough," the deputy mumbled.

"This is my home," Jacob said quietly. "And I intend to stay."

Dodd relented. "For now, it is. But not for long if I have anything to say about it."

"If this runaway was seen a few days ago, why are you looking for him now?" Samuel asked, trying to ease the tension. "He's likely long gone."

Sheriff Dodd got down from his horse and came close to the wagon. "Trail went cold. We're checking places he could be hiding."

Jacob shrugged. "You're welcome to look around, Sheriff."

Dodd was distracted, eyeing the wagon. "What are you carrying, Zook?"

"Produce. I buy a load from Jacob every week and deliver it to my customers."

Dodd reached up to grab a crate, shaking it gently. "What customers?"

"The tavern past the village, along the old highway, some folks in Chestertown."

"Stop by the courthouse when you get to town," Dodd said. "My missus may want some of this. How often do you come by?"

"Once a week," Samuel replied. "Usually Tuesday."

Dodd turned to Jacob. "You should sell it yourself, Yoder. Keep all the profit. I thought you folks were smart."

"If I did that, I'd have less time to farm," Jacob said. He tried not to stare at the wagon, the runaway feet away from Dodd. "Maybe when my children are old enough to help."

"Ain't the missus expecting?" Dodd asked, strolling around the wagon.

"Yes, she is," Jacob replied. He wasn't sure what Dodd was doing other than keeping the wagon close until he figured out what to do. "The baby's coming soon. Before summer ends."

"Good for you," Dodd said, not that he meant it. He stopped at the end of the wagon, pushing crates to see if they moved. "You've got the makings of a real nice family. Shame you don't live someplace else."

"We work hard," Jacob said, ignoring the insult. Sometimes he felt like Dodd just enjoyed their verbal jousting and had long ago forgotten about buying the land. "And we mind our own business."

"Yes, you do," Sheriff Dodd muttered. He turned to his deputies. "Take a ride around the farm. See if you find anything."

"Can I go, Sheriff?" Samuel Zook asked. "My customers are waiting."

"Not just yet," Dodd said as the deputies trotted away. "I want to take a closer look."

Jacob shared a guarded glance with Samuel. Beads of sweat were dotting the back of his neck, his hands slightly trembling. He had to distract the sheriff, get him away from the wagon.

"Why do you crisscross the crates?" Dodd asked. "Seems it'd be harder to unload."

"It's more stable," Samuel said. "The load won't shift. Most of the roads are rutted."

The sheriff stepped onto a foothold at the rear of the wagon and pulled himself up on the bed. He stood on the narrow edge and scanned the load.

Jacob looked away, his heart thumping against his chest. Dodd was so close to the runaway he could almost hear him breathing. He prayed the man didn't move. The slightest shift would attract Dodd's attention.

Ruth came out on the porch and eyed the deputies riding around the outbuildings, sensing danger. She looked at Jacob and waved, a subtle offer to help.

Dodd kicked the rear crate. "Got any empty space up there, near the headboard?"

Samuel's eyes widened. "No, of course not. The bed is fully loaded."

When the sheriff wasn't looking, Jacob signaled Ruth, moving his hand back and forth.

She hesitated, but then grasped his request. She went to the edge of the porch, reached up, and rang a bell hanging from the rafter. The chime echoed across the yard.

Dodd turned, startled, and looked back at the house.

Ruth cupped her hands to her mouth and hollered. "Lunch is ready. Beef stew."

"Will you join us, Sheriff?" Jacob asked quickly, glancing at Samuel.

Dodd hesitated. "Don't you people eat strange food?"

Jacob chuckled, trying to act calm even though he wasn't. "It's beef stew. Not that strange, I don't think. It likely has the same ingredients your wife uses."

Dodd eyed his deputies. "What about my men?"

"They're welcome, too," Jacob said, willing to do anything to get the sheriff away from the wagon. "And so are you, Samuel."

"Thank you, Jacob," Samuel said. "But I have deliveries to make. I want to get home before dark."

Dodd no longer seemed interested in vegetables. He climbed down from the wagon. "You go on, Zook," he said. "But keep a look out for that runaway."

"I will, Sheriff," Samuel promised. "You'll be the first to know if I see him."

The sheriff turned to Jacob as the wagon pulled away. "Whenever there's trouble, you people seem to be in the middle of it."

"I don't see how," Jacob replied, hiding his relief. "We don't bother anyone. How are we making trouble?"

"A runaway close by, undercutting our local farmers, wearing funny clothes."

"None of that sounds like trouble to me, Sheriff. And you know it."

Dodd scowled. "I don't like you, Yoder."

"That's a shame, Sheriff," Jacob said as he glanced at Samuel's wagon moving toward Chestertown, the runaway safely hidden. "Because you don't even know me. We're good people. I farm my land and mind my business."

Dodd eyed him cautiously and started toward the house. "I think I'll have some of your missus' stew," he said, and then turned to his deputies. "Search the outbuildings. I'll be in the house for a few minutes."

"What are we looking for?" a deputy asked. "There's no sign of the runaway."

"Look for where he could have hidden," the sheriff said. He paused, glancing at the outbuildings. "And make sure you search the barn."

Chapter Eighteen

Coffey Green left her shack Monday morning just after the sun showed its face over rows of tobacco stretching to the horizon. A ramshackle wagon waited, the back filled with a dozen slaves, Molly and her daughters among them. Coffey was about to climb on for a ride to the fields when Zeb Payne approached. She eyed him anxiously, hiding her fear.

"Coffey, come here for a minute," he called, standing twenty feet from the wagon.

She suspected she knew what he wanted. But she couldn't stop it. Not unless she killed him. How could a soul be so evil? She walked meekly toward him. The other slaves remained in the wagon, some watching, some not. None knew the hell she was living. But they each lived their own hell, dressed in different disguises.

"Yes, sir, Mr. Payne," Coffey asked, her gaze trained on the ground.

"Miss Annabelle wants to see you."

Coffey cocked her head. "Miss Annabelle want to see me?"

"That's what I said, isn't it?" Zeb said, glancing at those in the wagon.

Coffey was confused. "Yes, sir, I just don't know why she would."

"Go over to the main house and see what she wants. Don't keep her waiting."

"Yes, sir," Coffey said but then hesitated. "Is it too early? The sun barely come up."

Zeb shrugged. "She wanted to see you before you

went into the fields."

"I'll go right now, sir." She looked back at the wagon, preparing to depart. "How do I get out to the fields?"

Zeb frowned. "Go see Miss Annabelle." He signaled the driver and the wagon pulled away, squeaking on wobbly wheels.

Coffey was nauseous—as she always was whenever she was alone with Zeb Payne. She took a few tentative steps toward the main house, watching the wagon roll away. She expected Zeb Payne to send her back to her shack as soon as no one was looking. But he walked away and untethered his horse. Without another word, he rode away.

Something had changed, but she wasn't sure what it was. She looked at the main house, the chimneys poking over tree tops. With a last glance at Zeb Payne riding to the fields, she walked down a worn trail past the kitchen. A few house servants milled about, getting the morning meal ready for the Banks family.

What could Miss Annabelle want? Was it about Zeb Payne—what Miss Annabelle had seen, or thought she had seen? Or was it something different? For a brief instant she felt a glimmer of hope. When she reached the mansion, she quietly went in the back door.

"What are you doing here, Coffey?" Phoebe asked. "Ain't you supposed to be in the fields?"

"Mr. Payne said Miss Annabelle want to see me."

Phoebe eyed her strangely. "What would Miss Annabelle want with you, child?"

Coffey shrugged. "I'm just doin' what I was told."

"Miss Annabelle came down for breakfast a few minutes ago. I ain't about to disturb her."

"Can you just ask what she wants? I need to get out to the fields 'fore Mr. Payne gets riled up. I don't need no whuppin'."

Phoebe hesitated, hands on her hips. "I'll ask her, but I don't like it. And neither will she."

Coffey waited by the back door. She was afraid to go inside, knowing she didn't belong. A few moments later, Phoebe returned.

"Come on," she said. "Miss Annabelle want to talk to you while she's havin' her breakfast."

"I don't know any more than you," Coffey protested as she followed. "I just don't want no trouble."

Coffey hadn't spent much time in the main house. But every time she did, she was awed by the wealth on display—crisply painted white trim, bright wallpaper that felt like silk when she furtively touched it, landscape paintings that seemed so real it was as if she looked through a window, crystal chandeliers hanging from every ceiling.

Phoebe led her into the dining room. Annabelle sat at the end of the table, biscuits, cider, and a bowl of porridge before her. "Come in, Coffey," she said when she saw her in the doorway.

Coffey shyly took a few steps into the room, eyes lowered. Phoebe stayed beside her, very protective. "Mr. Payne says you wanted to see me, Miss Annabelle."

"Yes, I did," Annabelle said.

"Did I do something wrong?"

Annabelle chuckled. "No, of course not," she said and sipped her cider. "I wanted to be the one to tell you."

Coffey wasn't sure what she was talking about. "Tell me what, Miss Annabelle?" she asked, wondering what sort of trouble she'd caused.

"You won't be working in the fields for a while," Annabelle said simply.

Coffey didn't understand. "I won't?" she asked, confused. "Where else would I work?"

"We've rented you out to Adrian Reed. You know Mr. Reed, don't you?"

"Yes, ma'am, I do. But I don't know what you telling me to do."

"Mr. Reed will send a wagon for you," Annabelle said. "He'll take you to his sawmill, just down the road. You'll work for him each day, and he'll provide meals and a place to stay. He'll bring you back on Saturday. Monday morning, he'll come get you again."

"What am I gonna do for Mr. Reed?" Coffey asked. She was anxious, afraid of the unknown. Was she walking from one disaster to the next?

Annabelle shrugged. "I don't know, but I'm sure he'll explain it to you. Hopefully it's better than the tobacco fields."

Coffey couldn't hide her glee. "I suspect anything is better than the tobacco fields, ma'am." She realized Annabelle was helping her, doing what she could to make life easier, ensuring she avoided Zeb Payne.

Annabelle smiled. "I think you'll enjoy it. Unfortunately, you won't take direction from Mr. Payne for a while. Actually, you'll see very little of him. Is that a problem?"

Coffey sighed with relief, unable to believe her good fortune. "No, Miss Annabelle, not a problem at all. But I suspect Mr. Payne won't like it much."

"It doesn't matter what Mr. Payne likes."

Coffey shrugged. "If you say so, Miss Annabelle. But he still gonna try to tell me what to do. You just know he will."

Chapter Nineteen

Coffey didn't know what to expect when Adrian Reed's wagon came to get her. The driver was an older man, his face partially masked by a grizzly white beard. He nodded as he pulled up along the lane to the main house by the path that turned off to the slaves' quarters, and remained on the bench seat. He made no effort to assist as she climbed up in the wagon—not that she expected him to.

She got in the back, the bed littered with wood shavings. There were no benches—it was open—so she sat in the very back with her legs dangling over the end. As soon as she was settled, the driver wiggled the reins, and the wagon jerked forward. She grasped the side, holding it for support, and watched as Hickory Hill began to fade in the distance.

She had left the plantation many times, usually visiting Chestertown or another nearby village with an overseer to purchase items for the house. The trips were rare since they grew or raised almost all the food they needed—chickens, pigs, cows, a variety of vegetables. And many household items, like wooden ladles used for cooking, were made at the plantation.

The ride didn't last long. The driver led the horse down the lane and out to the road, heading south toward the harbor at Rock Hall. A few miles farther, past the fields of the plantation and perched along the mouth of an inlet where it spilled into the bay, the main office, shipbuilding operations, and sawmills for Reed and Sons sprawled along a peninsula that bordered the bay to the west and the harbor to the east. As the wagon came up to the sawmill, a handsome man with brown hair stood on the porch, waiting.

Coffey knew Adrian Reed, one of Annabelle Banks' suitors, a man who had been friends of the family ever since she arrived at the plantation. He smiled and nodded as the wagon stopped, and Coffey climbed down from the back.

"Good morning, Coffey," he said as he came toward her.

"Hello, Mr. Reed," she said. Her gaze met his, and she quickly averted it, staring at the ground. She didn't want to show any disrespect.

Adrian Reed eyed her closely, not speaking. He hesitated, almost as if he questioned his decision to rent her, and an awkward silence prevailed.

"Is everything all right, Mr. Reed?" Coffey asked anxiously. She didn't know what to expect. Would he be like Zeb Payne or Jack Dunn? Zeb Payne didn't whip anybody like Jack Dunn used to, but in some ways he was worse, pretending to be good when he was pure evil.

"Yes, of course," he said, rubbing his chin. "I'm wondering what we can have you do. You're such a tiny lady. You can't help logging crews. Do you know anything about lumber or sawmills?"

"No, sir, I don't."

"How about bookkeeping? Can you read and write?"

"I can't read, sir. But I know my Bible, mostly from stories other folks tell. Mainly Molly."

"Who's Molly?"

Coffey paused. It was hard to explain. Folks didn't understand that several families were squeezed into one slave shack. "I've known Molly since I came to Hickory Hill ten years ago," she said, keeping her explanation short. "I live in her house, with her two young'uns."

"You'll stay in my house through the week," Adrian

said. "I'll bring you back to Hickory Hill on Saturday afternoon and then pick you up again Monday morning."

"Yes, sir," she said. She wasn't sure she liked the arrangements—not that it mattered. She supposed Mr. Reed paid good money for her.

He hesitated, his thoughts returning to business. "Can you do numbers at all? Addition and subtraction?"

She frowned. "No, sir, I can't. I don't even know what that is."

"What can you do?" he asked softly, trying not to offend.

"I can cook or tend fields. I know all about tobacco and wheat."

Adrian crossed his arms, his lips pursed. "Do you know anything about trees?"

Her eyes widened. "Oh, yes, sir, I do. I know a whole lot about trees and plants. Phoebe taught me all about them."

His interest was piqued. "Tell me what you know."

"I know what plants are good and which are bad."

He looked at her quizzically. "I'm not sure I understand."

"Some plants can kill, but others can cure. They make for good tonics and such."

"How about trees?"

"I know how to make them grow and what the parts can be used for."

He seemed interested. "Tell me."

"I can make them grow faster, covering the scedlings with different plants and leaves, or I know what grows good together—like corn, beans, and squash—and what don't."

"Do you know how lumber is made?"

"No, sir, I don't. But I know everything on a tree can be used for something. Firewood or kindling, and stuff can be made from roots and bark."

He cocked his head. "What are roots and bark used for, other than firewood?"

"You can boil some roots and make tea or a tonic that's good for cuts and bruises. Some resin even get used for cream the white ladies use."

Adrian chuckled. "What kind of cream is that?"

"They put it on their face to make their skin smooth," she said. She leaned closer, sharing a secret. "Some say it keeps them young. They don't get no wrinkles."

He paused, his thoughts wandering. "Coffey, I think this is going to work out nicely."

Chapter Twenty

Adrian listened to Coffey intently.

"Phoebe like oak trees the best," Coffey said. "She call it sacred. Leaves are good for cuts. And if you powder the root, it can heal folks who get real sick."

Adrian was determined not to underestimate her, which was easy to do. She was slight, barely five feet, and so soft-spoken he sometimes strained to hear her. It had even been difficult to get her to talk at first, she was so shy, respectful and polite. She had a vulnerability he couldn't identify, masked by a woman who pretended to be stronger than she was. It wasn't fear, or at least it didn't seem like fear, but a part of her was fragile. Maybe she had once been broken and had never fully mended.

"The inside of the bark is good for healin', too," she continued. "And you can make tea from the roots. It helps sick folks feel better."

"Let's walk a bit," he said, interrupting her. He hadn't expected so much information. Especially from a woman he had known for so many years but had barely spoken to.

"Yes, sir," she said, an apprehensive look on her face. "I didn't talk too much, did I?"

"No, it was interesting," Adrian said, thinking of potential applications for the waste that was generated during the shipbuilding process.

She chuckled. "You just sayin' that to be nice."

"No, I'm not," he said, his eyes twinkling.

"You ain't playin' games with me, are you, Mr. Reed?"

He grinned. "No, of course not. I just never

expected so much information. You're a very smart young lady."

"I ain't smart at all," she said. "I told you I don't know numbers."

"A lot of people don't know numbers," he assured her. "Even some who think they do."

She smiled. "I don't say much, usually, but sometimes when I get to talkin', I can't stop. Phoebe and Molly always tease me."

"You can say whatever you want around me. I'll never tease you."

He took her past the sawmill to a small clearing near the water. It was littered with debris—roots, branches, bark, broken bits of timber. "Most of this will be used for firewood. The rest will be burned as waste."

"Oh, no, sir," Coffey said. "You can use all of this. Just like I told you. Especially them oak roots."

"We use pine, oak, and hickory for shipbuilding. What can our waste be used for?"

"Well, each tree a little different, sir. Do you want me to tell you about it?"

"Yes, tell me everything."

Coffey shrugged. "Alright, you asked. Just tell me when I need to shut up. Or I might talk forever."

He liked her. She was a good person, making the best of the life she'd been given. "No, go on. I'm listening."

"I'll start with hickory," she said. "Best use for scrap is to smoke meat, but you already know that. But you can boil the nuts in water. The oil splits up, and you can use it for cooking or mix it with water and make hickory milk. Some folks even use it for butter or cream."

Adrian was listening closely. He was a businessman, searching for profit potential. He hadn't considered using the nuts of the hickory tree. But he didn't see a huge market for hickory milk. "What about pine?"

"You can eat the nuts from the tree. And make broth from the needles."

Adrian wasn't interested. "Anything else?"

"Yes, sir, the resin. You steam it from the wood. It's a good tonic for bruises. And you can use the resin for candles, too."

"I didn't know that," Adrian muttered. Perhaps scrap from pine trees would offer opportunities. "How about oak—other than what you've already told me?"

"Brew the roots to make ale."

Adrian laughed. "Ale is easy to come by."

"Not for folks like me," Coffey said with a grin.

He chuckled. "Anything else?"

"Oh, yes, sir. The resin from oak makes skin pretty. Wrinkles go away."

Adrian smiled. "I never heard that before."

Coffey cast a serious look. "Oh, yes, sir, it does. That's the cream I was tellin' you 'bout. Miz Naomi use it all the time. But Miss Annabelle don't need nothing for her skin. Every inch of her is beautiful."

"Yes, it is," Adrian agreed, thinking. "She is very beautiful."

Coffey smiled shyly. "Some say you courting Miss Annabelle."

Adrian chuckled. "I am," he admitted. "Someday, I hope to marry her."

"I hope you do, Mr. Reed. I think you'd both like that."

He sighed, his thoughts wandering to a wedding that might never occur. Not if Naomi and Artemis Wentworth had anything to do with it. But he returned to business. "This cream that you make from the oak residue, do a lot of women use it?"

"I suspect so. It works real good. If more rich folk knew about it, they'd all be rubbing it on their faces."

"Yes, they would," Adrian mumbled. He paused,

pensive. "There's a big city across the bay called Baltimore. I bet ladies would pay for the cream, if it's as good as you say."

"Oh, for sure, sir," Coffey said, her expression serious. "They'd see. Just have to use it a few times."

"And the tonic, too," Adrian continued. "From the pine tree."

"Yes, sir, they would. It work real good. Heals cuts up real quick."

"Could you make it for me?"

She shrugged. "I suppose I could. I'd need some other stuff to mix in with it. But it all come from the forest. And some jars to put it in."

"I'll get the jars. You can get whatever else you need."

"If that's what you want, I can do it."

Adrian hesitated. "I have to talk to my father and brothers first."

"They the ones that build the boats?"

Adrian nodded. "They're usually over there," he said, pointing to a building past the sawmill. He looked back at all the debris. "Is there anything else you get from oak?"

"Oh, yes, sir," Coffey said. "You can eat the acorn. Just have to boil it first."

"And what if you don't?"

"If you eat too many you get real sick."

"Can you die?"

She shrugged. "I suppose. But other plants are better for killing. If that's what you want to do."

Adrian's eyes widened. Maybe he had underestimated her, after all.

Chapter Twenty-One

Adrian took Coffey to his house at the end of the day. "This is where you'll stay through the week."

The house was recently built for Adrian's family, assuming he soon would marry. It was spacious, tucked between trees in the cove, quiet and peaceful. The property bordered Hickory Hill, split by forest from the farthest field, and sat a few miles north of the shipbuilding operation at the harbor. It faced the water, the mighty Chesapeake, with frontage along the road that wound along the coast.

"You're welcome to wander the house whenever you choose," Adrian said as they stood in the foyer. He pointed to the right. "The parlor, with my study behind it."

Coffey looked at the spacious room, eyes wide. "You live here by yourself?"

"Yes, only me," he said, and motioned to the stairs. "Although there are plenty of bedrooms for a family when the time comes."

"Mr. Reed, you could fit a few families in here, not just one."

He chuckled and led her into the dining room. A crystal chandelier hung above an oak table, a buffet against the wall.

"Just this room is bigger than the hut where me and Molly stay."

He smiled. "But it's nowhere near as big as Hickory Hill."

"No, sir, you right about that."

"I'll show you the kitchen," he said when they

reached the end of the hall.

"The kitchen is outside at the big house. They don't want no fire."

"That's how they built those old mansions," he said. "Less heat in the house from cooking and less risk of fire."

"Do you want me to make your meals?" she asked.

He nodded. "And if you can do a little cleaning, too."

"Are you sure you want me staying in here?" she asked. "I ain't use to nothing like this."

"Absolutely," he said. "No different than the house servants at Hickory Hill."

"I suspect it is," she muttered. "They up in the attic."

"Come on, I'll show you upstairs."

They climbed the stairs, ending at a broad hallway with bedrooms on each side. "This is a beautiful house," Coffey said, shaking her head in awe.

"Thank you," Adrian replied. He pointed to the right. "My bedroom."

Coffey looked inside. "Big room," she said. "I don't know what you gonna do with all that space."

He chuckled and led her down the hall. "Spare bedrooms," he said, passing three more rooms.

"You can fit plenty of young'uns in here."

At the end of the hallway sat the servant's quarters, a small room separated from the house proper. "This will be your bedroom."

Her eyes opened wide. It was cozy, a bed with a mattress centered in the room, a bureau with a mirror against the wall. A small kitchen, fit into a narrow hallway, lay behind it. "Oh. Mr. Reed," she said, slowly shaking her head. "I ain't never stayed in a place like this before."

"I hope you enjoy it," he said. They turned down the hallway and started back down the steps.

"I can see the day when little feet are running up

and down these stairs," Coffey said.

Adrian smiled. "Not too far away, I hope."

"Good for you, Mr. Reed. All your dreams should come true. That's what Billy Giles always say. Everybody's dreams should come true."

"Isn't he the runaway?" Adrian asked, even though he knew he was.

"Yes, sir. Such a gentle man. He got all sorts of dreams."

Adrian noticed her face light up. "I suspect Billy Giles is more than a friend."

She laughed shyly, looking away. "Maybe he is."

Adrian chuckled. "Good for you. I hope you're together someday."

"We'll see, Mr. Reed. Whatever the good Lord brings."

He paused for a moment and then pointed to the kitchen. "I'll be away for dinner this evening, a prior engagement."

"I just fend for myself?"

"Yes, of course," he said. "You'll find fruit, vegetables, plates, mugs—everything you need. And there's meat in the smokehouse. Eat whatever you like."

"Yes, sir," she said, slowly shaking her head. "Mr. Reed, I ain't never been treated like this before."

He chuckled. "It's how you'll be treated when you're here."

"Lordy be," she said. "I be living like rich folks. A bed with a mattress and fine sheets, smooth and clean like nobody ever slept there."

He smiled. "Nobody has."

She hesitated, eyeing him cautiously.

"What's the matter?" he asked, confused by her expression.

She shook her head.

"No, don't," he said, lightly touching her arm. "You

can tell me."

"I just don't know why you being so nice," she said. "You ain't gonna make me do something I don't want to do, are you?"

He cocked his head. "I don't know what you mean."

She sighed, eyes lowered. "Is that why you want me staying up here? What my bedroom is for?"

He frowned once he understood what she meant. "No, Coffey, it isn't. Your bedroom is where you sleep and where you go when you want to be alone. Nothing more."

She gasped, eyes wide, and then chuckled and shook her head. "The good Lord done took me to heaven."

Chapter Twenty-Two

After he was confronted by Adrian Reed, Billy Giles ran through the forest, leaving broken branches and snapped twigs—an easy trail to follow. Gasping, his muscles aching, he didn't stop until he reached the marsh. He wasn't sure why Mr. Reed had let him go—and even pointed the way to freedom, but Billy wanted to get as far as he could before he changed his mind. He understood the risk Adrian Reed had taken. If anyone ever found out what he had done, he would be in as much trouble as Billy. The law didn't take kindly to those who helped runaways.

Billy was tired after staggering around all night and running through the forest during the day. He wondered how far he was from Hickory Hill—probably not too far. He had walked and run many miles; he was sure of that. But he had spent most of his time lost in the woods, wandering around in circles.

He needed rest, especially now that he'd found the marsh. He decided to sleep as long as he needed to. At dawn, he would start again. The marsh might be bigger than he thought, and he wanted to cross it in one day. After the marsh he would ford the stream, searching for a farm owned by the man with the strange name and funny beard, Jacob Yoder. He lay down among some foliage and drifted off to sleep.

His slumber was interrupted by shrieks and howls. At first he thought he was dreaming, but as the noise got louder, he started to stir, tossing and turning. When he heard it more clearly, he leaped to his feet. Dogs barking and men shouting—and they weren't far away. He staggered a few steps, disoriented, not sure where to go. The dogs were coming quickly, their yelps and cries echoing through the forest.

Dense limbs hid the sun. Only weak streams of light filtered through branches. He darted to a clearing and looked skyward. The sun poked over the horizon, its full face showing on the eastern sky. It was early morning. And now he knew which way to go.

He kept running, the marsh was just ahead, sprawling into the distance. Clumps of tall reeds with occasional spits of dry land dotted the soaked soil. The water was inches deep in some places, several feet in others. He stepped on one clump of reeds, saw another a few feet away and stretched, barely making it. Between reeds and occasional fingers of land that were barely a few feet across, he managed to move quickly, heading east.

Bloodhounds howled, driving closer. Billy hoped they would lose his scent when they reached the water. He moved as fast as he could, trying to stay dry. But the farther he went, the closer the dogs got, and a moment later, he heard voices, men talking.

"He's not far," Amos Quigg said, a voice Billy recognized. "He's real close. I can even smell the bastard."

"The dogs are heading into the marsh," a stranger added.

"Billy thinks they'll lose his scent in the water," Quigg said, laughing. "That's how damn dumb he is."

Billy was desperate. Only minutes away from apprehension, he waded through shallow water. He watched for snakes, breaking branches along the way, not caring if he left a trail. Distance was most important. He had to get as far away from the dogs as he could, and if he made it to the stream, he could lose them.

"The dogs got his scent," Amos Quigg said. "We just have to follow them."

They splashed through the muddy water. The dogs

barked and yelped, pulling their handlers forward. Wading through water wasn't enough to lose them; it didn't even slow them down. Billy glanced at the plants and reeds around him, searching for anything he could use to ward them off—something to hide his scent.

"Here's his trail," Quigg said. "Broken branches, footprints in the mud." He started laughing. "He may as well hang up a sign."

"Won't be long now," his partner said. "Dogs are hard to handle. They know he's close."

Billy ducked down and parted the reeds. He peeked back through. Far in the distance he could see Amos Quigg and his partner. Two bloodhounds pulled at the end of a leash. They were coming straight toward him. Billy crouched, bent at the waist, and moved through the water.

"This way," the other slave catcher said. "The dogs are fixed on him now. He ain't getting away."

Billy stepped onto a clump of land. Dense reeds covered most of it. He glanced at the sun, seeking direction, and crept across. On the other side, he stepped back in the water and, though he thought it only inches deep, it dropped off steeply, the water waist-high.

"We're close, Billy Giles," Amos Quigg yelled. "Better just give up, boy. The whipping won't be as bad."

"Over this way," his partner said. "Past that clump of reeds."

Billy moved faster. He reached another outcropping of land. He hid among the reeds, crouched over, hoping the water would kill his scent, anxiously eyeing the approaching bloodhounds.

"We're coming, Billy," Amos Quigg yelled. "Don't make me turn the dogs loose."

"They'd rip him apart," his partner said, laughing.

They were just on the other side of the reeds. Billy tried to stay calm. But he couldn't. His pulse raced. Sweat dotted the back of his neck. His hands trembled. But he kept moving through the water, sinking to different depths, then rising again as he crept across clumps of land.

He had to outsmart them. If he didn't, he'd be back at Hickory Hill. But first they would beat him to a pulp, if only to teach him and everyone who watched not to run away. And he'd never catch a single dream, never have his own land and a place to raise a family. Worst of all, he'd fail his momma, his daughter and Coffey Green. He had told them all he'd come back to rescue them, bringing them to the promised land, where all were free to do as they chose.

The water was waist-high. The dogs were gaining, fixed on his scent. He eyed the reeds, shrubs, any plants he passed, Phoebe Yates' voice echoing in his mind. 'Some plants kill, others cure,' she had told him. 'Most smell sweet but some stink bad. They hide scents real good.' He just had to find the right one. It was there somewhere, he just had to look.

He ducked behind a clump of reeds and scrambled forward, careful to stay out of sight. At the edge of the embankment he saw a plant with yellow blooms about two feet high, just what he'd been looking for. Phoebe called it stinking gum or the devil's dung; he didn't know the real name. She sometimes used it in cooking, but it had a pungent odor when it was raw. He pulled it from the ground and broke the root. A gummy resin oozed out. He rubbed it on his shirt and all over his body. When he reached shallow water, he rubbed the rest on the top of his trousers and the worn soles of his shoes where the water had leaked in. Then he kept moving.

"He's over this way," Quigg shouted.

Billy pressed on. The odor from the stinking gum would confuse the dogs. He was sure of it. But he had to be careful not to leave a trail—not a single footprint or snapped twig.

"He's gotta be straight ahead," the other man said.

"The dogs are headed that way."

Their voices were fainter. Maybe the dogs were losing the scent. The slavecatchers were confused, bickering about which way to go. Billy scurried through the water, moving as fast as he could. He crept through the marsh, moving slowly but steadily, making sure they couldn't see him. When he could barely hear them any longer, he glanced back.

Amos Quigg and his partner were stumbling through the marsh, chasing a ghost.

Chapter Twenty-Three

A buffet sat against the wall of the Banks' dining room, a silver tray laden with sliced venison resting upon it. Bowls of potatoes and peas sat beside a plate of warm cornbread with pitchers of water and apple cider, two open bottles of wine and apple pie completing the menu. Caesar stood at one end of the buffet, Phoebe at the other, waiting patiently, prepared to meet the slightest need Gideon, Naomi or Annabelle might have. As always, Gideon sat at the head, Naomi and Annabelle on each side, leaving a long, empty expanse of table that could comfortably seat sixteen diners.

"Has Amos Quigg found Billy Giles yet?" Annabelle asked.

"No, but he will," Gideon said. "He's found every slave he's ever been hired to catch."

They eyed each other cautiously, hesitant to speak in front of Caesar and Phoebe. After an awkward moment, Naomi turned to address them. "Can you leave us for a moment, please?"

"Yes, of course, Miz Naomi," Caesar said, sharing a guarded glance with Phoebe. "We'll wait in the hall. Call us when you need us."

When they had left the room and closed the door, Naomi turned to her husband. "I think we should sell Billy Giles as soon as he's caught. If he ran once, he'll run again. And next time, he'll convince others to join him."

Gideon placed his hand over hers, lightly caressing it. "But he's a good worker, one of our best. I would hesitate to part with him."

Naomi frowned. "It doesn't matter if he's a good worker or not. He's not worth the aggravation—or the expense should he run again."

Annabelle watched them squabble. It was rare that they disagreed. And when they did, her father almost always acquiesced, letting her mother have her way. She decided to offer a compromise. "I think he would stay if we gave him an incentive."

Naomi leaned back in the chair. "What are you talking about? He doesn't make demands. And he never will."

"I'm talking about something simple," Annabelle said, brows knitted.

"Like what?" Naomi asked, eyes wide. "I'm not rewarding him for running away."

"No, I understand. But we can give him something of his own to induce him to stay. Maybe a shanty just for his family."

"And burden everyone else?" Naomi asked. "No, we won't give him anything. It'll only give others a reason for mischief. We need to sell him."

"Why would you sell him if he's such a good worker?" Annabelle countered.

"Because he'll fetch a good price, and we can buy another," Naomi replied, her expression stern and passive. "Someone more appreciative of what we do for them. It's a simple business decision."

Annabelle was aghast. "But his mother and daughter would be heartbroken. And they do all the sewing you're always so quick to boast about. How could you be so cruel to them? They're like family to us."

"Oh, Annabelle," Naomi scoffed, her faced wrinkled with disgust. "If he cared about them, he wouldn't have left to begin with."

"But he does care about them," Annabelle insisted. "I know he does."

"Then why did he run?" Naomi asked.

It was a battle Annabelle was bound to lose. But she was determined to fight it anyway. "Maybe he intends to come back for them once he knows the escape route."

Naomi sighed and shook her head. "He's not coming back," she insisted. "He's not capable of caring for anyone but himself. He doesn't have emotions like we do."

Annabelle rolled her eyes. "Mother, not only is that not true, it's harsh. I'm sure you don't mean it."

Naomi shrugged. "Maybe not," she grumbled. "But he shouldn't have run off."

"Billy is a person just like us," Annabelle continued, struggling not to raise her voice. "He's an ambitious man with hopes and dreams, someone who wants a better future for his daughter." She leaned forward, sharing a secret. "And he wants to marry Coffey Green."

"Then why did he run?" Naomi asked. "Doesn't that prove my point? If he loves Coffey Green, why abandon her?"

"Enough," Gideon said loudly, raising his hands. "It's not a discussion for the dinner table."

They returned to their meal, a cloud of tension cloaking the room. Gideon didn't lose his temper very often. It took a few minutes for everyone to calm. But Naomi wasn't finished discussing slaves. "Whatever possessed you to rent Coffey Green to Adrian Reed?"

"He needed help, and she was all I could spare."

"Are you serious?" Naomi asked. "Coffey Green isn't much bigger than a child. How can she help build ships?"

Gideon shrugged. "I really don't know. But Adrian seemed happy to have her. He must have something for her to do."

"But why rent her out?" Naomi asked. "Especially when we're shorthanded to begin with."

"Because I asked him to," Annabelle said firmly.

Naomi paused. "Whatever for?"

"To protect her."

Naomi cocked her head. "Annabelle, you're not making sense. Protect her from what?"

Annabelle hesitated. It wasn't her secret to share. But it was better that she did. "Zeb Payne has been taking liberties with Coffey that he has no right to take."

Naomi's eyes widened. "Are you sure? Because that's a serious accusation."

"Zeb Payne is a perfect gentleman," Gideon said. "And he's the best overseer we've ever had. He would never do anything like that. The other slaves would rebel if they found out."

"Maybe he doesn't care."

"But that's absurd," Gideon said. "He understands the risk."

"You may not know him as well as you think," Annabelle declared.

Chapter Twenty-Four

Naomi listened to Annabelle's accusation. If it were true, she could rid herself of a possible threat before it materialized. She still wasn't sure if she had ever met Zeb Payne before, but he knew her. His expression had proved it during their introduction. Whether planned or accidental, though, his arrival was problematic.

"Gideon, Annabelle is right," Naomi said cautiously. "We know very little about Zeb Payne."

Annabelle put her fork on her plate and gave her mother a strange look. "Are you *agreeing* with me?" she asked, dumbfounded. "I can't ever remember you agreeing with me."

"Don't be ridiculous," Naomi scoffed, hiding her true motive. "If Zeb Payne is harassing servants, we'll end up with a dozen runaways, not just Billy Giles. I don't want that to happen."

Gideon frowned. "We have a suspicion, nothing more. The man has good character and he's a brilliant overseer."

"But we don't even know him," Naomi stressed. "You met him at an auction and got a reference from his friend. For all we know, he could be a thief or murderer."

Gideon sighed. "You're right, I could have done more of an investigation into his background. But he knows how to run a plantation. We'll have record profits this year, and much of that is due to him. He's done nothing to make me suspicious of his behavior. He's a perfect gentleman."

"I'm sure Coffey Green doesn't agree with you," Annabelle said tartly.

Gideon didn't reply. He picked at his meal and sipped his wine.

"I'm sorry," Naomi said with distaste. "I just don't like the man."

"You've only met him once," Gideon said. "And spoke to him briefly on a few other occasions. You don't know him. Or what he does for Hickory Hill."

"No, I don't," Naomi said. She had to tread carefully, weave suspicion where it might not exist. "But we don't need a rebellion. You know what's happened down south. They've had several uprisings."

Gideon frowned. "We don't know why slaves rebel in other locations and I don't really care. We treat our people well."

"Coffey isn't being treated well," Annabelle mumbled. "Nobody deserves what happened to her."

"You don't even know if it's true," he countered.

"I know what I saw," Annabelle said. "How can you deny it?"

Gideon eyed his daughter, face firm. "It's easy enough to find out. I'll ask her."

Annabelle's eyes widened. "No, you won't. She's a private person. She would never discuss it."

"She may think we wouldn't believe her anyway," Naomi added.

Gideon was skeptical. "No one would have believed her, at least until now. What's changed?"

Naomi had to temper her comments. She may have gone too far. "I just don't want any discontent."

Gideon eyed mother and daughter. "We won't know what happened unless we talk to Coffey and Zeb."

"I think we should respect her privacy," Annabelle said.

Naomi wasn't about to give up so easily. Suspicion had been cast on Zeb Payne. She wanted to ensure it stayed there. "I still don't like the way he was hired. It was a rash decision. We know nothing about him."

"We needed an overseer, and we needed one quickly," Gideon said defensively. "He was available, and he's doing a fabulous job."

"Why don't we just find out more about him?" Annabelle suggested.

Naomi was quiet, afraid of what might be revealed. She didn't need anyone digging up buried secrets. "It's not that important," she mumbled. She would fight the battle differently—if she had to fight it.

Gideon looked at her, eyes wide. "A minute ago, you wanted the man fired because he may or may not have taken liberties with a slave. Now you want to ignore it."

Naomi shrugged. "If you're pleased with his performance, then why bother?"

"I'll make some inquiries," Gideon promised, trying to please them both.

"Don't," Naomi said. "No one cares anyway." Her feigned indifference had planted seeds of doubt—just as she had hoped.

"Coffey cares," Annabelle muttered. "She has no one—no mother, father, or siblings."

Gideon frowned. "I know that," he reminded them. "I rescued her at the auction."

"She's grateful, I'm sure," Annabelle assured him. "But she still has no one to confide in."

"She has Phoebe," Naomi offered. "Molly, too."

Annabelle shook her head. "Not with something like that." She paused, eyeing her parents sternly. "Don't either of you breathe a word."

"We won't," Naomi promised, glancing at Gideon.

He nodded, face firm. "I know what we can do," he said. "I'll ask Artemis Wentworth to look into Zeb's background. He's a solicitor with contacts all over the country."

"Or we could just ask Zeb," Annabelle suggested.

"I'd prefer not to," Gideon said. "He's too good to lose. I don't want to offend him, especially if he's done nothing wrong."

"But why bother if you're satisfied with his performance?" Naomi interjected. She couldn't let anyone conduct an investigation. Not with what might be found. "It's a simple solution. Tell him to keep his hands off Coffey. If he doesn't, fire him."

Gideon eyed them skeptically. "I don't want to accuse him without better evidence."

Annabelle frowned. "If you want evidence, I'll get it."

"Just let it go," Naomi insisted. "If there is an issue, it's been solved. Coffey has been hired out to Adrian Reed, at least temporarily."

"I know what I saw," Annabelle insisted, not willing to surrender. "I can't forget it, and I can't ignore it."

"I'll mention it to Artemis," Gideon said. "But for now, we won't let Zeb know we suspect him."

Naomi returned to her dinner, wondering how she could stop what she'd started.

Chapter Twenty-Five

After dinner, Annabelle was playing Mozart's "Minuet in G Major" on the piano. Naomi sat on the sofa, doing needlepoint, Gideon beside her, reading a newspaper. When someone knocked on the door, she stopped playing and smiled. She knew who it was.

Caesar came down the hall and answered the door. They could hear muttered voices, the front door closed, and Caesar appeared in the parlor. "Mr. Reed has come to call."

Gideon Banks folded his newspaper and put it on the table. "Show him in."

Adrian entered a moment later. "Good evening," he said, nodding to Gideon and Naomi.

Annabelle turned on the piano bench to face him. "Hello, Adrian. It's nice to see you."

Naomi Banks cast a stern look at her daughter, which went unnoticed—or ignored.

"It's nice to see you, too," a blushing Adrian Reed replied.

"Please sit, Adrian," Gideon said, motioning to a chair. "I suspect I know why you're here."

Adrian sat across from them. "Actually, Mr. Banks—"

"Coffey Green is all I can spare," Gideon said, interrupting him. "And Zeb Payne only agreed to a temporary loan. At least until we find the runaway."

"Coffey is a good worker," Annabelle interjected. "I'm sure you're pleased."

"Yes, I am," Adrian said. "She's a resourceful young woman."

Naomi chuckled. "Adrian, don't be ridiculous. I can't imagine her doing anything productive."

Adrian hesitated as if he didn't want to discuss it. "I think she'll work out nicely."

"Not for long, I'm afraid," Gideon said. "Zeb Payne has already complained that he's short-handed. But we did have an agreement."

"It's only been a few days," Annabelle said. She knew why Zeb Payne wanted Coffey back, and she wanted to protect her and keep her with Adrian as long as she could.

"Yes, I suppose," Gideon muttered. "And I'm sure Amos Quigg will find Billy Giles. Mr. Payne will be pleased when he does."

"Thank you, Mr. Banks," Adrian said. "I appreciate your help."

"What do you have her doing?" Naomi asked curiously. "She can't do more than cook and clean, can she?"

Adrian shrugged. "Actually, she knows quite a bit about trees."

Naomi looked at him wide-eyed. "Surely, you're joking. Especially given your family's history."

"No, she's quite knowledgeable," he said. "Very shy, though."

"I can't imagine what she might teach you," Naomi sniped.

"She's actually very resourceful," Adrian replied. "She's offered possibilities for some of our waste."

"Intriguing," Naomi replied, hiding a smirk.

"I do need all the help I can get, so I'm pleased you let me rent her," Adrian said with a smile, as if he wanted to avoid sparring with Naomi.

"I hope you didn't waste a trip," Gideon said. "Because I can spare no more."

Adrian grinned sheepishly. "Actually, sir, I came to

see Annabelle."

Annabelle smiled and quickly stood. "I'm pleased that you did," she said. She walked over and took his hand, urging him from the chair. "Let's go for a walk. It's a pleasant evening."

"Annabelle, there's no need to throw yourself at the man," Naomi uttered.

"I don't see why not," Annabelle teased as she led Adrian to the door.

They left the house and walked down the brick pathway that led to the bay, beds of roses lining the path. "Shouldn't we have stayed in the house?" Adrian asked. "I want to do what's proper."

"I thought the bench overlooking the water would be a better place to sit."

"It is," Adrian agreed. "But I don't want to offend your parents."

Annabelle stopped and turned to face him, her lips inches from his. "Why would you care about my parents?"

"Because," he stuttered. "If I, I mean when I ask—"

She kissed him, wrapping her arms around him, pulling him close. He seemed surprised but returned her kiss with enthusiasm. When he broke away, she kissed him again.

"When you ask what?" she asked, her heart racing.

He sighed, his gaze fixed on hers, as if hoping for a future he could barely imagine. "When I ask for your hand."

She kissed him again, her body against his, innocent caresses hinting of more. "Just ask," she whispered. "I'm ready and so are you."

He kissed her lightly on the lips, then the cheeks and forehead. "Let me speak to my family first. And then I'll ask your parents."

"You do it however you want. I know tradition is important to you," she said, wanting him to feel comfortable. "But it doesn't matter to me at all."

"But Annabelle, it has to be this way," he insisted. "Why offend both our families when we don't have to?"

She took his hand and led him to the bench, hidden from the house. They sat, and she snuggled up close. "Just be quick about it."

"What about Artemis Wentworth?"

"What about him?" she asked, not really caring.

"Everyone knows he's courting you."

She shrugged. "So are you."

"But you could choose him."

She kissed him again, hungrily this time. When they broke apart, she smiled coyly. "Tell me, do you still think I'll choose him?"

Chapter Twenty-Six

After Adrian left, Annabelle slipped back inside the main house, trying to avoid Gideon and Naomi. They were still in the parlor and, as she tiptoed past the opened door to go upstairs, they heard her.

"Annabelle, come in here," Naomi called.

She paused, hoping to avoid a confrontation. "What do you want?" she asked, staying in the hallway.

"We need to talk to you," Gideon said. "It's important."

Annabelle sighed and made her way into the parlor. She sat across from them on a Queen Anne chair. "What is it?"

"You need to behave yourself," Naomi scolded. "Stop acting like a street walker."

Annabelle rolled her eyes. "What are you talking about?"

"Adrian," Gideon said.

"What about Adrian?" she asked as innocently as she could.

Naomi eyed her daughter, face firm. "If he wants to court you, he should do so properly."

"He does need our permission," Gideon added.

Annabelle paused. She knew the discussion was more about Artemis Wentworth than Adrian Reed. "He asked for your permission weeks ago. And you gave it. He doesn't have to ask again."

"But your situation has changed drastically," Naomi said.

Annabelle hid a smile. Her mother's drama was

almost unbearable. "What has changed, Mother?"

"Don't pretend you don't know," Naomi said.

Annabelle's eyes flashed. "I won't stop seeing Adrian just because Artemis Wentworth expressed an interest."

Gideon looked at his daughter, almost apologetically. "Annabelle, I only want what's best for you. But Artemis deserves consideration. He's a very good match."

Annabelle frowned. "A very good match for whom?"

"Don't be ridiculous, Annabelle," Naomi scoffed. "He's a prosperous attorney with an impeccable reputation."

"Soon to enter politics," Gideon added. "He might even be president someday."

Annabelle sighed. "That sounds wonderful for Artemis Wentworth. It really does. But it isn't the life I want."

Naomi shook her head, lips pursed. "Annabelle, you could be the most powerful woman in the country!"

"Which means what exactly?" Annabelle needled.

"You'll never find a better suitor," Gideon offered, his tone much softer than Naomi's.

"I already found the best," Annabelle countered.

Naomi rolled her eyes. "Adrian Reed?"

"Yes, Adrian Reed."

Naomi sighed and shook her head. "Annabelle, you're living out a fantasy created by two childhood playmates. It's different now. You're a grown woman with bright prospects."

"He's hardly the man Artemis Wentworth is," Gideon said softly. "At least in some respects."

Annabelle frowned. "I wouldn't agree."

"You have a chance to marry a man who could change the course of history," Gideon pleaded. "What more could you possibly ask for?"

Annabelle hesitated. She realized her father wanted her to be happy, regardless of who she chose to marry. She wasn't so sure about her mother. "Adrian builds ships, also a noble profession."

"No, his father and brothers build ships," Naomi clarified. "Adrian cuts down trees, the dregs of the family business, the tasks they could hire out to just about anyone."

Annabelle felt her pulse beginning to race. "Adrian is brilliant."

Naomi started laughing. "And he's relying on a slave to offer business improvements. No, you have it wrong. Artemis is brilliant."

"But I love Adrian, Mother."

Naomi frowned. "Love? You have no idea what love is. You're little more than a child. Don't let a fluttering heart fool you. Or some pact made by two childhood playmates. You know nothing."

"I know I want Adrian," Annabelle insisted. She paused, waiting while emotions subsided. "I do agree with you. Artemis is a nice man. He'll always be a close friend. But he's not Adrian and he never will be."

An awkward silence consumed the room, crowding those who sat within it. After a few tense minutes, Annabelle rose to go.

"Wait," Gideon said, motioning for her to remain. "I want you to promise me something."

Annabelle sighed. "What?"

"Don't do anything rash," Gideon requested. "Give each man an equal amount of time."

"And after four or five months, you can make your decision," Naomi suggested.

Annabelle looked at each of her parents in turn, searching for sincerity. She trusted her father, but her mother would have to prove herself. "I agree on one condition."

Naomi's eyes widened. "You don't give us ultimatums."

Gideon waved his hand, signaling silence. "What's your condition?"

"I'll wait for three months," she said. "And I'll spend equal time with both Artemis and Adrian. But at the end of the three months, I shall decide who to marry. Not you."

Chapter Twenty-Seven

The grizzled driver brought Coffey Green back to the plantation in his wagon just after noon on Saturday. The Banks were hosting another gathering, smaller and less formal than their dinner party. It was an afternoon affair with about ten guests, tables set under shade trees along the side of the main house, with chairs and benches scattered about the lawn. Phoebe Yates and Caesar, directing a handful of other house servants, prepared for guests to arrive.

Coffey went to the shack she had called home only a week before. For the first time, she noticed the crooked planks that made the walls, weathered and gray, the gaps between them stuffed with mud, branches, and newspaper. She shivered, a brief memory of winter winds invading, when no number of threadbare blankets was ever enough, the cold creeping through every crack and crevasse to chill her bones.

The door opened as she approached, and Molly stepped out, a stocky woman about thirty. "Coffey Green," she said. "It's so good to see you."

"It's good to see you, too," Coffey said, giving her a quick hug. "But I don't miss the tobacco fields none."

Molly laughed. "I don't blame you. But it's good to have you back. Even if it's only for a couple days."

Coffey smiled, pleased by the warm greeting. But she wasn't happy to be back. Adrian Reed was good to her. And she knew it.

"Come on," Molly said. "I'm going over to help Phoebe and Caesar."

"Where's the young'uns?" Coffey asked, looking

around the clearing as they crossed the lawn.

Molly pointed to two girls kicking a ball of yarn between two shacks. "Staying out of mischief," she said and then leaned closer. "At least for now."

They walked along the worn trail that led through the trees to the lawn where the festivities were about to be held. When Phoebe saw them coming, she grinned and came toward them. "Coffey," she said, giving her a warm hug and holding her tightly. "Is Mr. Reed treating you right?"

"Yes, ma'am," Coffey said. "You wouldn't believe it. I got my own bedroom and even a little kitchen. And the bed has a white folk's mattress and sheets."

Phoebe looked at her, eyes wide. "That's better than I got. And I been with Miz Naomi my whole life."

"Except in Africa with your voodoo queen momma," Molly said as they all laughed.

Coffey shrugged. "I sure ain't complaining. I like it fine with Mr. Reed."

"I wouldn't complain none, either," Molly said, eyeing the house servants as they prepared for the party. "I'm gonna go help out with dinner."

"I'll be over in a minute," Coffey said as Molly walked away.

"I'm sure glad you got it so good," Phoebe said. "Mr. Reed seems like a real nice man."

"Oh, he is," Coffey said. She leaned closer, whispering. "I sure hope he marries Miss Annabelle."

Phoebe frowned. "Ain't gonna happen if Mr. and Miz Banks have their way. They want Miss Annabelle to marry Artemis Wentworth."

"Who's that?" Coffey asked.

Phoebe pointed to a sloop that had just docked at the wharf. The captain was helping a man step off the boat. Dressed in blue trousers and tailored top coat with a white ruffled shirt, he had thick blond hair and blue eyes. He strolled across the lawn as if he owned the plantation or could buy it at a moment's notice.

"That's him there," Phoebe said, "just getting off the boat. He's some fancy lawyer or some such. Running for politics, they say. Come from across the bay."

"He a handsome man," Coffey remarked, watching Wentworth approach Naomi Banks.

"He sure is," Phoebe said. "Looks mighty fine. But Miss Annabelle still like Mr. Reed better."

"I sure hope she picks him," Coffey fretted.

Phoebe shrugged. "I suppose we'll see soon enough. Come on, we better get ready. Folks are coming now."

Coffey helped Phoebe, three other household servants, Molly, and Caesar with servings and preparations. They had prepared a wide variety of food: smoked beef, trout, potatoes, corn, broccoli, beans, cake and pie, all served with cider, beer, water or white wine. Coffey and the other women trouped back and forth to the outdoor kitchen, bringing trays of food that Phoebe and Caesar then served.

Coffey peeked around the corner at those in attendance. Miss Annabelle was talking to Artemis Wentworth, the man Naomi and Gideon Banks wanted her to marry. She was just about to go back to work when her gaze met Adrian Reed's. He nodded, gestured to Annabelle, and shrugged.

Coffey smiled. She felt good that Adrian Reed would share his secret—his affection for Miss Annabelle. Even though it wasn't much of a secret. But she was honored just the same.

After dinner, when the men gathered down by the water to smoke pipes and cigars, Phoebe, Annabelle, and the younger female guests approached.

"Coffey, can you take Miss Annabelle and her friends over to see the little ones?" Phoebe asked.

"Of course," Coffey replied, wiping her hands on the front of her apron. It was a common request. The young ladies liked to play with children, regardless of their color, and did so often during gatherings. "Come along, we'll go right now."

They walked through the grove of trees toward the seventeen shacks in the clearing. Most of the slaves were still in the fields, but the children of those who helped with the party were playing outside, along with an infant who belonged to the woman watching them. The white women fussed all over them, playing games with a half dozen small children, all under the age of ten, and taking turns holding the baby.

After the white women left, Coffey went back to her shack. She got her stuff sorted, planning to spend the night and next day before returning to Adrian Reed's. She heard the door open.

"Is that you, Molly?" she asked, turning.

Zeb Payne flashed a devilish grin. "No, it's me." He stood in front of her, blocking her path to the door, and raised his hand to caress her cheek. "It's good to see you, Coffey."

She felt sick, bile rising in the back of her throat. She lowered her gaze to the floor. "I don't want no trouble, Mr. Payne."

"You won't get any, Coffey," he said, breathing hard. "I'm just here to visit."

"Molly coming back with her young'uns," Coffey said. She tried to step around him.

He grabbed her roughly and pulled her back in front of him. "I didn't see them on my way here." He leaned close, kissing her forehead and then her cheeks, grinding his body against her.

"Please don't, Mr. Payne," she begged. "They gonna be here any minute."

"We have time," he mumbled, moving his hands up

and down her body. "But I don't like to rush. After today, we're gonna do it a little different."

"We shouldn't be doin' nothin', Mr. Payne," Coffey pleaded, shivering when he touched her. "We really shouldn't."

He ignored her, moving her to the straw mattress against the wall. "From now on, you bring supper to my house every Saturday night. Around six is fine. Do you understand?"

"Yes, sir. I understand."

He pushed her onto the bed. "Then we'll have more time together."

Coffey clenched her eyes closed and tried to think of a place far away. She would dream, like Billy Giles had taught her, about being free, maybe on a small farm.

Zeb Payne yanked her dress up. "Tell me, so I know you understand."

Coffey started to sob. "Every Saturday I bring supper to your house."

"Good girl," he said, grunting and gasping. "That's a good girl."

Chapter Twenty-Eight

As dusk shadowed the day, Jacob Yoder returned his plow to the barn. He had no runaways to harbor, nothing to hide. He was leery of Sheriff Dodd, who not only abhorred the Amish but was determined to destroy them. His bitterness seemed more than a dispute over five hundred acres of land, but Jacob wasn't sure what it was. Maybe Dodd was just a bully who badgered those who were different. But he was now suspicious for good reason—more than one runaway had been seen nearby. Jacob vowed to be more careful. He couldn't risk his family. It wasn't fair to them, regardless of how righteous the cause might be.

He was tired, dirt smudged on his face and trousers, his back muscles tight, clenched like fists. A hundred acres was too much for one man to manage, even after he'd left swatches of land fallow. It would get easier when his children were older and able to help. His daughter Elizabeth did what she could at a tender age; Eli was too young for anything but trouble. Ruth tended the family garden, smoked meat, and picked fruit and vegetables. She was a good partner, both in business and marriage. But he couldn't lean on her as much with the baby coming soon.

He had almost reached the house when he saw a figure at the edge of the marsh. At first, he thought it was an animal. But as he kept watching, he realized it was a black man, hunched over to minimize his profile, frantically looking back over the path he had taken.

The stream was wide, a tributary that ran to the river. It was dangerous and misleading, the current strong, especially after heavy rains. It was also deceiving. Varying depths surprised anyone who tried to cross it. The man waded into the water, and, as it got deeper, he tried to swim, struggling and fighting, but not making much progress.

"Ruth!" Jacob called as he ran by the house. "Ruth, I may need help."

She appeared a moment later, two little ones trailing behind her. She followed her husband, not asking questions. As he hurried toward the stream, so did she, keeping a watchful eye on the children.

Jacob paused at the bank. The black man flailed, wrestling the water. He abruptly emerged, standing upright, too confident for a stream that was soon to fight back. Staggering forward, he stepped into a trough and disappeared. Seconds later, his head bobbed up, and he fought his way forward, unable to swim but not surrendering to the current. Halfway across, he grew weary. Each time his head dropped beneath the surface, it took more time to reappear, his eyes wide with fright.

"Help!" he hollered when he saw them on shore.

"You can make it," Jacob called. "Just be careful."

Ruth kept the children close. "You may have to go in and get him."

"Who is that man?" Elizabeth asked, pushing in front of her momma.

"Get back, Elizabeth," Ruth said. "Stay out of father's way."

Jacob watched the man's progress. "He'll never make it if he panics."

"He's past halfway," Ruth said. "Not much farther."

The man kept moving. He tried to swim when the water was deep and wade when it was shallow. When he was close enough for Jacob and Ruth to clearly see his face, he stepped into a gully and disappeared.

"Help me, please!" the man called as his head popped above the surface.

"He's not going to make it," Ruth said.

Jacob kicked off his shoes and rushed into the water.

"What's papa doing?" Elizabeth asked.

Ruth stepped back from the water's edge. "Stay near me."

The children obeyed, watching closely. "Can I help, mama?" Elizabeth asked, holding Eli's hand.

"Not right now," Ruth said, watching warily. The stream was treacherous.

Jacob sloshed through the water. When it got deeper, he started swimming. The black man moved toward him. Floundering, his arms flailing, he made little progress, inching toward the shore, growing weaker.

"Don't panic," Jacob said, edging closer. "Stop thrashing and stay calm. Lay on your stomach and use your arms. Part the water as you would shrubs in the forest."

The black man listened. He stopped kicking and thrashing. His head barely above the surface, he used his arms like Jacob had told him, ever so slowly shuffling toward shore.

Jacob swam after him, reaching him a moment later. "Just follow me in," he said, propping him up.

The man calmed. He sensed survival and did what he was told. A minute later they reached the bank, and Jacob dragged him out of the water.

He fell to his knees, breathing heavily, eyes wide. "Thank you," the man gasped. "Thank you so much. I wouldn't have made it without you."

"The stream is more dangerous than it looks," Jacob said. "It's worse after heavy rains."

"I'm much obliged," the man said, staggering to his feet. He scanned the landscape, as if afraid of what he might see.

Jacob watched him closely, certain he was a runaway. "You've nothing to be afraid of," he said.

"You're safe here."

The man relaxed noticeably. "Thank you," he said, nodding to Ruth and the children. "I won't bother you none."

"Are you sure you're all right?" Ruth asked.

The stranger nodded. "Just take a minute to catch my breath. Thought the good Lord was coming' to get me for a minute."

Jacob glanced nervously up and down the shoreline, hoping he hadn't been seen. He couldn't risk another visit from Sheriff Dodd.

"Feelin' a little better now," the man said, taking large gulps of fresh air. He looked at the children. "Real nice family."

Ruth smiled. "You're very kind. Jacob will get you settled, and I'll bring you some food. You're probably famished."

"Yes, ma'am, I am. Been eatin' nuts and berries."

Jacob offered his hand. "Jacob Yoder and my wife Ruth. We'll help you."

"Billy Giles," the man said as he grasped Jacob's hand with a sigh of relief. "I run off from Hickory Hill. They chasing me. Another runaway told me I could trust you."

Jacob nodded. "You can. But we have to be careful."

"I'll do whatever you need me to," Billy said. "Especially after you saved my life."

"Come on," Jacob said, glancing back at the marsh. "Hurry. We have to hide you."

Chapter Twenty-Nine

Billy followed Jacob Yoder to the barn. He kept looking over his shoulder, afraid Amos Quigg and his bloodhounds might not be far behind.

"Sit a moment," Jacob said once they entered. He pointed to a bench beside the first horse stall. "My wife will bring some food."

"I'm much obliged, sir," Billy said, studying the strange man before him.

Ruth appeared a few moments later in her plain gray dress with a white smock and bonnet, her dark hair pulled back. She carried a basket with her, which she set on the bench beside him.

"Chicken, potatoes, and corn," she said. "Along with apple cider. Do you need dry clothes?"

"No, thank you, ma'am," he said. "I'll dry out real quick. I do appreciate your kindness, though."

Ruth smiled and left, lightly caressing Jacob's arm as she passed.

"Hmm, this is sure good," Billy said as he ate his first forkful of food.

"Ruth is an excellent cook. I was blessed. I couldn't ask for a better wife."

"No, sir, you couldn't," Billy agreed. He eyed Jacob, his black trousers and suspenders, a white shirt and broad-brimmed hat, clothing so different from those at the plantation. He suspected Jacob was a simple man who valued more in life than money. "You look just like my friend Jimmy said you would."

Jacob chuckled. "We're Amish. Five families who

came from Pennsylvania."

"Thanks for helping me," Billy said, smiling faintly. He didn't know who Amish were or where Pennsylvania was. But he would add both to his list of things to learn once he was free.

"You still have a long road ahead of you," Jacob said. He went to the door and peered out, studying the stream and marsh beyond. "How close were those chasing you?"

"I lost them in the marsh. At least I think I did. A man named Amos Quigg, his partner, and two bloodhounds."

Jacob kept his gaze trained outside. "I don't see them," he muttered and turned to Billy. "I have a secret room. Not much, but it'll keep you safe. You'll have to hide in there. I'm sure they're still looking for you."

When Billy finished eating, Jacob led him into the first horse stall. He tugged on a rectangular board above the stone foundation, hooks at the top holding ropes and reins, coiled and tidily stored. He pulled the board aside to expose an opening, three feet high and eighteen inches wide. It led to a tiny cave with a plank floor, roof, and sides that was carved into the side of a knoll. It was only four feet high, four feet deep, and six feet long. Two-inch wooden ports on each side were masked by vegetation, letting in air and light with views of the stream and road beyond. Two smaller ports, knotholes in the planks, faced the barn. It was cramped, hot, and dirty, but a good hiding place. An empty wooden pail lay against the far wall.

"I'll get you a bucket of fresh water," Jacob said as Billy climbed in. "And I'll bring breakfast in the morning."

Billy got settled and removed his damp clothes so they would dry faster. He lay down on a straw mattress against the back wall and soon fell asleep.

The following day, Jacob Yoder brought Billy his

meals and helped him out of the cave so he could stretch and get some exercise. It didn't seem as if anyone had followed him. Hopefully, he had lost Amos Quigg for good. He spent the day in the cave, dreaming about all he was soon to see, a life better than he could even imagine, coming back for his momma, daughter and Coffey Green. A nice plot of land, like what Jacob Yoder had, near a stream with a barn and livestock. He'd work the land and get his daughter off to school where she could learn like the white folks, and he and Coffey could start a live together, have a few young'uns of their own. He didn't need much, just like Jacob Yoder didn't need much. He simply had to get settled and go back and get his loved ones. He smiled when he thought about their reactions when he showed them his new home, so proud to be a free man.

Billy was eating his supper, talking to Jacob Yoder, when a wagon rolled down the lane from the main road, coming toward the barn.

"His name is Samuel Zook," Jacob said. "He's my closest friend—you can trust him. He'll take you to the next location."

"Am I leaving now?" Billy asked. "Because I want to thank your missus before I go."

"No, not today, but soon," Jacob said as the wagon drew closer.

Samuel Zook halted his wagon by the barn, the back loaded with empty crates. Jacob went out to greet him, and Billy watched them unload the wagon, stacking the crates by the barn. When they'd finished, they came inside.

"Samuel Zook," Jacob said, making introductions. "This is Billy Giles from Hickory Hill."

"Pleased to meet you, sir," Billy said, nodding to a man who looked and dressed like Jacob Yoder. He briefly made eye contact before averting his gaze to the ground out of respect.

"Nice to meet you, Billy," Samuel said. "I'll be

taking you on the next leg of your journey."

"Thank you, sir. I'm much obliged to both of you. I'm just a stranger, but you gave me food, hid me, helped me get free. I'll never forget it."

Samuel looked at Jacob. "It seems the right thing to do."

Billy looked at them humbly. "I couldn't be more thankful for your kindness."

"Let's get you free, first," Samuel said. "Now that I know you're here, I'll make the arrangements and take you away the next time I come."

"Samuel buys my fruit and vegetables and sells them to his customers," Jacob explained. "We'll hide you on his wagon, surrounded by crates."

"It's not a long ride," Samuel assured him. "Less than an hour."

Billy was confused. "Where do I go after that?"

"Someone else takes you to the next location," Jacob said. "You keep moving, from one place to the next. It's like a railroad, but you stop at every station."

Billy sighed, feeling overwhelmed. It suddenly didn't seem that simple, not as he had imagined. He had to ask a few questions. "I only seen a train a few times. I know it moves goods and such. And I know it can go real far. Is that what you mean—that I have a long way to go?"

Samuel glanced at Jacob. "It'll take about a week," he said. "And then you'll be safe."

"A man can go a long way in a week," Billy said, starting to have doubts. "I left my loved ones behind. Was gonna come back and get them."

"You'll make it," Jacob assured him.

"We've helped others do the same," Samuel added.

Billy sighed, studying each man in turn, judging their sincerity by the look in their eyes. He realized that he didn't have much choice. He had to trust them. "If you tell me what to do, I'll do it."

"It won't be much longer," Samuel promised.

"Soon you'll be living the life of a free man," Jacob said.

Billy was moved that strangers would do so much to help him. "Someday I'll pay you back for all you done for me, both of you. I swear."

Jacob glanced at Samuel. "There's no need."

Billy didn't know what to say. He studied the strange men before him, the first he had met that weren't obsessed with money. Even Mr. Banks, who seemed a decent man, kept buying up land, horses, carriages, paintings, furniture—even though he had enough a long time ago. But he still wanted more, bought through the sweat and tears of men and women like Billy and Coffey Green. But these Amish men were different. They worked the land themselves, they had the same dreams he did,

"Just live a life we'd all be proud of," Samuel said. He looked at an amber sky, streaks of pink stabbing clouds, the sun starting to set. "I'd best be going. I'll be back in a day or two to get you."

Billy nodded, his eyes bright with hope. "Thank you so much, sir."

"Best get you back in the cave," Jacob said.

Billy climbed in, and Jacob closed the door behind him. He could hear the two men leaving, the kind souls who were helping him find freedom.

Chapter Thirty

The following morning around 8 a.m., the secret door opened.

"Come on out, Billy," Jacob said. "It's safe. I have breakfast for you."

Billy crawled through the opening and into the empty horse stall. "That smells real good, Mr. Yoder."

"Eggs, bread, and some pannhass," Jacob said.

Billy sat on a bench and took the plate. "What's pannhass?" he asked, studying what looked like fried bread and meat mixed together.

"Some call it scrapple," Jacob said. "It's meat scraps and trimmings mixed with flour and spices."

Billy took a piece with his fork and put it in his mouth. "Hmm, it sure does taste good."

Jacob smiled. "Not everyone likes it. Especially when they know what's in it."

Billy stopped chewing and looked at him. "I thought you said it was meat trimmings."

"It is," Jacob said. "Everything that has no other purpose."

Billy was beginning to understand what scrap meant. But it was delicious. After a brief pause, he ate more. It was too good not to eat, no matter what it came from.

"Do you like it?" Jacob asked.

"I sure do. You give me the finest food I ever ate. Your missus is the best cook around, I'm sure."

Jacob smiled. "She's a loving woman with many skills. I'm very fortunate."

"You are," Billy agreed. "A nice family, a good piece of land. Heaven—at least it seems that way to me." He then paused, frowning.

"What is it?" Jacob asked.

"I feel like I should work for my keep, help you out in the fields."

"It's too dangerous. Someone might see you."

"But I gotta give back somethin' for your kindness."

"All you have to do is hide until it's time to leave."

"How long do you think that will be?" Billy asked, taking a sip of cider.

"A few days at most. The longest anyone has stayed was just under a week. It's hard, cramped up in the cave. But this is only the beginning. Once your route is set, it moves quickly."

Billy was quiet. "I didn't know it took so long. I thought I'd be a free man in a few days."

Jacob shrugged. "No, I'm sorry. We can't take any risks and neither can you."

Billy sighed. "Just ain't working' like I thought it would. Sometimes I don't think things through, just do want I want. And it always ends up wrong."

"In a few months, you'll have everything you ever wanted."

"But I'm already missin' my momma and daughter."

"I know it's hard," Jacob said. "But you can always go back."

Billy shook his head. "No way I can go back now. I crossed Miz Naomi. And she can be evil when she sets her mind to it."

"Who's Mrs. Naomi?"

"She run the plantation," Billy said. "Most think her husband Mr. Gideon does. But it's really her."

Jacob could see the torment in his eyes. "It'll be all

right," he assured him. "There's just a few ruts in the road."

"I surely hope so," Billy said. "I don't want much, Just me and my loved ones livin' free."

Jacob nodded. "I understand. All I need is my farm and my family."

"That's good enough for me, too," Billy said. "I got a woman who's a little bit of heaven herself. Someday we gonna have some land with little ones running 'round it."

Jacob smiled. "It's a good dream to have. I couldn't ask for more, nor would I want it." His smile faded, thinking of the risks he took sheltering Billy. It wasn't fair to Ruth and his children. And nothing was more important to him.

Billy ate more scrapple, chewing thoughtfully. "But as soon as I'm settled as a free man, I have to come back."

Jacob looked at him, understanding. "For the woman you love?"

Billy nodded. "And I gotta rescue my momma and little girl—her momma got sold a long time ago, and we ain't seen her since." His paused, his eyes misty. "Ain't nothing hurts more than losing someone you love, torn away from you like that."

"I can't even imagine," Jacob said, even though he could. He had left a large family behind in Pennsylvania. It was devastating—enough land for his seven siblings, but not for him?

"It's hard. It really is."

"Maybe someday you'll find her."

Billy shook his head. "Been too long. Four or five years. My Betsy was just a baby when Miz Naomi sold her off."

Jacob cringed. Maybe it was worth the risk, helping runaways escape. He could feel Billy's pain—and others like him.

I'll take them with me," Billy continued. "My woman, Miss Coffey Green, is just the sweetest thing you'd ever want to see. Got a mind of her own, though. Can be sassy when it moves her."

Jacob chuckled. "I hope it all works for you. A runaway I helped last year came back to get his brother, so I know it can be done."

Billy chuckled. "Lately I been wishin' I could stay here, work for you—so I can eat your wife's cooking."

Jacob laughed. "I wish you could, too. I need the help."

"Maybe someday," Billy said. "Never know what the good Lord is gonna bring."

Jacob grabbed an empty pail. "I'll get fresh water so you can wash."

Billy returned to his breakfast. He could hear Jacob out by the pump, the handle squeaking as he filled the bucket.

"Hello, friend," a voice called. "Can I have a minute of your time?"

Billy froze. It was Amos Quigg.

Chapter Thirty-One

Adrian entered a conference room at Reed & Sons on Monday morning, finding his father and older brothers already waiting. He was always amused by how stern they looked. They lived for the business—building exceptional ships was their dream. Adrian never seemed to satisfy them—no matter how hard he tried.

Thaddeus Reed sat at the head of the long oak table, his muttonchop sideburns meticulously trimmed. The windows behind him overlooked the shipyard, three slots of varying sizes. The largest, reserved for ocean-going ships, had the most activity, with dozens of workers milling about a partially-assembled vessel. It took a year to build a single ship, but they were prized, so perfectly were they constructed. The middle slot was used for boats that prowled the bay, barges and fishing trawlers, with an annual quota of eight that was sometimes exceeded. A barge currently being built was nearing completion. The smallest slot, which had the largest production rate, was reserved for small fishing and transport vessels with a goal of two per month. Stacks of lumber, planks and beams, sat behind each slot, a warehouse storing more lumber adjacent to the sawmill.

Adrian's older brothers, James and Jeremiah, flanked their father. They resembled him, with light hair and blue eyes, while Adrian favored his mother Sarah, a quiet woman who left the family business to her husband and sons, having little to do with it. She most delighted in spoiling her grandchildren, much to the annoyance of James and Jeremiah.

"What did you want to discuss?" Thaddeus asked as Adrian sat at the opposite end of the table.

Adrian eyed his father, who already glanced at his watch. He suspected it really didn't matter what he had to say. "I rented the negress Coffey Green from the Banks family."

His father frowned. "How do you justify the expense? I had hoped to secure a strong male, maybe two or three. She certainly can't do any logging, which needs the most support. She can't help us."

"But she can," Adrian countered. "She knows much about trees, including different uses for waste."

James Reed laughed. "Adrian, she can't know more than us."

"We need to increase production," Jeremiah said. "Renting a female slave doesn't help achieve our goal."

"We can't fill the orders we have now," Thaddeus continued. "Your brothers and I plan to expand, maybe on the other side of the harbor if land can be purchased at a reasonable price."

Adrian hesitated, always eyeing tomorrow. "I would suggest expansion include steel-hulled ships with steam engines."

James rolled his eyes. "We have a long history building superior sailing vessels."

"Which will continue for generations to come," Jeremiah added.

Adrian sighed, not convinced. He offered no rebuttal. "I do think we can turn our waste into product," he said. "Coffey has shown me—"

"Nonsense," Thaddeus declared.

Adrian realized they weren't interested. They would refute whatever he said. But he intended to say it anyway. "She knows uses for roots and resins. Tonics to treat illness and cream for women's faces that makes wrinkles disappear. What woman wouldn't pay to look younger?"

The brothers shared wide-eyed glances, hiding smiles. Thaddeus simply glared at his youngest son. "Are you daft, lad? We've no interest in slave sorcery."

Adrian chuckled and shook his head. "Father, they're viable products, much in demand. I checked with several merchants and wholesalers in Baltimore. All are willing to purchase them for resale."

Thaddeus rolled his eyes. "It doesn't matter. They're not products we're interested in."

"We make ships, not cosmetics," James said.

"It would ruin our reputation," Jeremiah protested. "Can you imagine what our competitors would say?"

Adrian was quiet, gauging his family's reaction. He had failed, at least in fostering a new enterprise. He changed the subject. "I have something else to discuss."

Thaddeus again glanced at his watch. "What is it? We've work to do."

Adrian paused, steeling his resolve. "I've decided to ask Gideon Banks for Annabelle's hand in marriage."

"Adrian, how did you turn out so different than your brothers?" Thaddeus asked, eyes wide with disbelief.

"Artemis Wentworth intends to marry Annabelle," James said. "Don't embarrass yourself."

Thaddeus frowned. "If this is something you and Annabelle dreamed up, it won't succeed."

"It seems that Wentworth's prospects are better than yours," Jeremiah said with a hint of compassion.

"He's a man with a bright future," Thaddeus said. "A likely governor in a few years."

"But my future is bright, also," Adrian protested.

Thaddeus chuckled. "Selling tonics and cosmetics—like a travelling salesman?"

Adrian blushed. "I intend to proceed with this business enterprise."

Thaddeus leaned forward. "You do so on your own. No link or reference to the family business."

"And you bear the cost of slave and product," James added.

Adrian sighed, determined to proceed. "I'm sorry you all feel this way. But I will continue."

"And you'll fail," Jeremiah mumbled.

Adrian stood, nodding to his family. "I'm starting right away," he said. He moved toward the door but paused, turning to face them. "And I will marry Annabelle Banks."

Chapter Thirty-Two

Coffey Green was confused. "What you tryin' to say, Mr. Reed?"

"I want you to use parts of trees to make the items you were telling me about."

"Firewood?" she asked. "Or collect nuts to eat."

"No, tonic and cream for women's faces—what you make from pine oil."

"The cream come from oak, the resin in the bark," she clarified.

"Yes, that's what I want you to do."

She was confused. He wasn't making much sense. "It only takes a little time to make cream and tonic. And one batch lasts a while."

"I want you to make many batches. And I want to put it in jars with labels to sell in Baltimore."

Coffey was embarrassed; she didn't understand. "Mr. Reed, I don't know my letters and such. I don't know what labels is."

"I'll teach you to read and write," he said, trying to be patient. "But you shouldn't tell anyone. Slaves aren't permitted to know their letters."

Coffey knew knowledge was like a key. It unlocked doors that otherwise remain closed, paths now unavailable. "I would like to learn to read and write."

"Then I shall teach you," he said. "Every evening after dinner."

"I don't understand," she said, his motive not clear. Most slaves never learned their letters. Some were given written passes to go into town or to nearby plantations. If they could read and write, they could forge passes and escape. "Why would you care about me?"

"Because you're helping me," he said. "So I'll help you, too."

She sighed, baffled. "You teach me to read and write, and I make a batch of tonic and face cream."

"I teach you to read and write, but that's not part of the work I have for you," he explained. "I want you to make nothing but tonic and face cream."

She looked at him, eyes wide and head cocked. "What about the trees, all you said you needed me to do?"

"You can help me when you have time."

"Mr. Reed, you sure are mixin' me up."

He hesitated, not sure how to explain it. "Coffey, I talked to men who will buy your tonic and cream to sell in stores in Baltimore. Maybe Annapolis and Washington, too."

She shrugged. "I can make as much as you want. I'll fill buckets if you tell me to."

"Yes, that's exactly what I want," he continued. "I'll set up a workshop in the barn. You tell me what you need, and I'll get it. I've already bought hundreds of glass jars, and I've spoken with a gentleman who can make the labels."

"What is labels, Mr. Reed?"

"It's a message, an explanation, the words written on paper affixed to the jars that describe what's inside—so people know what they're buying."

Coffey scratched her head. "I'll do whatever you want, Mr. Reed. But there's something that don't make no sense."

"What's that?"

"Why don't people in Baltimore make their own tonic and cream?"

"Because they don't know how."

She hesitated. "Why wouldn't we teach them?"

He chuckled. "Because they have no interest in learning."

Coffey shook her head. "If you say so, Mr. Reed. I guess some folk are just plain lazy, buyin' stuff they can make themselves."

"People do it all the time," he said. "They buy vegetables even though they can grow their own."

She was starting to understand. "Yes, I suppose so."

"We'll call the cream *Coffey's Cream* and the tonic *Green's Medicinal Tonic*."

Coffey chuckled. "You sure are fixing to do this, ain't you?"

"I am," he insisted. "And if it works, you'll be well rewarded."

She shrugged. "If you say so. I just can't believe folks gonna buy it."

"Oh, they will, believe me. I'll use the money we get to cover expenses: labels, jars, and the cost to rent you. We split what remains."

Coffey's eyes widened. "You gonna give me money?"

He nodded. "But it's our secret. We're business partners. You'll be paid for your work."

Coffey couldn't believe what she'd heard. For the first time in her life, she understood how powerful knowledge could be. It was a lesson she would never forget.

Chapter Thirty-Three

Gideon Banks occasionally sought legal advice from Artemis Wentworth, so he seemed the appropriate choice to investigate Zeb Payne. Naomi went with him on the appointment, even though she usually did not. But if they intended to get information, she needed to control what they discovered, keeping hidden what had to stay secret.

Artemis's main office was in Annapolis, close to the state capital and legislative offices. But he had been born and raised in Chestertown, and he sometimes stayed in the family home where his sister and her family currently resided. A Federalist-style brick building three-stories high with green shutters, Artemis had an office on the first floor to manage his business interests on the Eastern Shore. Located around the corner from the courthouse, it had been designed with style and grandeur befitting a man who might one day be governor of Maryland or even president of the United States.

Caesar guided the carriage to the front of the building, hitched the horses, and opened the door. A raised stone by the road's edge served as a step down to the cobblestone pavement. He reached out his hand, helping Naomi out of the carriage. Gideon followed.

"We shouldn't be long," Gideon said as Naomi wrapped her arm in his. "An hour at most."

"I'll be waiting right here, sir," Caesar said, eyeing the shade cast by a sprawling oak.

Gideon led Naomi inside. A sitting room with cushioned chairs opened into a hallway. They sat and waited. Artemis came in a moment later.

"Gideon," he said, shaking his hand. "Naomi, I'm surprised to see you. You don't normally come."

"I thought I would get out for a bit," she said, acting as innocent as she could. "I may want to run a few errands while we're in town."

"It's good to see you," Artemis said. "Come back to my office."

He led them down the hall to an open door on the right. The office was large, sun spilling through two broad windows behind a mahogany desk. Bookshelves filled with law books lined one wall, a narrow marble fireplace on another with a portrait of Artemis's father, Sinclair, above it. He was still an active member in the law firm's Annapolis office.

"What can I do for you?" Artemis asked as they sat in plush leather chairs in front of the desk and he sat behind it.

"We're concerned about our overseer," Naomi said, glancing at Gideon.

Artemis sat back in the chair. "Mr. Payne? I met him at the dinner party. He assisted with the carriages."

"Yes, Mr. Payne," Naomi confirmed. "He was hired with no references."

Gideon shrugged. "I needed someone quickly after Jack Dunn died."

Artemis nodded. "Jack was synonymous with Hickory Hill, he was there so long. I understand your haste in replacing him. It must have been daunting without him."

"It was a difficult role to fill," Gideon admitted.

"How did you meet Mr. Payne?" Artemis asked.

"At a slave auction in Annapolis," Gideon said. "A gentleman attending provided character references."

"Do you know the man who gave the reference?"

Gideon shook his head. "No, I didn't."

"Did you talk to Mr. Payne's prior employer?"

Gideon shifted in his chair. "No, I didn't. But I do

know it was a large plantation in Virginia. And I believe he oversaw a sugar plantation prior to that."

"According to him," Artemis clarified.

"Yes, according to him."

"What makes you suspicious?" Artemis asked. "Is he having difficulties managing the plantation?"

"No, not at all," Gideon said. "He actually does a phenomenal job, better than Jack did. Hickory Hill will reap record profits this year, largely due to Zeb's efforts. And he's only been in our employ a matter of weeks."

Artemis's eyes widened. "Why question his background if he's obviously competent?"

Gideon hesitated, as if wondering himself. "He's more than competent. He's a likeable man, helpful and polite." He shifted in his chair. "For example, we got Annabelle another horse."

"Snowflake," Naomi interjected, even though she knew they were rambling. "A beautiful white filly."

"But I told Zeb that Annabelle was interested in riding competitions, so he built a course by the stables to mimic the one in Annapolis."

"He sounds like an absolute treasure," Artemis said. "Why question him at all?"

Naomi sighed, feigning concern. "We received a complaint. Apparently, he's been mistreating one of our servants."

"A female," Gideon added with distaste.

Artemis nodded, face firm. "I think I understand. And rather than risk discontent or outright rebellion among your servants, or doubt the word of Mr. Payne, you want me to check if his history might justify termination—like repeated examples of similar behavior."

"Exactly," Gideon said. "You've captured it perfectly."

"I think a query to his prior employer would be sufficient," Naomi said, anxious to control any investigation. "No need to trace the man back to birth."

"Do you know the name of his former employer?" Artemis asked.

Gideon frowned. "I believe it was a Mr. Dickson, just south of Norfolk."

Artemis scribbled the information on a piece of paper, looked up at the pair, and smiled. "I'll see what I can find out."

"Thank you so much," Gideon said as he rose.

"How long will it take?" Naomi asked.

Artemis shrugged. "Only a few weeks, depending on speed of correspondence."

Gideon looked at his wife. "I suppose we can endure a few more weeks of mystery."

"Yes, of course we can," Naomi agreed.

"Thank you, sir," Gideon said as they turned to leave.

"Oh, Artemis," Naomi said, as an afterthought, smiling sweetly. "Why don't you come for dinner tonight?"

Artemis frowned. "I'm sorry, Naomi. But I have an afternoon commitment. I'm afraid I would arrive too late."

"Come after dinner then," she offered. "You can spend some time with Annabelle. She's so anxious to see you."

Artemis nodded, smiling. "I can assure you the feeling is mutual."

Chapter Thirty-Four

Annabelle Banks wanted to marry Adrian Reed, but her parents insisted Artemis Wentworth was the perfect match—an ambitious man with a bright future. She had to placate them and appear interested, even if she had no intention of choosing him as her husband.

She had spent some time with Artemis, mainly as acquaintances at social functions. He was polite, intelligent, attractive—qualities most women admired. But she felt no spark in his company; her heart didn't flutter like it did when she saw Adrian Reed. Even so, she would try to be impartial, if only to honor her parents' wishes, and give each man an equal amount of her time. She had no choice.

"Artemis is coming to visit after dinner," Naomi said as they enjoyed their meal.

"Why didn't you invite him to dine?" Annabelle asked, not that she cared.

"I did, but he had a prior commitment," Naomi said, leaning closer. "I suspect it involved his political ambitions."

"He seemed quite anxious to see you," Gideon added, sharing a furtive glance with Naomi.

"It'll give you a chance to spend time alone," Naomi said, flashing a rare smile. "I'm excited about the potential, both for you and the family."

"I do enjoy his company," Annabelle said. She knew how badly her mother wanted a son-in-law who might serve as a senator and Maryland's governor. "And he's a nice man, interesting to talk to. But we really don't have much in common."

"Nonsense," Naomi scoffed. "Ask him about his future. You'll be fascinated."

"Especially after what Thaddeus Reed told me today," Gideon said, chuckling.

Annabelle frowned. "What's so funny?"

"It seems your other suitor has some crazed scheme for the family business," Gideon said. "Thaddeus was livid when he told me."

"What might that be?" Annabelle asked, annoyed before she heard a word.

"Apparently Adrian has some damn fool idea about making perfume."

Naomi laughed. "Perfume? But they're shipbuilders."

"Not perfume," Gideon said, searching for the right description. "Face cream, that's it. And some sort of medicinal tonic."

Naomi's eyes widened. "Where did he ever get such a ridiculous idea?"

"Coffey Green told him about it," Gideon said. "And he's daft enough to try it."

They were interrupted by Caesar who appeared at the entrance. "Mr. Wentworth is calling," he said. "He's here to see Miss Annabelle."

"Show him in to the parlor," Naomi said. She turned to Annabelle. "Spend some time alone with him. You'll be impressed."

Annabelle left the dining room, prepared to play any role required, and went in the parlor. "Hello, Artemis," she said, greeting him warmly.

He stood by the piano, looking at sheet music. "Miss Annabelle," he said, nodding respectfully.

"Please, sit," she said, motioning to two cushioned chairs with an oval table between them.

She smiled as encouragingly as she could. She had to admit he was handsome, with thick blond hair and blue eyes, always immaculately dressed. She wondered if she was the only woman he pursued. She doubted it, although women pursuing him was more likely.

"Your mother invited me to call," he said. "We had a business appointment earlier."

"Yes, I'm aware," she said, smiling politely.

"I do look forward to any opportunity I have to spend time with you."

"You're too kind," she said sweetly. "But I enjoy it as well."

He leaned back. "I'm in Chestertown once a week. It's a convenient time to visit."

"Annapolis is only a short ferry ride, if that's easier."

"At times it is. Although I prefer to take my own boat and use your dock, as I did for the picnic."

"You're always welcome, regardless of how you get here."

"Thank you so much. I'll remember that." He leaned closer, whispering. "And I'll take advantage of it."

She laughed. "Please do," she said, although she wasn't sure why she did. She thought it best to change direction and not offer too much encouragement. "I must admit that I do find your political aspirations intriguing."

"It is an interesting avenue to explore."

"A natural transition for a lawyer of your stature, I would think."

"Yes, so it seems," he said and shrugged, trying to be modest. "What started as a whisper has become a clamor, I'm afraid. Those in high places demand my candidacy."

She looked at him with fresh perspective. "Really? For state or federal office?"

"Federal, for now. I intend to serve six years in the senate and then run for governor of Maryland. With exposure from those two offices, the presidency is within my grasp."

"Absolutely amazing," she said, feigning surprise even though her parents had described his ambitions several times. "My Lord, I never dreamed I would know a future president."

He chuckled and cast a flirtatious grin. "Perhaps you'll share the journey."

She smiled, although she didn't find the offer as intriguing as he did. "Is politics lucrative?"

He shook his head. "Not if you're honest, it isn't. I earn more in my current practice, especially in Annapolis. But politics does offer a chance to give back to the community, to make a contribution to mankind, perhaps better the lives of constituents."

"Do you have a specific agenda?" she asked. She hadn't thought he'd be driven by helping others. Her limited impression was of a man more self-centered, interested in his boats and houses.

"No, nothing specific. Not yet anyway. My financial backers will provide input. I have to consider their interests as well as the people I represent."

Annabelle hesitated, finding conflict between his claim to honesty and the need to appease those who supported him financially. "Do they have any common goals?"

"Oh, yes, of course," he said, and then chuckled. "They're businessmen." He paused, pensive. "Most are interested in expanding the country from Atlantic to Pacific."

"By making territories into states?" she asked, familiar with a topic that dominated public debate.

He nodded. "It's a lengthy process, but certainly worth pursuing."

Annabelle knew the very issues he discussed were tearing the country apart—along with what expansion offered. "What about slavery?"

His brow furrowed. "A more difficult topic. Compromise seems the surest solution."

"A slave state is added for each free state?" Annabelle asked. She knew that slavery made plantations profitable. She also knew what slaves endured—whipped or sold off or abused like Coffey Green. As each day passed, it became harder for her to justify, regardless of what her parents might think.

"Yes, or perhaps limit slavery to all points south of a certain latitude. But it's far more difficult to address than most realize. I'll try to explain."

Artemis Wentworth continued talking, describing the Utopian future he hoped to create. But Annabelle wasn't really listening. Was he an honest man? She wasn't sure. He certainly seemed compromised. Did he realize it? Maybe not. But it didn't matter.

She was dreaming about Adrian Reed.

Chapter Thirty-Five

"**M**rs. Jackson," a voice called from the trees that bordered the back lawn of Hickory Hill. "Mrs. Jackson!"

Naomi froze, her worst fears confirmed. She recognized the voice and the name—from twenty-five years before. She pretended it didn't apply to her and kept picking flowers from the bed that bordered the vegetable garden.

"Mrs. Jackson," the voice called again. It was Zeb Payne, using a name from her past to hint that he controlled the present.

She ignored him. She didn't look up, acting like whatever he was doing had nothing to do with her.

"I'm sorry," he said, feigning confusion as he came closer. "I meant Mrs. Banks."

Only when addressed by her current name did she glance up, looking at him oddly. "Excuse me?"

"I've wanted to talk to you alone ever since I got here."

She eyed him cautiously, like the fly that spies the spider. A flicker of fear danced in her eyes, but she tried to hide it. "What do you want?"

"We know each other," he said, smiling and friendly. "St. Lucia. I'm sure you remember."

She cocked her head. "St. Lucia? I've never been there."

He hesitated. For a brief instant he wasn't sure if he had the right person. "My father's boat," he continued, but with less confidence. "You fled St. Lucia on my father's boat. The night your husband was murdered."

She shook her head. "I'm sorry, but that wasn't me. You must be thinking of someone else."

"I shouldn't say murdered," he said, chuckling. "They never determined the cause of death. But his safe was opened, all his money gone, so it seemed like foul play."

She shrugged, her heart beginning to race. "I'm sorry, but I don't know what you're talking about."

"My father's boat," he insisted. "It was about twenty-five years ago. You and the black woman, your servant, came on board. We took you out to the channel, to the bigger ship."

Naomi slowly shook her head. "No, I'm sorry. It wasn't me."

Zeb Payne acted like he hadn't heard her. He glanced toward the main house where Phoebe was hanging the wash. "I'm not sure about her," he admitted. "Phoebe— is that her name? She looks a little worn, if you know what I mean. I could be mistaken."

"She's buried two sons," Naomi said coldly. "Enough to make anyone age, don't you think?"

He cringed. "Sorry. I didn't know."

"I'm afraid you're mistaken about both of us."

"I don't think so," he said firmly, the friendly smile still pasted on his face. "You look the same as you did that night—the most beautiful woman I ever saw."

She shifted uncomfortably. Feigning mistaken identity was becoming difficult. She clipped the last of the flowers she needed. "I'm sorry, Mr. Payne. I've never been to St. Lucia. You're confusing me with someone else."

"It's not likely, but I suppose I could be," he said, pushing his hat back on his head, his tone sharper.

"I'm sure you are."

His friendly expression vanished abruptly, replaced by an icy glare. "Actually, Mrs. Banks, I'm sure that I'm not."

Her face tightened. "What are you trying to say, Mr. Payne?"

His hungry gaze wandered down the curves of her slender frame and back up to her face. "I don't make many mistakes. Especially with a woman who looks like you."

"I should smack your face," she declared.

He laughed. "But you won't," he said lewdly. "Why make it worse than it is?"

"I don't know what you're talking about," she said tartly and started to walk away.

"I guess I shouldn't have said anything," he said with arms crossed.

She turned. "It's not that you said anything, Mr. Payne. It's that I don't know you, and I never have."

He slowly shook his head, smiling again. "I suggest you think about it, Mrs. Banks. I'm sure we can come to some sort of agreement. And if we do, I'll never mention it again—not to anyone."

Naomi was trembling. "We have nothing to discuss, Mr. Payne."

"You'll change your mind," he called as she walked away. "You have no other choice."

Naomi quickened her pace, her heart racing.

"And Naomi," Payne hissed. "I've been very careful about what I've drank ever since I came to Hickory Hill. Rufus Jackson should have done the same."

Chapter Thirty-Six

"**I**'m looking for a runaway," Amos Quigg said to Jacob Yoder.

Billy put his plate down on the bench, his breakfast half eaten. He looked at the secret door, partially open, and back to the barn entrance. He could see their shadows nearby.

"I followed him into the marsh," Quigg continued. "Had my dogs tracking him, but I lost him. Must have crossed the stream, just across the way, I suspect. Darn fool would pick the hardest place to ford."

Jacob shrugged. "I haven't seen anyone."

"Unless he drowned," Quigg said. "Don't know if the bastard can swim."

"Sorry, but I've seen nothing—not a body or a person. I farm my land and mind my business."

Billy quietly moved across the horse stall. When he reached the hidden cave, he eased into the cramped space, pulling the door toward him. But it latched from the outside. He couldn't close it. At least not all the way.

"Fetching some water for your horses?" Quigg asked.

"Just to wash them down a bit, cool them off," Jacob said.

Their voices were louder, they were coming closer. Billy pulled the door as tight as he could. But it wasn't flush. If anyone looked close enough, they would find him.

"Mind if I look in your barn?" Quigg asked. He was feet away, probably at the threshold.

"There's nothing in there but hay and horses,"

Jacob said. "Some cows at the other end, plows and equipment—not much else."

"Is that your breakfast?" Quigg asked.

Billy realized Quigg had come in the barn anyway, ignoring Jacob's meek protests.

"Yes, I was eating when you came," Jacob said.

Amos Quigg chuckled. "No, friend, you weren't. You were fetching a pail of water at the well. I saw you as I came up close."

"Some of the water is for me," Jacob said. "To have with my breakfast."

"Cider looks good enough to me," Quigg said. "What is that? Looks like pie."

"Shoofly pie," Jacob replied. "My wife makes the very best. And scrapple—at least that's what the locals call it. It's meat scraps and flour."

"Looks mighty tasty," Quigg said.

"I can have my wife get you some breakfast."

"No, that's all right, Mr..."

"Yoder. Jacob Yoder."

"Mr. Yoder, I appreciate that. But I got a runaway to catch. Good money for this one,"

Billy's fingers were cramping. He clenched the door, holding it tight to the frame. Sweat dotted his forehead. He barely breathed.

"I'll just walk to the end of the barn and have a quick look if you don't mind, Mr. Yoder."

"I already told you I haven't seen anyone," Jacob protested.

"Oh, these runaways are real crafty, believe me. You don't know 'em like I do. Most do anything to get away. No thoughts at all to the investment their owner made in 'em. They get fed and clothed, a warm place to live. Better than they'd ever do on their own."

Quigg's voice was trailing off as he walked to the other end of the barn.

Billy pulled at the door. A sliver of light shone through where it wasn't completely closed. If Quigg came into the stall, he would see it didn't fit tight. Billy didn't move, his heart racing, his fingers aching. Several minutes later, he heard Quigg coming closer.

"If you could keep a watch, I'd appreciate it," Quigg said. "Just let Sheriff Dodd know what you see. I already stopped in to talk to him." He paused and then chuckled. "Sheriff doesn't like you much, does he?"

"No, he doesn't like any of us," Jacob replied.

"He said he planned to buy this land for his boys to farm."

"He can buy land anywhere in the county," Jacob said. "He doesn't like us because we're different."

Quigg laughed. "You are different, friend. Funny clothes and beard. Strange food. Sheriff said he'd run you all out of here if he could."

"But he can't," Jacob said firmly. "And he won't."

"He said he had a runaway a few days back. Someone seen him in the stream, right about here."

"The sheriff came with his deputies," Jacob said. "They looked around but didn't find anything."

"Well, like I say. Damn runaways are crafty. May have outsmarted the sheriff." Quigg started laughing. "Likely outsmarted you, too."

"I didn't see anything."

"No, I suspect not."

Billy listened, his heart thumping in his chest. He knew by their voices that they stood at the barn entrance. A few minutes more, and he would be safe.

"I'll be on my way," Quigg said. "But I'll be in the area. May stop by again."

"I'll be sure to tell the sheriff if I see anything."

"I appreciate that," Quigg said. "If you help the sheriff catch the runaway, make sure you tell him to wait for me to come get him so I can get paid."

"I will, Mr. Quigg."

"Finish your breakfast, friend. Mighty peculiar you left it there to begin with."

Chapter Thirty-Seven

Jacob Yoder had heard about Amos Quigg, but it was the first time he had ever come on his farm. Quigg was known to be tenacious, rarely failing to find his prey. His sudden appearance forced Jacob to fear for his family. Sheriff Dodd was enemy enough, hateful of the Amish and determined to drive them off the Eastern Shore—and now he suspected Jacob harbored runaways. Adding Amos Quigg to the mix spelled disaster.

Jacob waited until dark before he went back to the barn, carrying a basket of food. He had to be cautious. Since late afternoon, Amos Quigg had been camped at the edge of his property on a slight knoll that rose above the flat landscape which stretched from the side of his barn and crested at a twist in the stream. Jacob stayed in the shadows, crossed the lawn, and kept close to the wall when he reached the barn. He paused before he entered, studying the terrain. Quigg sat beside a cook fire. Jacob waited, making sure he wasn't watching, and went inside. He entered the horse stall and opened the trap door.

"Come on out for a minute, Billy." He cast one last glance at the barn entrance.

Billy crawled out of the cave, his trousers smudged with dirt, beads of sweat on his brow. "It's been gettin' real hot in there," he said as he stood, stretching.

"We have to be careful," Jacob warned. "Amos Quigg is camped on the edge of my farm, by that bend in the stream."

Billy's eyes grew wide. He slowly shook his head. "That man is evil." He took a swig of water from a bottle. "He like a bulldog. Got his teeth into me and won't let go."

"He almost caught us this morning. I wasn't expecting a visitor."

"He snuck up on you is what he did. Shouldn't have to live scared like that. And you do it for me." He sighed, face firm. "I should get along. You got to keep your family safe. He a dangerous man."

"But you can't leave now," Jacob warned. "Not with him hovering over us like that."

Billy quietly ate his dinner. After a moment, he looked up. "Can't you do something about him? Maybe tell the sheriff. A man ain't supposed to bother hard-workin' folk."

Jacob shrugged. "He's not on my land. He seems to be watching the road, not the farm. But he's got a good view from that knoll."

"He watching' you, too. It just don't look like it."

"But there's not much I can do about it, not now," Jacob said, afraid the danger was greater than he suspected. "He'll leave in a few days. When he gets tired of waiting."

"Must be a way to outsmart him," Billy muttered as he kept eating.

"I'm not so sure. He's very good at what he does. Samuel Zook told me he's never failed to find a runaway—even trailed one all the way to New York. I don't like him watching my farm or the road. I have enough problems with Sheriff Dodd."

"Seems like the sheriff wants you out."

"He does. My friends, too. All five families that came down from Pennsylvania. He tried to stop us from buying the land because he wanted it for his sons."

Billy's gaze wandered the barn. "Who built this?" he asked. "Put together real good. So is the house."

"We did," Jacob said. "The families that settled here. We built each other's barns and houses, helping each other out. And we still do."

"Well, they done right, I'll tell you that. If you don't

want to farm, you can always build."

Jacob chuckled. "I have thought about it. But I'd rather build furniture, not houses or barns."

"Something you'd be good at, I'm sure. You have dreams, too. Just like me."

"Yes, perhaps," Jacob said, smiling. "But I have a family to feed. And for now, I can only do it by farming."

"You'll figure it out," Billy said. "Be makin' furniture in no time."

Jacob sighed. "Not if the sheriff has any say in it. He's still trying to force us out—over a year after we bought the property."

"He just a bitter man, all eaten up inside."

"I suppose," Jacob muttered. "A bad man to have as an enemy,"

"He don't like you 'cause you different. It don't have nothin' to do with land."

Jacob nodded. "That could be true."

Billy chuckled. "Then he must hate my folk. We surely different. Just think about what he'd do if I was his neighbor."

Jacob smiled. "Maybe you will be someday."

"Ain't never gonna happen if Quigg catches me, though."

"We won't give him the chance. As soon as he leaves, we'll move you. And after you get settled in your new home, you can come back for your loved ones. Winter is best, though. They don't watch as closely."

"I'll leave now if you want," Billy said, chewing on a chunk of warm bread. "I can go when it's dark, make my way down the road."

"No, it's too risky. And you don't know where to go."

"I'll be all right," Billy assured him. "Just point which way."

Jacob eased back to the entrance and glanced out at

the knoll. Amos Quigg hadn't moved. He sat by his fire. A hint of cooked bacon wafted on the breeze. "You should be safe here."

"Let me finish my dinner, and I'll be on my way," Billy said. "It's best. Ain't worth risking your family. You got too much to lose."

Jacob hesitated. "It's too dangerous."

"Too dangerous for you," Billy said. "I'll manage just fine."

Jacob studied the runaway, determined to do what was right. He was a better man than most—especially Quigg and Sheriff Dodd.

"There ain't no other way," Billy continued. "I got to go."

Jacob nodded grimly, even though he would rather he stayed. "I suppose it's best. I don't like it, but Quigg is sneaky, a danger to everyone."

"Which way do I go?" Billy asked, wiping his mouth, his meal finished.

Jacob studied him a moment more and then relented. "Go out the back end of the barn and turn right when you get to the road."

"I'll only travel at night," Billy said. "And watch the sun for direction."

"East," Jacob said, pointing. "And north. You want to make your way northeast."

"I best be going now. I can put some distance between me and Quigg 'fore dawn. Thank you for all you done. And thanks to your missus, too."

"You can always come back if you get into trouble," Jacob offered. "Or when you return for your family."

Billy nodded. "I appreciate that. They good people."

"Should you take a weapon—a knife or gun?"

"Oh, no, sir," Billy said. "Don't want to be tempted to use it."

Jacob nodded and extended his hand. "Just be careful. Take the bottle of water with you."

Billy looked at his hand, as if he hadn't expected it, and then shook it firmly. He met Jacob's gaze and nodded respectfully. Thank you," he said, as he grabbed the bottle.

"God be with you."

Billy went to the back of the barn. He paused at the doorway and looked out, glancing in both directions. Then he vanished in the night.

Chapter Thirty-Eight

Adrian Reed readied his two-seat buggy, eager to visit Annabelle Banks. As he trotted to the road and started the short trek to Hickory Hill, he mulled over the risk he was taking with Coffey Green. He had used part of his savings to hire her and purchase what she needed to make the beauty cream and tonic, offered her a portion of his barn for use as her workshop, with tables staged for her use in preparing her products, and he'd provided an area outside for a smoke pit—an integral part of her process. It wasn't a substantial financial investment—he wasn't too concerned about it—but his workload had increased, not decreased, as he'd expected it would have when he'd rented her. Hopefully it was short-term, and their enterprise would prove successful.

He didn't interface with her much. He left the house early every morning and only saw her during dinner or while teaching her to read and write. She didn't need oversight. She was a good worker—she already had two crates of product ready to ship—and he trusted her to do what was right. She was also a good person—he'd known that as soon as he'd met her.

When he arrived at Hickory Hill, Annabelle was leaving the stables. A love of horses had been their initial bond, all those years ago when they shared the same tutor. And that bond had only grown stronger. She waved, smiling, as he brought his buggy to a halt. When had she captured his heart: age five, ten, fifteen, twenty-two, or every minute he had known her?

It was a special evening, and he was nervous with

anticipation. He intended to ask Gideon Banks for Annabelle's hand in marriage—if she approved— regardless of the ridicule he had received from his family. He had abandoned his original plan to wait until winter. All had changed with the arrival of Artemis Wentworth.

He climbed from the buggy and tied his horse to the hitching post. "Good evening," he said as Annabelle came to greet him. "Were you riding Snowflake?"

"Yes, I was," she said. She gave him a quick kiss, and they started across the lawn. "She's such a great horse. I'm eager to show her in competition."

"I'm sure she'll do well," he said as they climbed the stairs to the lower balcony. "A beautiful horse. And a beautiful rider."

"How sweet," she said. She smiled, glanced at the nearest window to ensure no one watched and kissed him. "I've been waiting for you."

He was encouraged. "Should I speak to your father tonight?" he whispered anxiously.

She frowned. "No, I'm sorry. You can't. There's a complication."

He pulled away, fearing the worst. "Have you changed your mind?"

She chuckled. "No, of course not. Don't be silly. It's my father. Or my mother actually."

"She disapproves?"

"My parents insist that I entertain both you and Artemis courting me for at least three months before they'll discuss marriage. I'm to see each of you once a week."

Adrian frowned. "Then my father and brothers spoke the truth."

"They knew?"

He nodded. "No doubt your father spoke with mine, probably on matters unrelated. But I'm sure our courtship was discussed."

Again Annabelle glanced at the open window to

ensure no one peeked out. "I feel like a convict, the way my mother watches over me," she whispered. She turned to Adrian, leaning toward him. "They don't know that I've already decided." She took his hand and squeezed it firmly.

He smiled, relieved. It seemed a formality he must endure. Three months wasn't that long. A fall wedding would be nice. But challenges existed. "We still have to convince them. And I'm no match for Artemis Wentworth."

"You're twice the man Artemis Wentworth is."

Adrian smiled at the compliment. But he was doubtful, sensing a contest he couldn't win. "I'm not sure all would agree. Some say he'll be governor one day, maybe even president."

"Artemis says it most of all."

Adrian chuckled and then kissed her. His lips lingered.

She didn't resist. She encouraged him and then reluctantly pulled away. "My parents may be watching."

"Shall we walk down to the bay?" he asked. "We would have more privacy."

"No, we can't. Not yet. I'm sure my mother will observe us closely for a week or two. Making sure I give Artemis equal consideration."

He sighed. "It's only three months. Well worth the wait."

She kissed him again, acting as if she didn't care who watched. "That was for my mother, in case she is watching. I love to torment her."

He chuckled and gently pulled away. "Best not to irritate her."

"I'm not sure that's possible."

Adrian thought it better to change the subject—and to avoid more kisses. He didn't want to anger Naomi, should she be watching. "I may not be able to rent Coffey for long," he said

"Why not?" she asked, perplexed.

"She can't do the physical labor I need done, so I have to work harder to compensate. And my family insists that I pay for her through earnings and savings. It's a financial component I hadn't expected."

"But the cost isn't substantial," she said, eyebrows knitted. "I would think the business would absorb it."

He studied her closely. She seemed more concerned than he would have expected. But he didn't know why. "She's not really working for the business."

She cocked her head. "What is she doing?"

"When Coffey first came to the sawmill, I asked her about trees. I was surprised to learn she knew many uses for parts we discard—roots, resin, needles, acorns."

"Phoebe Yates taught her, I'm sure. She's shown many servants how to use natural remedies—Billy Giles, too."

"Where did Phoebe learn so much?"

"Her mother was some sort of voodoo queen in Africa. At least that's what Phoebe tells everyone. But once I asked my mother about it, and she just laughed. Sometimes the servants talk nonsense. Passes the time, I suppose."

"Regardless, Coffey did know what she was talking about. She mentioned two products that I found very interesting. One is a—"

"Cream that women use on their faces," Annabelle interrupted.

"Yes," he said surprised. "It supposedly makes them look younger."

"It does. My mother has some. Phoebe makes it for her. I suppose I should use it, too."

"Nonsense," he scoffed. "Don't tempt perfection."

She smiled and kissed him. "A wonderful response, Adrian Reed."

"The other product is a tonic for cuts and bruises."

"I'm familiar with that, too. Phoebe put some on her hand when she burned it in the kitchen."

"Did it work?"

She nodded. "Healed in a few days with no scar. And it was a nasty injury."

"Excellent," he said, starting to feel more comfortable.

"My father mentioned something about all of this."

Adrian frowned. "I'm sure my father told him. In unflattering terms, most likely."

She looked at him, perplexed. "But what will you do with a jar of beauty cream and healing tonic?"

"It's much more than that," he said. "I set up shop for Coffey in my barn and made arrangements with a man in Baltimore to distribute and sell them. I even made labels— Coffey's Cream and Green's Medicinal Tonic."

Her eyes widened. "Adrian, that's brilliant."

He smiled broadly, glad to have her support. "She's a hard worker. I'm sure she'll do well." He decided not to share their financial arrangement, at least not yet.

Annabelle didn't quite understand. "Is that what she does for you—works all day making cream and tonic?"

He nodded. "Yes, mostly, although sometimes she helps nurture some of the seedlings we plant. She works hard, too. You should come by and see her."

She smiled slyly, hinting at an ulterior motive. "I'll do that," she said. "And then I can see you, too."

Chapter Thirty-Nine

As the small cutter pulled away from Adrian Reed's dock, he assessed the risks he was taking on its cargo. He'd personally covered the expenses—Coffey's rental and all the necessary supplies—and provided labor needed to get roots and bark required for a process he didn't pretend to understand. He'd endured the ridicule of his family, though his mother supported him and always would, and he was exhausted, performing his usual tasks for the family business as well as supporting Coffey. But it seemed worth it.

He smiled as he looked at the roll of bills he held in his hand. He had learned much in the last few weeks. An endeavor he never would have considered—straying from the family business—had been conceived and realized, even though in its infancy. It had taken courage. And regardless of the smirks and insults hurled by his father and brothers, he had done it. Even if he failed in this first attempt, he was strong enough to try again. If he didn't, his role would never expand beyond planting seedlings and choosing trees to harvest.

Next, he would evaluate future expenses, allocate some of the money he'd received to cover them, and split the profits with Coffey. It was an arrangement that would make most shudder for the mere implications of what it might become, if nothing else. But it seemed the right thing to do. Maybe he did it because Coffey was such a good soul with a heart as big as the universe. Would he act the same if he had rented a broad-shoulder buck instead? Probably not, but he didn't know why. He just felt she deserved more from life, and, if he could help her get it, he would. When he really thought about it, he realized all those in bondage deserved what Coffey did—the same freedoms he and his family enjoyed. And he suspected most knew it was true. Only a few clung to beliefs of superiority, like Naomi Banks. But her views had nothing to do with race. If her slaves had been Irish or German or Italian, she would have treated them the same. He had seen enough over the years—slaves sold, former friends scorned, land owners ruined—to know that he never wanted to count Naomi Banks as an enemy.

He left the dock and went into his house where his study offered generous views of the bay. Bookshelves lined the walls, filled with leather volumes he was fond of collecting—English poetry, philosophy and history. Paintings by local artists of Eastern Shore landscapes, from farms to forests, ships to shores, occupied the remaining wall space. His oak desk was centered in the room overlooking the bay, and, when he sat behind it, he sometimes felt like master of the universe—especially given his good fortune.

He removed a ledger from the top drawer, the expenses for his and Coffey's business enterprise carefully documented. He laid the bills on the desk and counted out what he needed for expenses. He calculated the cost for jars and labels—enough remained for two more shipments. They were losing money. But not much. They were just getting started, and costs were always excessive at the outset of any new enterprise. He took what he had allocated for jars and labels and split it in half. But then, as an afterthought, he took his share and combined it with Coffey's. He would take nothing from their first sale. It would serve as an incentive to a woman who had spent her entire life in servitude, to show what the world could actually offer her.

Adrian left his study and found Coffey in the barn, hard at work. She stopped when she saw him approach, a kerchief wrapped around her head, wet with perspiration.

"Our first batch has been sold," he said. "Off to Baltimore merchants."

Coffey smiled and shook her head. "I still can't believe folks pay good money for stuff they could make themselves."

Adrian laughed. "Someday, I'll take you to Baltimore. Then you'll understand."

She shrugged. "Maybe I will. But it all seems silly to me."

He paused, not sure how to describe profit. "We won't know how successful we'll be until our next few orders are placed. But keep making products until we know for sure. Assume the best."

"I'll do whatever you want me to, Mr. Reed," Coffey said. "You payin' good money for me, and I want to make you happy."

"Is this better than Hickory Hill?" he asked, hoping to improve her life in a measurable way.

She started laughing. "Oh, Lordy, is it better," she said. Then she paused, a cloud crossing her face. "You don't even know, sir."

Adrian eyed her closely. She kept a secret close to her heart. He suspected it wasn't good. Maybe someday she would share it, and he could help her. "As in any business enterprise," he then said, "profits are divided among partners."

Coffey laughed. "I ain't no partner, Mr. Reed. I just do what you tell me."

He showed her the slender stack of bills, not much, a pittance to him but a fortune to her—the only money she had ever earned. "Here's your share," he said. "But I strongly suggest you let me hold it for you. If anyone at the plantation saw you with it, they might assume the worst."

Her eyes widened. "This is mine?"

"All yours," he said. He wouldn't tell her he had

taken nothing for himself. "It'll be different with each sale, but your stack of money will keep getting bigger."

She looked at the money and then at him. "Mr. Reed, I don't know what to say."

The expression on her face made it all worthwhile. Adrian was determined to continue, even if he never made any money at all.

Chapter Forty

"**D**oes Miz Naomi know you off to see Mr. Reed?" Caesar asked as the carriage rambled down the dirt road.

"Why would she care?" Annabelle asked. She wasn't sure if she could trust him. He'd been a house servant for many years, longer than she'd been alive, and he shared a mutual respect with her parents—at least with Gideon. Naomi never let him forget he was a servant. No longer a slave, but still a servant.

"Because of the courting going on," Caesar said. "Miz Naomi wants to make sure Mr. Reed and Mr. Wentworth get the same attention. That's all I'm saying."

She frowned. "Do you intend to tell my parents what I'm doing?"

"No, Miss Annabelle, of course not. I wouldn't do that."

"Then why does it matter?" she asked, satisfied he was sincere.

"I just don't want to get all caught up in the middle of this, should your momma find out. That's all."

Annabelle hid a smile. Everyone was afraid of her mother. "There's no need to worry. I'm actually visiting Coffey."

"Oh, you didn't say that, ma'am. I suppose that's different."

"Don't worry, Caesar," Annabelle said, chuckling. "I won't let my mother bully you."

Caesar smiled. "I don't think anyone can stop that. Not even you."

Adrian Reed's house was built along a cove, his

property adjacent to the southern boundary of Hickory Hill. It was a short journey, only a couple miles. Farther south lay the harbor at Rock Hall where Reed & Sons was located, shipbuilding slips, an office and the sawmill.

"If you could pull up to the barn," Annabelle said. "That's where Coffey works."

Caesar brought the buggy to a stop. He climbed from the carriage and opened the door, helping Annabelle out.

"I just want to visit for a few minutes," she said.

"Are you sure Coffey isn't with Mr. Reed? Maybe we should call at the house, right and proper, before we go traipsing all over the property."

Annabelle smiled. "It's all right. I told Mr. Reed I was coming to visit Coffey. He isn't home anyway. I'm sure he's at the harbor or in the forest somewhere."

Caesar sighed. "Whatever you say, Miss Annabelle. Do you want me to come with you?"

"No, you can wait here. I won't be long."

She walked through the open barn and found Coffey at the far end. Two long plank tables were set near the back door, glass jars stacked on top of them. Wooden crates sat on the floor. As Annabelle approached, Coffey turned and saw her.

"Miss Annabelle," she said, smiling as she came toward her. "It's good to see you. If you came for Mr. Reed, he ain't home just now."

"No, I thought I would pay you a visit," Annabelle said. "Just to see how you're doing."

"Oh, Miss Annabelle, that's so kind. I appreciate that." Her eyes widened and she slowly shook her head. "You wouldn't believe all that's happened."

Annabelle smiled, glad to see Coffey so happy. Especially with what she had witnessed—and could never forget. "Tell me all about it," she urged. "I can't wait to hear."

"I got my own room in the house," Coffey said proudly. "All I do is clean a little and get Mr. Reed's supper." She leaned closer, ready to share a secret that might be better kept. "And he's teaching me to read and write."

Annabelle arched her eyebrows. "Really?" she asked. It was illegal for slaves to read and write, even though a few could.

"He surely is," Coffey said. "But I'm not supposed to tell." She bent over and wrote in the dirt with her finger. "Look at this. C-o-f-f-e-y. Coffey."

"That's wonderful," Annabelle said, still concerned. "But you must promise not to show anyone else."

"I won't, Miss Annabelle," she said, still excited. "But that ain't the half of it. Mr. Reed has me makin' tonic and cream. Most days, that's all I do. But sometimes he needs somethin' else done."

Annabelle already knew about their business. But she wanted Coffey to tell her about it. She picked up a glass jar and read the label. "What does he do with it all?"

"A man comes in a boat to get it," she said. "He gives money to Mr. Reed and takes it all to Baltimore."

"He sells what you make?"

"Yes, he does," Coffey said, standing upright and smiling. She looked through the barn, out at Caesar, to make sure he couldn't hear. Then she leaned close to Annabelle and whispered. "Mr. Reed even gives me some of the money he makes."

"He pays you?" she asked, not sure she understood.

"Yes, ma'am, he does. "But he holds the money for me. I'm saving it to buy my freedom from your daddy."

"That's marvelous, Coffey," Annabelle said, not sure her father—or her mother—would agree. "Isn't it wonderful working for Mr. Reed? Your whole life is changing—all for the better."

Coffey beamed. "It surely is. But I do miss Phoebe,

Molly and the children." She smiled shyly. "And Billy Giles."

Annabelle knew about their relationship—gossip traveled quickly around the plantation—but she pretended she didn't. "Coffey, I had no idea you and Billy were in love."

She nodded. "Yes, ma'am, I suppose we are. Ain't much happened yet. But he made some promises, and I like the sounds of them."

Annabelle didn't understand. What promises could a runaway make? "He still hasn't been found," she said delicately.

Coffey looked away as if she knew more than she was willing to share. "Maybe he'll never be found."

"Which doesn't say much for your future with Billy."

Coffey started to speak but hesitated. She changed the topic. "Is Phoebe doing all right? I got to see her at the picnic you all had."

"Phoebe's fine. She misses you. But you'll get to see here on Saturday."

"Yes, ma'am, I will." Coffey frowned, fear and shame crossing her face. "But she ain't all I'll see."

Annabelle noticed her reaction. "Zeb Payne?"

Coffey nodded. "It ain't never gonna stop, Miss Annabelle. I know it ain't."

"I spoke to my father," she said, not sharing the investigation Artemis was conducting. "He's watching Mr. Payne closely."

"Ain't gonna do no good," Coffey muttered. "You know that."

Annabelle's face firmed. "It'll end, Coffey. I promise. One way or another."

Chapter Forty-One

Naomi sat in a straight-backed chair in her bedroom while Phoebe ran a silver brush through her blonde hair. "We have a problem," she said softly.

"What might that be?' Phoebe asked. "It sure ain't your hair. It's as soft and shiny as the day we met. Ain't hardly any gray, neither, Miz Naomi. Just a strand here and there."

Naomi chuckled. "Only the beginning, I'm sure. I've been blessed, having you look after me, or I'd have many more."

"I've been blessed, too, Miz Naomi. I could have done a lot worse. You gave me a good life, considerin.'"

Naomi sighed, her thoughts on Zeb Payne. "I hope it's not about to come crashing down."

Phoebe stopped brushing. "What do you mean, Miz Naomi?"

"Zeb Payne."

"Is it him? The boy on the boat?"

Naomi nodded. "He says it's him."

"I been thinking about it, and he does favor that boy, that rusty-colored hair. But I can't hardly tell after twenty-five years."

"He's not sure about you," Naomi said. "But he seems certain about me."

"Then he don't know his own self."

"Oh, he does, believe me. He knows how Rufus died, too."

Phoebe gasped, her hand to her mouth. "How's he know that?"

"The doctor must have done tests and run his mouth about the results."

Phoebe returned to brushing. "Ain't soundin' good. What's he gonna do?"

"He suggested I think about it. He wants to come to an agreement."

"He want money," Phoebe declared. "Sure as I'm standing here."

"I'm not so sure," Naomi muttered, thinking about what Zeb Payne had done to Coffey. But she didn't say anything. Phoebe had all but raised Coffey once she'd arrived at Hickory Hill. Phoebe would kill him—in minutes or hours, not days.

"What are you gonna do?"

"I don't know yet," Naomi said. "He said he's going to be careful about what he drinks."

Phoebe started laughing. "Then he ain't as smart as he thinks. He don't know how Rufus died, he just think he does. Or he'd be real careful about what he ate, not what he drank. Damn fool doctor probably thinks whatever killed Rufus was in the whiskey. It was real smart what you did, spilling the glass by the body."

Naomi smiled faintly. "I'm not proud of it, but we had to do it. Rufus was an evil man who deserved what he got. I don't regret it."

"Neither do I, Miz Naomi. But now we got Mr. Payne to deal with."

Naomi frowned. "I think he knows everything. I may have no choice but to bargain with him."

"And give him money?"

She hesitated. "If that's what he wants, yes."

"What else could he want? It ain't like you gonna give him Hickory Hill."

"No, I'm not," Naomi said, scheming on a solution. "But if we come to an agreement, he has to leave. And quickly."

"May take a while to work things out."

"I can't delay long," Naomi said. "Gideon hired Artemis Wentworth to check Payne's background. I have no idea what he'll find."

"Only one person on God's green earth knows you come from St. Lucia, and that's me. Ain't no way Artemis Wentworth or Zeb Payne gonna find that out."

Naomi sighed. "I'm not so sure."

Chapter Forty-Two

Annabelle smiled, nodding politely while Artemis Wentworth spoke, feigning fascination with every word, just like her mother and father did. She picked at her cod, toyed with her bread, occasionally sipped her cider, giving every indication she listened intently while her thoughts wandered far away.

She much preferred the group setting—her mother had invited Artemis to dinner—to private moments they might be forced to share. It was easier to maintain the charade, to pretend she seriously considered living her life with Artemis Wentworth even when her heart had been stolen by Adrian Reed, never to be returned.

"You can count on my enthusiastic support for your political endeavors," Gideon said. "Whatever effort you deem most helpful."

Artemis nodded respectfully. "I'm most appreciative. I have strong financial backers—I'm in a much better position than my opponents. If I could only garner support from the people, especially the lower social classes."

"I've no doubt you will," Naomi said, head cocked, as if shocked the entire world wasn't as enamored with Artemis Wentworth as she was. "Especially once your policies are presented."

"I surely hope so," Artemis said. "All will realize that I only seek to serve."

Annabelle took a forkful of food, eyeing Artemis skeptically. He sought to serve, but for whose benefit? She was confused by his wealthy backers. To her, it meant that Artemis was bought and paid for before he ever reached the senate floor. But maybe that's how politics worked. It seemed power was most important. Everything else was secondary to such a considerable degree that the peoples' interest might never be served at all.

Artemis noticed her staring at him. "Of course, nothing would make my life more complete than having Annabelle share it with me."

"Aww, that is so sweet," Naomi said. "Isn't it, Annabelle?"

She smiled. It was sweet, although she wasn't sure it was sincere. Artemis Wentworth was a smooth talker. That's why he had such a bright future as a politician.

"I'd be the envy of every man alive," Artemis continued, eyeing Annabelle.

"She does have other suitors," Naomi warned playfully, upping the ante to force the outcome. "But Gideon and I have stressed what a perfect match you would make."

"I would hesitate to leave Hickory Hill," Annabelle interjected, offering any possible obstacle to their union, which her parents already considered a foregone conclusion.

"Nonsense," Gideon said. "Your sister married well and has lived in New York for several years. She never regretted leaving."

"She is very happy," Naomi added, nodding to Artemis.

"And we rarely see her," Annabelle mumbled. "I must consider my parents, with a sister far away and a brother in the army, home to visit only once or twice a year. It would be a lonely existence for them if I departed."

"Oh, Annabelle," Naomi scoffed. "You'd be just across the bay." She turned to Adrian. "We've never had a politician in the family before."

Artemis chuckled. "I'm not a politician yet. But I suppose we'll know in November."

"I predict your support will grow, and you'll soon be unstoppable," Naomi said, glancing at Annabelle. "I suspect we have the next senator from Maryland seated at our dinner table."

Artemis pretended to be modest but failed, his face beaming. "It's much too early to tell. My opponent is quite popular, especially in rural counties out west. I do need to work hard to earn the people's vote."

"I've no doubt you'll prevail," Gideon said. "And soon you'll sit in the senate chambers."

"What do you think, dear?" Naomi asked. "You've barely said a word."

Annabelle smiled politely. "It does sound fascinating."

"Is there anything you would like to add?" Gideon asked. "A question or concern you might want clarified?"

Annabelle felt trapped, not wanting to commit to a future she didn't want, not even hypothetically. "No, not really," she said as the door opened and Phoebe entered. "Especially now that dessert is served."

They all laughed and eyed the pie that Phoebe set on the buffet. "It looks delicious," Artemis said. "I'm honored to be your guest."

"You're more than welcome," Naomi replied, a smile pasted on her face. She turned to Annabelle. "Why don't you take Artemis for a walk after dinner? You can rest on that charming bench by the bay and watch the sunset."

Annabelle forced a smile. Her mother must have spied on her and Adrian, stealing kisses on a bench that wasn't as secluded as she had thought it was.

Chapter Forty-Three

Coffey came back to Hickory Hill early Saturday afternoon. The slaves were still in the field, but she knocked on the shanty door anyway. When no one answered, she entered, finding everything just as she had left it the week before, except for a child's wrinkled dress on the bed and two empty mugs on the table.

She went back outside, was about to sit on the porch when she saw Phoebe at the edge of the clearing, in the humble graveyard tucked between trees. She stood alone before two crooked crosses, the graves of her sons who had each died young.

Coffey watched her, unable to even imagine her pain. Ten minutes quietly passed, and Phoebe turned, wiped her eyes with the back of her hand, and started across the clearing. As she came closer, she saw Coffey on the porch.

"Coffey Green, how are you?" Phoebe asked, sadness still etched on her face.

Coffey gave her a quick hug. "I'm doing real good," she said. "How are you?"

"I miss havin' you around, but all else is good. Miz Naomi treats me right."

"You deserve it," she said. She paused, made sure no one eavesdropped, and leaned closer. "Mr. Reed pays me money for the work I do. Just like the white folk. He keeps it safe for me."

Phoebe looked at her, eyes wide. "He gives you money for what?"

"I make tonic and cream, just like you showed me. I

put it in jars with writings on 'em and Mr. Reed sells 'em to a man in a boat."

Phoebe looked at her, head cocked. "What does a man in a boat do with cream and tonic?"

Coffey chuckled. "He takes it to Baltimore, and white folks buy it."

Phoebe cast a skeptical glance. "They pay money for a jar of cream they could make themselves?"

Coffey nodded. "I didn't believe it none, either. But Mr. Reed told me it's true. Said it's no different from folk buying bread or corn at the market."

Phoebe shook her head. "It make no sense at all to me."

"But it's true, I swear. I got money to prove it."

"Why's he giving you money? He already pays Mr. Banks to rent you."

"Because he's a good man."

"They a lot of good men. But none of 'em paying black folk. Nobody at Hickory Hill get paid."

Coffey sighed. "I'll explain it all like Mr. Reed done told me. When he get money from the man in the boat, he takes for his self what he already spent—for jars and such."

"And to rent you?"

"Yes, ma'am," Coffey said. "He showed me—all written up in a book. And he gives some of what's left to me. Just like white folk do."

"Child, I ain't never heard of that before. Except for free blacks, like the reverend. Folks give him money for preaching."

"I'm gonna save up and buy my freedom from Mr. Banks," Coffey said triumphantly.

"You make sure Mr. Reed holds it," she warned. "'Cuz Zeb Payne gonna think you stole it."

"I will," she said. "Mr. Reed looks out for me."

Phoebe was quiet for a moment. When she spoke,

her tone was barely above a whisper. "I got my freedom not long ago."

"When you got old enough to be free."

Phoebe nodded. "It's what they do here on the plantation. Most slaves get freed when they too old to work the fields."

"Why did you stay?" Coffey asked, thinking of how important freedom was to Billy Giles.

"Miz Naomi needs me," Phoebe said. "I been at her side more than twenty-five years."

Coffey hesitated, eyeing her friend. "But that ain't no reason, Phoebe. You could still stay friendly with Miz Naomi if you were free. She could get another servant."

Phoebe sighed, as if she wondered if she had made the right choice. "It ain't what folks think it is. Where was I gonna go?"

Coffey's eyes widened. "You could go anywhere you wanted."

"And do what?" Phoebe asked. "Still gotta live— find a place to stay and get food to eat."

Coffey was quiet, wondering what she would do. "I suspect it ain't as easy as it seems," she said. "Especially when you got nowhere to go."

"No, it ain't. I just stayed doing what I know. Miz Naomi's good to me. I ain't complainin'."

"I'm still gonna get settled somewhere once I'm free," Coffey said, undeterred. "Maybe in Chestertown with some of the other free black folk." She smiled shyly. "Or maybe with Billy Giles."

Phoebe frowned. "Billy still ain't been found. They gonna whip him to death if he get caught."

"He won't get caught," Coffey said coyly and leaned closer. "He gonna come back and get me. His momma and daughter, too.

Phoebe smiled. "You dream big, child. That's good. You're young, you should have dreams. But just make sure it's what you want. And if it is, you gotta do somethin' before it's too late."

Coffey sighed, not sure she understood. "How much money does it cost to be free?"

"A lot more than you got, that's for sure. And it ain't Mr. Banks who gonna say if you free. It's the missus. I love that woman like a sister, but she got a mean streak in her like I ain't never seen before. Don't ever get her riled up."

Coffey was quiet. Phoebe's expression said more than her words did. There was much she didn't know— about Phoebe and Miz Naomi, and about living free. But she would learn. She turned abruptly and smiled. "I'm gonna tell you another secret. Mr. Reed is showing me stuff I never knew before. He's teaching me my letters."

Phoebe eyed her warily. "Why would he do that— unless he got good reason?"

Coffey wasn't sure she knew the answer. After a moment, she shrugged. "Maybe he just a good man."

Phoebe breathed a tired sigh, her gaze on the big house. "Child, even good people do evil."

Coffey shook her head. "No, he's a good man. I'm sure of it."

"You'll know soon enough. You don't know about people until they do something you ain't expectin'. You're not like me. I can see what people all about, what they even thinking sometime. My momma taught me how to see right into someone's soul."

Coffey hid her smile, never having believed the voodoo claims about Phoebe's mother. "If you can see Mr. Reed's soul, you gotta tell what's in there."

"I will," Phoebe said, not explaining why she hadn't yet bothered to look. "It may not be what you think, though, so you gotta be ready."

"Yes, ma'am, I will. But I think you'll find a good man."

Phoebe shrugged. "Only the Lord know the answer to that."

Coffey knew she was naive. She didn't know Adrian Reed well, but he was good to her. She couldn't imagine him changing into something ugly like Zeb Payne who was pure evil and probably always had been. Whenever she came back to Hickory Hill, he managed to get her alone. She had avoided him so far, but he would find her when he came back from the fields, He'd watch her shack, and the minute Molly and the young'uns were gone, he'd appear out of nowhere. Or he would grab her when she brought dinner to his cottage that evening.

Coffey hadn't told a soul what Zeb Payne was doing. Only Miss Annabelle shared that secret. If Phoebe ever found out, she would kill Zeb Payne deader than dead. And she'd make him suffer, too.

Chapter Forty-Four

Sunday was a day of rest for all slaves, including those at Hickory Hill. But this Sunday was special. Nat Brown, a serious young man who worked hard and was unusually quiet, was marrying Minty Jones, a fine-looking woman known for her love of conversation. Some joked Minty would talk so much that Nat might never say a single word again.

"Molly said that Mr. Banks give all the food and drink for the wedding," Coffey told Phoebe. "He can be such a good man sometime."

"Miz Naomi behind it," Phoebe said with a hint of distaste. "She wants her people married and raising families."

"Then they won't run off," Coffey muttered.

Phoebe motioned to a nearby shack, a gray-haired woman and a young girl sitting on the porch, watching the preparations. "It didn't stop Billy Giles none. He left Venus and little Betsy." She turned to Coffey. "And he left you, too."

Coffey looked at Betsy. "Poor little girl. She's so sad, lost without her daddy."

"Venus is just as bad, missin' her son," Phoebe said. "Poor woman. Billy don't know what he did to them when he run off. So busy dreamin' he doesn't think sometime. Always lookin' for someplace better. Got his loved ones right here. Ain't nothin' better than that."

"He'll be back," Coffey said softly. "I know he will."

Phoebe wasn't listening. "Maybe we should ask

Betsy to help us some. Be good to keep her busy."

Coffey nodded. "Hey Betsy," she called. "Can you help us get the vittles out?"

Betsey turned to her grandmother, spoke a few words, and then ran over to help. "What do you want me to do?"

"Set up these glasses in nice rows on the table, next to the cider," Phoebe said.

A few minutes later the reverend arrived, a free black named Tice David. He was a kind man, admired by all, who helped those he could. Most of the slaves didn't understand why he was free and they weren't, but they liked him just the same.

"Coffey, will you come here for a minute?" Annabelle called.

"I'll be back, Phoebe," Coffey said. She hurried over to Annabelle.

"Can you help me weave these flowers through the trellis?" Annabelle asked. "It'll make a nice backdrop for the ceremony."

"Sure, Miss Annabelle." Coffey helped decorate, the white paint on the trellis chipped and faded, some of the wood rotted. It had once been in the garden at the big house. But when it fell into disrepair, Mr. Banks had given it to the slaves.

"Here comes Nat," Annabelle said, pointing.

"Don't he look handsome. All dressed up like that."

Annabelle smiled. "He's wearing one of my father's outfits. Venus and Betsy fixed it up, along with Minty's dress. It used to be my mother's."

"I bet she gonna look real pretty," Coffey said.

"She will, I'm sure," Annabelle agreed as they finished the trellis. "Here comes my parents now."

Gideon and Naomi Banks arrived nicely dressed, mingling with their slaves as they always did for special occasions. A few minutes later, the Reverend David took his place at the trellis. The slaves and guests all gathered around as Nat Brown stood beside the reverend. Gideon went over to one of the slave shacks, standing upright, waiting patiently.

Those attending formed an aisle to the preacher, looking back to the shack were Minty Jones lived. She only kept them waiting a few minutes more. The door opened and, with all eyes turned in her direction, Minty crossed the porch and came down the crooked steps, taking the arm of Gideon Banks.

"Just don't seem right," Phoebe mumbled.

"What don't?" Coffey asked.

"Mr. Gideon pretendin' to be her daddy. Especially when ole Jack Dunn worked her daddy to death."

Two slaves sitting under a shade tree provided the music, one with a fiddle, the other with a banjo. Gideon led Minty Jones down the aisle formed by those attending, walking slowly toward the reverend.

Coffey watched the ceremony, eyes misting. It was good, all people together, black and white, at such a happy event. Mr. Banks was giving Minty away just like her daddy would have, God rest his soul—even though Phoebe didn't like it much. When they reached the reverend, he offered a brief sermon, and, as all watched with happy faces, Nat Brown and Minty Jones exchanged vows. As the preacher pronounced them man and wife, they shared a kiss, the guests hooting and hollering and cheering them on.

When the ceremony ended, the bride and groom and their guests made their way toward several tables filled with food—venison, ham, and fish, superbly cooked and served with yams, corn, and broccoli, along with sweet desserts. Provided by Gideon and Naomi, it was the best meal any of the slaves had eaten in some time. They ate and drank, mingled and danced, as the musicians kept everyone entertained, all laughing and having a great time.

Zeb Payne stood among the trees at the edge of the clearing, watching the festivities but not socializing with anyone. He probably thought no one noticed him, off by himself. But Coffey Green did.

And so did Naomi Banks.

Chapter Forty-Five

Billy Giles went as far as he could, stumbling through darkness, staying just off the road. Without the sun to guide him, he could only guess if he went the right way. Jacob Yoder had said to go northeast. He wasn't sure the road went that way, but it seemed close. He stayed near it, passing through fields and forest, eating what nature provided—blackberries, hickory nuts, different leaves and grasses—and stealing whatever he could from farmers' fields.

He slept during the day or hid in the forest until it was dark. But when he came to a village, he wasn't sure what to do. It was surrounded by fields, so he had no place to hide. He kept to the edge of town, traveling around it, trying to stay on the same road. But he was exposed, whether it was dark or not, and could easily be seen should anyone come. When he saw a simple stone church, a graveyard beside it with tombstones poking skyward, he approached it cautiously, just as dawn was breaking.

He waited outside, leaning against the wall, listening for any sign that someone might be inside. When he heard nothing but silence, he approached the door and turned the knob. It wasn't locked. He opened it slowly, trying to avoid squeaky hinges, and stepped inside. It was deserted. An altar stood at the far end, windows behind it and rows of wooden benches reaching toward the door. A sparse building, small and functional with little decoration, it served one purpose. It's where people came to praise the Lord. It was eerily quiet as it should be. Billy said a brief prayer, thanking the Lord for looking after him. He crossed the plank floor to a bench along the far wall and lay down, closing his eyes.

***

He was awakened roughly by someone shaking him. He bolted upright. "Who are you?" he asked, rubbing his eyes and jumping to his feet.

At first the man didn't reply. He simply glared at Billy. He was older, a graying beard cut close to his gaunt face. "Roger Simpkins. I help out the reverend."

"I only set a spell, Mr. Simpkins. I must have drifted off. I'll be on my way now."

"What made you think you could traipse in here uninvited?"

"I'm sorry, sir," Billy said, slowly collecting his wits. He started for the door but the man blocked his path.

"You're not a runaway, are you?"

"No, sir," Billy lied. He had to appease the man, apologize, and get on his way. "Not a runaway. Just travelin'."

Roger's eyes narrowed. "I'm sending someone for the sheriff."

"Wait," Billy said. "No need for the sheriff. I'll be on my way real quick."

Roger stepped back, eyeing him coldly. "You're lying, boy. I know what you're doing. And you belong in jail." He turned abruptly, toward the door.

Billy grabbed his arm. "Please, sir. I don't want no trouble."

"Get your hand off me," Roger snapped, wrenching away. "I'm getting the law."

"Please," Billy pleaded, grabbing his arm again.

Roger turned, a scowl on his face. "I said to keep your hands off me!" He swung his fist, hitting Billy in the jaw.

Billy was stunned, even though the blow wasn't delivered with much force. He blinked, blood trickling from his lip.

The man hit him again, harder. "I'll teach you to lay a hand on me."

Billy made no effort to defend himself—it wouldn't be proper in a house of the Lord. He stood still and took it, another blow, and then one more. But when Roger reared back, ready to swing again with much more force, Billy's anger rose. "Stop!" he said sharply, shoving him away.

Roger stumbled. His arms flailed as he tried to keep his balance. He sprawled backwards a few steps and fell. His head hit the stone wall, a jagged rock smashing the base of his skull. He lay on the floor, eyes closed. A trickle of blood dripped from his head.

"Oh, Lord, what have I done," Billy moaned. He bent over him, shaking him gently. "Sir, you all right?"

Roger was still, eyes closed.

Billy placed his hand on his chest, searching for a heartbeat. He thought he felt something but wasn't sure. He lifted Roger's head. Blood wet his hair. Billy stared in horror, not sure what to do. Roger was dead, he was sure of it.

A door at the back of the church opened and slammed closed. "Hey, what are you doing?" a man shouted.

Billy bolted out the entrance.

Chapter Forty-Six

Jacob Yoder went out to his barn just after dawn. The knoll beyond his field was empty, with no sign that Amos Quigg had ever been there. Jacob wondered when he'd left—soon after Billy did, or at dawn, less than an hour before? Regardless of when, Jacob knew where. Quigg was trailing Billy. And Jacob suspected he was getting close. Amos Quigg was tenacious, a lion stalking his prey.

Had Billy escaped? Maybe he'd found his way northeast to a kind soul who would help. Or had he stumbled through the countryside, lost, tired, and afraid? Jacob hoped he was safe, that no one had caught him. And if he wasn't, he prayed the trail didn't lead back to his farm. His priority was Ruth, the baby she carried, Eli, and Elizabeth. He could no longer forget that.

Jacob wasn't fated to be alone for long. The day after Billy scampered off, Samuel Zook's wagon came down the road, loaded with empty wooden crates that Jacob would fill with fruits and vegetables. The large garden was tended by Ruth and the children, and they did well, selling a wagonload each week through Samuel to local businesses. Sometimes Ruth would add needlepoint or a quilt, or Jacob would use his woodworking skills to build a cabinet or bench, even a bureau. Samuel paid them upfront, making a small margin when he sold to his customers. For a growing family, miles from where they were raised, the extra money helped. They carefully saved their earnings, hoping to add more acreage to their holdings.

"Good morning, Samuel," Jacob said, greeting his friend as the wagon came closer.

"Best to pull close to the barn," Samuel called, steering the wagon off to the right.

Jacob walked beside him. The message was clear. He had additional cargo.

Samuel brought the wagon to a halt. "Let's unload these first," he said, pointing to the crates on the side of the wagon closest to the barn.

Jacob studied the terrain, along the stream and the opposite side, and then up on the knoll where Amos Quigg had camped. When he was certain no one was watching, he helped Samuel, grabbing the first crate.

"I've got a young woman and her daughter, can't be more than four or five years old," Samuel said softly.

Jacob arched his eyebrows. "A woman and child?" It was rare—almost all of the runaways were men. But sometimes they came back for their families once they knew the route.

Samuel nodded, grabbing a crate. "Tired and hungry, too. They've been on the road for a while."

"Where did they come from?" Jacob asked as he removed another crate, close to exposing mother and daughter.

Samuel glanced back at the road to make sure no one was coming. "Farther south. Down in Virginia."

Jacob's eyes widened. "They've come a long way. I'm surprised they made it this far."

"I'll take Billy today, too," Samuel said. "That'll make room for these two."

Jacob paused, lips pursed. "He's gone already."

Samuel stopped, crate in hand. "What happened? He didn't get caught, did he?"

Jacob shook his head. "Amos Quigg, the slavecatcher, was camped on the knoll," he said, pointing toward the turn in the stream. "Supposedly watching the road."

Samuel frowned. "He suspects you. He wasn't

watching the road."

"I know. That's why Billy left."

"To protect you?"

Jacob nodded.

"Any idea where he went?"

"Not really," Jacob said. "All I could tell him was to head northeast."

Samuel sighed. "It gets a little harder each time, doesn't it?"

Jacob fixed his gaze on Samuel, his eyes offering an apology. "Today will be my last delivery. I have to protect my family."

"I understand," Samuel said, passing no judgment. "I don't blame you."

"First Dodd, and then Quigg. I want to help, I do. But I can't risk getting caught."

Samuel nodded. "It's dangerous work, regardless of how good the cause may be." He grabbed another crate and looked back towards the stream. "Let's get these two inside the barn."

They paused to check landscape again, up on the knoll, out to the road, along the stream and the marsh behind it, making sure no one observed them. Then they removed the last few crates.

"Come on down," Jacob said once they were free. "Are you injured at all?"

"No, we just tired and hungry, sir," the woman said. She helped her daughter climb down, and they entered the barn, standing near the entrance.

Jacob eyed the runaway. She was young, not far past twenty, and dark, like charcoal. Her daughter was light brown, mixed race, most likely. Jacob didn't need to know what she might be running from. He could guess. "What's your name?"

"I'm Haney Mills, and this is my daughter Chloe." A flicker of fear flashed in her eyes. "I know we at your mercy, sir. But we good people."

"You're a brave woman, Haney Mills," Jacob said, putting her at ease. He leaned over to the little girl. "And so are you, Chloe."

The girl looked up at him. "You have a funny beard."

"Chloe, that's not nice," Haney scolded.

Jacob laughed. "It's all right. She's not the first to say that."

"My momma say I'm a good girl," Chloe said.

Samuel chuckled. "And your momma always tells the truth."

Jacob smiled, watching them. "My name is Jacob. I'll be taking care of you for a little while."

"We much obliged," Haney said. "We really are."

Samuel sighed, glancing up at the sun to gauge the time. "I'll wait a while, leave the wagon here to block the view. Should anyone show up unexpected."

Jacob nodded. "Haney, I'm going to get food and water. Why don't you and Chloe stretch a bit, walk around here in the barn? You'll be hiding in a cramped space, likely for hours at a time."

"We go anywhere you say, sir. Glad to have the help."

"I'll be back in a minute," Jacob promised.

He left the barn and started toward the house. A moment later, Ruth came out, carrying a basket full of food, Elizabeth behind her with a jug of water. They met halfway to the barn.

"The more I try to protect you, the more you insist on getting involved," Jacob said, worried for her welfare.

"I share your life," Ruth said simply. "Everything you do, we do together."

Chapter Forty-Seven

Adrian left the forest, guiding his horse to a little-used trail adjacent to Hickory Hill plantation. He was dirty and tired, his horse bathed in sweat. He had marked different trees for cutting, thinning the forest to allow others to reach maturity. It was a practice he'd learned from his grandfather, who had remained active in the family business until the day he'd died.

He had been close to his grandfather, closer than he was to his father or older brothers. He suspected his siblings' age difference created the distance, but he couldn't say for sure. His older brothers favored their father, in both appearance and disposition, as well as their grandfather, who'd transferred his knowledge of trees, lumber, and shipbuilding to his descendants. Adrian favored his mother. Not much different from other families, he supposed.

His horse was tired, so Adrian let him walk, nudging him into a light trot occasionally. When they reached the crossroad that led back to Adrian's house, a rider approached—the new overseer at Hickory Hill, Zeb Payne.

"It's almost dusk, Mr. Reed," Zeb called as he came near. "A long day for you."

"I haven't been in this part of the forest for a while," Adrian said. "It took me longer than I expected."

"What were you doing, marking trees to cut?"

Adrian nodded. "We need to do some thinning so stronger trees have room to grow. I'll be out here all day tomorrow, too."

"That right?" he asked, his tone flat. "And how's Coffey doing? Has she managed to help at all?"

Adrian was guarded, not willing to share their business venture. "Yes, she has," he said. "She has a good knowledge of the forest, different uses for parts of the tree that we usually discard."

"I wouldn't have guessed that," Zeb said, surprised. "I suspect a strong man would be more helpful. Someone who could swing an ax or haul wood."

Adrian's face brightened. "If you have such a man to rent, I'd be most appreciative."

Zeb shook his head. "No, not just yet, Mr. Reed. But we seem to be doing fine without Billy Giles. I was thinking when he comes back, I could make him available."

"If he ran away, why would you expect him back?" Adrian asked, his thoughts drifting to his brief encounter with Billy in the forest.

"Because Amos Quigg is after him. Billy won't be gone long."

Adrian hesitated, wondering what would happen to Billy once he got caught. He suspected Naomi might want revenge. Maybe he could help him. "I'll be glad to take him. If that works for you."

"It sure does," Zeb said. "But I should warn you, he's not easy to handle. A good worker, though—when he sets his mind to working. I've got no complaints there."

"He'll do fine," Adrian assured him, trying not to sound too hasty. Billy could help the logging crews. "I don't expect any problems."

"Then it should work out for both of us. I'll have Coffey back to bundle picked tobacco, and that should free a hand for picking."

Adrian realized he had been tricked. "But I'd rather keep Coffey. I've already trained her."

Zeb cocked his head. "Billy's a smart man. Strong, too. Whatever Coffey is doing, he'll do better. You'll be glad you made the swap."

Adrian's face stiffened. "I'd prefer not to. Coffey does fine."

Zeb was quiet for a moment, briefly glancing down the road. "I need to do what's best for Hickory Hill, Mr. Reed. I'm sure you realize that."

"I understand," Adrian said, suspicious of his motives. Did he want Coffey back that badly? Probably not. He just wanted to rid himself of Billy before he ran away again.

"I'll ask Mr. Banks," Zeb said. "He can decide." He leaned forward, as if sharing a secret. "Well, Mrs. Banks will decide."

Adrian smiled but didn't reply, trying to be polite. He would ask Annabelle for help. She would intervene on his behalf. Gideon would do anything for Annabelle—he always had.

"Surely you understand," Zeb continued, smiling wryly. "I'm only thinking of the household."

Adrian didn't reply. He had said too much already. Best to let Annabelle defend his interests.

Zeb eyed him closely, sensing he was wary. "I expect Mrs. Banks will want Coffey back to help Phoebe, anyway."

Adrian didn't know what he was talking about. But he wanted to find out—as carefully as he could. "Phoebe can run the household herself," he said. "She's been doing it for years. She shouldn't need help from Coffey."

"I've no doubt," Zeb agreed, a little quickly. "She's a hard worker, very efficient. I'm told she's been taking care of Mrs. Banks for years, even before she came to Maryland."

Adrian shrugged, puzzled by what he inferred. "I wouldn't know. Naomi and Phoebe have been at Hickory Hill as long as I can remember."

Zeb pushed his hat back on his head, a mischievous

twinkle in his eyes that he couldn't quite hide. "I only thought with the wedding coming—surely you know all about that. Phoebe might need help. It'll be a huge celebration—lots of planning and preparation. You know Mrs. Banks. She'll insist on the biggest gala the Eastern Shore has ever seen."

Adrian was quiet, his heart sinking as he digested Zeb's comments. He had two questions. And although he normally wouldn't be so bold as to ask them—especially to a plantation overseer, he had to have answers. "Did you know Naomi before she came to Hickory Hill?"

Zeb Payne smiled faintly, as if he might have misspoken. "I know *of* Mrs. Banks," he said, vaguely correcting his original statement. "But everybody around here does."

"I'm sure they do," Adrian said, still curious. "But I don't know where she came from before Hickory Hill. I'm surprised that you do, being so new to the plantation."

"She came from Baltimore, I was told. At least that's where she met Mr. Banks. He was telling me the story. It's a real fairy tale romance."

"Yes, I suppose it is," Adrian muttered, wondering why he didn't know more. Maybe he did once and had forgotten. Or maybe he had never thought to ask.

Zeb chuckled and slowly shook his head. "And this wedding she's planning could be the biggest celebration folks around here have ever seen. At least if Mrs. Banks gets what she wants."

Adrian kept a smile pasted on his face, even though he suspected something had gone horribly wrong. "What wedding is that? I didn't know they had anything planned."

Zeb looked at him, head cocked and eyes wide. "Miss Annabelle and Mr. Wentworth," he said, showing disbelief. "Mrs. Banks told us all it's coming, just not sure when. I'm surprised you didn't know."

Chapter Forty-Eight

Adrian went to Hickory Hill uninvited. He had to know if Zeb Payne had been telling the truth, and he couldn't wait until his planned visit. Caesar opened the door when he arrived and looked at him quizzically but made no judgement.

"May I see Miss Annabelle?" Adrian asked.

"Yes, of course, Mr. Reed. Please come in."

Caesar led him to the gentlemen's parlor. Adrian waited, pacing the floor, admiring the seascapes that hung on the walls and glancing out windows. But his mind was racing, scrambling puzzle pieces that might not fit.

A moment later, Annabelle came in. "Adrian, what a surprise," she said, eyeing him curiously. "I didn't expect to see you this evening."

He glanced to the hallway, not knowing if anyone eavesdropped. "May I speak to you for a moment?"

"Yes, of course," she said. She took his hand and led him to the sofa. "Let's sit down."

He paused, ill at ease. "Can we find a more private location?" He leaned closer, whispering. "I don't want anyone to hear us."

Her eyes widened. "Is everything all right?"

He nodded. "I have something important to tell you. And a few questions to ask."

"We can go out to the stables and see how Snowflake is doing," she offered.

"Let's go out back instead," he suggested. "Someone might be tending the horses."

Lines of concern etched her face. She studied him

closely for a moment and then led him down the hallway.

When they reached the rear entrance, Naomi appeared, likely alerted by Caesar. "What brings you here, Mr. Reed?"

Adrian knew she wasn't pleased. But he couldn't help it. "I have a few questions for Annabelle. It'll be a brief visit. Just a few minutes."

Naomi eyed him sternly. "I'm sure Annabelle explained the courting schedule."

"Yes, she did, Mrs. Banks. And I apologize for violating it."

"This couldn't have waited?"

"I suppose it could have," he said. "But I was passing Hickory Hill, and it seemed an opportune time to visit."

"Except it's not fair to Mr. Wentworth," Naomi scolded. "You do realize that, don't you?"

"Yes, I do," Adrian replied. "And I apologize. I promise I won't be long."

Naomi glared at Annabelle but replied to Adrian. "See that you aren't."

Annabelle rolled her eyes. "Come on," she said, taking Adrian's hand.

They went out on the porch. Naomi followed, watching as they started down the steps.

They crossed the lawn, walking toward the bay. "She's not too happy to see me," Adrian said wryly.

"She's never happy to see anyone," Annabelle grumbled.

Adrian waited a moment and then turned. Naomi had gone, but he wasn't sure for how long. Annabelle led him to the bench tucked among the foliage, overlooking the bay. As soon as they were seated, she leaned over and kissed him.

He didn't resist but didn't let the kiss linger. Naomi would soon call for their return, and he needed information.

"I saw Zeb Payne today."

"Where did you see him?" she asked, more interested in the kiss than the discussion.

"On the road between our properties. I was inspecting the forest."

"Is that why you've come? Because of something he said?"

"Yes, two things, actually."

She sighed. "I can only imagine. You shouldn't let him aggravate you."

He smiled weakly. "Sometimes it can't be helped."

"I'm willing to bet whatever he said is false."

Adrian wasn't sure where to begin. "He claimed he knew your mother before she came to Hickory Hill. But when I pressed him, he said he hadn't known her personally."

Annabelle was quiet for a moment. "What was he implying?"

"I'm not sure," he admitted. "Did you parents meet in Baltimore?"

"Yes, they did. Is that what he said?"

Adrian nodded. "He said your father told him a story about how they met."

"Maybe he did," she said. "But it's really not that important. Why would it bother you?"

"Because he seemed uncomfortable after I challenged him, as if he regretted saying it."

She was quiet for a moment. "Do you think he's hiding something?"

Adrian shrugged. "He could be. His behavior was odd."

She frowned. "I wouldn't believe anything he said. He was only trying to irritate you. And apparently, he did."

He hesitated, not sure how to reveal the rest. "There's more."

She looked at him, still concerned. "What else?"

Adrian paused, collecting his courage. Zeb's revelation had been painful, which was his likely intention. "He said your mother is planning a wedding, a huge gala that all on the Eastern Shore will envy."

"It's no secret that I'll marry this fall," she said, squeezing his hand tightly. "It doesn't surprise me that she's planning the wedding."

"Zeb didn't seem to know that we're courting."

She looked at him strangely. "I don't see how he doesn't."

"He claimed you were marrying Artemis Wentworth."

She frowned. "I'm not. And you know that."

"I'm so relieved," he said and sighed. Then he kissed her.

She chuckled. "You should know better than to believe that nonsense."

"Maybe he was only teasing or playing a practical joke." He paused, his brow furrowed. "But why would he do that?"

"Who knows?" she asked, snuggling up close. "I don't really care."

"Where would he get that information? He seemed quite certain."

The back door opened, and Naomi stepped out on the porch "Annabelle," she called. "it's time for Mr. Reed to leave."

Annabelle looked at Adrian and rolled her eyes. "I think I know who told him."

Chapter Forty-Nine

When Adrian left and Annabelle came back in the house, her mother was waiting in the hallway.

"You're wasting time, dear," Naomi said. "Your sister Emma chose her husband in only a few weeks."

Annabelle's face firmed. "I can choose right now if you prefer, Mother."

Naomi frowned. "I'm sure you could. But it would be the wrong choice." She hesitated, as if wondering whether to reveal a secret. "Someday I'll tell you what happens when you pick the wrong man."

"What would you know about marrying the wrong man?" Annabelle retorted. "You have a fabulous husband. The whole world knows it. Except for you."

"Don't be ridiculous," Naomi scoffed. "I love your father. I always have."

"I'll love my husband, too. Which is why *I* need to choose him—not you."

"It shouldn't be difficult," Naomi said. "You only have two suitors. A wealthy man whose future may include the White House and a man who cuts down trees. The comparison is revealing to most."

Annabelle glared at her, hands on hips. "Will you support me, regardless of who I choose?"

Naomi didn't answer, rolling her eyes instead. "Your father and I had significant influence into your sister's selection. She almost made the same mistake you're about to make. She wanted to marry Joseph Crawly from Rosemount plantation, down near Cambridge. But in the end, she did what was right."

"If she loved Joseph Crawley, why did she do what

was right by marrying a man no one even knew?"

"Because she now lives a fairy tale," Naomi said sharply. "Her husband is a prominent banker, she owns a beautiful mansion, and her children lead lives any would envy."

"And we see them every year or two," Annabelle grumbled. "I'm still lost without her. I suppose I don't understand why her current husband was the best choice. Was it for Emma, because she loved him, or was it for you and the social status you seem to crave?"

"Because he makes Emma very happy," Naomi insisted.

"How do you know? No one ever sees her."

"Annabelle, don't be ridiculous."

"Is that what you want for me? Marriage to a man I don't love just because he's rich and famous?"

"Artemis is a man you'll learn to love. He's far superior to the childhood playmate you're currently obsessed with. Adrian couldn't compete with you intellectually then, and he still can't now. You'll lead a boring life married to him."

Annabelle's face flushed with anger. "It's not an obsession, Mother. It's love. And you can't seem to recognize it, because you don't know what it is."

Naomi ignored her. "Just think of the life you'll live—the wife of a senator, perhaps first lady."

"Is that the life you always wanted?"

Naomi frowned. "Don't be silly, Annabelle. I see your future. It's bright and promising. Hopefully, within days if not a few weeks, you'll see it, too."

Annabelle crossed her arms. "You see the future you wish you had. Not the future I want."

"That's absurd. I want what's best for you. I don't understand why you can't see that."

Annabelle shook her head and stormed down the hall. She went out the back door, started walking toward the bay, but decided to go to the stables instead. Snowflake always managed to calm her.

She veered off to the left, cutting through the grove of trees that split the main estate from the stables, livestock pens, and workmen's shack. It was lush, foliage growing profusely, hiding in the shade cast by limbs of towering trees.

Motion caught her attention. She wasn't sure what it was. An animal or one of the slaves on his way to the carpenter's shack? She advanced cautiously, fearing the creature might be wild, when she saw Phoebe, bent at the waist. A basket lay on the ground beside her, filled with mushrooms. Others sprouted in clumps from moss underneath the trees. They were golden, funnel-shaped with meaty heads, gill-like ridges under the stem.

"What are the mushrooms for?" Annabelle asked.

Phoebe bolted upright, eyes wide, her hand to her heart. "Good Lord, Miss Annabelle, you near scared me to death. I thought you was a ghost or something."

Annabelle chuckled. "I'm sorry. I didn't mean to startle you."

"Well, you sure did, child."

"I was on my way to see Snowflake."

Phoebe slowly shook her head. "You sure love that horse, don't you?"

Annabelle smiled. "Everyone loves Snowflake."

"Whatever you say, Miss Annabelle," Phoebe muttered and starting picking again.

"Are the mushrooms used for cooking?"

"Yes, ma'am. To season my stew. These are my favorite, taste like pepper. They cook up real nice mixed with butter or cream." She leaned toward Annabelle and smiled. "And mixed with wine, they even better."

Annabelle laughed, eyeing the mushrooms. She pointed to a rotted tree trunk where smaller mushrooms with tiny caps were growing in clusters. "What about those?"

"Oh, no, Miss Annabelle," she said, eyes wide. "They poison. You cook them up, add a little whiskey to hide the taste, and then eat 'em, you be deader than the rotted tree they came from."

Chapter Fifty

Naomi had to do something about Zeb Payne, and she had to do it quickly—before Artemis Wentworth found out who he really was. But she wasn't quite sure what to do. First, she had to determine just what he knew and how much he was bluffing. Somehow, she had to stop him—or her entire life would unravel.

She wanted to meet on her terms when she'd be fully prepared, not like their last encounter when she'd been taken by surprise. She also had to be certain they were alone, far from any prying eyes and ears. But she couldn't just go to the overseer's cottage and confront him. She had no way of knowing if he was even there—or if he was alone. She had to lure him to her, at the time and place of her choosing.

She decided two issues needed resolution: her past and Coffey Green's present. And somehow, to fix both, she had to get Zeb Payne to leave Hickory Hill forever. If she couldn't, she would be forced to take more drastic action— as revolting as it might be. But if it came to that, she had to plan it perfectly. Just like the murder of Rufus Jackson.

Naomi watched from the balcony as wagons carrying slaves returned from the fields. Zeb Payne came back last, a few minutes after the others. He followed the drivers to the stables, ensured the horses were cared for, the wagons parked beside the barn.

She still hadn't determined where to meet him. She walked around the balcony, circling the entire house, looking for hidden locations that couldn't be seen from the house. There were many: the trees that flanked the mansion, the far corner of the flower garden, the back end of the stable, the carpenter's shack, the rear of the kitchen. But only one location was also visible from the overseer's cottage—the far corner of the flower garden. It was the only safe place to meet him, at least for now.

Naomi crept downstairs, determined to bait Zeb Payne. But she didn't want anyone to see her. She paused in the foyer and peeked into the parlor. Annabelle was playing the piano, an extremely difficult piece by Chopin she had been struggling to master. Naomi passed by, tiptoeing down the hall. She glanced in Gideon's study. He sat by the window, using the remaining daylight to read a book. She crept past his doorway, ensuring he wasn't disturbed, and went out the back door.

She passed the kitchen and smokehouse, both empty. When she reached the vegetable garden, she went just beyond it, where the flower beds were planted. She stood in the far corner and turned in a circle, scanning the landscape, ensuring she couldn't be seen from anywhere else. Zeb Payne's cottage was visible through the trees.

She waited patiently, moving little, pretending to admire the flowers. Her ploy worked. It wasn't long, not ten minutes, before Zeb Payne came through trees, a cocky grin on his face.

"You must be looking for me," he said as he approached.

She didn't reply, eyeing him coldly. She despised him, both for what he did to Coffey and what he was doing to her.

He came to the edge of the flowers, standing so close she could see the lurid gleam in his eyes. He was enjoying the trap he had set. "Here I am, ready to talk."

Her face was firm, eyes angry. "What do you want?"

He sighed, pushing his hat back on his head. "My daddy was best friends with a police inspector down in St.

Lucia, a man named Burton. I bet you didn't know that."

She shrugged. "I bet I didn't care."

"Maybe not, ma'am," he said. "But Inspector Burton told my daddy everything. He loved fishing. Spent a lot of time on my daddy's boat."

Naomi knew she was in trouble, but she wasn't sure just how much. "Get to the point."

He sighed as if it took an effort to continue. "Inspector Burton claimed you poisoned Rufus Jackson, who died a horrible death. Even made Doc Jones sick when he saw the body."

"I don't know what you're talking about."

Zeb started laughing. "You're one cold woman, Naomi."

"Only around certain people."

"The inspector told my daddy that, too—about how cold you were. He said you killed Rufus Jackson without shedding a single tear. At least not any real ones. Who could do that? Makes a man wonder."

"I want you out of here."

"Oh, no," he said, chuckling. "That's not gonna work. I've got a big mouth, liable to tell everyone willing to listen that Rufus Jackson was murdered—and who did it. And you know what else I'll tell them?"

"I can't wait to hear," she said, scowling.

"Inspector Burton knew exactly how much money was in the safe hidden behind the painting of Soufriere harbor." He looked at her sternly. "You stole a lot of money, Naomi."

She turned away, cringing. It was far worse than she'd thought. She waited a moment, gathered her thoughts, and spoke in a measured tone. "If I wanted you to vanish, and keep your mouth shut forever, how much would that cost me?"

He shrugged. "There's more to the story, Naomi."

She frowned. "I can't wait to hear it."

"You gave my daddy a few gold pieces to keep quiet. And he did. Even though the inspector was his closest friend, my daddy never told him where you went. Always said he thought you headed to New Orleans."

"Your father was an honorable man. It's a shame his son didn't inherit that trait."

He ignored her. "That's loyalty, Naomi. My daddy carried your secret to his grave. And that should be worth a lot of money."

"How much do you want?" she asked bluntly.

He hesitated, his gaze fixed on hers, assessing whether she would cooperate. "You come to my house tomorrow night. Same time. Just when I get back from the fields. And you bring some money."

"How do I know how much to bring?"

"I'll let you know if it's enough."

She shook her head with disgust. "Fine. I'll come to your house."

"Good," he said, nodding. "We're making progress. There's just one more thing to discuss."

She frowned. "What is it, Mr. Payne? What else do you want?"

He reached out with his hand, touching her blonde hair where it laid on her shoulder. "You're just as fine as you were twenty-five years ago." He met her gaze, grinning lewdly. "Sometimes money just ain't enough. Sometimes, you have to give just a little bit more."

Chapter Fifty-One

Coffey Green poured syrupy liquid from a glass pitcher into small jars, preparing another batch of Coffey's Cream. She had finished filling the first jar and moved to the second when a horse neighed at the other end of the barn. A moment later, footsteps shuffled across the dirt floor.

"I'll have another batch of cream real soon, Mr. Reed," she called.

"Hey, Coffey," a man said with a throaty whisper. "How are you?"

She spun around, almost dropping the pitcher. "What are you doing here?"

Zeb Payne stood behind her, a smug grin on his face. "I thought I'd come visit. It isn't right we don't get to see each other much, is it?"

Coffey felt like she would vomit. "Mr. Reed due back any minute," she said softly, avoiding eye contact, praying his image would disappear. But it didn't. She closed her eyes, summoned her strength, prepared to do anything to avoid what was about to happen.

Zeb reached out and caressed her cheek. "Yesterday Mr. Reed told me he'd be gone all day. He's out in that stretch of forest by Hickory Hill."

Coffey's face firmed. She was determined to protect herself. But she wasn't sure how. She glanced at her work bench. A knife rested on the far end of the table. A mild soul, she had never wished harm on anyone—not until now. She would kill Zeb Payne if she could. And it seemed like as good a time as any.

"You don't seem happy to see me," Zeb said with a

lewd grin. He wrapped his arms around her and pulled her close.

Her body stiffened. She could smell him, fresh from the fields, feel the perspiration on his neck. "I got work to do, Mr. Payne," she said, repulsed.

"You can rest a bit, it's all right." He yanked away her head scarf, letting her hair spill free. "I won't tell anyone."

"I got to finish, or Mr. Reed ain't gonna like it."

"Mr. Reed doesn't have to like it," he muttered, kissing her lightly on the lips.

She stepped back and glanced at the table. The knife was too far away. She had to find something else. "I ain't gonna let this happen, Mr. Payne. Not anymore. It's done with."

"I decide what happens," he said, breathing heavily, his voice husky. "Not you."

"I swear I won't tell a soul," she said, looking away. She scanned the barn for a weapon or an escape path, she didn't care which. "You just stop touching me and be on your way."

Zeb started laughing." Oh, Coffey. You talk like a white woman sometimes." He gestured toward the workbench and the house beyond. "All of this nonsense made you forget what you are." He grabbed her roughly, pulled her close, and put his arms around her, his hands groping her.

"Stop it," she insisted, squirming to break free. "I done found the strength to fight you. And I'm gonna do it."

He was astonished, eyes wide. "Who do you think you are?" he hissed.

"A woman who don't want to do this." She put her hands on his chest, pushing him back.

"You do what I tell you to do," he barked. He grabbed her roughly and swung his fist, punching her under her left eye.

Coffey stumbled back against her work table, knocking the pitcher to the ground. It shattered, spilling cream in the dirt. She fell hard, the room spinning. Blackness came and went, sound muffled and faraway. She blinked, her vision hazy, her head swimming.

"Maybe now you'll do what you're told," Zeb scolded. He climbed on top of her, forced his knees between her legs, pulled up her dress.

Her face swelled, and her cheek throbbed to match her pulse. She resisted, kicking, punching, screaming. "Stop!" she hollered. "You stop right now!"

"Don't fight me, Coffey! You like it as much as I do. You know you do."

Tears streamed down her face. Resistance seemed futile—he was too big, too strong. The pitcher lay beside her, shattered into a dozen pieces, cream oozing in the dirt. She reached for shards of glass, remnants of the handle closest, a sharp edge showing. It was just beyond her grasp. She fought, wriggled and cried, twisted her torso—she wasn't able to stop him. But as her body shifted, she inched closer to the handle.

"Ain't you the wild one today," Zeb said, pinning her down, struggling to subdue her.

Coffey touched the handle with her fingertips. But she couldn't pick it up. She rolled it toward her as Zeb fumbled with his pants. She stretched as far as she could and grabbed it. Jagged end out, she swung her arm in an arc, plunging the glass in his back. She shoved it deep and yanked downward, ripping skin and muscle.

"You crazy bitch!" he howled. He reared up and punched her in the mouth.

Her lips split, trickling blood. She lashed out again, wielding the broken glass, swinging it back and forth. He raised his arms, shielding his face. She cut his hands and forearms, thrusting the glass toward him.

He leaped off of her. "Damn you, woman!"

She scrambled away, crawling across the dirt floor. As soon as she was free, she leaped to her feet and ran. She raced out of the barn, crossed the clearing and darted into the woods.

"Come back here, Coffey!" Zeb screamed. He reached behind his back, ran his hand along the gash, cringing as he touched it. Blood dripped from his hands and forearms, several slices tearing the skin but not going much deeper.

"You'll pay for this!"

Chapter Fifty-Two

Adrian came back from the forest later that afternoon. He had marked trees to be cut and would schedule a logging crew to harvest and transport them to the harbor. It was challenging to keep the sawmill fully stocked with timber, especially as production increased in the shipyard.

He led his horse into the front stable and removed his saddle. Coffey was at the far end of the barn, her tables, crates, jars, and product stacked around her. Adrian removed the tack from his horse, got him hay and water, and then walked toward her, past his wagon and buggy.

"How are you today, Coffey?" he asked as he approached.

"Not good, Mr. Reed," she said, her back to him. "I fell and broke a pitcher. I'm so sorry. Take the cost from the money you give me so you can get a new one. I need to pay closer mind to what I'm doing."

Adrian came closer. She wasn't acting herself, glad to see him when he came back from the forest. She was despondent, anxious, mumbling. "It's only a pitcher," he said, minimizing the impact of such a minor mishap. "If we don't have another in the house, I'll buy one."

"Thank you, sir," she said. "I am sorry. Just clumsy."

"It's nothing to worry about." He eyed her closely as she minded her work, hunched over the table, talking softly. Something wasn't right. "You didn't get hurt, did you?"

"I couldn't finish up the batch of cream, neither," she continued, not answering his question. "Spilt so much when the pitcher broke."

He couldn't understand why she was so upset. "As long as you're all right. That's all that matters. We can always make more cream. And a broken pitcher means nothing. It's the cost of doing business. People fall. Things break. Product gets spilled."

"If you say so, sir."

He hesitated, worried she seemed so depressed. "Why don't you quit for the day? Relax a little before dinner."

"I couldn't do that, sir. Not after all the bad I did."

"Don't be silly," he said, touching her arm and turning her toward him.

"But Mr. Reed—"

He gasped, eyes wide. "Coffey, my Lord!" he exclaimed. "What happened to you!"

Her left eye was purple, almost swollen shut. Her cheek was badly bruised, her lips torn and swollen. "I tripped and fell, sir," she muttered. "Like I told you."

"Tripped where?" he asked in disbelief. "Are you all right? Should I fetch a doctor?"

"No, sir, I'll be fine. I can doctor myself."

"Where did you fall?" He scanned the barn, searching for something she could have tripped over. "That's a horrible injury. We need to take care of you."

"I can do it, Mr. Reed. I put some tonic on it. Be better in a few days."

"But, Coffey, they're terrible bruises. You look like you've been beaten."

"I'm just clumsy is all, sir," she replied, eyes lowered.

She was hiding something. But he didn't know why. "Coffey, no one gets hurt that badly from a fall. Tell me what happened."

"I did fall, Mr. Reed, and just got hurt bad."

"Show me where you fell," he said, eyes narrowed.

"Right over there," she said, pointing toward the entrance.

"Where?" he asked. "Show me exactly."

"I was coming in the barn when I tripped and hit my face on the edge of the table, knocked the pitcher off and broke it."

He was quiet, eyeing her closely. Regardless of what she said, he suspected she'd been punched. "Did anyone visit today?"

"No, sir, Mr. Reed. Miss Annabelle came the other day. But no one today. Just me here by myself."

"Tell me what happened," he insisted. "I'll protect you. I promise. But I can't help if you won't tell me."

"I just tripped, Mr. Reed."

Adrian sighed. He didn't believe her. But why wouldn't she tell the truth? She could have fallen, it was possible. Although it didn't explain injuries to different parts of her face—her mouth and eye. He strongly suspected she had been punched. But he didn't know who had done it or why.

He went back to the barn entrance and bent close to the soil, studying tracks—horses' hooves, wagon wheels, footprints—searching for a sign someone had been there. Many markings marred the soil, but he couldn't tell which were his and which might belong to someone else—either friend or foe. Only Coffey knew the truth.

But why wouldn't she tell him?

Chapter Fifty-Three

Billy raced from the church, slamming the door closed behind him. He stumbled across the lawn, paused briefly to study the landscape, and sprinted toward a nearby field.

The man in the church chased him. "Stop him!" he yelled as he ran out the door.

"What happened, Reverend?" called a man from a neighboring farmhouse. He stood beside a broken buggy with three others, tinkering with the back wheel.

"He split Roger's head open," the reverend hollered. "Most likely killed him."

"Let's get him!" one of the men yelled. "Come on! I can track him."

"I'll check Roger and then find the sheriff," a second man said.

"I bet there's a nice reward for him, too," the reverend called.

Billy raced across the field, drawn to a forest in the distance. When he turned to look behind him, four men followed, the reverend and three of his neighbors.

"You best stop now, boy," the tracker called. "I *will* find you."

Get him before he kills someone else!" yelled another."

Billy dashed across the field and into the forest, staying along the edge. Breathing heavily, not knowing which way to go, he stumbled over a tree root. He fell fast and hard to the forest floor.

"Circle around," the tracker called. "We'll trap him."

Billy got up quickly. One knee of his britches was torn, his leg scraped and bleeding. He started running as panic overtook him. He looked back and saw his pursuers split up. Two ran along the field at the forest's edge; two trailed him into the forest. Billy scrambled through the foliage, not sure where he was or where the forest led. In his haste to escape, he ran blindly in different directions, confused and disoriented, breaking twigs and branches. If the tracker was as good as he claimed, they could follow him easily.

He gasped for air; his heart raced. But he had to stay calm, no matter how hard it was. If he didn't, he'd get caught for sure. He not only had to lose his pursuers, he had to come out of the forest near the road. Then he could follow it to freedom like Jacob Yoder had told him. When he came to a clearing, he glanced skyward. He guessed from the sun's position that the road still ran northeast. But the forest didn't. The road was off to his right where two pursuers waited.

"There he is!" someone yelled. "Just up ahead."

Billy darted through trees and shrubs. He could escape if he kept his wits. He ran as fast as he could, breaking everything in his path, leaving an easy trail to follow. But it didn't matter. Not as long as he was faster than they were.

A few minutes later, he heard them shouting—but they weren't as close as they had been. He was getting away, but he was losing track of the road. He slowed and went to his right, knowing the forest would yield to the field, the road just beyond it.

It took several minutes, but he reached the edge of the trees. A farm field sprawled beyond, waist-high wheat blowing in a soft breeze. An acre or more across, the road wound off in the distance. He risked a look back. The reverend and one of his neighbors moved along the forest fringe, sometimes wandering into the undergrowth.

An oak sprawled beside him. Its branches spread in all directions. Stout limbs wandered into the forest and spread across the edge of the field. The reverend and his friend weren't tracking him. It didn't seem like they knew how. They wandered cautiously, peering through foliage, looking for him. The tracker and his partner combed the woods. They were closing in, pinching him between them.

He saw no plants that could hide his scent, not that it mattered. They didn't have dogs. Only four men, close to catching him. They tracked impressions he left in the moss, broken twigs and branches. They were tedious, meticulously moving forward. Each time they caught sight of him, they raced toward him. He still managed to lose them, but he might not be able to the next time. He had to outsmart them. They wouldn't give up.

Billy reached to the oak's lowest branch. He pulled himself up, climbed to the next, and then hoisted himself to the limb above it. He sought the densest foliage, not the highest branch. When he found it, he crawled along the limb and stretched out along it to minimize his profile. He scanned the forest, looking through leaves. The reverend and his friend were close, walking along the forest's edge. He couldn't see the tracker and his partner, but he kept his gaze trained to where he thought they were. They posed the greatest threat.

A moment later, the reverend and his friend walked underneath the tree. They never looked up. They kept going, peeking through the brush, ensuring no one came out of the woods, guarding the approach to the road.

Billy waited, barely breathing. When the reverend was a hundred feet away, the tracker and his partner approached, partially visible through the trees. They followed his path, checking for broken branches. In minutes they would reach the tree. He climbed down, carefully stepping from limb to limb, warily watching all four pursuers.

Once he got to the ground, he crept along the edge of the forest, but in the opposite direction. As he went back the way he had come, he was cautious, moving slowly and carefully, breaking no branches or twigs. If he could get to the road, they would lose his trail among all others who had traveled upon it.

He made his way back to the church. When he reached the edge of the woods, he used the forest as a screen and ran across the field. He crept around the church to the road and ran a half mile back the way he'd come. He rushed into a grove of trees on the opposite side of the road and found a thicket. He crawled inside it and waited, exhausted, listening for his pursuers. When an hour passed and no one followed, his eyes drifted closed.

He awakened when someone kicked his leg. He bolted upright, eyes wide. Amos Quigg, Sheriff Dodd, the reverend and three townsfolk all stared at him.

Amos Quigg started laughing. "Billy, you're one dumb son-of-a-bitch."

"We're taking you to jail," Sheriff Dodd said. "You killed a man. And we're going to hang you, right and proper."

Chapter Fifty-Four

A storm threatened as dusk approached. Black clouds consumed the sky, ignited by streaks of lightning. Jacob Yoder came in from his farthest field, his step slow and heavy, the hair under his broad-brimmed hat matted with sweat. His stomach growled as he neared the house, the aroma of crackling meat wafting on the breeze. He smiled. Hard work always paid handsome rewards. Ruth had a nice supper waiting, and he could play with the little ones afterward. But first he had to feed Haney and her daughter who were still hiding in the barn.

He jeopardized his family's safety by helping runaways, and the risk had intensified with Sheriff Dodd's suspicions. But slavery was wrong, and he did what he could to right it—in his own small way. If he could make a few lives better, it was all worthwhile. But the risks had begun to multiply. And now his children were starting to question the strangers who mysteriously came and went. Maybe he could help in a different way—donate food or clothing, rather than sheltering those who so desperately sought their freedom.

As he neared the house, rain started falling, little more than a drizzle. He glanced at the road and paused. Three figures approached, two on horseback, the third walking, his hands tied behind his back. A tether was fixed around his waist, strung to the pommel on a rider's saddle. The bound man shuffled; his feet were loosely secured, allowing just enough motion for him to move. As they turned off the road onto the farm, Jacob recognized Sheriff Dodd and Amos Quigg. Their captive was Billy Giles.

"Evening, friend," Amos Quigg called as a crack of

thunder shook the sky. "We caught that runaway we were looking for."

"I can see that," Jacob replied. "Does he need to be tied like that?"

"He sure does," Dodd replied, looking at Billy with contempt. "He killed a man while making his escape. We're taking him to jail now."

"We had a helluva time tracking him down," Quigg added. "Don't plan on losing him again."

As they came to a halt, Jacob shared a furtive glance with Billy and received a subtle nod in return. It was too late for Jacob to help, but Billy would keep their secret.

"I was wondering, friend," Quigg said, "with this storm brewing and a hard day behind us, could we stay in your barn tonight? Maybe get some of that fine food your missus makes."

Jacob hesitated. If they stayed in the barn, Haney and Chloe were in danger. And so was his family. "Chestertown is only a few miles away. It shouldn't take you much longer."

"It'll take an hour or more dragging him along," Dodd said. He looked up at the darkening sky, the rain falling faster. "No man should be out in this storm."

"We'd be much obliged," Quigg continued, rubbing his scruffy face with his hand.

"Yes, of course," Jacob said reluctantly. "I'll ask my wife to prepare more food."

"Doesn't have to be much," Quigg said. He pointed to Billy. "The boy can eat whatever slop you got."

Jacob hurried to the house, turning just before he entered. Quigg and Sheriff Dodd were getting settled at the edge of the barn, very near the stall where Haney and Chloe were hidden. Billy was still bound, tethered now to a rail on the side of the stable.

As Jacob walked in, Ruth was setting the table. "Sheriff Dodd and a slave catcher came with Billy, the runaway." He eyed his children as they helped their momma. "They're spending the night in the barn. They've asked for food."

Her eyes widened. "We have plenty," she said, recognizing the danger. "But can you get them away from the barn, even for a few minutes?"

He hesitated. None of the options were good ones. "I could ask them to come in," he said reluctantly.

She shrugged. "It seems safest. Don't you think?"

He nodded. "Yes, I suppose."

She motioned to the children. "I don't know what they've seen."

"Or what they may say."

"They're innocent and naïve. They'll say whatever comes to mind."

Jacob frowned. "It might be more dangerous bringing them here."

"It'll get worse if you can't warn our guests."

Jacob nodded. "I'll ask them in. But I'll need an excuse to go back out."

He left the house and hurried to the barn. If Haney or Chloe made even the slightest noise, everything would unravel. And he'd be in jail, leaving two children and a pregnant wife.

Quigg waited at the entrance; Dodd leaned against the stable rail. "My wife has supper ready," Jacob said. "She invited you all to table."

Quigg scrunched his nose as if fighting a horrendous smell and motioned to Billy. "You don't want that dog at your dinner table."

"I'll bring his meal out to him," Jacob said, the perfect excuse to return.

"We can't leave him alone," Dodd interjected. "Not after killing a man in cold blood."

"Tell your missus we're much obliged," Quigg said. "But if she could send some food out, we'd appreciate it all the more."

Jacob left, staying close to the building to avoid the wind and rain. He couldn't do anything now but pray—and hope Haney remembered what he'd told her. But a woman and child had needs that a man might not. It wasn't as easy as it seemed.

"They're staying in the barn," he told Ruth when he went back to the house.

She pursed her lips. "They're here with a purpose, not for shelter from the storm." She filled three bowls with food and put them in a basket with bread and cider. "They suspect you."

"You're right," he agreed, afraid he had gone too far, done too much. Ruth always offered a quiet wisdom, able to see what he could not. "I hadn't thought of that."

"And if Billy committed murder, they plan on tying you into it somehow."

He nodded grimly. "Dodd would like nothing more."

"Just be careful," she warned. "Don't show any hint you've ever seen Billy before. I'm sure they're watching you closely."

Jacob thought about the furtive glances they'd shared. Had anyone noticed? He wasn't sure. "I promise to be cautious."

"What about the woman and her daughter?" Ruth asked. "Do they understand the danger?"

"I'm sure they must. I can't get a message to them anyway."

"She can hear them talking," Ruth said. "She knows what to do."

"I sure hope so. It'll be disastrous if she doesn't."

Chapter Fifty-Five

Zeb Payne had duplicated the equestrian course at Annapolis in the field behind the stables. He had many desirable qualities, loyalty to Hickory Hill among them, and Annabelle often appreciated his efforts despite the evil that stole his soul. He seemed like two different people— one a man you came to love and the other who made you fear for your life.

She practiced riding for an hour each day under the watchful eye of Luke, one of Zeb Payne's assistants. He had some equestrian experience in a competitive environment.

"You're doing well," Luke said as she finished her ride and helped her dismount. "I see a grand champion before me."

Annabelle chuckled. "Snowflake is the champion. Not me. I don't deserve anything."

"No, you do, too, Miss Annabelle," Luke said as he led the filly away. "You've been working hard."

Annabelle went back to the house, over an hour before dinner would be served. She sat at the piano, determined to master the Chopin piece that had proven so difficult. After she had been playing for fifteen minutes, someone knocked on the door. She paused, wondering who it might be, but then continued.

A moment later, Caesar interrupted her. "Mr. Reed is here to see you, Miss Annabelle."

"Mr. Reed?" she asked, rising from the stool.

"Yes, ma'am. Should I show him in?"

"Of course," she said. It was his second visit in only

a few days. Her mother wouldn't be pleased.

"Hello, Annabelle," Adrian said as he came in, flushed and anxious. "I'm sorry to intrude."

"You're not intruding at all," she said, noting his expression. She motioned to a chair. "Is anything wrong?"

He sat in front of the fireplace "It's about Coffey."

"Is she all right?" Annabelle asked as she sat beside him, an oval table between them.

"Yes, but she's had a horrible fall."

Annabelle's hand moved to her mouth. "How badly is she hurt?"

"Her left eye is close to swollen shut, and her mouth is badly bruised. At first, I thought her jaw might be broken."

"My Lord!" Annabelle exclaimed. "All from a fall?"

He shrugged. "That's what she claims."

"Is she in pain?"

"She must be. It hurts to even look at her. She's been applying tonic, said it helps."

Annabelle eyed him closely. "You seem skeptical."

His face firmed. "How did she get two nasty bruises from a single fall?"

Annabelle sat back in the chair. "What did she say happened?"

"She was coming in the barn and tripped, banging her face against the table."

Annabelle hesitated. "It seems like a reasonable explanation."

"She had to hit more than the table if she has two bruises."

"Maybe she did."

"I didn't see anything else she could have struck."

Annabelle tried to envision the accident. "Maybe she banged the table and hit the leg on the way down."

"The bruises are bad," he stressed.

Annabelle started feeling nauseous, connecting threads she wouldn't normally consider. "Do you think someone hit her?"

"It sure looks like it. It's hard to imagine a fall could do that much damage. She took two hard blows to her face."

"Did anyone visit her?" Annabelle asked, her pulse starting to race. She had her suspicions. But she couldn't share them.

"I asked, but she said she was alone. And I looked for tracks in front of the barn, but I couldn't tell much."

Annabelle feared the worst—Zeb Payne. "You seem certain someone beat her."

He sighed. "I don't know what to think. But it does look like she was punched in the face. Though I think she would confide in me if she'd been assaulted."

Annabelle frowned. She wasn't so sure. "I'll go to see her. I'm sure she'll tell me what happened. And she could have fallen. We don't know that she didn't."

Naomi walked in and interrupted them. "Adrian Reed, what brings you here again? These unexpected visits are becoming a habit."

"Good evening, Mrs. Banks," Adrian said, standing. "I had something to tell Annabelle."

"Isn't that what you said the other day?" Naomi asked. "When you violated the courting agreement the *first* time?"

"My apologies, ma'am," he said with a slight bow. He turned to Annabelle. "I'll be on my way."

"I would ask you for dinner," Naomi continued, "but I've already invited Artemis Wentworth. It might get awkward." She looked at her daughter. "Shouldn't you get yourself ready, dear? You can't wear your riding outfit."

"Yes, of course," Annabelle mumbled. "I'll change. I didn't know we were expecting a visitor."

"I had plans to surprise you," Naomi said sweetly.

"I know how much you enjoy Artemis's company." She turned to Adrian. "I'll show you out, Mr. Reed."

"I'll let you know if I find anything out," Annabelle said as he started to leave.

"I'll do the same," he promised, and nodded to Naomi. "Good evening, Mrs. Banks."

Naomi walked him to the door and then returned to the parlor.

"What time is Artemis arriving?" Annabelle asked.

Naomi looked at her strangely. "Artemis?"

"You said he was coming to dinner."

Naomi cocked her head. "Did I say that?"

Annabelle folded her arms across her chest. "Yes, you did."

Naomi sighed. "Oh, dear. What was I thinking? Artemis is coming tomorrow night."

Chapter Fifty-Six

"I don't know why you can't talk to Coffey on Sunday, Miss Annabelle," Caesar said as he helped her climb off the buggy outside Adrian's barn. "You were just here last week."

Annabelle hid a smile, amused by how badly her mother intimidated him. "If I want to visit Coffey, I will."

"But Miz Naomi isn't gonna like it one bit."

"Don't be silly," Annabelle scoffed. "She won't even know. We won't be gone that long."

"Oh, she'll find out, Miss Annabelle, believe you me. She's probably wondering where I'm off to right now."

"Not if you don't tell her," Annabelle said.

His eyes widened. "You know sure as I'm standing here that I can't do that. When Miz Naomi wants something, she gets it. Always has and always will."

Coffey had seen them arrive and came out to greet them. "Hi, Miss Annabelle. Hello, Caesar." She stepped from the barn's shadows into the sunshine.

Caesar was handling the horse when he saw her. "My Lord, Coffey Green! What happened to your face?"

"I fell," Coffey said, eyes averted.

"Fell on what, woman?" Caesar asked, eyes wide. "Looks like someone beat you senseless."

Annabelle cringed and stepped closer. The bruises were bad, worse than Adrian had described. "Oh, Coffey," she said, touching her arm to reassure her. "What a nasty fall that must have been."

"You must have fell down a mountain to get banged up like that," Caesar continued.

"I fell just out back," Coffey said softly.

Annabelle took her by the arm. "Come on, let's visit," she said as she led her toward the back of the barn.

"I'll be waiting right here, Miss Annabelle," Caesar called. "And you take care of that face, Coffey Green."

"It'll be just fine in a few days," Coffey said as they walked away. "Been puttin' my tonic on it."

"You better put more than tonic on it," Caesar declared, and then sought the shade of a sprawling oak.

Coffey and Annabelle went to the far end of the barn, where Coffey's products were staged on several tables. "Did Mr. Reed tell you I was hurt?" Coffey asked.

"Yes, he did. He's very worried about you."

"Ain't much," Coffey said. "I'll be as good as new soon."

Annabelle knew with only a glance that Coffey hadn't fallen. "Tell me what happened."

Coffey's gaze met hers as if she realized Annabelle couldn't be fooled. She lowered her eyes to the ground. "I told Mr. Reed I fell."

"I know you did, he told me. But you didn't, did you?"

Coffey shook her head. "No, ma'am. It was Mr. Payne did it."

Annabelle's hand moved to her mouth. "Oh, Coffey, that's horrible!" She squeezed her arm reassuringly. "What did he do, beat you?"

Coffey nodded. "Yes, ma'am. Just 'cause I didn't give him what he wanted, I suspect."

Annabelle grimaced. "You could have been killed."

"But you told me I didn't have to put up with him none. And I decided I wasn't gonna."

Annabelle cringed, slowly shaking her head. "Coffey, it's horrible what he does to you. I can't even imagine what you go through."

"I ain't gonna live in fear no more."

"But you can't fight him on your own. You need help."

Coffey chuckled. "I did just fine, Miss Annabelle. He never got what he wanted, neither. Not even close."

"It doesn't look like you did fine, not with those bruises," Annabelle said, tenderly touching her cheek. "How badly does it hurt?"

"Yesterday was worse, my whole head was pounding. Today's a little better."

"What did Adrian say?"

"Oh, he's such a good man, Miss Annabelle. But he didn't believe me when I said I fell. I had to tell the same lie over and over."

Annabelle shook her head in disgust. "Tell me what happened."

Coffey stared at the ground. "It ain't the kind of thing folks talk about."

Annabelle looked beyond the barn where two wooden chairs were set in the shade. "Come on, let's sit and talk."

Coffey followed her out behind the barn, and they sat down. "Do you want anything to drink, Miss Annabelle? I can fetch some cider or water."

"No, thank you. I want you to tell me what happened. You can trust me."

Coffey knew she spoke the truth. She hesitated, started to speak and stopped, but then began again. "Mr. Payne showed up at the barn. Said Mr. Reed was in that patch of woods out by Hickory Hill and would be gone all day."

"And then he made advances?"

Coffey nodded, her eyes vacant and misty. "He surely did. But I fought back."

"Is that when he hit you?"

"Yes, ma'am. The first time."

"What happened next?"

"He shoved me to the ground. I dropped a pitcher full of face cream on the floor, and it broke into pieces. When Mr. Payne climbed on top of me and started fumbling with his pants, I grabbed a jagged piece of glass and sliced his back and arms."

Annabelle's eyes widened. "You cut him?"

"Yes, ma'am, I did. I cut him real good. He'll have scars, I'm sure.

"My Lord, you are brave," Annabelle declared. "You have a lot of courage packed in that tiny package."

Coffey chuckled. "You should've heard him howling the first time I stuck him."

"Is that when he started beating you?"

"Yes, ma'am. He was plenty mad. But I cut him some more, and then ran away."

Annabelle's face firmed. "He'll be back."

Coffey smiled. "I don't think so, ma'am. I may be beat up some, but you ain't seen him."

"It doesn't matter," Annabelle muttered. "He'll never give up."

"I ain't so sure, Miss Annabelle. He surely didn't expect what he got. And I'll beat him off again, just as sure as the sun shines."

Annabelle frowned. She suspected Zeb would seek revenge. And it might be worse the next time. "I need to tell my father."

"No, you can't, Miss Annabelle," Coffey pleaded, reaching out to touch her arm. "I don't want nobody to know."

Annabelle slowly shook her head. She didn't know what to do. But she wanted Coffey prepared. "Do you have any way of protecting yourself if he comes back and gets violent?"

Coffey shrugged. "Yes, ma'am, I do. I got a thick hunk of wood by my working table. I can beat him off with that."

Annabelle wasn't convinced. "It's time we did something with Mr. Payne. It's never going to end unless we do."

Chapter Fifty-Seven

"**H**ow much money does he want?" Phoebe asked as she unbuttoned the back of Naomi's dress, getting her ready for bed.

"He wouldn't tell me," Naomi said. "He wants to prolong this, make it as painful as possible. He thinks I'm helpless."

Phoebe helped Naomi slip her arms out of the dress. "He ain't too smart if he thinking that."

"He's definitely in control, at least for now."

"How do you know you can trust him?"

"I can't," Naomi said. "But I want him gone before Artemis Wentworth has time to learn anything about him."

Phoebe shrugged. "He may not find much. We don't even know if Zeb Payne is his real name."

"I thought about that," Naomi said. "But there's no way for us find out."

"Are you sure he the young boy on the boat the night we left?"

Naomi stepped out of her dress. "He claims he was."

"I guess he gotta be," Phoebe said as she helped Naomi remove her undergarments. "Else he wouldn't know so much."

"What if he's just a fraud?" Naomi asked. "Maybe he heard the story from someone else, and he's trying to make money from it."

"I don't know, Miz Naomi. Lordy, what a mess."

Naomi thought about Zeb Payne taking liberties with Coffey. "Whoever he is, real or fake, he's an evil man."

"I seen him at the wedding, hiding in the trees, too highfalutin to come near us black folk. I don't like him one bit."

Naomi slipped into her nightgown. If Phoebe knew about Coffey, Zeb Payne would already be dead. And maybe he should be. But Naomi wasn't ready to risk all she had in life by killing him. At least not yet.

"What are you gonna do?" Phoebe asked.

"I'll bring him some money tomorrow night."

"I wouldn't give him much. He only gonna want more."

Naomi nodded, waiting as Phoebe turned down the bedsheet. "I think you're right. I'll give him a few gold coins. Enough to attract his attention but not much more."

"If we lucky, he'll take it and run."

"I doubt that he will," Naomi said as she climbed into bed. She lay on her back, her head on the pillow. "Stay a while longer."

Phoebe sat on a straight-backed chair by the window. "If this man is as nasty as you say, maybe you better not go yourself."

Naomi was quiet for a moment. "He won't get violent. He can't afford to. I'll expose him if he does."

"But then he exposes you," Phoebe said. "You'd best be real careful."

Naomi sighed. "I was surprised he knew so much. But it seems the inspector told his father everything."

"That inspector didn't seem too smart to me. Neither did the doctor."

"I told you Zeb Payne knew Rufus was poisoned. But he thinks it was the whiskey."

"Then let him go on thinking that."

"He also knew about the safe. And how much money was in it."

Phoebe eyed her warily. "Are you sure he's gonna

take the money and go?"

Naomi frowned. "I don't know. Evil people have a way of staying evil, if you know what I mean."

It was quiet, each lost in her own thoughts. "You don't have to give him any money at all," Phoebe then said softly.

"I do if I want to get rid of him."

"Give him some money tomorrow," Phoebe suggested. "If he don't take it and clear out, I got a better idea."

Naomi's gaze met hers. "What's that?"

"We take care of him the same way we took care of Rufus Jackson."

Chapter Fifty-Nine

It took a few days before the swelling eased on Coffey's face, but the purple bruises remained dark and ugly. She was going back to Hickory Hill on Saturday, and, although she planned to tell everyone she fell, she doubted they would believe her. The gossip wouldn't last long, though. They all had their own battles to fight, struggles to overcome, scars from wounds that never healed. They weren't too interested in hers.

What she dreaded most was bringing Zeb Payne's dinner on Saturday night. She trembled just thinking about it. But it might not be as bad as she suspected. He never had come back to Adrian's barn. A part of her doubted he ever would. He'd probably gone his whole life without anyone stopping him from getting what he wanted. But she had stood up to him. She had beat him. It felt good, a small victory, but a victory just the same. She smiled at the thought of him tending his wounds. He might not be so anxious to grab her next time. But she was ready anyway. She had found a knife in the back of the barn—not the cleaver she used to prep ingredients for her tonic. It had been dropped by someone and long forgotten. Slender enough to carry, it was rusty and dull but cleaned up nice. And if Zeb Payne ever came near her again, she would stick it in his gut.

Adrian Reed came home later that afternoon, his clothes dirty from the forest, his face flush from the sun. "Hello, Coffey," he called as he walked through the barn. "How's everything going?"

"It's going real good, Mr. Reed," she said. "I'm gettin' faster makin' everything. Got me a nice way of doin' things."

"That's great," he said. "The more you make, the more we sell, and the quicker we'll make money."

She cocked her head. "If you ain't making money, how come you paying me?"

He grinned, his gaze fixed on hers. He pointed to two chairs out back underneath the shade cast by a large oak where she had talked to Annabelle. "Let's sit a while," he said. "And I'll explain it to you."

She looked at him, eyes wide. "You want to sit with me?"

"Sure," he said, smiling. "We'll chat."

"All right, if you say so," Coffey said. "You want me to get us some cider?"

"Sure, that'll be nice."

She went in the house and filled two mugs. When she came back, he was sitting under the tree, looking out on the bay. A cutter sliced the water, destined for parts unknown, its sails billowing in the breeze. It made for a pretty picture, cottony clouds floating above the boat, deep blue water stretching around it. She handed Adrian a mug and sat down.

"Let's talk about our business," he said.

"I didn't know we wasn't makin' no money. Seems silly to keep doing it."

"It's not uncommon for a new business to lose money at first," he explained. "It takes a while for a product to become popular."

"Then why do it?"

"Because each week we lose less money. It another week or two, we'll break even. Then we'll start making money."

"But if we ain't makin' money, why do you pay me?"

Adrian chuckled. "Because we're partners. I want you to know how much I appreciate you."

She was confused. "But you already renting me."

"Yes, I am. But that's different. That's between Gideon Banks and me. The money I pay you is between you and me."

Coffey shrugged. "If you say so, Mr. Reed. I do whatever you tell me."

He paused as if wondering how to word what he was going to say. "I was told that Mr. Banks might want you back at Hickory Hill. He intends to send Billy in your place."

She smiled. "Billy long gone. They ain't gonna catch him."

"Everyone seems to think that Amos Quigg will find him. When he does, that's when you may have to go back, and Billy may come here."

"I don't want to go back. Besides, Billy don't know how to make creams and stuff anyhow."

"He wouldn't make cream," he said. "That's a business you and I started. He would work with the loggers."

"Then you don't have anyone to make stuff."

"Exactly," he said. "And that's what I plan to tell Mr. Banks if he makes this offer. I'm going to do everything I can to keep you."

"I would like that," she said. "You good to me, Mr. Reed. And I know it."

"You have a huge heart, Coffey. You deserve the best. It just may take a while to get it." He paused, sipped his cider, and gave her a pained expression, as if he had something difficult to discuss.

She knew something was on his mind, but she didn't know what it was. "You got something bad to say?" she asked, prompting him.

His gaze met hers. "Did anyone come to the barn

the day you fell?"

Coffey looked away. "No, sir."

He hesitated, watching her closely. "I think someone did, and I think it was Zeb Payne."

Coffey's eyes widened, but she recovered. "Nobody came."

Adrian sipped his cider. "I'm very fond of you, Coffey. You know that, don't you?"

"I suspect you are, sir. It shows by how good you treat me. When you look at me sometimes, too."

He kept his gaze fixed on hers. "If I find out that Zeb Payne beat you, I'll kill him. I swear."

Chapter Sixty

Billy Giles sat in the dirt, tethered to a horse stall in Jacob Yoder's barn. Any dreams of chasing rainbows would soon be replaced by a jail cell. Death by hanging would likely follow. His feet were bound, his hands spaced so he could eat when his food came. A separate rope was looped around his neck, the opposite end slung over a corner post.

He couldn't believe he had killed a man—someone's husband, father, uncle, son—and he prayed for the soul of the life he had taken. He had never wanted to hurt anyone. He was a simple man trying to see all that the world might offer, to live happy and free with his loved ones. But now his mamma, daughter and Coffey Green would never know what had happened, hearing only the worst from Amos Quigg or Zeb Payne.

Jacob Yoder came back to the barn, a slicker draped over his white shirt and black suspenders. He carried a basket filled with food, a checkered cloth draped over it. The wind whipped the fields, kicking leaves and ringing the dinner bell hanging on the porch in an uneven cadence. The lashing rain formed puddles that flowed through wrinkles in the ground like miniature streams.

"It sure smells good," Amos Quigg said as Jacob set the basket down.

Billy fixed his gaze on Jacob Yoder while taking his plate. He then cast a furtive glance at the secret door, arching his eyebrows. When Jacob offered a subtle nod, he knew someone was hidden inside.

"Much obliged to your missus," Sheriff Dodd said. "I don't like you people, never did. It's no secret I wanted this land for my boys. But I do admit she's a good cook."

Billy waited for Jacob's reply, but it never came. He wondered how long the sheriff had badgered him. Probably since the day he had arrived.

"Best food I ever ate." Amos Quigg said, his mouth full while he talked. Little chunks of half-chewed food dropped on his shirt. "And I don't mind saying so."

"My wife will be pleased to hear that," Jacob said. He sat on a bench across from them, eyeing the rope wrapped around Billy.

Amos Quigg noticed. "Don't feel sorry for him none, friend. He's already killed one man. Dangerous as heck, too. If I didn't have him tied up, he'd fight to get away and then run down the road to nowhere."

Jacob nodded but didn't reply.

"Why do you care, Yoder?" Dodd asked. "Unless you know him."

Jacob shook his head. "No, I don't."

"I'm not so sure," Dodd said, glancing between them. "You look like you do, eyeing each other like cousins or something." He chuckled. "Maybe you're brothers."

Amos Quigg laughed, briefly choking on dinner.

"I have compassion for a hog-tied man," Jacob said with disdain. "Anyone would."

Dodd frowned. "He's a killer, Yoder. Or don't you understand that?"

"I ain't killed no one," Billy said, speaking for the first time. "The man in the church grabbed me, so I pushed him. He fell, couldn't be helped."

Dodd shook his head. "You don't get it, do you? It doesn't matter if he fell. Or how he fell. He's still dead. Now you're gonna fall, too—from a hangman's noose."

"Will you be leaving in the morning?" Jacob asked bluntly, his face firm.

Dodd glanced at Billy. "We've got to. I need to get him in jail before he kills someone else."

"Best place for him," Quigg agreed. "I got to get over to Hickory Hill. Given the goings-on, I can still collect my reward. Zeb Payne will have to pay a little more, though. Make it right for the dead man's family and pay the sheriff for all his trouble. I'd leave at dawn, except…"

"Except what?" Jacob asked, irritated.

"Breakfast would be real nice," Quigg said, grinning. "Some of that scrapple your missus makes."

"We're up at dawn," Jacob said. "I'll bring out breakfast. But then you leave."

"We sleeping in the stable?" Billy asked.

Dodd glared at him. "You'll be sleeping where I tell you to."

"Can we move away from the horses?" Billy asked. "Get away from the stink."

Dodd started laughing. "What would you care? You don't smell any better."

Quigg scanned the back of the barn and turned to Jacob. "You need to think like a caged animal to understand him. Something back there caught his eye. And now his tiny brain is thinking about running again."

"Before he hangs," Dodd added.

Jacob looked toward the back of the barn. "There isn't much there except for tools and hay."

"Tools," Quigg repeated. "Probably saw something to cut the rope."

"I'm just saying it might be better sleeping," Billy protested.

"We'll sleep right here," Quigg said. He laughed. "I sleep with one eye open. Just so you don't try anything."

Billy wanted to warn whoever hid behind the secret door. "We're staying here the whole night?" he asked loudly, almost shouting.

Dodd elbowed him. "Will you shut up? What in the heck are you yelling about?"

Billy glanced at Jacob. He wanted to send a signal,

to let him know he would do what he could to protect him and his family.

"That was mighty fine eatin', friend," Quigg said as he handed his plate to Jacob. He drained the rest of his cider and gave him his mug.

"I'm finished, too," Dodd said, handing over his plate. "Give the missus my compliments."

"I'll do that," Jacob said as he laid the empty plates in the basket. "Is there anything else you need?"

Quigg eyed Billy and shook his head. "No, sir. But thank you. We had best get some rest."

Jacob took Billy's plate and mug and put them in the basket. "I'll bring breakfast out at dawn," he said. He left the barn, the rain no longer falling as hard.

Billy waited until he was a few feet away. "Thanks for supper," he hollered. "I'm sure breakfast will be just as tasty."

Quigg smacked him alongside the head. "Will you stop shouting. You'll wake the dead. Lie down on the floor like a good dog. I want to fix that rope a little tighter."

Billy did as directed while Quigg tethered his feet, arms, and neck to the corner post. He could barely move. It would be difficult to sleep.

"I'll be sitting right over here," Quigg said. "With a loaded shotgun, should you get anxious."

"And I'll be right beside him," Dodd added.

It took a while, but Billy fell asleep.

When he woke, weak rays from a rising sun painted amber hues across a pale blue sky. The rain had stopped, the clouds had gone.

He heard a child sobbing behind the secret door.

Chapter Sixty-One

Slumber was elusive, and Jacob Yoder woke several times during the night. What if Quigg and Dodd found Haney and Chloe? Billy would try to protect them, but he couldn't do much. Especially if they made noise. He worried most about Chloe, a naive child who might not know any better.

It was almost light when he and Ruth climbed out of bed. A golden line sliced the horizon, promising dawn. The rain had stopped, the storm passing, the moisture it left behind bathing fields and swelling streams.

With the children still asleep, Ruth started breakfast—eggs, scrapple, wheat bread, and sweet apple cider. Jacob went out to the henhouse to feed the chickens, warily watching the barn. He noted no activity; his guests must still be sleeping. When he went back in the house, he helped Ruth finish cooking and loaded the basket. He was carrying it out to the barn when the sun showed its full face, rising above distant trees.

Just as Jacob reached the door, he heard Billy shriek, a sharp, panicked cry. Jacob ran into the barn as Amos Quigg bolted upright, his rifle pointed at Billy. Sheriff Dodd rubbed sleepy eyes.

"A spider," Billy said, feigning fear. "Biggest one I ever saw."

Quigg shook his head and put down the rifle. "You dumb son-of-a-bitch. A spider? You're scared of a spider?"

"It woke me up," Billy mumbled. "Ran right across my face." He looked at Jacob. "That smells real good, Mr. Yoder."

"It surely does," Sheriff Dodd said, sticking his

hand out for a plate. "I'm gonna miss you folks once you're gone."

Jacob ignored him, suspecting Dodd liked to taunt him and nothing more. He handed a plate to Amos Quigg.

"Hmm, looks mighty tasty," Quigg said, licking his lips. "Thank your missus for me."

"I will," Jacob said. He got Billy's plate. "Will you untie him?"

Quigg paused, enjoying a mouthful of scrapple. "He can scoot up to eat. Go ahead boy, sit up."

Billy rolled to his side and slid to his rump, his back against the pole. The tethers holding him bunched and knotted. He set the plate on his knees.

"I'll put your cider beside you," Jacob said.

Billy nodded. "Thank you, sir."

Jacob knew there was no spider. The scream had been a warning to Haney and Chloe, a message that someone bad was still just beyond the door. They had to hold on, be still. Help would come soon. It worked. It was quiet, the only sounds coming from Amos Quigg and Sheriff Dodd noisily eating their breakfast.

"This is mighty good, friend," Quigg said, glancing up at Jacob. "I could make a habit of coming round for breakfast."

Jacob nodded but didn't reply. To most people, he would have extended an invitation. But most were good. Amos Quigg was not. "When do you expect to be moving on?"

"Soon as we're done," Dodd said. "Got to get him jailed. Too dangerous."

"Are you sure you got the right man?" Jacob asked, eyeing Dodd sternly. He doubted Billy would harm anyone, let alone kill them.

Dodd was taken aback. "Why would you care?" he asked, eyes narrowed.

"He seems a gentle man," Jacob said, nodding to

Billy.

"He killed a white man, friend," Quigg interjected. "Ain't no doubt about it."

"Was he provoked, or defending himself?" Jacob asked. "Or don't you care?"

"We'll sort it all out before we hang him," Dodd said, glancing at Quigg and grinning.

Quigg wiped his mouth with his sleeve. "And I got to get my money, too. Hung or not."

"If Zeb Payne pays you," Dodd said.

"He's got to, near as I can tell," Quigg said. "Paper says to catch the runaway and return him, which I am."

"Along with a few extra expenses, like the law and the dead man's family," Dodd added.

"I can't help it if he killed somebody," Quigg said.

"It was an accident," Billy insisted. "He fell."

Dodd glared at him. "Will you shut up? No one's talking to you."

Jacob shook his head, compassion etched on his face. "What happens next? Is there a trial?"

Dodd laughed. "No need for a trial. We know he's a killer."

"Zeb Payne has a say in this," Quigg countered. He pointed at Billy. "He is Banks' property."

Dodd frowned. "Doesn't mean he can't be hung."

"Who's Zeb Payne?" Jacob asked.

"The overseer at Hickory Hill," Quigg replied. "Got a lot of power, that one. Real loyal to the family, too."

Jacob knew little about the plantation, other than it stretched for miles. "How many acres is Hickory Hill? And how many slaves?"

"It's a big spread," Quigg said, looking at Billy. "Do you know how many slaves, boy? Seventy, eighty?"

Billy nodded. "A few more if you count the young'uns."

"They got four thousand acres or so," Quigg said.

"Been buying up land the last twenty-five years."

"Do they all work the fields?" Jacob asked, unable to fathom an army of imprisoned people forced to work for one man. "It's just me, here, although Ruth and the children help."

"Most of the slaves work the fields," Quigg replied. "But they have hifalutin' ones, too. House slaves. They're smarter than the rest."

"I suppose they take care of the family," Jacob said.

Quigg nodded. "Cooking and cleaning, minding the children if they have any. Take care of vegetable gardens, too." He looked at Billy and chuckled. "I'll tell you the damnedest story you'd ever want to hear."

Jacob couldn't imagine what it was. He shrugged, offering no objection.

"Two of the house slaves at Hickory Hill, Caesar and Phoebe, were old enough to be freed. Most plantations around here offer freedom when a slave turns forty-five. But they had nowhere to go, so they stayed, kept right on serving their masters. They knew how good they had it. But not Billy. He's too damn dumb. Had to run off and kill somebody."

Billy finished his breakfast. He seemed as eager to leave as Amos Quigg. But Jacob knew why—he was protecting the hidden runaways.

"Come on, boy," Dodd said. He handed his mug and plate to Jacob, grabbed Billy's and did the same. "It's time we got going."

Quigg rearranged the ropes that bound Billy. "Get moving."

Billy stumbled out of the barn. "Thanks for your kindness, Mr. Yoder."

"You're welcome any time," Jacob replied, knowing Billy would understand what he meant. He looked at Dodd. "Where are you taking him?"

Dodd motioned to Billy. "The jail in Chestertown."

"Then I have to talk to Zeb Payne," Quigg said. "Maybe Gideon Banks can buy his way out of a hanging."

"Billy might be saved?" Jacob asked. He wanted desperately to help him. But he didn't know what to do.

"It's possible," Dodd said. "Mr. Banks can pay off the dead man's family—assuming they convince townsfolk it was an accident. Otherwise, Billy hangs in a day or two."

Quigg saddled up their horses. "We're much obliged, friend. Tell your missus her meals are right good."

"I will," Jacob said, walking with them from the barn.

Dodd stopped. "One last thing, Yoder."

"Yes, what is it?"

Dodd nodded toward Billy. "He seemed real comfortable here last night. Like he's been here before."

Jacob shrugged. "I don't know what you're talking about."

Dodd stepped closer, inches away. "After I hang him, I'm coming back for you."

Chapter Sixty-One

Adrian sat in his office at Reed and Sons, scanning his accounting ledger. His efforts with Coffey were soon to bear fruit. As he studied the numbers, and as he had told Coffey, the trend was positive. Each week showed measurable improvement. In the upcoming week, he expected to break even or turn a small profit. From that point forward, the business would grow with accelerating earnings. And he intended to expand—Annapolis, Washington, Philadelphia. He might even add more products.

He was interrupted by a tap on his opened door. His father stood in the entrance. "Adrian, we'd like to speak to you in the conference room for a moment."

Adrian took one last glance at the numbers. "Sure. I'll be right there."

He closed his ledger and left his office. He didn't want to keep them waiting. When he entered the conference room, his father Thaddeus sat at the head of the table, flanked by his brothers. Adrian sat at the opposite end. He eyed the long, empty expanse between them—a symbol of their fractured family.

"We have a few items to discuss," Thaddeus said, glancing at his brothers. "First I'd like to talk about the slave you rented."

"Coffey Green."

"Yes, whatever her name is," Thaddeus muttered. "I talked to Gideon Banks yesterday. He wants her returned, but he's offering another slave—the runaway that's expected to be apprehended shortly."

Adrian suspected the proposal came from Zeb Payne. Why would he want Coffey back, and why would he offer a much better field hand in her place? It made no sense. Zeb must have a motive. Adrian was determined to find out what it was.

His father coughed and shook his head. "Are you listening to me?"

Adrian frowned. "I'm sorry, sir. I've got a lot on my mind."

"You seem to be in another world lately," Thaddeus said. "I'm worried about you."

"We've noticed it, too," Jeremiah added. "You seem to have lost interest in the business."

Adrian wasn't sure what to say. If he was honest with his family and himself, he would admit they were right. "I was thinking about Coffey. I don't want to lose her."

"Then you have two issues you're not likely to solve," James said. "First, you don't own her, Gideon Banks does. And second, she's not worth the cost."

Jeremiah nodded in agreement. "She's barely five feet tall. She can't be cutting trees."

Thaddeus studied his youngest son, face firm. "Why do you insist on keeping her? I hope you didn't start that foolish business you were talking about."

Adrian hid a smile. "I did," he said. "And since I pay for Coffey personally, it doesn't matter what I have her doing."

Jeremiah grinned. "You're making women's products?"

"I am," Adrian said proudly. "Coffey converts our waste—roots and bark—into desirable merchandise. We've been selling it in Baltimore."

His father arched his eyebrows. "Are you serious?"

Adrian nodded. "Absolutely. We haven't turned a profit yet, but the trend shows we will this week. The products are gaining popularity, and I intend to expand distribution."

James glanced at his brother. "Didn't you mention perfume?"

"No, it's a tonic for abrasions and a face cream for ladies."

They exchanged glances, chuckling and shaking their heads. "But we build ships," James stressed. "And you're making beauty cream. It'll destroy our reputation."

Adrian shrugged. "Good business is good business. Is it not?"

"We want no part of it," Thaddeus said. "You can do whatever you want with your own time and money, but don't link this nonsense to Reed and Sons."

"I won't," Adrian promised. "I've yet to choose a name for the company. But I certainly shan't soil your reputation."

Thaddeus studied his youngest, pensive. "If you're using scraps from our process, shouldn't you pay us?"

"Should I charge you a fee for hauling it away?" Adrian countered. "It does save you from burning it."

Thaddeus frowned. "We'll let it go for now."

"What about the runaway?" James asked. "Will he be making cream after you return the woman? The logging crews could use a good man."

Adrian had no intention of giving up Coffey. He just wasn't sure how to keep her. "I'll discuss it with Gideon when I visit Annabelle."

"That's another thing," Thaddeus said, sitting upright. "Where is this courtship going?"

Jeremiah chuckled. "Nowhere, I suspect. Not with Artemis Wentworth as his competition."

"Annabelle and I have a special relationship," Adrian said, ignoring him. "And we always have. It's only strengthened over time." Sometimes the family made him feel like an outcast, but he wasn't sure why. Maybe he intimidated them. He dreamed big, challenged the status quo, was willing to take risks. They weren't. He threatened them.

James frowned, glancing at his father and brothers. "Apparently it's not as special as her relationship with Wentworth—not according to reports we've received."

"Adrian, you're our brother, and we love you," Jeremiah said. "But Artemis Wentworth just argued a case before the Supreme Court. He's likely our next senator."

"Some openly support a Wentworth presidency," James added.

"He does have a promising future," Thaddeus stressed.

Adrian shrugged. "So do I."

"Consider this," his father said, rubbing his chin thoughtfully. "I was talking to Lucas Crane in Chestertown the other day. His daughter Amelia is ready to marry."

Adrian was quiet for a moment. "What does that have to do with me?"

"She's attractive," James offered. "Black hair, blue eyes."

"Intelligent, too," Jeremiah added. "She would make a good wife."

"Yes, she would," Adrian agreed. "If I were looking. But I'm not. I've already found my wife."

"That's the point," Thaddeus said delicately, as if to spare his son's feelings. "You should be looking. You haven't found a potential wife, you've lost one."

Adrian sighed. "I haven't been declined any more than Artemis Wentworth has been accepted."

"Rumors suggest Naomi Banks will announce the engagement shortly," James said, almost apologetically.

"She intends to marry Wentworth," Jeremiah said. "It's better you hear it from us first."

Adrian was quiet. Annabelle had promised she wouldn't marry Artemis Wentworth. She wouldn't deceive him. But his family seemed sincere, certain they were right, and concerned for his future. Now he was worried.

"Amelia Crane is a good woman," his father continued. "Give her a chance. Her father's plantation isn't as large as Hickory Hill, but it's still a considerable enterprise."

"Probably two or three thousand acres," James added. "Maybe more."

"I admit that Amelia Crane is a wonderful woman," Adrian said. "But I still plan to marry Annabelle Banks."

"That's the problem, son," his father said with a rare display of affection. "Annabelle doesn't plan to marry you."

Chapter Sixty-Two

"She still claims she fell," Adrian said to Annabelle, referring to Coffey. They sat on the front porch at Hickory Hill during his scheduled visit. "But I have my suspicions."

"She told me she fell, too," Annabelle said with some hesitation. "I went to visit her."

"Her bruises are mending," he said, moving closer. "The tonic works wonders."

Behind them, someone raised the sitting room window higher, the curtains fluttering in the breeze. Naomi was always nearby to keep romance from blooming.

Adrian shook his head slightly and smiled, nodding toward the window. "Can I not sit this close?"

Annabelle took his hand and squeezed it. "You can sit as close as you like."

His family was convinced Annabelle would marry Artemis Wentworth, so concerned they'd shown a tenderness rarely expressed. He broached the topic. "Is it still a contest?"

She looked at him, head cocked. "Is what still a contest?"

"I can't compete with Artemis Wentworth," Adrian said softly, his gaze meeting hers.

"Artemis is a nice man with a bright future."

He hesitated. She hadn't answered his question. Was she toying with him or deliberately being evasive? "My father suggests I search for a bride elsewhere. And my brothers agreed."

"I don't know why you would." She paused a moment more, smiled and leaned closer, kissing him on the lips.

The window in the sitting room slammed shut and then reopened. Adrian cringed. "She didn't like that."

"Too bad," Annabelle said. She kissed him again, her lips lingering.

Adrian reluctantly pulled away. "If your parents are sure you'll choose Artemis, why is your mother standing guard?" he whispered.

She chuckled. "My parents like Artemis because of what he might become—not because of what *I* can become."

He smiled. "I often thought you were smarter than our tutor while we were growing up."

She playfully smacked his arm. "Not true. But I wish it were."

"I do understand your parents," he said. "For their generation, tradition and social standing are most important."

"But I have a bright future, too. And meaning no offense to you, it's not tied to a man."

Adrian admired her independence, one of her most desirable traits. "You can be whatever you choose, married to me or not."

"I wish my parents understood that."

"They can't," Adrian said, surprised he defended them. "They value status and security."

"I don't care about either," she said, but hesitated. "Although having money is nice."

"They'll realize, if they haven't already, that you'll do whatever you want to do. You're different than your sister, Emma."

Annabelle was quiet, perhaps thinking of a sister she loved and missed.

"Have you made a decision yet?" Adrian asked, not sure he wanted to know the answer.

She touched his chin, turned his face to hers, and

kissed him, long and lovingly. "What do you think?" she then asked.

Nothing was better than her kiss. But he couldn't stop thinking about his family's warning. "Are you kissing Artemis, too?"

She laughed, amused by his jealousy. "No, I'm not. And I'm not doing anything else, either."

He smiled. "Good. That makes me happy."

"You should be happy. Because I plan to make you even happier."

"Shall we go sit by the bay?" he asked. "We'll have more privacy."

"No, you will remain on the porch," Naomi called sternly from the sitting room.

"Mother, will you leave us alone?" Annabelle groaned.

"I was adjusting the drapes and happened to overhear," Naomi said.

Adrian cringed and leaned close. "She's been listening the whole time."

Annabelle shrugged. "Who cares?"

"This is ridiculous," he whispered. "If you've already chosen me, why continue this charade?"

"Because my parents insist."

He was quiet for a moment, pensive. He was starting to feel desperate—the longer the courtship lingered, the less chance he had of winning her hand. "Should I ask your father again?"

She shrugged. "You can, but I'm not sure what he'll say."

Adrian stood. "Take me to him."

Annabelle led him inside. Gideon Banks was in his study, sitting in front of the fireplace, a newspaper spread before him.

"Father, Adrian would like to speak to you," Annabelle said.

Gideon folded the paper and put it beside him. "Leave us for a minute, Annabelle."

"I'll wait on the front porch," she said to Adrian.

After she had gone, Gideon motioned to a chair. "Please, sit."

Adrian sat across from him and took a deep breath, gathering his courage. "Sir, I would like to ask for Annabelle's hand in marriage."

Gideon nodded, face firm. "Your intentions are known and have been for some time."

"I promise to make her happy," Adrian said. "She'll have a good life."

"Yes, I'm sure she will," Gideon said, his eyes showing sympathy. "It's just too soon for a decision."

"But we've courted for months. And we've been together since childhood."

"But another suitor is involved—Mr. Wentworth. He deserves the same opportunity you have—access to Annabelle so she can make the right decision."

Adrian sighed. "Your answer, then, would be no."

Gideon leaned forward. "It's just too soon, Adrian, that's all. It's not personal. I told Annabelle to see you and Artemis once each week for three months. And then a decision can be made. A month has barely passed, let alone three."

"I understand, sir," Adrian said, his heart heavy. "Thank you for your time."

He rose and left the room, finding Naomi in the hallway, eavesdropping. She cast a condescending glance as he passed.

Chapter Sixty-Three

Annabelle sat beside Artemis Wentworth, her parents across from them in cushioned chairs. The parlor windows were open, capturing a gentle breeze that bathed the room. They were continuing discussions from dinner, largely focused on politics and Hickory Hill. Artemis dined with them weekly, yet Adrian was rarely invited. But Naomi controlled the courting schedule, and Annabelle clearly understood her motive.

"How is everything on the plantation?' Artemis asked.

Annabelle glanced at the others. When no one spoke, she did. "I'm almost ready for the equestrian event in Annapolis. I'm competing in dressage and show jumping."

Gideon smiled. "I'm very proud of you. Snowflake is a beautiful horse with wonderful conformation. She'll show well."

"Luke thinks she'll win every event," Annabelle said. She turned to Artemis. "He's one of our field hands who knows quite a bit about horses."

"He raced when he was younger," Gideon added. "Before he came to Hickory Hill to assist the overseer. He has a long history in equestrian events."

"He thinks Snowflake was born to show," Annabelle continued. "A filly like that comes along once in a generation."

Artemis didn't seem interested in Snowflake or the competition. As soon as there was a pause in the conversation, he changed the subject. "Is your tobacco yield as good as last year?"

"Better," Gideon replied. "This should be our best season yet."

Artemis cocked his head. "How did you do it? Different techniques?"

"No, I think we owe it all to Zeb Payne," Gideon said. "He's extremely efficient—using some techniques he had learned at prior plantations."

Annabelle hid her anger, knowing what Zeb had done to Coffey. She wanted to tell them, to let everyone know what an evil man he really was, but she had made a promise, and she wouldn't break it. "Did you find anything interesting about Mr. Payne?"

Artemis frowned. "I did promise background information. But I've yet to receive replies to my inquiries."

"We're in no rush," Naomi said hastily.

"Although we are interested in what you learn," Gideon said. "If nothing unseemly is uncovered, a frank discussion with Zeb should solve the problem."

"Assuming he chooses to stay at Hickory Hill," Naomi said.

Annabelle looked at her oddly, wondering what she meant. "Why would he leave? He seems quite content. And father thinks highly of him." Her face grew firm. "Even though I don't."

Artemis looked at her, eyes wide, her venom surprising him. "Would he leave of his own accord, due to better opportunities? Or are you assuming our investigation will demand his departure?"

"No, we're pleased with his performance," Gideon said. "And as far as I know, Zeb isn't looking for employment elsewhere."

"Good overseers are in demand, however," Naomi countered. "I've heard whispers at a women's club I belong to. And who knows what opportunities he might have been offered?"

Gideon frowned. "None, that we know of."

"His prior employer thought the same," Naomi argued. "Until he left abruptly to come to Hickory Hill."

"It would solve our problem if he left, wouldn't it?" Annabelle asked, hoping it were true.

A tense silence settled over the room, but Naomi hastened to end it. "We have resolved another issue. We've been told that Amos Quigg captured our runaway."

Gideon frowned. "Although there were complications—additional costs."

Artemis shrugged. "Sometimes apprehension results in property damage. Is that what happened?"

Gideon glanced at Naomi. "We don't know any specifics. Zeb Payne is going to Chestertown to find out what happened."

"What are your intentions, once the runaway returns?" Artemis asked.

"I want him sold," Naomi said. "If he ran once, he'll run again. We don't need the aggravation."

"But he is a good worker," Gideon offered.

"And his mother and daughter do our sewing," Annabelle muttered. "They'll be heartbroken."

"They're heartbroken now," Naomi said sharply. "And have been ever since he deserted them."

Artemis shifted in his seat, immersed in a family squabble he'd like to avoid.

Naomi noticed his reaction. "Do you have plans for the election?" she asked, changing the subject when she realized he was uncomfortable.

"Yes, I do. Some campaigning this fall."

"I'm sure you'll find an interested populace," Gideon said. "The nation seems so divided."

"It does," Artemis agreed. "We're offering an interesting platform based on expansion of the nation, statehood for territories, business opportunities. We have a train tour planned with other candidates. We'll each present our positions and answer questions from the audience."

Annabelle sighed, bored. The discussion was no different than their dinner conversation, constantly repeated, slightly altered. It seemed politics was the only topic that interested Artemis.

"Annabelle, aren't politics fascinating?" Naomi asked, trying to keep her engaged.

"It seems perfect for Artemis," Annabelle said. "But I don't think the public is too interested. Not as long as they can feed their families and give more to the next generation than they received. I think that's what concerns people. Simple survival, the struggle to get ahead."

Artemis arched his eyebrows, not expecting a debate. "Politics is a complex universe, one that's difficult for anyone to master."

Annabelle frowned. "Isn't that condescending?"

His eyes widened. "I didn't intend it to be."

"If you underestimate the people," Annabelle said, "then they'll reject you."

Naomi intervened. "You'll perform brilliantly, as you do with everything else."

Annabelle was sickened by her parents' constant compliments. They never spoke highly of Adrian. She glanced at her mother, who noted her reaction.

"Enough political talk," Naomi said sweetly. "You've come to visit Annabelle, not us."

"Nonsense, Mrs. Banks. I enjoy your company," Artemis said, nodding politely.

Naomi smiled. "Why don't you and Annabelle walk along the bay? There's a bench by the water that offers privacy."

Artemis looked at Annabelle. "I would like that very much."

"Go ahead," Naomi prompted. "Annabelle will enjoy it, too."

Annabelle pasted a smile on her face. "We should go now, or we'll miss the sunset."

"Before you leave, Artemis, I do have one question," Gideon said.

"What is it, sir?"

"When does campaigning start?"

Artemis paused, considering dates. "In about eight weeks."

"Oh, my," Naomi said, her hand to her mouth. "How quickly time has passed."

"Early fall is best, so our views are fresh in voters' minds."

Naomi looked at Annabelle, eyes wide. "I suspect we'll have an announcement to make before then, won't we, Annabelle?"

Chapter Sixty-Four

Annabelle slept later than usual the following morning and had breakfast alone in the dining room. As she enjoyed her flapjacks, cider, and coffee, she contrasted Artemis and Adrian. Artemis barely acknowledged her in a group setting and seemed to have little interest in anything she said or did. It was almost like he courted her parents— among the wealthiest landowners on the Eastern Shore. And although Artemis was polite, handsome and charming, he was also calculating, logically assessing any situation. He had no room for emotion.

Adrian was different. He adored her. He had been crestfallen when her father refused his request to marry her, asking that he wait two more months. She understood what her parents were doing, even if Adrian didn't. They were stalling, hoping he tired of the chase, knowing his adversary had superior prospects. And if he did, he might take his family's suggestion and court Amelia Crane or someone from Chestertown or Annapolis. But then they didn't know Adrian like she did.

Most women seeking suitors envied Annabelle. They dreamed of a partner like Artemis Wentworth. But she saw it differently. Although she suspected Artemis would be a good provider, he would likely be a lousy husband, his goals and dreams supreme to all else— including a spouse. She had little doubt that he came first and always would. She wasn't sure she could cope with that. Maybe she was selfish. Or maybe he was.

The door opened, and Phoebe came in. "Do you want more flapjacks, Miss Annabelle?"

"No, thank you. But more honey would be nice. And some cider."

Phoebe poured more honey on what was left of her flapjacks and filled her mug with apple cider. "Have you seen Coffey lately?"

Annabelle cringed, thinking about the beating she'd received. She could only imagine Phoebe's reaction when she found out. "No, not for a week or so," she lied.

"I hope she comes back this weekend," Phoebe said. "I miss her when she's not around."

"We all do," Annabelle said. She suspected Coffey might want to hide her bruises and avoid Zeb Payne. "But I'm not sure she's coming this weekend. Adrian mentioned rushing to complete orders they have for face cream."

"Mr. Reed been real good to her, I hear," Phoebe continued. "I think she likes it fine, working for him."

"He's a good man," Annabelle said softly.

"And he's after a good woman in you, Miss Annabelle," Phoebe said, smiling at the woman she had helped raise.

"Thank you, I appreciate that."

Phoebe looked in the hall, making sure no one was nearby. "You gotta big decision to make. Two handsome men chasing after you."

"It's an easier decision than most think."

"Now, don't be hasty," Phoebe said. "Both are good people."

"But one is better."

"Very different," Phoebe said, not addressing her comment. "Mr. Artemis chats away, could talk to anyone for hours. Mr. Adrian is shy, barely talks at all."

"Which is preferred in many cases."

"Your mamma sure likes Mr. Artemis. Talks about him all the time." She headed for the hallway but turned and smiled. "But I just want what's best for you."

Annabelle finished her breakfast and went to the

stables to ride Snowflake. She was determined to do well in the competition and any that followed. She had one of the field hands saddle her horse, and she climbed on his back sidesaddle and started practicing, directing the filly across the course.

Her thoughts focused on Coffey. She realized she could do something to help her, regardless of what her parents might do. She could confront Zeb Payne, tell him she knew what he was doing, and to stay away from Coffey. Or she would make his life miserable—threatening to tell her parents about the beating. He wouldn't want to anger her father.

She finished riding and returned to the house. She kept busy the rest of the day, doing needlepoint, reading for a while and playing the piano, waiting until evening when she suspected Zeb would be back from the fields. She left the house and started across the lawn. She didn't even know if he was home—or if he was alone.

But she would go anyway.

Chapter Sixty-Five

Naomi knocked on the door of Zeb Payne's cottage, looking back through the foliage to make sure no one could see her. She waited, standing on the porch, collecting her courage. She refused to be intimidated.

A moment later, Zeb answered. "I was wondering if you would come," he said, motioning for her to enter.

The cottage was functional, clean and sparsely furnished. He led her into the parlor with broad windows offering a generous view of the bay, a stone fireplace, sofa, and chairs. Paintings of ships were spaced along the walls, just as they were in Hickory Hill. He motioned to a chair.

She sat down, upright and proper, not leaning back. She wanted to conduct business and leave. If she sat on the edge of her seat, acting as if she were ready to go, it might drive the pace of their discussion.

"I suspect you remember me now," he said as he sat down. "You probably talked to your servant, if it's the same one, about the night you fled Soufriere."

"Actually, I don't remember you at all," Naomi said sternly. "I'm beginning to suspect you're a fraud."

He grinned. "Really? Why would you suspect that? I gave you details that only the inspector or someone close to him would know."

"I have no idea what you're talking about."

He ignored her. "I never did determine motive. Neither did Inspector Burton. You didn't have to kill Rufus Jackson to steal his money. You could have robbed him and fled. He never would have found you."

She eyed Zeb warily. He had a thirst that had to be

quenched, the boy who witnessed a crime and spent his entire life wondering why it had been committed. "You didn't know Rufus Jackson," she said with distaste, knowing what she said would implicate her in his death. But she didn't care.

"No, I didn't know Rufus Jackson. And neither did my father. But most of the folks in Soufriere did."

"Not many offered compliments, I'm sure."

"No, they didn't," he agreed. "He wasn't a man the peasants liked, that's for sure."

Naomi didn't reply. She had no interest in discussing her past. She reached in her skirt pocket and withdrew a few gold coins. She handed them to Zeb.

"What's this?" he asked as he took them.

"I think that's adequate compensation," she said. "Enough to travel and start over. And I expect it to be a long journey."

Zeb started laughing. "Oh, Naomi, you are naïve, aren't you?"

She knew the negotiation wouldn't be easy. She had given him a meager amount because she knew, no matter what she offered, he would want more. But she feigned ignorance. "I don't understand."

"I'm insulted."

"Insulted?" she asked. "It's six month's salary."

"Six month's salary? To keep a secret? To spare you public humiliation and a murder trial? Not to mention all the money you stole."

"I think it's adequate."

"But I don't," he said. "And it's my opinion that matters, not yours."

She stood and prepared to leave, not wanting the altercation to escalate. "I'll consider more. But not much more."

"Yes, much more," he said. He followed her to the door and grabbed her shoulder.

She turned abruptly, casting an icy stare. "Do not touch me."

"Oh, I'll touch you, Naomi. Whenever and wherever I want. That's part of the deal."

"No, it isn't and it never will be," she said as she opened the door.

"When are you coming back?" he asked as he followed her onto the porch, his lewd stare traveling down the length of her body.

She paused, lips pursed, and resisted the urge to punch him. Maybe time would defuse a situation she couldn't control. "I can get away again in a few days. Same time—when you come back from the fields."

"Good," he said, reaching out to caress her blonde hair. "I can't wait to see you again."

Chapter Sixty-Six

Annabelle gasped, her hand to her mouth. She was stunned, witness to a sordid rendezvous she never could have imagined—with a promise of more to come. Her initial anger was doused by tears, their affair destroying all she had ever known.

She hurried to the far side of the cottage, not wanting to be seen, and peeked around the corner. A few seconds later, Naomi appeared, glancing in all directions, making sure she wasn't watched. She then walked briskly toward Hickory Hill.

Annabelle waited a moment more. Stray tears dripped down her cheeks, which she quickly wiped away. When Naomi crossed the clearing and entered the trees beyond, she followed, casting a wary eye on the cottage windows to ensure Zeb Payne wasn't watching. When satisfied she hadn't been seen, she scurried into the trees, close behind her mother as she passed through foliage.

Naomi hurried down the slender trail, glanced in all directions, and darted out to the lawn that stretched behind Hickory Hill. But she didn't go toward the house. She turned toward the bay. Fifty feet farther, she passed behind the flower beds and quickly crossed the lawn. When she reached the kitchen, and smokehouse beside it, she hugged the back walls, hiding in shadows.

It was a winding path. Annabelle found it confusing. She retraced her mother's steps, not getting too close. As she did so, she eyed Hickory Hill—windows, doors, and balconies. Naomi's movements weren't visible from the mansion. She was blocked by outbuildings or positioned at an angle that avoided detection. Her path had been planned, practiced and likely made on many occasions.

Annabelle hurried past the flower beds. A thousand thoughts consumed her, most hurtful, some enlightening. Zeb Payne had told Adrian that he'd known Naomi before she came to Hickory Hill. Had they once been lovers who fate had reunited? Or merely acquaintances? Although their age difference was no longer an issue—Zeb was six or seven years younger—it had likely been a deterrent twenty-five years earlier. Yet they both concealed their pasts, if it did exist, and the present, not caring who they hurt or destroyed.

Annabelle paused behind the kitchen, waiting while her mother entered the house, looking back toward the cottage before she did so. Naomi didn't want to be seen and neither did Annabelle. She stayed a few moments more, heart sinking, thoughts hazy, captured by a nightmare she couldn't conceive.

Her poor father. He had faults, like anyone else, but his love for her mother could never be questioned. His eyes twinkled when she entered a room, he tenderly caressed her whenever she came near him. He couldn't contain his affection—touching her hair, kissing her cheek, wrapping his arm around her. He ensured any wish she had was quickly granted. She wanted for nothing, material or emotional. Annabelle cringed, thinking of his reaction should the betrayal be exposed. His heart would shatter, never to be mended, his life crumbling on its shaky foundation.

Annabelle emerged from behind the kitchen, ensured her mother remained in the house and quickly crossed the lawn. She was nauseous, so shaken by what she had seen. She had never been close to her mother. They were too much alike—independent, opinionated, and headstrong. But she never would have imagined an affair. Regardless of Naomi's role at Hickory Hill—she could be cold and demanding—Annabelle had always believed that she loved her father as much as he loved her—and always had. She was then struck with a thought even more disgusting. Had her mother had other lovers, or just Zeb Payne?

Annabelle wanted to confront her but couldn't. She was too hurt, too angry. It was best to avoid her. She needed time to process what she had overheard, which sounded like a tender goodbye. But as she relived fragments of their conversation, an irrational rage consumed her. She had to destroy Zeb Payne—for all he had done to Coffey and for tearing her family apart.

She plotted the ultimate revenge, fully prepared to execute it.

Chapter Sixty-Seven

Coffey Green returned to Hickory Hill reluctantly. Not only did she have to confront Zeb Payne, but she had to explain her battered face to Molly and Phoebe. She was still bruised but looked much better than she had earlier in the week. The swelling had eased, and the purple blotches were fading, streaks of amber around the edge. Her tonic sped the healing.

When she got off the wagon late Saturday afternoon, Phoebe was resting on the front porch of the shack she sometimes shared with Molly and her two daughters. "What on earth happened to you, child?" she asked, eyes wide.

"I fell," Coffey said as she climbed the porch steps. "Got hurt real bad, but I'm doin' better now."

Phoebe got off her chair and looked closely at her face. A moment later, she stepped back, eyes angry. "You didn't fall. Somebody hit you."

"No, I fell," Coffey said, averting her gaze.

"Don't tell tales, Coffey Green! If Adrian Reed did this to you, I'll—"

"No, not Adrian Reed," Coffey insisted. "He a good man. He pays me and teaches me letters and such."

Phoebe put her hands on her hips. "Tell me who did it," she demanded. "Because I'll bury 'em before the sun sets."

Coffey knew she meant it. "I can't, Phoebe."

"Yes, you can, child. And you will."

"I'm gonna ask Miss Annabelle for help."

"Miss Annabelle?" Phoebe asked. "What she got to do with this mess?"

"Phoebe, stop. I'll take care of myself."

Phoebe tenderly touched her cheek. "It sure don't look like you can take care of yourself. I'll let it go for now. But I'm gonna find out who did this to you. Won't take me long, neither."

"I'll be just fine," Coffey assured her.

Phoebe sighed and opened the door. "You come inside a spell. Molly and the young'uns are down by the bay."

They entered the sparse shack, straw mattresses against the far wall. Phoebe fussed around the fireplace while Coffey sat on a straight-backed chair with a mended leg. "What are you doing?"

"I'm gonna get some tea," she said. "Made the leaves up special. It'll help with those bruises. And I have some salve to rub on 'em, too."

Coffey watched closely, wondering what Phoebe might offer that she didn't already know. "I used the tonic you showed me how to make. It's healing up nice."

"The salve is the same, just made from different stuff. But the tea helps from the inside."

Coffey was interested in both. Maybe she could make more products for Mr. Reed. "What's the salve?"

"Just something I made for Molly's children," Phoebe said. She approached Coffey, holding a hollowed sliver of wood, paste sitting in the recess. "Let me rub some of this on your face. Works real good. It's like the tonic, but better on bruises. The tonic fixes cuts and scrapes."

"Who taught you all this?" Coffey asked as Phoebe dabbed the paste around her eye.

"Another slave showed me a long time ago. Before I came to Hickory Hill."

Coffey was quiet. It was an explanation she had never heard before. Phoebe was wrapped in mysteries— some true, some not. "Can you teach me?"

"Sure. Let me bring this water to boil first." She set

the paste on a narrow table and poured water from a pitcher into a scarred pot Naomi had given her when she no longer wanted it. She set it over the small fire. "Take a while to boil."

"Show me the plants to make the salve," Coffey said. "Maybe I'll have something else for Mr. Reed to sell."

"I will, after our tea."

"Show me now, 'fore it gets dark. We can go while the water heats up."

Phoebe straightened up. "All right, should only take a minute. Come on."

They crossed the clearing where the shanties sat, close to the water and battered by winds that whipped off the bay, and they made their way through the trees that screened the big house from the overseer's cottage and slave shacks. When they reached the house garden, Phoebe pointed to an herb growing in the corner. "This is rosemary," she said. "You need it for the salve."

Coffey knelt, fingering the herb. "Can I dig up a few and take them back with me?"

Phoebe nodded. "Sure, child. Plant them so you got your own."

They crossed the back lawn, past the bench where Annabelle and Adrian hid to steal kisses, and into the trees that shielded the big house from the barn, livestock pens, and carpenter's shack.

"Most of the rest come from these flowers," Phoebe said when they reached the edge. "They marigolds. Like a lot of sun, so they grow here, by the livestock pens."

"I just crunch up a flower and herb and mix them? How do I turn it to paste?"

"I'll show you when we get back," Phoebe said. "There's other stuff, too. But it ain't hard."

They retraced their steps, moving through the underbrush. They had almost crossed the copse when Phoebe motioned for Coffey to stop. "It's Miss Annabelle."

"What she doing?"

"Look like she picking mushrooms," Phoebe said. She turned to Coffey with a start. "But they the wrong ones. They poison. I better stop her. She don't know what she's doing."

Coffey wasn't sure they should intrude. "Maybe we should let her be."

Phoebe didn't listen. "Miss Annabelle," she called.

Annabelle turned, eyes wide. "Phoebe, Coffey, hello. You startled me. I thought I was alone."

"We just come to pick some flowers," Phoebe said. "Gonna mix up some salve for Coffey's bruises."

Annabelle came closer, holding the mushrooms she'd gathered as she studied Coffey's face. "They look much better than they did the other day."

Coffey nodded. "They almost gone. Another few days, maybe."

"Miss Annabelle, you got the wrong mushrooms," Phoebe warned. "They poison."

Annabelle eyed them cautiously. "I know. I thought I might need them."

Chapter Sixty-Eight

Coffey knew exactly why Annabelle wanted poison mushrooms, but she was afraid of what might happen. What if Annabelle poisoned Zeb Payne and he didn't die? He would get revenge, and that was horrible to think about.

"You don't need them, Miss Anabelle," Coffey said. "I can take care of myself now. I done it once already."

Phoebe looked at them, head cocked. "What are you talking about?"

Annabelle sighed, her gaze fixed on Coffey. "We have a bad man amongst us," she said softly. "He has to be stopped."

Phoebe's eyes widened. "The man who did that?" she asked, pointing to Coffey's face.

Coffey nodded meekly. "I don't want no trouble. I'll fix it. And I have hope. My man will come get me one day soon."

Phoebe glanced at Annabelle and then Coffey. "What are you talking about?"

"I'm sorry, Miss Annabelle," Coffey said.

"Sorry about what?" Annabelle asked.

"My man, he gonna rescue me," Coffey explained. "Now I know you been real good to me and all, but he gonna make me free."

Phoebe cocked her head. "Billy Giles?"

Coffey hesitated. "Yes, ma'am."

Annabelle gave Coffey a sympathetic look. "But he ran away."

"I know, Miss Annabelle," Coffey said. "But as

soon as he set up like a free man, he gonna come back and get me. His momma and daughter, too."

"And take you back with him?" Annabelle asked.

Coffey lowered her eyes to the ground. "Yes, ma'am. I so sorry."

"Oh, child, that ain't never gonna happen," Phoebe said, wrapping an arm around Coffey's shoulders.

Annabelle hesitated. "Amos Quigg is chasing Billy down. We got word he already caught him—or he's close."

"Billy is comin' back," Coffey insisted. "He promised."

"Does Billy know about the man who hit you?" Phoebe asked.

Coffey shook her head. "I can't let him know that. Billy would kill him."

Phoebe looked at Coffey, who averted her gaze, and then to Annabelle. "Tell me who it is, Miss Annabelle. Because I'm gonna kill him myself."

"I can't," she said. "I won't betray Coffey's trust."

Phoebe moved close to Coffey. "I done raised you as my own, child," she said firmly. "Now you tell me so I can help you."

Coffey sighed, a stray tear trailing down her cheek. "Zeb Payne," she said. "I even told him Billy Giles was my man, but he didn't care."

Phoebe's face firmed. "I suspected as much," she muttered. "And you don't know the half of it." She turned to Annabelle. "You don't need those mushrooms, Miss Annabelle. I'll fix something a whole lot better."

"I have to take him dinner now," Coffey said. "Part of my Saturday evenin' chores. So ain't no time to fix anything."

"Don't have to be today," Phoebe said, eyes blazing. "But I'll take care of him real soon. I'll make sure it hurt real bad, too."

"You can't bring his dinner alone," Annabelle

warned. "It's not safe. We'll go with you."

"No, that'll make him suspicious," Phoebe said, already plotting. "And we can't have him suspicious. Not with what I'm gonna do to him."

"But I have to take his dinner," Coffey protested, worried about what would happen if she didn't.

"Bring his dinner," Phoebe said. "But set it down on the porch. Then knock on the door and run away."

"We'll hide behind the house and wait for you," Annabelle assured her.

"And if he chases after you, we'll kill him then and there," Phoebe said coldly. "Even if we gotta strangle the bastard to death."

Chapter Sixty-Nine

Amos Quigg and Sheriff Dodd yanked Billy Giles all the way to Chestertown, his hands tethered to Quigg's saddle. As the horse trotted down the dirt track, Billy was forced to follow, maintaining the same speed.

"Watch this," Quigg said, chuckling. He urged his horse to a canter, jerking Billy forward.

Billy started running, struggling to keep his balance. As the horse increased speed, he couldn't keep up and tripped, falling face first on the dirt road. "Stop!" he yelled. "Please, stop!"

Quigg kept his horse at the same pace, dragging Billy behind him. After a hundred feet he stopped and turned in the saddle, laughing.

Billy struggled to his feet. His clothes were caked in dirt and dust, his trousers torn. His hands and knees were scraped and bleeding, his face swelling where it had banged the road.

"You oughtta be glad I'm not sheriff," Quigg said. "You'd be begging to be hung."

They continued at a slower pace. Billy's hands and face stung, dirt smearing cuts and scrapes that crisscrossed his body. As he stumbled behind Quigg's horse, growing tired and gasping for air, he realized he wouldn't be chasing any rainbows. If he survived the march to jail, he wouldn't live much longer.

Chestertown was only a few miles from Jacob Yoder's farm, but it was mid-morning when they arrived. They put Billy on display, dragging him up and down the streets while residents watched from brick homes or shops, pointing at the hapless runaway.

"Got a bad one, Sheriff?" asked a man who was hitching his wagon.

"One of the worst," Dodd replied, looking back at Billy. "But don't worry. He'll get what's coming to him."

"I did nothin' wrong," Billy shouted.

Dodd laughed. "Be quiet, Billy. Or I'll hang you right now."

They made their way to the rear of the courthouse. A brick building over a hundred years old, it was too small to cope with the fast-growing region which served as an immigration hub in the bustling county seat.

Dodd dismounted and tethered his horse to a post. "Bring him inside," he said to Quigg.

The sheriff's office was cramped, two desks squeezed into the open floor space, three narrow jail cells against the outside wall. As Quigg brought Billy in and untied him, Dodd unlocked the iron gate to the first cell.

"You won't be here long," Dodd said. "The hanging should be quick."

Amos Quigg stood in front of the cell, grinning through iron bars. "You're right where you belong, boy. You did all that running for nothing. It got you nowhere. Should've stayed at Hickory Hill. You had it good. But you were too dumb to realize it."

Billy glared at Quigg but didn't reply. Why bother? It wouldn't do any good.

Dodd chuckled. "Don't be bothering my prisoner, Amos. He's gonna get all upset before his hanging."

Quigg grinned and turned toward the door. "I best get to Hickory Hill. I'll tell Payne what happened and collect my reward." He paused and took one last look at Billy. "It don't matter if you're dead or alive. As long as you're caught."

"Tell Payne the hanging is tomorrow morning," Dodd called as Quigg left.

A few minutes later the door opened, and Quigg

came back in. "Look who I found in town, out getting supplies."

Zeb Payne strode in behind Quigg. "I never would have guessed," Zeb said as he went to the cell. "A runaway is bad enough. But a murderer?"

"Be careful, Zeb," Dodd warned. "He's dangerous."

"I didn't kill nobody," Billy said, sulking in his cell. "It was an accident."

Dodd came closer. "Not only is he dangerous, but he lies, too."

"It's easy enough to prove, Billy," Quigg said. "We got witnesses down at the church."

"Take Zeb to the victim's family," Dodd said with a wink that didn't go unnoticed by Billy. "He should at least pay his respects, maybe pay for the funeral."

Quigg nodded. "I'll do it right now."

Zeb Payne looked at Billy and shook his head. "I'll talk to the family," he said. "And make things right the best I can."

Amos Quigg and Zeb Payne left, closing the door behind them. Sheriff Dodd sat at his desk, scribbling notes in a logbook.

Billy Giles sat quietly on the cot in his cell, wondering why Dodd had winked at Amos Quigg.

Chapter Seventy

Jacob Yoder set the basket on the wooden bench beside the first horse stall. It held two plates of eggs, scrapple, and ham along with hunks of homemade bread and mugs of apple cider. He went to the well, filled a pitcher of water, and set it beside the food.

He opened the secret door. "It's safe to come out. I brought some breakfast."

Haney crawled out of the cave, followed by Chloe. Their faces were drawn and streaked with sweat, their plain gray dresses smudged with dirt. Worn down by days in darkness, they sat on the bench, looking defeated.

Jacob handed each a plate. "It's still good and hot."

"Thank you, Mr. Yoder," Haney said as Chloe nodded. "We much obliged."

He was sympathetic, their forlorn appearance hinting they lacked strength to go much farther. "It shouldn't be much longer," he assured them. "The man who brought you will come back with his wagon. You'll go with him to the next hiding place."

"We go with that same man?" little Chloe asked, her dark eyes wide and innocent. She seemed confused, wondering why they hadn't just stayed with Samuel Zook instead of hiding in a cave.

"He's a good man," Jacob said, stilling any fears. "He'll take good care of you."

"What happens then, Mr. Yoder?" Haney asked, taking a bite of her bread.

"Someone else will help you, just like I did. And little by little you'll make your way to Philadelphia. Many nice people live there, and they'll help you get settled."

Haney shook her head and smiled. "It seem too good to be true. All those folks helpin' us along the way." She glanced back at the secret door. "I didn't think we'd make it with those men here last night."

Jacob hadn't thought they would either. But he didn't want them to know. "It was the sheriff and a bad man named Amos Quigg. He catches runaways and brings them back to their owners."

"Who was the other man? I heard three voices."

Jacob paused, not wanting to reveal Billy's dilemma. "A runaway Amos Quigg caught. They're bringing him back to Hickory Hill plantation. It's not far, along the bay."

"I hope that bad man, Amos Quigg, don't find us," Haney said, glancing at her daughter.

"He won't," Jacob assured them. "Just do what those helping ask, and you'll make it to Philadelphia."

"I sure hope so," Haney said. "Been a long way. We tired."

"Are you trying to find any friends or family?"

Haney shrugged and motioned to Chloe. "Her granddaddy run off years ago. Be nice to find him. Ain't never seen Chloe."

"The people in Philadelphia can help you," Jacob said. "They keep lists of runaways and where they settle. Some go all the way to Canada."

"Ain't never heard of Canada," Haney said. Then she laughed. "Ain't never heard of Philly Delphia, either."

Jacob smiled. "It's big city. Lots of good people."

Haney and Chloe finished their breakfast and went back inside the cave. Jacob returned the basket and dirty dishes to his kitchen and cleaned everything up. He was about to leave for the fields when Samuel Zook's wagon came winding down the lane.

"I promise this will be the last delivery," Jacob said

to Ruth as they watched anxiously from the porch. "No more risk."

She smiled, her hand lightly caressing her belly. "It's good what you do. It really is. But our family comes first. And with the children getting older—"

"I know," he said, interrupting her. He leaned over and kissed her lightly on the lips. "You're right, as always."

Samuel parked the wagon by the crates of fruits and vegetables that Ruth and the children had packed. He was loading the first crate when Jacob arrived. "Have you heard any more about Billy?" he asked.

Jacob nodded. "Quigg caught him. They passed through with Dodd last night on their way to Chestertown. They stayed in the barn to wait out the storm."

Samuel shook his head. "He should have stayed here instead of running off. He wouldn't have gotten caught."

"It's much worse," Jacob said grimly. "Dodd claims Billy killed a man while he was trying to escape. They plan to hang him."

Samuel sighed and shook his head. "I wish we could do something to help him."

"Me, too," Jacob said. "But it doesn't look like we can."

Samuel glanced in the barn. He could just make out the secret door. "What about—"

"They're safe," Jacob said. "But anxious to go."

"I don't blame them. Best get them moved."

"I told you that today will be my last delivery. I have to protect my family."

"I don't blame you," Samuel said as they finished with the crates. "Especially with the baby coming."

"Thanks for understanding. I want to help. I do. But I can't."

Samuel nodded. "You need to do what's best for you. No one begrudges you for that."

Jacob touched his arm lightly. "Let's go to the barn and get the runaways."

Samuel looked up, the sun rising. "I have a delivery for my least favorite customer around noon. I'll have to hurry."

"Who would that be?" Jacob asked, as they started for the barn.

"Sheriff Dodd."

Chapter Seventy-One

Annabelle spent most of the following day with Snowflake, mastering maneuvers the competition required. She tried to stay engaged, to not think about what she'd seen at Zeb Payne's cottage. It was best to pretend she didn't know, ignore what she'd overheard, not dissect an affair that could have endured for years. At least not yet. The time for confrontation would come. But for now, she had a more pressing issue to address.

Early that evening, she found her father in his study, looking at a ledger. "Where's mother?" she asked. She wanted to talk to him privately, without her mother's interference.

He shrugged. "She was with Venus earlier, getting a dress altered."

Annabelle was distraught, upset by both her mother's infidelity and her courtship with Artemis Wentworth. She wanted to protect her own interests and not be tricked or bullied into an unwanted marriage. But she was losing the battle, her mother stealing what had once seemed a certain victory from a beleaguered Adrian Reed. She would bring the fight to her father, where she had a better chance for success. He had spoiled her terribly as a child, always his obvious favorite, probably because she was the youngest and, in many ways, an exact replica of her mother. She saw no reason why he shouldn't continue to do so now that she was an adult.

When she remained in front of his desk, Gideon looked up from his ledger. He sensed she had something to discuss. He motioned to a chair.

She sat down but hesitated, scanning the room—the fireplace, paintings, bookshelves—wondering how she should start.

"Is this about Adrian?" he asked, knowing his daughter as well as she knew herself.

Her gaze met his, and she nodded, smiling faintly.

"I haven't denied him your hand. I only asked that he wait. I want you to appreciate Artemis for what he is, to understand his potential, before you make your decision."

"I understand," she said. "I know Artemis is a good man with a bright future, kind and compassionate, a perfect partner for most women."

He smiled. "But not for you?"

She slowly shook her head. "I love Adrian."

He sighed, arching his fingers together, and looked at her lovingly, always seeing the child she once was. "I want nothing but your happiness. But I don't want you hurt, either."

"I know," she whispered, not surprised by his response. He was such a good man, and he loved her so much. Why would her mother seek solace in the arms of another? Especially when a man so close to perfection already shared her life.

"Something is bothering you," he said, a quizzical look in his eyes.

She toyed with telling him. But she couldn't break his heart. When she summoned the courage, she would confront her mother. It would be an ugly scene, but she couldn't avoid it.

"Is it so difficult to wait another month, preferably two?" Gideon asked, assuming her turmoil was driven by a courtship she couldn't control.

"Not if you want me to. But you're not the one who concerns me."

He arched his eyebrows. "Your mother?"

She nodded. "Adrian's father told him to expect an

imminent wedding announcement. Did you speak to him?"

"I did," he admitted. "I told him your mother hoped for a quick engagement."

"Mr. Reed took it to the extreme. He's encouraging Adrian to court someone else."

Gideon sighed. "And that's the point of our discussion."

"Yes," she said softly. "Promise me you won't make an announcement or plan a wedding without my consent."

"Fair enough," he said. "I promise."

"What about mother?"

He frowned. "I'll talk to her. It'll be difficult to restrain her, but I will." He paused, his gaze fixed on the daughter he loved so much. "It is your husband, after all. Isn't it?"

"Yes, it is," she said, relieved. She came around the desk and gave him a hug, holding him tightly. "Thank you. I love you so much."

"I love you, too. Just remember, your happiness is most important."

She left the study and prepared for bed. But she lay there for hours, unable to sleep. Regardless of what her father had promised, she felt like her world was collapsing. She didn't know what to do—especially about her mother. She couldn't forget hearing her voice as she left Zeb Payne's cottage, promising to return. It seemed she visited often. What surprised her most was that her mother had managed to keep it secret on a plantation where gossip whispered in the wind. Did Phoebe know? It was hard to believe she didn't. Even the roundabout route her mother had taken to Zeb's cottage reeked of deceit. Annabelle kept asking herself why. Her father was such a good man— handsome, compassionate, successful, attentive. He doted on his wife. Yet she preferred another man.

Zeb Payne was handsome, well-built with thick

russet hair, a nice smile. He had proven his devotion to Hickory Hill many times over—building her equestrian course, introducing innovative techniques to better harvest tobacco, staggering deliveries to the docks to gain better pricing. He helped any who asked, always polite, and was admired by all who knew him. But few realized, as she did, that a monster lurked within—a man with flaws he couldn't control. She knew it. So did Coffey Green. And now Phoebe did, too. How could her mother not?

Annabelle had been tempted to tell Adrian about Zeb Payne—what he was doing to Coffey, and how he had beaten her. But he was a man who valued justice. He wouldn't ignore it; he would take action. He would kill Zeb Payne.

She began to wonder. With so many people wanting Zeb Payne dead, why was he still alive?

Chapter Seventy-Two

Naomi was resting in a rocking chair on the upstairs balcony, reading *The Pirate* by Sir Walter Scott, when Artemis Wentworth arrived by carriage. His driver tethered his horse to a hitching post and then helped him climb out. Naomi suspected his visit was important. He normally came by boat from Annapolis, so she assumed he had been working from his Chestertown office, but she had issued no invitation. He wasn't there for Annabelle. His visit suggested he had information about Zeb Payne. She had to know what it was. Protection of her past was paramount. She hurried inside as Caesar answered the door.

"I'm sorry to disturb you," Artemis Wentworth said as Caesar admitted him. "May I see Mr. and Mrs. Banks for a moment?"

"Yes, of course, sir," Caesar said. "Mr. Banks is in his study, and I'll summon Miz Banks."

"I'm coming, Caesar," Naomi called from the top of the stairs.

Caesar led Artemis down the hallway and tapped on the door to Gideon's study. "Mr. Wentworth is here to see you, sir."

"Show him in," Gideon called.

Naomi approached from the stairway. "Good afternoon, Artemis."

"Naomi," he said, nodding politely.

They entered the study. Gideon was behind his desk, turned to his chessboard to plot his next move. "Artemis, how are you?"

"I'm well, sir," Artemis replied. "I'm sorry to intrude, but I have some information regarding Mr. Payne."

"Please, sit, you're not bothering us at all," Gideon said, motioning to chairs in front of his desk. "Can I get you anything—whiskey, wine, cider?"

"No, thank you," Artemis said, glancing at his pocket watch. "I can't stay long. I have to catch the ferry to Annapolis."

"Have you learned anything interesting?" Naomi asked, unable to wait while pleasantries were exchanged. She was ready to refute anything he offered, suggesting mistaken identity or claiming outright falsehoods. She had no alternative.

"No, not really," Artemis said, glancing at each in turn. "Only a few details. Not as much as I would have liked."

"Is he a man with no past?" Naomi asked, hoping he found nothing substantial. Then she could pay off Zeb Payne and be done with him.

"Yes, for the most part," he muttered, brows furrowed. "Didn't you mention references?"

Gideon nodded. "I did, but it was word of mouth. A man at the auction who claimed to know him."

Artemis frowned. "You don't know who the man was, do you?"

Gideon pursed his lips, slowly shaking his head. "No, I'm afraid not."

"I can't seem to locate his prior employer, which is where I had intended to start the investigation. I've actually found very little, if anything."

Naomi sighed with relief. "Maybe we shouldn't waste any more of your time. We can closely monitor Zeb and then determine a course of action."

"I still think we're fortunate to have him," Gideon mumbled. "As we've already discussed, he's an excellent overseer, the best I've worked with. He's done wonders here at Hickory Hill. Everyone respects and admires him."

"My contact in Norfolk did know a man named

Payne," Artemis offered. "But it didn't lead anywhere."

"He had no relevant information?" Gideon asked.

"He did have something. But I don't know if it has any value. It'll take time to verify."

"Did he know which plantation Zeb oversaw?" Naomi asked. "He did mention he was last in Virginia."

"No, my contact knew no one named Zeb Payne employed at any of the Virginia plantations, at least not those along the coast."

"But you said he did know a man named Payne?" Naomi probed, her pulse starting to race.

"Yes, he did," Artemis acknowledged. "But the Payne he knew, and he couldn't quite remember the man's first name, arrived in Norfolk by ship a few months ago."

Naomi shifted in her chair. "Likely a different man. If he recently arrived by ship, what would he be doing at a slave auction in Annapolis?"

Gideon shrugged. "He might have been looking for work."

"But you said he was already employed," Artemis countered.

Gideon frowned. "Yes, that's what he told me. But I'm not sure it matters. He obviously has significant experience."

Artemis paused, as if hesitant to continue.

"What is it?" Gideon asked, noting his reaction.

Artemis shrugged. "Why would he lie if he had nothing to hide?"

"I suppose that's true," Gideon admitted. "I hadn't really considered it, but Zeb should volunteer information."

"But we've never asked him anything," Artemis said. "And that could be the next phase in checking his background, if we don't uncover anything further."

"You said he may have arrived by ship," Naomi said. "Where did it come from?"

"Soufriere, St, Lucia," Artemis replied.

Chapter Seventy-Three

Naomi feared Zeb Payne much more than she had before. She had hoped he heard a few rumors, knew some facts, and was more bluff than threat. But after Artemis discovered he had recently arrived from St. Lucia, it no longer seemed likely. Her worst fears had been confirmed, and she had to somehow get him to disappear before it got worse.

A massive sugar plantation spread through the valley between two peaks across from Soufriere, and she suspected Zeb had managed it. An extensive operation manned by hundreds of slaves, it explained how he produced results that others could not. But given his background and expertise, she was plagued by lingering questions. Why had he left St. Lucia? And why had he appeared at a slave auction so close to Hickory Hill? Had he planned it all? Had he somehow discovered where she was and, even after all the years that had passed, decided he could capitalize on a twenty-five-year-old murder? She might never know.

She had intended to double the money she had given him—a year's wages versus six months. But now she knew he was the boy on the boat the night she fled St. Lucia. She recognized the danger he posed. He wasn't conning her for a few dollars. It was much more serious. She was afraid, in more ways than one. What if she couldn't satisfy him, regardless of his demands? She couldn't deny that he knew exactly what had happened to Rufus Jackson—and who had killed him. Artemis Wentworth might soon know, too—especially if he pursued an investigation through contacts in St. Lucia. Even if he found nothing, he might then question Zeb Payne, and she would no longer be able to hide a secret she had kept for so many years.

Naomi watched from the balcony while the slaves returned from the fields, waiting until she was sure Zeb was back in his cottage. She quietly slipped out of the house, avoiding Annabelle, who seemed distant lately anyway, and checked on Gideon. He was occupied in his study, writing a letter, probably to Benjamin. She went out the back door, cautiously looked over her shoulder to ensure no one followed, made her way to the back of the smokehouse and kitchen, and then over to the garden. When she reached the corner of the flower bed, hidden from view by any at the mansion, she darted through the foliage to Zeb Payne's cottage.

He was waiting on the front porch, an arrogant smile pasted on his face. "I knew you would be here sooner or later."

"This is the last time," she said, stepping onto the porch.

He led her inside, and they sat in the same chairs they had occupied during her last visit. It was awkward, neither speaking at first.

"Can I get you anything?" Zeb asked. "Some whiskey?"

Naomi was alert and defensive. She knew he wanted more than money as he clearly stated on several occasions. It was best to avoid socializing. She had to pay him off and be done with him before anything happened that she couldn't control.

"Or I have cider," he continued.

"No, I'm fine. Let's get this over with."

He smiled, his gaze wandering to her bosom. "I think we should spend some time together."

She rolled her eyes and reached in her dress pocket,

withdrawing the coins. "Eight hundred dollars," she said. "One year's pay. Plus, the four hundred I already gave you."

Payne's eyes widened. He grabbed the coins and stacked them on the oval table between their chairs.

"Our business is now concluded," she said. "When will you be gone?"

He didn't reply at first. After a moment, he chuckled and eyed her coldly. "You still don't understand, Mrs. Jackson, do you?"

"Don't call me that," she demanded.

He shrugged. "Fine, Naomi. Twelve hundred isn't enough."

She sighed and fixed her gaze on his. "There comes a point, Mr. Payne, when your demands exceed any repercussions I might suffer, assuming what you say is true."

He chuckled. "I think we're both smarter than that."

"If you continue to make demands, I'll contact the sheriff myself."

"I doubt he cares. Why would he?"

"Because I'll confess to what happened in St. Lucia. And then I'll tell him you're blackmailing me."

He grinned. "You won't do that. And we both know it."

"Don't be so sure," she said sternly.

He studied her a moment more, a hint of uncertainty in his eyes. He seemed to gauge her resolve, wondering if she had the strength to do what she claimed.

"Extortion is a serious crime," she said and then paused dramatically. "And I'm sure you've committed others."

He looked away while he assessed her offer. After a moment, he fixed his gaze on hers like a poker player intimidating an opponent. "Let's compromise."

"Compromise how?" she asked suspiciously.

"Another four hundred," he said. "Bring it Saturday night."

"And you leave as soon as you get it?"

He nodded. "No one will notice me missing until Monday morning. I'll be long gone by then."

Naomi was satisfied. "Agreed," she said as she stood and started for the door. "Four hundred more on Saturday night."

"Wait," he said, getting up to follow her. He reached toward her, grabbing her arm.

She yanked her arm away and hurriedly crossed the room. She opened the door and stepped out on the porch. If she had to, she would scream. And she suspected he knew it.

"One more thing," he said.

She turned, glaring at him. "What do you want?"

He approached, standing close, his breath heavy and stinking of whiskey. He reached for her face, his fingers caressing her cheek. "You're part of the bargain, too, Naomi."

"No, I'm not part of the bargain, Mr. Payne."

He shoved her against the wall, pressing his body against hers. "I've never forgotten you, stepping on my daddy's boat, all pompous and pretty like you could take the world if you wanted. Been thinking about it ever since. I decided right then and there that I was gonna have you someday."

"But you're not, Mr. Payne," she said, squirming as she tried to get away. "And you never will.

"I'm not so sure," he said. He again touched her cheek, and then dropped his hand to her shoulder, slowly moving lower.

She smacked his hand away, twisted from his grasp, and stormed off the porch. She could hear him laughing as she hurried through the trees.

Chapter Seventy-Four

Billy Giles sat on the straw mattress in his jail cell. It might be the last day of his life if the sheriff's threats to hang him were true. He marveled at how quickly life could change. In a matter of seconds, he had killed a man with little more than a shove. But it didn't matter how much force he'd applied. The man was dead—someone whose family and friends now mourned his loss. Billy had ended his life, impacting all who knew him in ways they would never forget. He'd had no right to do it, regardless of how it had happened. He knew his Bible. He deserved to be hung.

It no longer mattered what happened to him. He had been blessed with life and had squandered it. Now his loved ones would suffer. He lay on the cot, wishing he could say goodbye to his momma, daughter, and Coffey Green, the woman he had hoped to marry. He worried about her the most. His momma and daughter could cling to each other, mourn his loss, and do what had to be done to live their lives. But they would never be the same, an empty ache would hold their hearts. Coffey Green was different. She had no one. She would hurt more deeply, mourn longer. She already knew pain, sold off as she had been, separate from her family and losing her heart and soul at the same time, always wondering what might have been. He'd made a lot of promises to Coffey. But none would ever come true.

Billy had always been a dreamer, eyes bright and smile wide. But his dreams had all vanished when he'd shoved the man at the church. He would never be free or see a city crowded with people and buildings. He would never know what lay at the end of rainbows. He wouldn't find what lurked on the other side of the bay or walk down a street without looking over his shoulder, waiting for Amos Quigg to grab him. But worst of all, he would never hold his momma or daughter, and he would never marry Coffey Green. He would die, mourned by a few, leaving no mark on mankind except for a daughter who treasured his memories. He had lived a life that no one wanted to mimic and most would forget in just a few days.

Around noon, the jail door opened, and a man walked in. He was dressed strangely, black trousers and wide-brimmed hat, a white shirt with black suspenders. His black beard grew only on the rim of his face, dropping down toward his chest. Billy sat up abruptly. It was a man he knew—Samuel Zook, whom he had met at Jacob Yoder's farm.

"Good afternoon, Sheriff Dodd," Zook said as he came in.

"Samuel Zook," Dodd said, getting out of his chair. "I've been expecting you."

"I have fruit and vegetables for your missus. Just like you asked."

"Good, she'll be pleased. I was hoping you'd come by today. She's been asking for you."

"It's a nice assortment," Zook said, not even glancing at Billy. "Peaches, apples, corn, tomatoes, broccoli. and lettuce."

"I'll take a little of everything."

Zook nodded. "I'll fill a crate and bring it in." He walked toward the door, paused, and turned. "I have some apple fritter bread, almost half a pan. Would you like some? No charge. My missus made it for me."

"Absolutely," the sheriff said. "You may be the strangest folks I've ever seen, but your women sure can cook."

"I'll bring it in after I get your produce."

Sheriff Dodd stood by the edge of his desk, waiting for Zook's return. He noticed Billy sitting on his cot, watching him. "What are you looking at?"

"Not a thing, sir."

"I can be nice to those Amish when they've got something for me," he confided in Billy. "Although I'd run them all out of the county for stealing the land my boys wanted if I could."

"I suspect there's plenty of land to buy."

Dodd shrugged. "Maybe there is. But my family wanted the five hundred acres those Amish took. They don't belong here."

"They treat you real good, mean as you are."

Dodd frowned. "Mind your business."

The door opened, and Zook came in, carrying a slender wooden crate overflowing with produce. "Should I set this by the door, Sheriff? You can get it on your way out."

"Yes, set it down there," Dodd said, pointing.

Zook put the crate on the floor. "I'll go get the fritter bread. Quite a bit left."

As Zook left, Dodd turned to Billy. "You keep your mouth shut and maybe I'll save some for you."

Billy sulked in his cell. "I ain't sayin' nothing."

The door opened, and Zook came in, carrying a pan. "I think you'll like this," he said, walking toward the desk.

"What do I owe you for everything?" Dodd asked as he approached.

Zook looked at the produce as he set the pan on the desk. "Same as last week."

Dodd took some money from his pocket and leaned away from Zook to count it.

As soon as the sheriff turned, Zook leaned on the desk, his hands on the edge. A set of keys on a round ring dangled from a nail tacked into the side of the desk. When Dodd wasn't looking, he grabbed the ring and shoved it in his pocket. The sheriff didn't notice.

But Billy Giles did.

Chapter Seventy-Five

Jacob Yoder was coming back from the fields when Samuel Zook's empty wagon turned off the road and rambled down the lane that led to his house. He hurried toward it, worried something had happened, and met Samuel at the barn.

"Is anything wrong?" he asked as the wagon came to a halt.

Samuel shook his head. "I moved Haney and Chloe to their next destination. They're on their way north."

Jacob breathed a sigh of relief. "I was worried. It's difficult with a child." He glanced at the house. Ruth stepped out on the porch and started to ring the bell for supper. When she saw him at the barn, she waved and went back inside. "Maybe now I can help in other ways."

"I'll think of something," Samuel said. "There's so much to be done to save those poor souls."

It was quiet for a moment, neither man speaking. Jacob sensed Samuel had something else to say but seemed reluctant. "Did anything else happen?"

Samuel scanned the barn, looked out toward the road, and then turned to his friend. "I have something important to discuss."

Jacob nodded, prepared to do anything to help his friend. "What is it?" he asked.

"Billy Giles," Samuel said. "When I brought produce to Sheriff Dodd, he had Billy locked up, ready for hanging."

Jacob frowned. "I wish he would have stayed here and waited for you. He'd be safe now, maybe even in

Philadelphia. Do you know when it is?"

Samuel shrugged. "It's hard to tell. Supposedly in the morning. But I didn't see any activity—no one in town demanding justice or any talk of a trial."

Jacob shook his head. "I wish I could do something to help him."

"Maybe you can," Samuel said, a sly grin on his face. "There's more to the story."

Jacob looked at him, head cocked. "More to what story? Billy killed a man. There's not much we can do."

"Oh, but there is," Samuel assured him. "Amos Quigg was talking to Zeb Payne, the overseer at Hickory Hill, while I was offloading produce. I heard every word they said."

"Quigg said he might be able to pay off the dead man's family to save Billy from hanging."

Samuel paused, as if hesitant to reveal what he had overheard. "There's a lot evil going on. Evil a good man couldn't fathom."

Jacob paused, confused by the cryptic message. He eyed Samuel for a moment, wondering why he didn't say more. "The world is full of evil," he mumbled, thinking about Billy and dreams he had that would never come true. "I suppose there's not much we can do about it."

Samuel chuckled, his eyes twinkling. "Actually, I think there is."

Jacob looked at him, confused. "I don't understand."

Samuel removed the keys from his pocket and held them up for Jacob to see. "I took the liberty of borrowing these from the sheriff's office."

Jacob's eyes widened. "Why would you ever do that? You'll hang beside Billy."

"I intend to put them back," Samuel assured him. He paused to study dark clouds blowing in on the horizon. "Another storm coming. We've had a lot of rain lately.

Good for the crops."

"What are you doing with the keys?" he asked, not interested in the weather.

"I'm going to let Billy out," he said simply. "With your help, of course."

"Samuel, we can't! What happens if we get caught? We both have families."

"We won't get caught. I have it all planned."

Jacob hesitated, not wanting a good man to hang, regardless of the crime he'd committed. He was quiet for a moment, thinking, and then wavered. "What's your plan?"

"We'll leave here just before midnight," Samuel said. "We go to the jail, release Billy, put the keys back where I found them, and lock the door on our way out. They'll never know what happened."

Jacob looked back at the house. He had a wife and two children with a third on the way. "I don't know if I can do it," he said softly.

"I can't do it without you," Samuel insisted.

"But it's too dangerous."

"We'll be fine," Samuel assured him. "I'll do everything, but we'll take your carriage. Someone may have noticed me at the jail today, selling produce to the sheriff. Too risky to take my wagon."

Jacob considered potential problems. "What if someone sees us?"

"Bring one of Ruth's cloaks, something with a hood. We'll cover Billy's head. Anyone looking from far way will think it's two men and a lady traveling late."

Jacob hesitated but then gave in. "All right, I'll help you. But we can't bring him here."

"Fair enough," Samuel said. "We'll take him to the crossroads, give him directions, and tell him he's on his own."

Chapter Seventy-Six

Coffey made porridge, sausage and dark rye bread for breakfast. She still thought it strange that the kitchen was inside the house instead of a separate building like Hickory Hill, but she liked it better. It was easier to cook and serve. She brought breakfast out to the dining room, cider and coffee already on the table.

Adrian Reed scanned a ledger while he sipped his coffee. He looked up when she came in and smiled. "I have an update on our business, Coffey."

"What's that, Mr. Reed?" she asked. She set down his bowl and put a plate of meat and bread beside it. "Are folks still buying our cream and tonic?"

"Yes, they are. We sell more every day. This week we'll turn a profit. Not huge, but we should have positive cash flow going forward."

She had no idea what positive cash flow was, but she was starting to piece different business terms together. "Does that mean we makin' money?"

He chuckled. "Yes, it does. And our business should continue to grow. I shipped sample product to vendors in Annapolis yesterday. We'll see how that market responds. Hopefully it does as well as Baltimore."

"I sure hope so. I'm making tonic and cream as fast as I can."

"And we sell it as fast as you can make it."

Coffey paused for a moment. She would have been reluctant to speak her mind only a few short weeks before, but Adrian Reed had given her confidence. "I was thinkin'," she said. "May be some other things we can make."

"What might that be?" he asked as he ate his porridge.

"I got some plants from Phoebe when I went to Hickory Hill. She uses 'em to make tea. It make folks feel better when they upset, I suppose. And a salve to rub on bruises, swellings and such. Different than the tonic we make for cuts."

Adrian put down his spoon. "I'm listening."

"It'd take a little bit of land, but I can get the stuff we need from her and grow it right here. We can try makin' some, see if folks like it."

Adrian was quiet, lips pursed. "Let's make some samples, and we can give them to our merchants. If there's an interest, we'll do more."

"Yes, sir," she said. "I'll dig up a small spot for growing behind the barn, where the sun shines all day. When I see Phoebe, I'll get what else I need."

"If the tea and salve become popular, you may need help," Adrian said. "You can't do it all yourself."

Coffey shrugged. "I'll do fine, Mr. Reed. I'll just work a little harder."

Adrian smiled. "You work hard enough now."

When he finished eating, she cleaned up the dishes in the kitchen and then looked in on him. He was in his study, reading the newspaper. "I'm gonna go out and get started."

He glanced at his pocket watch. "I'll be leaving shortly, too."

Coffey went out to the barn, lined up some empty jars on the bench, and started mixing ingredients. Twenty minutes later, Adrian Reed came out and saddled his horse. Just as he was about to leave, they heard a rider approaching, horse's hooves smacking the trail and echoing through the forest.

"Who can that be?" Adrian asked, tying off his

horse and walking to the entrance.

Coffey turned, eyes wide, her hand to her chest.

"Good morning, Mr. Reed," Zeb Payne said as he brought his horse to a halt.

"What brings you out here?" Adrian asked, rather abruptly.

Coffey feared the worst. She prayed he wasn't collecting her to bring her back to Hickory Hill. She'd stayed with Mr. Reed longer than Zeb Payne wanted. But she hoped no one cared.

"I came by to talk to Coffey," Zeb said, looking toward the back of the barn.

Adrian eyed him, face firm. "I discussed her rental with Mr. Banks. He agreed I could have her a little longer."

"Yes, I know," Zeb replied. He feigned a somber sadness, but a glint of revenge was housed in his eyes. "This is different, a little more serious."

Coffey felt her heart begin to race, a sickening feeling in the pit of her stomach. She started to cross the barn. "What is it?" she called.

Zeb Payne climbed off his horse, holding the reins in his hand. He waited until Coffey reached them and fixed his gaze on hers. "I'm afraid I have some bad news for you."

Coffey noticed pink lines on his hands and arms from where she'd sliced him, almost healed. "What's wrong?" she asked, her voice trembling.

"No one is ill at Hickory Hill, are they?" Adrian asked with alarm.

"No, sir, nothing like that," Zeb said.

Coffey was anxious, sensing disaster. She eyed Zeb warily, suspicious of what might be said.

Zeb hesitated, his expression showing sympathy. "It's Billy Giles."

Her eyes widened. "What about Billy?"

"I know you planned to marry, although I don't

know how since he ran away."

"What about Billy?" she snapped, her breath coming in labored gasps.

Zeb Payne sighed, glancing at each in turn. "Billy killed a man. He was running from Amos Quigg, and the man tried to stop him."

Coffey looked at him, eyes wide. She shook her head and took a few steps back. "No, it can't be true. My Billy wouldn't hurt nobody. He's a dreamer, not a killer."

Zeb frowned. "I'm sorry, Coffey, I really am. But a witness saw him do it. He got caught. He was never any good anyway. You should have known that."

She moved her hands to her heart, her eyes moist. "What happens now?"

"They're going to hang him," Zeb said, glancing up at the sun. "If they haven't already."

Chapter Seventy-Seven

Adrian's heart sank as tears dripped down Coffey's face. Zeb Payne painted a dismal portrait. If Billy wasn't dead already, he soon would be.

"It can't be true," Coffey mumbled. Her vacant stare showed every dream she had ever had, now gone forever. "Billy wouldn't do that. I know he wouldn't. He's a gentle man, kind and good."

Zeb shrugged. "Maybe you don't know him as well as you think. He did kill a man in cold blood. Takes an evil person to do something like that."

Adrian lightly touched his arm. "Easy," he said. "Just give her a minute. It's a lot to absorb."

Coffey's chest heaved as she sobbed quietly. "I don't believe it none. Not Billy. He ain't like that."

Zeb turned to Adrian, talking softer. "It isn't easy for me, either. I lost a good worker. And I'm short-handed as it is."

Adrian was disgusted. He struggled to control his emotions—anger, pain, sympathy. He suspected Zeb told Coffey so he could watch her suffer. He looked at her, at first defiant but now destroyed, and back to Zeb, feigning sympathy but gloating, as if he enjoyed the pain he'd inflicted.

"I may go in to Chestertown to see how it all turns out," Zeb continued. "You're both welcome to come along, if you like. Maybe see him for the last time."

Adrian cringed. It was such an insensitive comment. But when he saw the smug look on his face, he realized it was intentional.

Coffey's sobs shifted to a high-pitched wail. "Oh, dear Lord! Why do this to such a good man? Not my Billy. He don't deserve it. He really don't."

Adrian nodded to Zeb and motioned toward the barn door. They stopped when they reached his horse, both looking back at Coffey as she cried in agony and prayed to a God that didn't seem to hear.

"Thanks for telling us, Zeb," Adrian said with a hint of sarcasm. He was willing to say anything to make him leave. "It was good of you to ride over."

Zeb nodded. If he noted the bitterness in Adrian's tone, he didn't show it. "I thought Coffey should know. She was close to him."

"I think she needs some time to grieve."

Zeb climbed up on his horse. "It's better this way. Otherwise, she'd wait her whole life for a man that was never coming back. It's sad, really. I think she had some silly notion they'd live happily ever after."

Adrian felt his face flush. It was difficult to control himself. "We all have dreams, don't we? You can't blame her and Billy for having some, too"

Zeb shrugged. "I don't know that they can dream." He led his horse out to the road that wound back to Hickory Hill.

Adrian glared at him as he left. Zeb had enjoyed relating Billy's fate. But why? He seemed like he wanted to devastate Coffey. If true, it confirmed his suspicions. Zeb likely beat her, and he could guess why. He intended to find out for sure. When he did, Zeb would get what he deserved.

Adrian came back in the barn and approached Coffey. She still sobbed, her eyes clenched closed, her hands to her heart. He wrapped his arms around her, pulling her close. "We'll get through this," he said softly.

"It ain't right," she said, leaning her head on his shoulder and hugging him tightly. "He was such a good man. Just had some dreams, that's all. Ain't nothing wrong with that."

"No, it's not right. We'll never know what happened, what the truth really is."

"Ain't no truth ever came from Zeb Payne's mouth," she said bitterly. "I can promise you that."

"No," he said, consoling her. "He's a bad man."

Her body jerked, and the tears fell faster. "He a real bad man, Mr. Reed. You don't know the half of it."

"I think I do," Adrian whispered. "And someday soon he'll pay."

Chapter Seventy-Eight

Footsteps echoed in the hallway, and Annabelle abruptly opened her bedroom door. "We need to talk," she said sharply.

Naomi was walking toward her bedroom. She hesitated, startled by her anger. "We can talk whenever you like."

"How about now? It's important."

"Yes, of course," Naomi replied. She eyed her daughter warily, not knowing what to expect.

Annabelle's bedroom was spacious, a small suite. A narrow fireplace was perched against an interior wall, flanked by portraits of horses, a white canopy bed across from it. Two open windows gazed out over the trees that split the mansion from the plantation, amber fields of wheat stretching beyond the treetops, blowing in the breeze. Rows of tobacco sprawled in the distance, the crop that made so much money for Hickory Hill. In front of the fireplace, two cushioned chairs shared an egg-shaped table. Annabelle sat closest to the fireplace, Naomi beside her.

"What did you want to talk about?" Naomi asked with a puzzled expression.

"Several things, actually."

Naomi shrugged. "We can discuss whatever you like."

"Let's talk about Adrian Reed."

"Adrian is a nice man. I admire him and like him very much. I always have, ever since you were children."

Annabelle paused to frame her thoughts. "His father encouraged him to court Amelia Crane. He's under the impression that I'm soon to wed Artemis and claims an announcement is forthcoming."

Naomi sighed. "I've made no secret of my desire. I hope that you do marry Artemis."

"You would announce a wedding without my consent?" Annabelle retorted.

"No, of course not," Naomi said, bewildered by her anger. "I would like to announce your wedding to Artemis, but I never told anyone it was imminent."

Annabelle hesitated. Seeds of doubt had been planted, but she wasn't yet ready to concede. "Why would Adrian's father make such an assertion?"

Naomi shrugged. "I don't know. A misunderstanding, I suppose."

Anabelle wasn't sure she believed her. Her mother could be deceitful when it served her purpose, as she had seen throughout her childhood. "Why would he ask Adrian to court someone else?"

"Annabelle, I have no idea," Naomi said, sighing. "You'll have to ask Thaddeus Reed. He must not want Adrian to marry you. Neither do I."

Annabelle's resolve firmed. "It doesn't matter what you or Thaddeus Reed want. You should know that by now."

Naomi rolled her eyes. "Fine, Annabelle. In the end, it's your decision, whether you choose the wrong man or not."

Annabelle smirked. She sat back in the chair, arms crossed, now ready to confront her mother. "You know all about choosing the wrong man, don't you, Mother?"

Naomi looked at her strangely, head cocked. "What's that supposed to mean?"

"Has Artemis found anything more about Zeb Payne?"

"He's still making inquiries. But he does suspect Zeb may not be who he pretends to be. His past may not link to his present, at least as he described it."

"That's interesting," Annabelle scoffed. "So he's a liar. Then I suppose we can also assume Coffey is telling the truth."

Naomi hesitated, as if startled by the depth of her ire. "I have no reason to doubt Coffey. Proving what she claims may be more difficult. Acting upon it, almost impossible."

"Nothing will happen? Is that what you want?"

"I didn't say that."

"Then why is Zeb Payne still at Hickory Hill?" Annabelle asked smugly. "Especially since he's a proven liar and rapist."

Naomi was taken aback. "Your father and I need to sort everything out. We can't release the man without good cause—verified and proven. Or without a replacement."

"Really?" Annabelle asked. "Because I have a different theory."

Naomi cowered. "What might that be?"

"I think someone is protecting him."

Naomi looked at her, confused. "Who would protect him?"

"You would."

Naomi gasped, but then shook her head. "Don't be ridiculous."

"I'm not," Annabelle declared. "Although it does fit nicely with your lecture on marrying the wrong man."

"What are you talking about?" Naomi asked, incredulous. "You're not making sense."

Annabelle looked at her mother, lips pursed, shaking her head. "I saw you at Zeb Payne's cottage."

Naomi frowned but then rolled her eyes. "It's not what you think, believe me."

"It never is."

"I swear, Annabelle. You don't know what's going on."

"I think it's obvious. How long have you known him, Mother? Months? Or years?"

"It doesn't concern you."

"Yes, it does," Annabelle muttered with disgust. "My poor father."

Naomi eyed her sternly, aggravated. "What are you talking about?"

"I think you're having an affair with Zeb Payne. Maybe you always have been."

Naomi leaped from her chair, defiant. "You couldn't be more wrong, Annabelle. I hate Zeb Payne with every ounce of my being."

She stormed out, slamming the door.

Chapter Seventy-Nine

Once a month, women of privilege in the western part of the county gathered for tea and conversation, rotating as hosts. Limited to eight of the region's most well-known socialites, their husbands were among the wealthiest, all owning large plantations.

The guests began arriving at Hickory Hill early that afternoon in stylish carriages, black with gilt trim, all pulled by handsome chestnut horses. The women wore flowing dresses consistent with the latest fashions—green, lavender, and light blue—suffering in the summer heat. It seemed they tried to outdo each other, either with style, gossip, or some fascinating tidbit of knowledge not known to the rest of the modern world. Naomi counted none of the women as close friends—she really didn't have any—but always found useful information to glean at their gatherings.

Caesar met each attendee at the door when they arrived and led her into the parlor. Phoebe waited by a long table laden with lace doilies, tea, cider, and muffins ready to be served.

Naomi greeted her guests as they entered, smiling warmly, nodding politely. She couldn't focus, her thoughts drifting to her argument with Annabelle. She had been certain no one had seen her at Zeb's. But she'd been wrong. Her own daughter had been close enough to see, or worse yet, to overhear part of their discussion—just enough to get the wrong impression. It offered one more reason to rid Hickory Hill of Zeb Payne as quickly as possible—no matter what the cost.

As each guest arrived, Naomi led her to one of the chairs staged around the room so they could comfortably talk. A half dozen ladies attended, anxious to discuss all that had happened since their last meeting, new revelations about their lives, plantations, politics, and whatever gossip they may have heard.

"If the rain doesn't abate, I'm afraid the tobacco crop will suffer," said Rachel Callaway as they all got settled. "My husband may plant more grain next year."

"It is more resistant," Charity Shepherd said, accepting a cup of tea from Phoebe. "But not as profitable."

"Not as hard on the soil, either," said Susannah Crane, Amelia's mother.

Naomi listened with little interest. She eyed the women closely, seeking an opportunity to steer the conversation to gossip, especially about Amelia Crane and Adrian Reed. Her plans for Annabelle would be much easier if Adrian fell in love with someone else. Artemis would win her hand by default.

"You look lovely, Naomi, as always," Rachel Calloway said. She admired the indigo dress that flowed to the floor, accented with white lace trim on the neck and wrists.

"Venus, my seamstress," Naomi said. "She's marvelous. And she's training her granddaughter, Betsy."

"Do you rent her out?" Charity Shepherd asked. "My seamstress is adequate, but nowhere near as talented as Venus."

Naomi nodded. "I think we can come to some sort of arrangement."

"You'll likely need her more than ever," Rachel Calloway hinted. She leaned forward, as if sharing a secret. "Now that an announcement is soon to be made."

Naomi chuckled. "We may not be as close as some claim. Annabelle is keeping all options open."

"My Amelia is seeing suitors," Susannah Crane

said, eyeing the others as if to gauge their reactions.

Naomi knew she sought information to benefit her daughter. "Few eligible men are available. At least not on this side of the bay."

"Henry Rodgers," Charity Shepherd offered. "Melody's son. He's returning from Washington to start his own law practice."

"He's already expressed an interest in Amelia," Susannah Crane informed them. "As have others."

"Adrian Reed, I'm told," Rachel Calloway said. She glanced at Naomi, observing her reaction.

Naomi smiled. "Mr. Reed may be available. Although it's too early to say for sure."

"I've heard Artemis Wentworth plans an announcement shortly," Susannah Crane said, her face brightening, her daughter's prospects probably in mind.

Naomi shrugged. "We'll soon see."

Charity Shephard scanned the group with mild surprise. "Artemis Wentworth?"

"Only one of Annabelle's suitors," Rachel Calloway clarified.

Charity Shepherd smiled, expressing disbelief. "Apparently you haven't been to Annapolis lately."

Naomi sensed a revelation, as did the others. They leaned forward, listening closely to Charity Shepherd.

"It's been ages since I've been to Annapolis," Susannah Crane confided.

"Me, too," echoed Rachel Calloway. "Please, tell us what you've heard."

Charity Shepherd paused, enjoying their undivided attention. "I'm only surprised you haven't heard. I thought everyone knew."

"Knew what?" Susannah Crane asked. "Don't keep us in suspense."

"It's about Artemis Wentworth," Charity Shepherd said.

"What about him?" Susannah Crane asked, rolling her eyes.

"Yes, tell us," Rachel Calloway begged. "We can't wait to hear it."

"Sarah Harrison and Artemis Wentworth are inseparable. Artemis will soon ask for her hand."

Chapter Eighty

"**I** am ready to marry," Artemis said, glancing at Gideon and Naomi. He took his last forkful of apple pie. "I think it's the right time to start raising a family."

Annabelle caught Naomi eyeing her subtly, but she refused to acknowledge. They hadn't spoken since arguing about Zeb Payne. Naomi hadn't offered an explanation for her appalling behavior—she hadn't even attempted to. She'd simply stormed from the room, declaring her disdain for him. But to Annabelle, her actions proved otherwise.

"I suspect the right woman has captured your fancy," Naomi said, lacking any enthusiasm.

Annabelle cocked her head slightly. Naomi was acting strangely—her statement direct. More acidic than hopeful. She seemed distant, not showering Artemis with compliments like she usually did. Annabelle studied each in turn, searching for signs of discord. She saw none in Artemis. But her mother showed an aloof coolness—a behavior she often displayed quite effectively.

"I do realize you'll marry for love," Gideon said, furtively glancing at Annabelle. "But it also provides a political advantage. Voters will feel more connected to you."

Artemis smiled. "I suspect many do identify with newlyweds. It certainly won't hurt my chances for victory."

When they finished dessert, Annabelle and Artemis went out on the balcony and sat facing the lane that led from the road to the mansion. It was a pleasant evening, a gentle breeze from the bay easing the heat. They chatted briefly about the weather, the campaign, Annapolis—but

Annabelle was interested in a different topic.

"Have you learned any more about Zeb Payne?" she asked.

Artemis gave her a guarded glance. "I didn't know your parents had shared the results of my inquires, limited though they may be."

"Of course they did," she lied, having learned little from her mother. "I prompted the investigation."

Artemis seemed hesitant to discuss it. "He's a mysterious man," he said evasively. "A ghost."

She looked at him, head cocked. "Why would you say that?"

"So far, I've found little about him. And anything I did learn was conflicting—no two sources agreed. But I suppose that only suggests they're confused, thinking not of Zeb but someone similar."

"How will you learn the truth?" she probed.

He shrugged. "Quite frankly, it would be easiest to simply ask him. But your mother opposes direct communication."

"I'm not surprised," Annabelle muttered.

Artemis turned to face her, smiling. "Do I detect bitterness?"

She innocently shook her head. Artemis didn't need to know her suspicions. "She despises scandal."

"Oh, yes, of course. We all do."

It was quiet for a moment. Annabelle sensed an awkwardness not present in their prior conversations. She decided to press the issue she thought was driving it. "You're determined to wed before the election, aren't you?"

"I am," he said, his gaze averting hers. "In early September, most likely."

She hid her frown. She had no intention of being pushed into marriage with a man she didn't love. "It promises to be a busy autumn."

"Yes, it does," he agreed.

He avoided what had to be said, the question that begged to be asked. He watched a cardinal fly past, resting for a moment on the railing before fluttering away.

Annabelle took his hand and held it, not as a lover, but as a friend. "Artemis, you're a good man with great potential."

He smiled faintly, turning to face her. "But your heart belongs to another."

She nodded, her face a mask of compassion. "I'm sorry. Ours is a match my parents wanted so desperately to make."

"It would have been a good one, I'm sure," he said. "But you must follow your heart. Happiness can be so elusive. If you've found it, don't let it slip away."

"No, I won't," she said softly. "But I will always remain one of your closest friends and staunchest allies."

"More valuable, perhaps, than a wife could ever be," he joked.

She was pleased he took her refusal so well. It wasn't what she'd expected, especially for someone so accustomed to getting what he wanted. He didn't seem hurt or offended. But then she realized, for men like him, marriage wasn't necessarily about love. It was sometimes founded on opportunity.

"A man as charming and attractive as you must have many interested parties," she teased. "Some of the most beautiful women in the world, I'm sure."

He chuckled. "Yes, but not what you might expect. And none are my first choice. But life is often disappointing."

"I've no doubt you'll find happiness. Or it will find you."

He sighed. "I suppose so. It's an interesting time for me, a journey I never expected to take. But I'm enjoying it immensely."

Annabelle dreaded informing her mother. Naomi wanted her to wed Artemis so badly, whether she loved him or not. "Who will tell my parents?" she asked, cringing.

"I will," he said, always the honorable man. "Just before I take my leave."

Chapter Eighty-One

"Can you ask Annabelle to come in here?" Naomi asked Caesar after he had shown Artemis Wentworth to the door. She sat on the sofa with Gideon, his hand lightly caressing hers.

"Yes, sir," Caesar said. "She's just across the hall."

Annabelle came in a moment later. "Is this about Artemis?"

"It is," Gideon said. "I'm stunned, actually. I certainly wasn't expecting that."

Annabelle cringed. "I feel terrible," she said. "I hated to break his heart. But I thought it best. Especially after dinner, when he talked about marrying this fall."

"But you didn't break his heart," Naomi said curtly.

Annabelle looked at her, head cocked. "Why would you say that?"

Gideon was also baffled. "Yes, what do you mean? He was obsessed with Annabelle."

Naomi sighed, face firm. "Apparently not. I heard from members of my women's group that Artemis is about to make an announcement. It seems he and Sarah Harrison are all but inseparable."

Annabelle's eyes widened. "Sarah Harrison from Annapolis? That's the first I've heard her name mentioned."

"Me, too," Gideon admitted, glancing at his daughter with disbelief. "Are you certain? I'm sure Artemis would have told us, or at least let us know he was courting more than one woman."

"Why would he?" Naomi asked. "He knew

Annabelle had more than one suitor. He probably assumed that we knew he did, too."

Gideon shrugged. "He still should have said something."

"I think he's been chasing Sarah Harrison for quite a while," Naomi said. "But for whatever reason, he couldn't catch her. Annabelle served as bait so he could get what he wanted."

"Mother, that's cruel," Annabelle said crossly. "And it also isn't true."

Gideon pursed his lips. "But it does make sense. Her father is the richest man in Maryland. And a massive force in the political world."

"Sarah does seem the obvious choice," Naomi added delicately. "Especially if politics was his motivation."

"But Artemis never mentioned her," Annabelle said. "Not even once."

Naomi chuckled. "No, of course he didn't."

"But why would he do that?" she asked. "I was honest with him about Adrian."

"Because he wanted it to look like you refused him," Naomi said. "At least on this side of the bay. To ensure his maintained his political backing, I suspect. My friends said it's much different in Annapolis. Everyone is aware of their courtship."

"But he knew from the outset that I wasn't interested," Annabelle said. "Why would he waste his time?"

"I think you may have given him the excuse he needed," Gideon said.

Annabelle rolled her eyes. "What excuse? I love Adrian, and he knew it, Sarah Harrison or not."

Naomi pursed her lips. "Artemis was playing chess. You were playing checkers. You were the pawn he sacrificed to capture the queen."

Annabelle was quiet, pouting. "That's quite hurtful, if true."

Naomi didn't want her hurt. But she thought it best that she knew the truth. "I suspect he wanted Sarah all along. But she was hesitant. Or maybe her father was."

"And Annabelle served as the catalyst to get what he wanted?" Gideon asked, his hand still lightly caressing hers. "Is that what you're suggesting?"

"Exactly," Naomi said. "I suspect they'll announce their engagement shortly."

"I'm still not sure I believe it," Annabelle said. "Artemis always acted as if he wanted to marry me."

"Apparently, you were his second choice," Naomi muttered.

Annabelle glared at her mother. "That's a horrible thing to say."

"It's true, unfortunately," Naomi replied. "I don't like it any more than you do. He used the whole family, not just you. And to ensure we didn't turn on him, and perhaps support the opposition in his political campaign, he tricked you into playing the role of uninterested party."

Annabelle sulked briefly but quickly brightened. "It doesn't matter anyway. Now I can marry Adrian."

"Yes, you can," Naomi said slowly. She paused, formulating a plan. After a moment, she turned to her daughter, a sly grin on her face. "Are you interested in revenge?"

"Naomi, there's no need for revenge," Gideon scoffed. "It was a courtship that didn't progress. It happens all the time."

"No, it's different," Naomi insisted. "Artemis used Annabelle to get what he wanted, whether it was Sarah or political favors from her father."

"Or maybe Artemis did want to wed Annabelle," Gideon offered, "but Jeremy Harrison wouldn't support him politically if he did."

"It doesn't matter now," Naomi said, glancing at her daughter. "He used Annabelle, regardless."

Annabelle bristled, realizing she had been tricked. "No one likes to be toyed with," she declared. "Not even me." She turned to her mother. "What revenge are you talking about?"

"Let's announce your wedding before Artemis announces his. It'll make everyone on both sides of the bay think you rejected him—just as he claimed."

"But I did reject him," Annabelle insisted.

"You only think you did," Naomi said. "It was part of his plan."

Annabelle frowned. She wanted the world to know just how deceitful the great Artemis Wentworth was. But how could she, without appearing bitter over the rejection? "Who cares? It's done with," she said flatly. "I can marry Adrian. And if revenge means I can marry him sooner, then that's fine with me."

"I thought you would like that," Naomi said, smiling smugly. She turned to Gideon. "I suggest we make the announcement immediately."

Annabelle clasped her hands with excitement. "I'll talk to Adrian tomorrow."

Naomi smiled, scheming. "If you'd prefer, we can arrange the wedding quickly. Maybe even before Artemis announces his engagement."

Chapter Eighty-Two

Adrian halted his buggy at Hickory Hill, climbed out and tethered his horse to one of the hitching posts. As he started up the steps, the front door opened, and Annabelle rushed out. She crossed the porch to meet him, gave him a warm embrace, and took him by the arm.

"Come on," she said. "Let's go for a walk out back. I have wonderful news."

"You're certainly excited," he said as he followed her down the steps.

"You will be, too," she said. She led him along the brick walk that wandered around the house. "My mother knows you're coming, but I wanted to see you alone before we went inside."

They strolled down the lawn, flanked by trees, the kitchen and smokehouse tucked off to the right, the gardens behind them. They went to their favorite bench, gazing out at the bay as it stretched into the horizon. Sailboats sped across the water, from small craft to cutter. A steamship in the distance belched smoke, ferrying people and cargo from Rock Hall to Annapolis.

Adrian was leery of Naomi's reaction the last few times he had visited—a frosty reception at best. "Are you sure we should be out here? Especially if your mother knows I'm coming. She'll be angry if we don't do what she wants."

Annabelle leaned toward him and kissed him hungrily. "Is that a good enough reason to come out here?" she asked coyly.

He grinned. "I'm not complaining."

She wrapped her arms around him, pulling him

close. "It's so nice to see you."

"It's nice to see you, too," he said as she laid her head on his shoulder, and the scent of her perfume lingered on the breeze. "Though I have been worried."

She lifted her head. "Worried about what?"

He sighed. "My father still claims your mother is about to announce your engagement to Artemis Wentworth. He insists I court Amelia Crane."

Annabelle burst into laughter. "Your father couldn't be more wrong."

He arched his eyebrows. "He's not often wrong."

She turned toward him and took his hands in hers. "Artemis was here last night, and we agreed to end our courtship."

His eyes widened. "Really?" he asked. It wasn't what he'd expected, and, for a moment, he wondered if it was true. "You're not teasing me, are you?"

"No, I'm serious," she insisted.

"Artemis seems like a man who always gets what he wants."

"He usually does," she said. "But not this time. And there's much more."

"I can't wait to hear it," he said, still stunned.

"One of the women in my mother's tea circle said Artemis is about to announce his engagement to Sarah Harrison."

He was confused. "Sarah Harrison from Annapolis?"

"Yes, apparently they're inseparable."

Adrian paused. "I wouldn't have guessed that. They seem very different. Sarah is more of a scholar, a bookworm. Better suited as a librarian than a senator's wife."

"She'll still help him further his political ambitions. Or at least her father will."

He furrowed his brow. "Her father isn't a nice man.

Our business has had dealings with him in the past. I wouldn't want to count him as an enemy. Artemis may not know what he's in for."

She shrugged. "Why should we care? That's his problem."

"I'm sure politics had something to do with their marriage," Adrian mused aloud. "I can imagine negotiations between Artemis and Jeremy."

"Artemis once mentioned he was beholden to his financial backers."

"I'm not surprised," he said. "Some politicians are bought and paid for. I guarantee Jeremy Harrison will get what he wants, and you can be sure it's much more than wedding his daughter to a senator."

She leaned closer. "My mother didn't take the revelation well."

Adrian cringed. "No, I would think not. No one crosses your mother. Not if they're smart."

"She was actually quite angry," Annabelle continued. "Which did provide some enjoyment."

He laughed. "You're naughty, sometimes."

She shrugged. "I can't help it. But now my mother wants revenge."

Adrian sighed. "Why?" he asked. "It seems the decision was mutual."

"Artemis doesn't think we know about Sarah Harrison," she explained. "For my parents, he made it seem like I ended the courtship. But my mother learned he's soon to announce his engagement."

Adrian was quiet for a moment, considering all possibilities. "Are you suggesting that he only courted you to win over Sarah Harrison and force an agreement with her father?"

"Yes, exactly," she said. "And my mother didn't like that, believe me. Which is why she wants revenge."

"But can't you just go on with your life? You didn't

want to marry him anyway."

"That's exactly what I plan to do," she said, squeezing his hand. "But my mother thinks differently. Although you may like the revenge she has planned."

He hesitated, aware of how nasty Naomi could be. "What does she want to do?"

"She wants our announcement made before Artemis Wentworth makes his. Maybe the wedding, too, if we can manage it. That's her revenge. She wants to embarrass him and truly make it look like I rejected him, rather than he was never interested in me to begin with."

Adrian's head was spinning. Deceit wasn't among the traits he possessed, and he had a difficult time grasping what she said. "Then I only need to formally ask your parents for your hand?"

Annabelle nodded. "They're waiting in the parlor. My mother will ensure the announcement is in all the newspapers as quickly as possible, maybe even tomorrow."

"And the wedding?"

"Within the month, I would think. She only needs time to arrange it."

He chuckled, amazed at fate's twists and turns. He had arrived doubting he could compete against Artemis Wentworth. He would leave engaged to his beloved. "Let's go ask them," he said, taking her hand. "We're wasting time."

They hurried across the lawn, anxious to finalize the arrangements. "Guess what I want my parents to give me as a wedding present?" Annabelle asked.

He hesitated, thinking of all she loved. "Another horse."

She smiled. "I hadn't thought of a horse. But maybe I'll ask for that, too. Even though I love Snowflake above all else." She paused for a few seconds and then laughed. "Except for you, of course."

He squeezed her hand. "What else?"

"Coffey Green."

His face firmed. "I'm not sure I want to own a person."

Annabelle shrugged. "Then we'll free her. We can pay her a salary to look after us."

Adrian thought for a moment, his future becoming clear. "Or even better," he said. "She can be my business partner."

Chapter Eighty-Three

Billy Giles was awakened just after midnight when the tumbler in the door lock clicked. He jerked up in his cot, eyes wide, staring at the door. He could see nothing, only blackness. Seconds later, the knob turned, and the office door gently opened. A figure entered, clothes dark, followed by a second. The door quietly closed.

His heart raced. He barely breathed. He knew all about lynchings—some poor black man dangling at the end of a rope for looking at a white woman wrong. Or maybe some poor soul stole something, and an angry mob broke him out a jail and hung him from a tree. Billy had killed a man inside a church. Not many crimes were worse. The townsfolk had every reason to be angry, to come get him in the middle of the night. They wanted their own justice, not what Sheriff Dodd had planned. Now he feared for his life—a beating that would leave him close to dead before he was strung up to a tree with a noose around his neck.

He leaned back against the brick wall, afraid to move. Beads of sweat dotted the back of his neck, feeling cold on a hot summer night. He craned his head forward, his body trembling. Maybe they were friends of the man he'd killed, ready to drag him out of jail and make his last minutes of life more horrible than any could imagine. He suspected he had only minutes left to live, images of his daughter, momma, and Coffey Green drifting through his mind.

The intruders waited at the entrance, perfectly still. A dog barked, a door at a distant house slammed closed. A moment of eerie silence followed. One man stepped forward, the second behind him. He came up to the cell gate, fumbled with keys until he found the right one, and stuck it in the lock.

Billy closed his eyes. He mumbled a prayer, prepared to meet his maker. When the gate slowly opened, he opened his eyes, trying to see the blurred images coming to get him, the men about to hang him.

"Billy," a man hissed. "Come on. We have to hurry."

He squinted, trying to see. He leaned forward, eyeing shadows. "Jacob?" he asked. "Is that you?"

"Shh!" the second man hissed. "Be quiet. Come on."

Billy tiptoed across the cell. When he stepped in the office, Samuel Zook closed the gate and locked it.

"I'll return the sheriff's keys," Samuel said, chuckling as he hung them on the nail tacked in the side of the desk. "It was nice of him to lend them."

Jacob Yoder steered Billy to the door, Samuel Zook a few steps behind them. He opened it, eyed the alley behind the courthouse, and studied the streets and houses beyond.

"Cover yourself," Jacob said, handing a cloak to Billy. "Put the hood up."

Billy slipped the garment over his shoulders. "Can't get my arms through," he said. "Too small."

Jacob shrugged. "Just lay it on your shoulders and put the hood over your head."

Billy did the best he could, covering his head and upper shoulders. He followed Jacob into the alley. Samuel locked the door behind them.

"My carriage is around the corner," Jacob whispered.

They stayed in shadows, close to shrubs. Across the street, a candle flickered in a window. They crept past. When they reached the corner, the dog started barking again.

"Hurry," Jacob hissed.

A figure came to the window, a shadow against the curtain. They rounded the corner, not looking back. Billy kept his head covered, face down, wedged between Jacob and Samuel. Jacob's carriage sat on the edge of the road a hundred feet away.

Jacob untethered the horses from a fence and climbed up on the bench seat. "Sit between us," he whispered to Billy. "No talking."

Samuel and Billy climbed in. Jacob urged the horses forward, and they moved slowly down the dirt road. The clopping of the horse's hooves competed with the howling dog. When the carriage cleared the last residence and had traveled another quarter mile, Jacob spurred the horses into a trot, and they sped down the lane.

Tree limbs hung above them; a shy moon peeked from cotton clouds that marred the sky. When they had gone almost three miles, they reached the crossroads, close to Jacob's farm, and he stopped the carriage.

"You're safe now," Samuel said.

Billy exhaled, many tense muscles relaxing at once. "I don't know how to thank you. They was gonna hang me."

"Actually, they weren't," Samuel said. "They just acted like they were."

Billy was stunned. "I'm not sure what you saying, but tomorrow was the day I was gonna die."

"It was a con," Samuel said. "I heard Amos Quigg tell Zeb Payne."

Billy was quiet. "I don't understand."

"The man you shoved didn't die," Samuel explained. "He's got a nasty cut on his head and some swelling, but he's alive and well."

Billy breathed a sigh of relief. "Praise God. I don't want to kill no one."

"You didn't," Samuel assured him.

Billy's relief turned to anger. "Why did they do all that? Put me in jail and tell me I killed someone."

"Because they squeezed more money out of Zeb Payne. They claimed the man you shoved was close to dying, and they needed to pay off his family. The sheriff wanted money, too."

"But why act like I was gonna hang?"

"It was Quigg's idea," Samuel said. "He knew you'd never learn the truth. He thought you'd be so grateful to Zeb Payne for paying off the dead man's family and saving your life that you'd never run again."

Billy shook his head in disbelief. "And Mr. Payne went along with it?"

Samuel nodded. "Reluctantly, but he was worried about the money. He's loyal to Hickory Hill, I'll give him that much. But in the end, he said he'd do anything that scared you enough to keep you from running again."

Billy sighed. "I didn't think Zeb Payne cared if I was dead or alive."

"Oh, he does," Samuel said. "He wants you alive so you can make money for Hickory Hill."

"When was they gonna tell me?"

"Tomorrow morning, from what I overheard," Samuel said. "When they took you out to hang you, Sheriff Dodd was going to explain what happened and turn you over to Amos Quigg. For a fee, of course."

"Oh, Lordy, Lordy, ain't some men evil?" Billy muttered. "I can't believe how their minds work. Who thinks of things like that?"

"Devils do," Samuel Zook muttered.

"You right there, Mr. Zook. Satan himself must have dreamed all that up."

"But you still have a problem, Billy," Jacob said.

Billy smiled. "I ain't got no problems, Mr. Yoder. I'm alive and well."

"But I can't take you back to my barn," Jacob said. "I almost got caught with the last runaways I had. I can't take risks any more. Not with the baby coming."

"No, you can't," Billy agreed. "You got yourself a nice family and a good plot of land. Don't do nothing to lose it."

Jacob grasped Billy's hand and shook it firmly. "I'm glad you understand."

"I do, Mr. Yoder, I surely do."

Jacob pointed at the crossroad. "If you go right and travel for a few days, you'll eventually get to Philadelphia."

Billy turned to shake Samuel's hand. "Thanks for saving me."

"You're a good man, Billy. You deserve to be saved."

Billy took off the cloak, folded it, and set it on the bench seat. He climbed down from the carriage and stood in the road. He turned and looked to the left. "Where's this road go?"

"Back to Hickory Hill," Jacob said.

Billy stood there for a moment, thinking. He looked up at the carriage. "Much obliged to all you've done for me. I can't thank you enough."

"Good luck," Samuel Yoder said.

"And take care of yourself," Jacob added.

Billy waved his goodbyes. When the carriage was out of sight, he turned left toward Hickory Hill.

Chapter Eighty-Four

Naomi tugged a cord hanging from the ceiling beside her bedroom fireplace. It rang a bell in Phoebe's room, just above.

A moment later, Phoebe tapped on the door. "You need me, Miz Naomi?"

"Yes, can you come in for a minute? I have a lot to tell you."

Phoebe entered, looked at her anxiously, and closed the door behind her. "Is everything all right?"

"For now, it is," Naomi said, motioning to a chair by the fireplace. "But we have to plan a wedding quickly."

"Miss Annabelle marrying Mr. Wentworth?" Phoebe asked. Daylight was fading, so she lit an oil lamp on the table between them.

Naomi frowned. "No, I'm afraid not."

Phoebe cocked her head. "I'm sorry to hear that. I know you was hoping she would."

"He told Gideon and me that Annabelle loves Mr. Reed."

"Well, I suspect she does, Miz Naomi."

"I know, but I had hoped Artemis could charm her, steal her away."

Phoebe chuckled. "Lord knows he tried. Or at least he seemed to."

Naomi pursed her lips. "I'm not so sure."

"You don't think he did?"

Naomi shook her head. "Mr. Wentworth always intended to marry someone else, a woman that could further his political career."

Phoebe's face stiffened. "He just used Miss Annabelle to speed it along."

Naomi nodded. "It seems so."

"Then who's getting married?"

"Annabelle and Adrian Reed."

Phoebe's eyes widened. "Aww, that's nice. They do love each other, Miz Naomi. Anybody can see that."

Naomi reluctantly agreed. "Yes, I know. I should have realized Mr. Wentworth had an agenda. But I don't like to be played for a fool."

"No matter now, anyways. When is the wedding?"

Naomi looked at her lifelong friend and smiled. "As soon as we can plan it."

"Oh, Lordy," Phoebe said. "I better start to get it ready."

"I'll create the guest list over the next couple days, so you know how many people to cook for."

Phoebe rose to leave. "I'll think up some dishes, and you can decide if that's what you want folks eatin'. A wedding out back, by the bay, would be nice."

"Yes, it would," Naomi agreed as they walked to the door. "It's such a beautiful view."

Phoebe hesitated. "I sure hope nothing spoils it, like that scoundrel Zeb Payne."

Naomi frowned. "I've given him eighteen months pay to leave Hickory Hill and never mention St. Lucia again."

"Is he gonna do it?"

"No, he wants more."

Phoebe's eyes widened. "More than all that money?"

Naomi nodded. "He wants two years pay. I have to bring more Saturday evening."

"And he gonna leave right quick?"

Naomi shrugged. "He promises to leave Saturday night. If he does, no one will notice he's gone until Monday morning."

"He best be gone," Phoebe huffed. "Or he'll get what Rufus Jackson did."

"I hope to avoid that," Naomi mumbled. "One dead man on my conscience is enough."

"I hope you can, Miz Naomi. But I'm not so sure. Does he want anything else?"

Naomi sighed, eyeing her confidant. "He wants to take liberties he has no right to take."

Phoebe frowned and shook her head. "Just like he did with Coffey Green."

Naomi nodded. "I've denied him so far. But I'm sure he'll insist. Unless he only enjoys watching me squirm."

"Is he just makin' threats?"

Naomi hesitated. "I'm not sure. He's more aggressive every time I see him. But why would he take such a risk?"

"What if he don't care?"

Naomi wasn't sure what she would do. "I just have to get through Saturday night."

"I know just the thing," Phoebe assured her, lightly touching her arm. "I be right back."

Phoebe stepped out, closing the door behind her. Naomi paced the floor, wondering what she had to offer. It was only a few minutes before she returned.

"Looky here," Phoebe said, closing the door behind her. She reached down into her knee-length stocking and withdrew a home-made stiletto. She handed it to Naomi. "Take this with you. Fits nice in your stocking. And it kills real quick."

Chapter Eighty-Five

Annabelle wasn't expecting a knock on her bedroom door. The servants had been dismissed, most of the household already in bed. She frowned when she opened it. Naomi was waiting in the hallway.

"What do you want, Mother?" she asked. "Is Zeb busy?

Naomi ignored her and entered. "I want to talk to you," she said as she sat near an open window, a light breeze rustling the curtains.

Annabelle was so disgusted by her mother's affair with Zeb Payne, that she didn't even want to look at her. "Maybe I don't want to talk to you."

Naomi rose as quickly as she had sat down. "That's fine. We don't have to talk." She walked toward the door. "It was actually about your wedding."

"Wait," Annabelle urged. "Come and sit."

Naomi stopped, her hand on the doorknob. "Why should I?"

Annabelle rolled her eyes. "Please, come back. Tell me what you had to say."

Naomi returned to the chair and waited while Annabelle sat beside her. "I talked to Phoebe," she said. "We thought it would be nice to have the wedding out back, by the bay."

Annabelle already knew what she wanted. "A ceremony at Hickory Hill would be perfect. And I want a backdrop behind the minister, maybe a trellis filled with flowers."

"We can have whatever you want. A floral

backdrop would be beautiful, all the color splashed against the bay in the distance."

"Adrian and I have a few different dates we're considering."

"We'll need to finalize a guest list, too. Do you know who you'll invite?"

"No, not yet," she said, thinking about family, friends, schoolmates, those she knew from equestrian circles, Adrian's family, their friends, customers—it was overwhelming.

"Do you want a large formal wedding or a casual affair with fewer guests?"

"Adrian prefers a small wedding, probably family and a few friends. But I don't want to omit someone and have them hurt."

"We need to choose the date and develop the guest list so we can send the invitations."

Annabelle thought about Adrian's suggestions. "It shouldn't take long. I'll talk to Adrian tomorrow. Is Emma coming from New York?"

"If we give her enough notice, she will. But your brother can't come, not from New Orleans."

Annabelle pursed her lips. "Weddings are for family."

Naomi shrugged. "We can delay it, push it toward the end of fall. Emma will come, regardless. It'll just be difficult for Benjamin."

"I don't want to delay it," Annabelle said. "It already seems like we've waited forever."

"Your brother and sister have known Adrian their entire lives," Naomi said. "I'm sure they'll be very happy for you, whether they're here or not. I'll get letters off to Emma and Benjamin in the morning with proposed dates. If they come, they can always stay here for a few weeks."

"Yes, I suppose," Annabelle muttered. "I do miss them."

"We all do. And they miss us, too," Naomi said. "The announcement will run in the *Baltimore Sun* and *Annapolis Gazette* this Sunday."

Annabelle chuckled. "Artemis won't like that."

Naomi shrugged. "Too bad. He shouldn't have used my daughter like he did."

Annabelle was wary of her mother's sudden cooperation. She suspected an ulterior motive, which was so consistent with Naomi's character. "But you would have been quite content if I had married him instead of Adrian."

"It doesn't matter what I wanted," Naomi said. "You've made your decision, and so has Artemis."

"No thanks to you," Annabelle mumbled.

"Annabelle, it's over. I only want you and Adrian to be happy."

"Like you and father are happy?" Annabelle snapped, unable to forgive what she'd overheard at Zeb's cottage.

Naomi turned, eyes flashing. "Your father and I are very happy. And we always have been."

"Zeb Payne might not agree."

"I should smack your face," Naomi snarled. She sprung from the chair and started for the door.

"But you won't," Annabelle said smugly. "Because I know your secret. And you're terrified I'll reveal it."

Naomi eyed her daughter for a moment, anger shifting to sadness. She sighed, walked back across the room, and sat beside her. "It's time you knew the truth."

Chapter Eighty-Six

"**I** was born in Soufriere, St. Lucia," Naomi began. "My father was wealthy, involved with trade, sugar mostly, but other products as well. My mother was sickly—she never adapted to the tropics—and she died of fever when I was very young."

Annabelle sat back in her chair. "I thought you were from Baltimore," she said crisply.

Naomi shook her head. "No, although I met your father in Baltimore."

"Does he know you're from St. Lucia?"

Naomi hesitated. "No, he doesn't." It was a pivotal moment. Her relationship with Annabelle would forever change if she told the truth. It could be better, founded on trust, or it might no longer exist.

Annabelle's face firmed. "How many other secrets have you kept?"

Naomi didn't answer. "I married young," she continued, determined to reveal everything. "I was only seventeen, wed to a man named Rufus Jackson who was much older than I was."

Annabelle listened, doubt and betrayal housed in her eyes. "You had another husband?"

Naomi nodded. "I did. We were married almost two years."

Annabelle's face flushed. "Does my father know?"

"Yes, he does. I was a young widow when I met him."

"In Baltimore? Or is that another lie?"

"I left St. Lucia and came to Baltimore. Phoebe was

with me. Then and now."

"Why am I just hearing this?" Annabelle snapped.

"Because it's time I told the story. But before I continue, you must swear you will never repeat it."

Annabelle hesitated, knowing what she was about to hear might change her life forever. "I won't tell a soul," she promised.

Naomi searched her face for sincerity. When she found it, she continued. "Rufus Jackson was the richest man in Soufriere. He dabbled in everything—politics, shipping, farming, real estate. He was the envy of everyone, and I was his wife, the most prominent woman in the entire city, almost a queen to the poor."

Annabelle slowly shook her head, her mother's fascination with social status now explained. "I don't know you at all," she whispered. "You're a total stranger. My whole life has been a lie."

"You don't know who I was," Naomi said. "But you know who I've become. And that's what's most important."

Annabelle kept her gaze fixed on her mother. "You said you were a widow when you met my father."

Naomi nodded. "I was. But it's a long story."

"Tell me," Annabelle urged. "Even though I may not like what I hear."

Naomi sighed, framed her thoughts, and continued. "My father fell ill. Since my husband was such a successful businessman, my father trusted him with his holdings. After several weeks passed, my father's health improved. He sought to regain control of his assets."

Annabelle was listening intently, her initial anger fading. "Rufus wouldn't give them back, would he?"

Naomi shook her head. "No, he wouldn't. It turned out that Rufus Jackson wasn't a brilliant businessman. Or the envy of everyone. He was a swindler, a fake and a fraud, a con man who stole whatever he could get his hands on, usually wrapped in some sort of legal framework. He took from the rich. He took from the poor. And he got away with it because he terrified everyone, even the police."

"What did your father do?"

"There wasn't much he could do," Naomi said. "Or me, either. Rufus was devious, and very good at what he did. After my father became a pauper, his health declined rapidly. He died soon after. We were devastated."

Annabelle knitted her brow. "Who is we? You and Phoebe?"

"And my older sister, Jenna."

Annabelle's eyes widened. "I have an aunt?"

Naomi nodded. "Yes, you do. She left St. Lucia after our father died, the pain unbearable. She emigrated to Australia. I haven't seen her in many years. But we do exchange letters."

"Does father know you have a sister?"

"Yes, of course he does."

"Will I ever meet her?"

Naomi shrugged. "It's a long journey. I've invited her to Hickory Hill many times, but I'm not sure she has the means to get here, or the time. I'll extend the invitation again, making it clear she comes at our expense."

"What happened to your husband?"

Naomi frowned, disgust written on her face. "He was nasty in so many ways, beyond belief for those with a heart and soul. After my father died and Jenna left, I realized what a monster he really was. I couldn't face those he swindled, the pain in their eyes. I had to leave him."

"Is that when you came to Baltimore?"

Naomi shook her head. "No, not yet. It got even worse, too much for anyone to endure. I tried to leave, but he wouldn't let me."

Annabelle pursed her lips. "How could he stop you?"

An awkward silence ensued. Naomi eyed her

closely, seeking compassion, searching for just a thread of understanding. She quietly stood, turned her back to her daughter, and lowered her dress. Then she slid her chemise down her back.

Annabelle gasped. "My Lord!" she exclaimed. She stared at her mother's back, marked with ugly red and purple welts.

"He beat me with a whip," Naomi said. She raised her chemise and dress back up to her shoulders and sat down.

Annabelle cringed, closing her eyes tightly, as if trying to will the image away. She took Naomi's hand, holding it tightly. "I am so sorry. I never knew." She hesitated, both compassion and curiosity etched in her eyes. "But I'm sure father does. He must."

Naomi nodded. "Of course, he does. But he doesn't know where I came from or what I did next."

Annabelle leaned closer, still holding her hand. "What did you do next?"

"I killed Rufus Jackson."

Annabelle gasped, her hand covering her mouth. "You *killed* him? How?"

"Yes, I killed him," Naomi said, the first time she had ever admitted it. "With Phoebe's help. We made a potent poison and mixed it in his dinner. It killed him, but he suffered horribly before he died." She looked away, her finger dabbing a stray tear from her eye. Then she fixed her gaze on Annabelle's. "I enjoyed watching him suffer."

Annabelle shivered but passed no judgment. She sighed, let go of her mother's hand, and leaned back in her chair. "You didn't get caught?"

Naomi shook her head. "No, but I came close. That night, when the authorities came, they first assumed he had suffered a heart attack. But then they took samples from a whiskey glass—they suspected poison—and they were returning the next day to investigate further."

"Is that when you and Phoebe fled?"

Naomi nodded. "I knew whatever remained of my father's fortune was in a safe hidden in Rufus's study. I opened it and took everything—most of which has since been invested in Hickory Hill. I had arranged for a small boat to take us out to the channel, to a waiting ship. We booked passage and went to Baltimore."

Annabelle slowly shook her head. "For all these years, you got away with murder."

"Until now," Naomi said.

Annabelle looked at her, head cocked, and a vague understanding crossed her face. "Zeb Payne?"

Naomi nodded. "The boat that took us to the clipper was owned by Zeb Payne's father. His closest friend was the inspector who investigated the murder."

"What a terrible coincidence," Annabelle muttered.

"No, it isn't a coincidence," Naomi said. "Zeb Payne has spent his entire life trying to find me. He finally succeeded. And he knows everything."

Chapter Eighty-Seven

Jacob Yoder and Samuel Zook left Billy Giles at the crossroad and returned to Jacob's farm. The night was still, a faint rustling in the trees, rows of corn and wheat swaying gently in a damp breeze. They felt sure no one had seen them in Chestertown during the jail break or when they'd made their escape. At least no one had wandered the streets. A resident may have peeked from a window, but they would have only seen shadows leaving by carriage in the dead of night.

It was just before 2 a.m. when Jacob steered the buggy into the barn.

"Not a word to anyone," Samuel Zook said as the climbed from the carriage.

Jacob nodded. "A word has never been spoken, at least not from my lips."

"Which is why I sought your help in the beginning. No one else."

"I'm honored," Jacob said, suspecting his friend hoped for further collaboration. "But this is my last. No more for me."

"My thanks for all you've done," Samuel said, lightly touching his arm. "You've helped so many people. They'll never forget you."

Jacob nodded, proud of his successes, as he helped Samuel get his horse ready. They spoke no more, words weren't needed. The bond between them could not be broken, the adventures they shared never forgotten, the lives they'd changed too many to mention.

"I'll come by for produce in a few days," Samuel

said as he climbed up on his horse and led it from the barn.

The rain started just as Samuel rode off, hard and steady. Jacob unharnessed the horses and put them in their stalls. He grabbed the pitchfork, tossed them hay and went to the door, waiting to see if the rain might ease. When it didn't, he sprinted to his house, pausing on the front porch to catch his breath. A crack of thunder shook the heavens, a streak of lightning snaked behind it. The rain came harder, shallow lakes forming where the soil was too soaked to absorb it. The stream rose higher on its banks, already swollen from recent rains.

Jacob went inside, gently closing the door behind him. He quietly removed his boots, the kitchen still fresh with the aroma of Ruth's stew. He paused to enjoy it, so grateful for the blessings he had received—a good family, his farm, a rewarding life. He had all a man could want, and he thanked the Lord for providing it. He crept to his bedroom and undressed, putting his clothes over a straight-backed chair against the wall.

Ruth leaned up on one elbow, watching him in the dark. "Is everyone safe?"

"Yes," he whispered, not wanting to wake the children, "All went as planned."

She sighed with relief. "No one saw you?"

"No, we were in and out quickly."

"That ends it," she said, her tone firmer than she typically spoke to her husband.

He climbed into bed and wrapped his arms around her, her warm back against his stomach. "Yes, that ends it," he promised.

They slept late, awakened by the children. Ruth started breakfast while Jacob went out on the porch. The rain still fell but had tapered off, and he ran across the field to the hen house. He fed the chickens, collected a few eggs and hurried back to the house.

Eli and Elizabeth were eating flapjacks and

scrapple, drinking cider. Jacob went over to Ruth, stood behind her at the stove, and wrapped his arms around her. He lowered his hand to her swollen belly, gently caressing it.

"It won't be much longer," Ruth said. "Two weeks, maybe three."

He kissed the top of her head, so grateful for such a wonderful woman, and helped her finish breakfast. They sat and ate, neither speaking much, smiling as they listened to the children ramble. It was different now, and as much as they wanted to help others, they no longer could. It was time to focus on family, without the stress and fear.

After breakfast, Jacob stepped outside. The rain had slowed to a drizzle, the fields too wet to work. He went to the barn and grabbed a damaged harness, sat on a bench by the barn door, and started to mend it.

"Thought the rain would never stop," Sheriff Dodd said.

Jacob jumped, looking up. "I didn't hear you approach."

Dodd made no apology. His face was stern, his eyes cold. "You didn't see that runaway come through, did you?"

"What runaway?" Jacob asked, his heart racing.

"Billy Giles."

Jacob shook his head. "I haven't seen anyone. Not with all the rain."

"He's missing," Dodd said. "Wasn't in jail when I went by this morning."

Jacob shrugged and tended the harness. "I don't know where he could be."

"Where were you last night, around midnight?"

"Asleep," Jacob said curtly.

Dodd stared at him, face firm. "I don't like you, Yoder. And I make that known."

"Yes, you do, Sheriff. Quite often."

"And I'd run you out if I could. No matter how good your missus cooks."

Jacob sighed, tired of their constant combat. "You've made that clear, too, Sheriff."

"But if I find you've been harboring runaways, you'll wish you never met me."

Jacob didn't reply. He focused on the harness.

Dodd watched him, hands on hips. "I'm going to look around."

"Go ahead," Jacob said, not raising his eyes.

Dodd started on the other side of the barn. He rummaged through equipment—harnesses, the wagon and carriage—and then searched through stores of hay and feed. He ended at the back, pens that sheltered livestock from bad weather. But with the sun poking through clouds, the pens were empty, cows and pigs outside. Dodd came back through, stopping to search when he felt the need.

"I'll find it," he said when he reached Jacob.

"Find what?"

"Wherever you hide them."

"Who are you talking about?" Jacob asked tersely.

"The runaways," Dodd said, looking out as the weak sun fought to dry remnants of rain. "Maybe they're in the smokehouse."

"Go look," Jacob said, hoping he would leave.

Dodd entered the first stall, moving around the horse to the far wall. He paused, eyeing the stone foundation.

Jacob tensed. He didn't look, pretending to work the harness. He tried to stay calm, to not seem interested, but his hands trembled.

Dodd was inches from the secret door. He touched the panel that extended past the foundation, reins and rope hanging from hooks at the top. He stepped back and studied it.

"Is something wrong, Sheriff?" Jacob asked, trying

to distract him.

"Maybe," Dodd mumbled. He turned to Jacob. "If the other side of the barn is for storage, why hang rope and reins inside a horse stall?"

"It's where I use them," Jacob said, his heart racing.

Dodd grabbed one of the hooks and tugged. The panel creaked. He tugged harder, and the door burst open, exposing the cave tucked in the knoll.

"I store Ruth's preserves in there," Jacob said hastily.

Dodd laughed. "I'm not stupid, Yoder. And neither are you." He poked his head inside. "I see sunlight. Air holes maybe. Stinks of sweat, too."

Jacob didn't reply. There wasn't much he could say. He couldn't deny it, although he hadn't been caught with an actual runaway. He wasn't sure what Dodd could prove in a court of law—if anything.

Dodd leaned out of the cave and closed the door. "You're in a lot of trouble, Yoder."

Chapter Eighty-Eight

Adrian got his buggy ready late Saturday afternoon. He hitched a horse and pulled it just outside the barn. "We're ready," he called to Coffey.

She was attaching labels to jars of cream at the end of the barn. As she approached the buggy, she looked at him strangely. "What are you doing, Mr. Reed? The older man takes me back to Hickory Hill in the wagon. Don't say much, real quiet, but he don't bother me none, neither."

"Not today," Adrian said. "I'm taking you."

She smiled shyly. "But Mr. Reed, I can't go in the buggy with you."

"Why not?"

She moved her hand to her mouth, as if asked the unthinkable. "It ain't proper. Everybody knows that. Folks would talk, say bad things about you."

Adrian laughed. "Who says it isn't proper?"

"All folks—white or black. I can't ride in a buggy with my master. It ain't right."

"Don't be silly," he said. "I'm not your master. I'm your business partner. And it's my buggy. I decide who rides in it."

Coffey shook her head. "If you say so, sir. But you makin' a real mess for yourself."

He offered his hand, helping her climb up. "Not so bad, is it?"

She smiled. "Wait 'til you see the look folks give."

"I don't care, and neither should you." He climbed in beside her, snapped the reins, and the buggy jerked forward. "It's a short ride. We won't see anyone anyway."

Coffey was quiet while they got underway, a sullen look on her face. She didn't seem eager to go back to Hickory Hill—not after losing Billy.

Adrian felt the sadness her eyes showed. "It'll be hard at first," he said softly. "But easier as time passes."

"Ain't never gonna get no easier for me, Mr. Reed," she said, eyes misty. "They done stole my heart. I ain't never gonna get it back."

He wasn't sure what to say. "It may help spending time with those who loved him."

"I do gotta talk to Miss Venus, Billy's momma, and his daughter Betsy. Just pay my respects and such. I bet they hurtin' real bad."

"Everyone who knew him is hurting. He was a good man."

"He just wanted to be free," she said, struggling to understand why he was dead. "That's all. Talked about it all the time. He used to say, 'Coffey, I know there's a big world out there.'"

Adrian smiled. "He had dreams, just like you."

"I can't dream as big as Billy did," she said, eyes wide. "No, sir. No one can. He was always askin' what was across the water or at the end of a rainbow. Or he wondered why the reverend was free and he was a slave."

"He wanted a better life," Adrian said. He hoped talking about Billy was helping her, like a catharsis. "We all do."

"He had big dreams for his daughter, too," she continued. "He loved that little child so much. Wanted her to learn her letters, maybe go to school someday."

Adrian was touched by what she said, simple dreams most take for granted—traveling across the bay, learning to read and write, wondering how other people lived. He hadn't told Coffey she would be free after he married Annabelle. It wasn't his place. But listening to her made him wish he could free all the slaves, give them the life they chose, whether they wanted to stay on the plantation or explore the unknown. It should be their decision. They wouldn't be property; they wouldn't be owned.

As they approached Hickory Hill, Coffey grew quiet, as if she wondered whether she had the strength to face those in pain.

"Don't do anything foolish," Adrian said softly.

"I don't know what you mean, Mr. Reed."

"I think you do," he said. He referred to Zeb Payne. And she knew it. "The time will come for justice. It just isn't today."

She hesitated as if she wanted to speak but was afraid to. "If you say so, Mr. Reed."

"It's not because I say so, but because it's a battle you can't win. Not alone. His time will come. Be patient."

"I understand," she said. "I know you're right. You always are."

Adrian turned into Hickory Hill and went down a slender lane that led to the bay. The cluster of slave shacks were nestled in the clearing.

"I'll be back to get you Monday morning," he said. "We'll ride in the buggy again."

She laughed as she climbed out of the coach. "If you say so, Mr. Reed."

"Promise you'll be careful."

"I will, sir. I always do what you tell me."

Chapter Eighty-Nine

On Saturday evening, after the slaves had come back from the fields, Naomi hurried across the back lawn. When she reached the smokehouse, she peeked around the corner, looking back at the mansion. No one sat in the chairs sprinkled around the balconies, bathed by bay breezes. Curtains swished in open windows, but no one appeared. The upper floor, quarters for house servants, was eerie and still.

She crept forward, stopping at the corner of the flower garden, hidden from the house. Her breath came quick, her pulse rapid. She tried to calm herself. In minutes it would be over. Zeb Payne would be gone. She took one last glance in all directions. When she was satisfied no one was watching, she scurried through the trees that screened the cottage from the rest of the plantation.

She approached slowly, listening. It was quiet, not a sound from inside. The porch was empty. For an instant she wondered if he was there. But he must be. She had something he wanted. He wouldn't risk losing it.

She took a deep breath, seeking courage she couldn't find. She had to keep control, outsmart a man who was stronger—if a physical altercation ensued. It would be different from prior visits. This was the last, when all was at stake. He would insist on taking everything, even what she refused to give. She climbed the porch steps and paused at the door. Trying to steady a trembling hand, she knocked twice. She had to be brave, not intimidated, not afraid.

The door swung open. Zeb stood, grinning. "I've been waiting for you." His gaze met hers and scanned her body, stopping when he liked what he saw. "I'm looking forward to finishing our transaction." He eyed her lewdly. "Every bit of it."

"It'll be quick," Naomi said, sounding braver than she felt. She strutted past him into the parlor.

He closed the door. The tumblers clicked, the door locked.

She sat frozen in the same chair she had been in during her last visit. She tried desperately to pretend nothing was wrong.

Zeb sat beside her, the tiny table between them. He looked at her expectantly. After an awkward moment, he reached out his hand. "You owe me four hundred dollars."

She took coins from her pocket. Ignoring his outstretched hand, she set them on the table. She didn't want to touch him. "This finalizes our agreement. Sixteen hundred dollars. Two year's wages."

He grabbed the coins, stacking them. "Doesn't seem like enough."

"But it is," she said firmly. "More than enough."

He enjoyed aggravating her. "I haven't decided where I'll go. Texas, maybe Louisiana."

"I really don't care. As long as you're gone."

"I'll leave tonight. As soon as we're done."

"We are done," she said, standing.

He started laughing. "No, we're almost done."

Naomi was trembling. But she had to be strong. "You will never breathe a word about me, Hickory Hill, or St. Lucia."

"My mouth is closed," he assured her as he rose from his chair. "But if it wasn't, you couldn't do anything."

"I'll track you down," she said coldly. "No matter where you are." She didn't finish her threat. She didn't have to. The implication was enough.

He took a step closer. "Aren't we brave?" He chuckled and touched her hair, caressing the silky strands. "So nice."

She pulled away and turned toward the door. She took only a few steps when he grabbed her arm and spun her around.

"We're not finished." He was breathing heavy, his eyes evil.

"Oh, yes, we are," she insisted, wrenching away.

He grabbed her again, wrapping his arms around her. "I've been waiting for this," he muttered, his stinking breath hot and wet.

"Let me go!" she demanded, twisting her torso.

"Not a chance," he grunted.

"Stop it!"

He yanked her to the floor and pinned her down.

She lay on her stomach. He sat on her back. She squirmed, kicked, swung her arms. "I'll scream," she threatened.

He laughed. "And I'll punch you. Not in the face, though. Too beautiful. But it'll hurt. I promise."

"Let me go!" she screeched. "If you do, I won't tell the sheriff."

He grabbed her shoulders. With surprising strength, he flipped her on her back. He wedged his knees between her legs, prying them open, grabbing her hands.

She tried to push him away. "Stop! You can't do this!"

"Oh, yes I can," he snarled. "And I will."

"No!" she insisted, eyes clenched closed, trying to pull away.

He forced her hands over her head. Pushing them together, he clenched them with his left hand, freeing his right. "You'll love this as much as I will."

"Stop it! Please!"

A coarse grin crossed his face, lust lit his eyes. He pushed her legs farther apart. With his free hand, he fumbled with his trousers. He yanked her dress up and clawed at her undergarments. Ripping them from waist to thigh, he exposed her.

She squirmed, twisting her wrists. When he touched her flesh, she groaned, raised her legs, pretended to cooperate.

"Oh, that's better," he moaned, distracted, his hand touching, his fingers probing.

She wrenched her hand away and grabbed Phoebe's knife from her stocking. Before he could react, she plunged it into his torso, just under his armpit.

"Ahh!" he cried. The blade pierced muscle and dug deep. "What are you doing!"

She twisted the blade, making it hurt. She withdrew it, shoving it in his side.

Anger flashed in his eyes. He leaned up and swung his fist, hitting her hard in the abdomen.

Air was forced from her lungs. She gasped, choking, fighting to breathe. She poked him weakly with the knife, stabbing his chest, neck, stomach. He tried to grab her, but she swung wildly. Most of her thrusts barely pierced him. But some sank deep.

He hit her again and again, in the stomach, ribs, her breasts. But each blow got weaker, some missed completely. Blood oozed from his gashes, dripping steadily where the knife had done damage. It stained his shirt and spilled onto her dress, warm and sticky, oozing into puddles and drenching the cloth.

She stabbed frantically, freed her other hand, and pushed him away. He tumbled off, falling to the floor, stunned and groaning. She scrambled to her feet, fighting to breathe. Her body ached, the pain intense. She sprinted for the door.

He grabbed her foot, pulling sharply. She tripped, falling. He yanked her towards him. "You'll pay for this, Naomi!"

She kicked him in the mouth

He twisted away, spitting blood. "You're done for."

"Let go of me!" she screamed, kicking the side of his head.

"Never," he grunted. He tried to rise, struggling.

She scrambled to her feet and ran to the door. She turned the knob. It didn't open.

He stumbled upright, his body wavering as he staggered toward her.

She fumbled with the lock, her hands shaking.

Chapter Ninety

Coffey Green climbed from Adrian Reed's buggy and crossed the clearing to her shanty. The aroma of beef cooking mixed with chimney smoke and drifted on the bay breeze. Children played in the grass, running and laughing. Their parents sat on porches, resting after a hard day's work, chatting with neighbors.

She stepped on the crooked porch—one end of the roof dipped lower than the other. She eyed the weathered bench where she had often sat and chatted with Billy, and she tapped on the door. A moment later, it opened.

"Coffey, honey, you ain't gotta knock," Molly said.

"I feel like I'm bustin' in." She glanced around the empty shack, a table and a few old chairs, straw mattresses. It hadn't changed since she'd seen it last.

Molly laughed. "It's your home, too."

"I ain't here much. At least not lately."

"Coffey, I'm so sorry about Billy," Molly said, misty-eyed, hugging her tightly. "Zeb Payne told us what happened."

"Thank you," Coffey whispered, a few tears trailing down her cheeks. "He was a good man, he really was."

Molly gently pulled away. "He was a dreamer. Had all kinds of plans, didn't he?"

"He did," Coffey said, wiping her eyes and forcing a smile. "I wish I could be more like him."

"That man asked a thousand questions," Molly continued as she moved toward the fireplace. "How come the reverend free and I'm not? What's Baltimore? How come the sun sinks over the bay?" She stopped, chuckling. "He was different, our Billy."

"Yes, he was," Coffey said as she sat on a straight-backed chair. "I miss him."

"We all do, honey. It's hard."

"I'm gonna stop and see Venus and Betsy in a bit."

"They hurtin' bad," Molly said. "Poor people."

Coffey sighed. It would be difficult—too much hurt, tears, and pain. But she had to see them, pay her respects. "Where's the girls?" she asked, referring to Molly's daughters.

"They runnin' around somewhere. I was just cookin' up some stew. Do you want some?"

"It sure smells good. But I'll get some later. I gotta bring dinner to Zeb Payne."

"He's a stern master but seems fair," Molly said, stirring the pot that hung over a tiny fire. "Gets a lot of work outa us."

"Yes, he does," Coffey muttered but shared nothing else.

"I work so hard in the fields I don't do nothing when the day is done. Same with my girls. They gettin' good with tobacco, though."

Coffey was quiet, thinking of Billy and Adrian Reed. Both could see a future where children didn't work the fields. But now their days remained unchanged as months became years, until a lifetime had come and gone. Her heart broke for the poor children who wouldn't see anything but Hickory Hill. They'd never know how the rest of the world lived. Just like her and Molly and Phoebe and Caesar.

Molly turned, head cocked. "You all right, Coffey?"

She nodded and forced a smile. "Just dreamin' a little myself."

Molly chuckled. "Like Billy."

Coffey nodded and stood. "I best get Mr. Payne's dinner for him. Ain't no rest until I do."

"I'll save you some stew," Molly promised.

Coffey left, passing the trellis where the slave wedding had been, the flowers brown and withered. She went to the kitchen, but Phoebe wasn't there. Another house servant had dinner ready for Zeb Payne, tucked in a basket and covered with cloth to keep it warm. With a sense of dread, because she knew what would likely happen, she took the basket and went to his cottage.

She heard noises as she approached—shouts, screams, threats—people struggling. She hurried up onto the porch, and, as she reached the front door, someone fumbled with the lock.

"Let go of me!" Naomi Banks screamed.

"Never," Zeb Payne grunted.

Coffey put the basket down. She took out the knife she'd found in Adrian's barn. It was old and rusty but had cleaned up sharp. Just as she touched the door, it flung open. Naomi Banks ran out, her dress soaked with blood. Zeb Payne followed, a few feet behind, his arm stretched out, his fingers inches from her shoulder. His shirt was splattered with blood, his face contorted with rage.

"Come back here!" he screamed.

He crossed the threshold onto the porch. Coffey thrust her knife into his stomach, just below his ribs.

"Coffey!" he shrieked. He stared, stunned, not moving.

She took every ounce of hatred, shame, and desperation she had and turned it into strength. She shoved the blade in to the hilt, twisting and turning, cutting up his insides.

Naomi stared at the knife in his belly. Eyes wide, face pale, body trembling, it still wasn't enough. She leaped forward, her stiletto high, and stuck it in his right eye as far as it would go.

Zeb Payne screamed, a hideous screech that echoed off the bay. He fell straight back, dead before he hit the floor.

Chapter Ninety-One

Adrian held the reins loosely, steering the buggy down the dirt road that led from Hickory Hill to his home. Fields of wheat and tobacco, along with some corn, yielded to trees as he approached his property. He had almost reached his house when a figure in the distance darted from the edge of the road into the foliage. Visible for only seconds, almost a shadow, it vanished as quickly as it had appeared. He kept his gaze fixed on the location, searching for movement, unable to believe what he'd seen. Was it a man? Or a ghost?

He stopped his buggy where the figure had faded. "Billy," he called.

It was quiet. Tree branches blew in the breeze, a few birds sang. A squirrel scampered up and down a tree, watching him curiously. "Billy," he called again. "It's Adrian Reed. You're safe. Come on out."

Branches parted a moment later. Billy stepped out on the road. "I thought that was you," he said.

Adrian stared at him with disbelief. "I thought you were dead."

"No, they was just givin' me a good scare. Tricked Zeb Payne first. Got more money for Amos Quigg."

"Weren't they going to hang you?"

"They wanted me to think so, scare me real bad so I'd never run off again."

Adrian cocked his head. "You didn't kill a man?"

"No, sir, turns out I didn't. They just made me think I did."

Adrian sighed and shook his head. "I don't

understand."

Billy explained. "I shoved a man when he tried to grab me. He fell, banged his head against the wall. Got a nasty gash on his head, but he wasn't dead."

"Zeb Payne told Coffey and me that you were in jail, ready to be hung," Adrian said, still not sure what had happened.

"I was, sir. But they was only waitin' until Amos Quigg got more money from Mr. Payne."

"So they never intended to hang you?"

Billy shook his head. "No, sir. Only wanted to make me think Zeb Payne saved me so I'd stay loyal to Hickory Hill and everyone else would, too. They thought it was funny."

Adrian paused, shaking his head. "What demented mind dreamed this up?"

"Amos Quigg, mostly. But Sheriff Dodd helped."

"I understand paying damages to the man you injured, like a fine levied for assault. But why would they let you think you had killed someone?"

"Mr. Yo—." He hesitated, not saying the name. "The man who helped me get away told me Amos Quigg wanted me to suffer."

Adrian's eyes widened. "You escaped?"

Billy looked at him sheepishly. "Yes, sir. Busted right out of jail. Didn't hurt nobody, though."

Adrian frowned and shook his head. "Oh, Billy, this could be bad. I suspect you're in quite a bit of trouble, more than you realize."

Billy shrugged. "I suspect so, too, sir."

Adrian was still putting pieces together. "I'm not sure why Zeb would tell Coffey they planned to hang you. Especially if he knew they weren't."

Billy frowned. "Probably told my momma and daughter too."

"I'm sure he did. But why?"

"Because Zeb Payne is pure evil, that's why. He wanted everybody to think he saved me, that he's such a good man. But he a child of the devil."

Adrian would never understand the hate that lived in some hearts. "What are you doing out here, so close to Hickory Hill? Aren't you worried about getting caught."

Billy shrugged. "I got half a mind to beat Zeb Payne senseless."

"That would only make it worse. You're in enough trouble."

"I come to get my momma and daughter. And my woman, Coffey Green. We gonna escape together."

Adrian sighed. "You'll never make it, not now. Everyone will be looking for you. You'll only put your loved ones at risk."

"I don't know what else to do."

Adrian was quiet, creating a plan. "I think I know," he said after a moment. "I'll take you to Mr. Banks. We'll say you came back voluntarily."

"They'll whip me good and make it worse than before."

"No, they won't. Mrs. Banks mentioned selling you after you were caught."

"Then I don't know where I'll go. And I'll never see my momma or Betsy or Coffey again."

"I'll buy you," Adrian assured him. "But it'll be different. I'll make you a free man. You can work for me if you like."

"That ain't no freedom, sir. Much as I'm obliged."

"I'll pay you to work *with* me."

Billy's eyes widened. "Pay me like white folks?"

"Yes," he said. "I pay Coffey now. She helps me." He chose not to share that Coffey would soon belong to him—even though he found it distasteful.

Billy shrugged. "That sounds real good, Mr. Reed. But I don't think Miz Banks will go along."

"I'll worry about Mrs. Banks," Adrian said. "Come on, get in the carriage."

Billy hesitated. "You want me to ride with you?"

"Yes, I do. Come on, get in."

"If you say so, sir." Billy climbed in and sat beside him. "I can't believe you doing all this just for me."

"You're a good man, Billy. You deserve to be happy. Let's go see Mr. Banks."

"Can I stop and see my folk first? They all think I'm dead."

"Yes, of course," Adrian said. It only seemed right. Even though he had to speak to Gideon and Naomi before Sheriff Dodd or Amos Quigg tracked Billy back to Hickory Hill. "But only for a minute. We need to make all of this right."

Adrian retraced his route, guiding the buggy back to the clearing clustered with slave shacks. "I'll wait here," he said to Billy when they arrived. "But hurry."

Billy ran to his momma's shack. He was gone for a few minutes, emerging with tears of joy in his eyes. He next went to Coffey Green's shanty. Molly answered his knock, hugged him tightly, and they talked for a moment. He came back to the buggy.

"Molly say Coffey went to bring Zeb Payne his supper."

Adrian had a sickening feeling. He climbed out of the carriage and tethered his horse. "Come on," he said. "Let's go find her."

Chapter Ninety-Two

"It's used to store preserves," Jacob Yoder insisted, referring to the cave. His palms were sweaty, his heart raced. Dodd had caught him, and now he had failed his family when they needed him most.

Dodd laughed, shaking his head. "It's for runaways. I know it and so do you. I finally got you, Yoder."

Jacob shrugged, feigning confusion. "There's no runaways here."

"It doesn't matter," Dodd said. "I knew you were up to something."

"I'm not up to anything," Jacob protested. "I'm raising my family and farming my land."

"And hiding runaways," Dodd muttered, glancing around the barn. "He came through here, didn't he?"

"Who?" Jacob asked, feigning ignorance.

"Billy Giles."

"I don't know what you're talking about."

Dodd grabbed Jacob's arm. "Where did he go?"

Jacob didn't reply. But his gaze shifted to the stream, the marsh beyond, toward Hickory Hill.

"The marsh!" Dodd exclaimed. "He's gonna hide out for a few days, isn't he?"

Jacob shrugged. "I haven't seen him, Sheriff."

"You're a horrible liar, Yoder. Stick to your Bible."

"I only want to be left alone."

"Too late," Dodd said, looking past the stream to the marsh. "I'll be back for you. And it won't be good." He stormed out of the barn, climbed on his horse, and started toward the stream.

"Sheriff, where are you going?"

"I'm gonna find Billy."

Jacob grabbed the horses' reins. "No, don't. You can't cross the stream, not after all this rain."

"Get out of the way," Dodd demanded. He flung his foot forward, kicking Jacob in the mouth.

Jacob's head snapped back. He fell to the ground, dazed. Blood oozed from his lip into his beard.

Dodd urged his horse forward, heading for the stream.

"Sheriff!" Jacob yelled. He leaped to his feet and ran after him. "Not the stream."

Dodd ignored him. He galloped to the water's edge. When his horse hesitated, he forced him into the water, smacking his rump. "Come on, boy, go!"

Jacob ran to the stream. It was deceiving, wider, deeper, the current strong. "Sheriff, don't! Go around. Take the road."

Dodd never looked back. He forged across, fighting the current. But the farther he went, the more his horse struggled. Its torso twisted, the depth past his belly. Dodd dug in his boots and smacked his rump. But they fought the current, made little progress, and started to drift downstream. Struggling, he turned to come back.

Jacob dashed to the barn. He grabbed a coil of rope and sprinted back to the stream. "Ruth!" he yelled. "Ruth, help me."

She came out on the porch. When she saw what was happening, she hurried toward the stream, her left hand supporting her stomach. Eli and Elizabeth trailed behind her.

Jacob reached the bank. Dodd's horse fought the water, making it back to shore.

Dodd had vanished.

"Sheriff Dodd!" Jacob yelled.

The day was quiet. Only a few birds chirped. The

water rippled, but Dodd's head wasn't bobbing above the surface.

"He went under!" Ruth screamed. She pointed toward an oak on the far bank. "Right over there. Give me the rope."

Jacob hesitated. He looked at her swollen belly. "No, it's too dangerous."

"Give it to me," she insisted. "I'll be fine."

He handed her one end. He kicked off his boots, wrapped the other end of the rope around his waist, and waded into the water.

Ruth wrapped the rope around the trunk of an oak. She held it firmly, dug her shoes into the soil with legs straight, and braced herself. "Stay here," she said to the little ones. "Don't get too close."

Jacob sloshed farther into the stream. He fixed his gaze on the tree Ruth had pointed at, swimming toward it. The bottom was uneven; sometimes he scraped it, sometimes it dropped away. He moved his hands through the murky water, reaching, feeling, searching. He was almost at the far bank when he saw Dodd's arm snagged on a branch, hanging over the water.

Jacob grabbed him, yanking his head above the surface. "I've got him!" he yelled to Ruth, swimming toward shore.

"I'll pull you in," Ruth called. She turned to the children. "Walk with mommy. Away from the water."

Ruth unwound the rope from the tree and started toward the house, shoving her shoes in the soil, the rope over her shoulder. The children walked beside her, watching as she tugged. The rope was taut, the tension helping.

Jacob came closer. He pulled Dodd, holding his head above the surface. "He's got a nasty cut on his forehead."

"Just get him to shore," Ruth shouted.

The current was strong. They plodded on, fighting. He towed Dodd, Ruth tugged. Once they passed midstream, there was less resistance and he swam quicker. A few minutes later he dragged Dodd on shore, up on solid ground.

Jacob laid him on his back. His face was pale, blood trickling from his head. "He's unconscious. And he swallowed a lot of water. I don't know if he's breathing."

Ruth hurried to the sheriff, stretched out and motionless. "Roll him on his stomach," she said, tugging on Dodd's arm, helping to turn him.

Jacob rolled him over. He looked to Ruth. "What now?"

"Wrap your arms around his waist and yank, like you're lifting him."

Jacob did as she directed. Dodd was lifeless, made no sounds, but water spilled from his mouth.

"Do it again," she urged. "Hurry!"

A second attempt had the same results. But after the third try, Dodd coughed, spitting water. He choked, gasping, and struggled to his knees. He paused, breathing heavily, blinking, then sat up in the mud, pale and disoriented.

"Yay," Eli and Elizabeth cheered. "He's all better."

Ruth leaned forward, lightly touching his forehead. "Are you all right, Sheriff?"

"I think so," Dodd said, eyes vacant. "But I'm not sure."

"Rest a minute, and we'll get you inside," Jacob said. He put on his boots, waited until the color came back to Dodd's face, and helped him rise.

"I'll bandage that gash," Ruth said. "And set you by the fire to dry out."

Dodd rose, unsteady. He looked at the family around him. "You saved my life," he mumbled.

"You would do the same for us," Ruth said, passing

no judgment. She never did.

Dodd eyed each in turn. A single tear trickled down his cheek, but he quickly wiped it away. "I think you're right," he said. He seemed to recognize who he had been—and what he should become. "I suspect I would."

"Come on," Ruth urged. "We'll take care of you."

Dodd staggered, leaning on Jacob. "I didn't see anything in the barn," he said softly.

Jacob nodded. "Thank you, I appreciate that. But from now on, I'll be focusing on my family. Nothing else."

Dodd nodded, eyeing the young family, seeing what he had never seen before. "You'll get no more trouble," he said. "Not from me." He reached down to muss Eli's hair. "Now, what are the little ones' names?"

Chapter Ninety-Three

Naomi gasped and stepped back, eyes wide. Zeb Payne was sprawled on the floor, face up. The stiletto stuck in his right eye; Coffey's knife was imbedded in his abdomen.

"He sure dead now, Miz Naomi," Coffey muttered, looking at her wide-eyed.

Naomi held her hand to her mouth, staring at the carnage. A crimson puddle oozed onto the porch, trickling from stab wounds. Her dress was stained; drips splattered her torso. The bodice was soaked with blood, and the cloth by her left breast stuck to her skin. Her undergarments had been torn nearly away, one side intact, the other hanging loosely down her thigh.

She stared at the corpse, unable to look away. Breathing heavily, feeling faint, she wasn't sure what to do. She had killed the second man in her life—far more brutally than the first. But both had been warranted. Would a court of law disagree?

"We gotta do something, Miz Naomi," Coffey said, her hands clasped over her heart. "Or we gonna be in a lot of trouble."

Naomi took a deep breath. Her pulse slowed; her body stopped trembling. "We have to get rid of the body."

"We better do it quick, 'fore someone comes along."

"We can't do it alone," Naomi mumbled. She was dazed, unable to think. "I need Phoebe. She'll know what to do. I'll go get her."

Coffey looked away from the body. "Don't let nobody see you. Or we be caught for sure."

"I won't," Naomi said. "I'll change my clothes and come back with Phoebe."

"I'll get some scrubbin' stuff. We gotta clean up this mess real good."

Naomi hurried from the cottage and paused in the trees. It was dusk, forty minutes before dark. She looked at the mansion. Candles flickered in windows—Gideon's study, Annabelle's bedroom, the servants' quarters on the third floor. Gideon and Annabelle were occupied. It was only the servants she had to avoid—and anyone who might come out on a balcony to catch the bay breeze.

She couldn't wait for darkness. She stumbled across the lawn, gasping, trying to fix her disheveled hair. Unable to think, she smoothed her wrinkled dress with her hands. But it was covered with blood. Wrinkles didn't matter. She paused at the garden, hidden from the house, and randomly yanked flowers from the far bed. Gathering a large bunch, she held them across her chest. They covered most of the stains, not all. She had to get to her room to change clothes. And she had to wash the blood seeping through her dress, soiling her skin. It made her nauseous.

She put her head down and hurried across the lawn. Not looking up at balconies, ignoring windows that faced her, she could only hope that no one watched. She cringed as she got closer. It was unlikely she could avoid the servants. When she reached the back door, she opened it slowly, listening, and then peered inside. No one approached. She crept down the hallway.

"Is that you, Naomi?" Gideon called from his study.

She froze. Not sure what to do, she waited as seconds ticked by. She couldn't go forward; she would have to pass his open door. Only the servants' stairs at the back of the house would let her get to her room without being seen.

"Naomi?" he called again.

She leaned against the wall, afraid to move. If he

came out into the hall, he would see her. When she didn't hear him moving about, she tiptoed to the servants' staircase. On the third step, the boards creaked. She paused, listening, but heard nothing. She pressed her body closer to the wall where the stairs were stronger and edged upward, avoiding the worn center of each step where thousands of footsteps had passed before hers. When she reached the second-floor landing, she could hear servants on the third floor, their voices faint.

Annabelle's bedroom door was closed, candlelight flickering underneath it. Naomi crept past to her bedroom. She hurried inside, closed the door, and leaned against it, sweat dotting her forehead. She tried to think. She had to be calm, cunning, rational. Eyeing the rope by the fireplace, she tugged it, ringing the bell to summon Phoebe in the room above.

A moment later, a light tap landed on the door. "Miz Naomi? You called me?"

Naomi came across the room and opened the door. "I need help."

Phoebe came in. She gasped, her hands to the side of her face. "My Lord, Miz Naomi. You hurt bad! Oh, Lord! What we gonna do!"

"No, I'm not hurt," Naomi said, grabbing her by the shoulders, trying to calm her. "It isn't my blood."

Phoebe quieted. A vague understanding crossed her face. She lowered her hands, her gaze fixed on Naomi's. "You killed him."

"I had to. I swear. I had no choice."

"I believe you, I do." She stepped away, looking at Naomi's dress. "Oh, Lordy be, what a mess."

"He wouldn't stop," Naomi insisted. "So I kept stabbing him. Then Coffey came, and she stabbed him, too."

"Where Coffey now?"

"She's getting something to clean up the mess.

Blood splattered everywhere."

"We got to get you out of those clothes. And then we got to get rid of 'em. Bury 'em, maybe."

"The corner of the garden," Naomi mumbled. "Where the flowers are. It can't be seen from the house."

Phoebe nodded. "Fine, we bury 'em there."

"We can remove the plants, bury everything, and put the flowers back."

Phoebe touched Naomi's shoulders and turned her around. She unbuttoned her dress. "I'll cut off the bloody parts. Less to bury."

Naomi slid the dress over her shoulders and stepped out of it. "My undergarments, too."

Phoebe looked, suspecting the worst. "Oh, my Miz Naomi. That bastard did deserve to die."

"I killed him before he got too far."

"We don't have to bury 'em," Phoebe said. "Just give 'em here, with the scraps from your dress. I'll make somethin' with them so nobody knows."

Naomi took a fragment from the dress and went to a washbasin on her bureau. She dabbed it in the water, washing away the smeared blood. Her whole body ached, bruises across her torso, purple and tender.

Phoebe wrapped the stained shreds from the dress into a ball, the rag included, and put it on the floor by the door. "Let's get you dressed."

"We have to get all this done tonight," Naomi said. "While it's dark."

Phoebe got undergarments and another dress out of the wardrobe. "Let's hurry then. We best get started."

Naomi slipped into her clothes. Phoebe pulled it up over her shoulders, and she slid her arms in.

"Where's the body?" Phoebe asked softly as she buttoned up the dress.

"On the cottage porch, by the front door."

Phoebe finished buttoning and gently turned Naomi

around. "We got to bury the body, too."

Naomi nodded, understanding. "At least it's Saturday night. No one will look for him until Monday morning."

"We gotta get started," Phoebe said. She grabbed the soiled shreds.

Naomi opened the door. Annabelle stood on the other side.

Chapter Ninety-Four

"What are you doing?" Annabelle asked, her gaze shifting to the bloody bundle.

Naomi started sobbing, tears trailing down her cheeks. "I killed him. I had to."

Annabelle's eyes widened. "What?" she hissed. She turned to Phoebe, looked at the clothes, and back to her mother.

"Come on, Miss Annabelle," Phoebe said gently. "You got to help us. We got a real mess to clean. Can't nobody ever know what your momma did. We gotta make it look like nothin' ever happened."

Annabelle looked at Naomi but saw a stranger instead. Her mother had always been strong, no cracks in the wall that seemed to surround her. Now she was close to collapse. It was startling, an image she couldn't have imagined only minutes before.

"Will you help us?" Naomi asked, eyes begging, her voice quivering.

Annabelle nodded, the decision easy to make. "Yes, of course. I'll do whatever has to be done. But we better hurry. Especially if it's as bad as you say."

"You right, Miss Annabelle," Phoebe said. "We gotta get going."

They hurried down the hallway, hoping Gideon didn't suddenly appear. But it was early, he would be tucked in his study for several more hours. They heard murmured conversations from the servants on the third floor but no one close or coming down the steps. When they reached the back stairs, Phoebe stopped.

"Let me go down first," she said. "If nobody's there, I'll wave for you to come."

Annabelle wrapped an arm around her mother's shoulder and pulled her close. "It'll be all right," she whispered. "I promise."

Phoebe appeared a moment later and waved for them to follow. They crept down the stairs, through the hall and out the back door.

Naomi led them along the route she had so often taken, to the back of the kitchen and smokehouse, across the lawn to the corner of the garden. "We can bury him here, along with the soiled clothes," she said. She pointed to the mansion. "No one can see us."

Annabelle looked back at the house, then at the kitchen and smokehouse, both vacant. "We have a lot of digging to do if we're going to bury him."

"Then we got to cover it all up," Phoebe added. "Make it look like nothin' happened."

Naomi peered through trees to the cottage and then eyed the garden. "We'll have to take out the flowers, dig the grave, and put everything back the way it was. No one will see us if we're careful."

Annabelle pursed her lips. How would they ever have time? And all without being seen. "Where's the body?" she asked, her mind racing.

"At the cottage," Naomi said, wiping a few stray tears from her eyes.

Annabelle doubted they could get away with murder, although her mother and Phoebe had done it once before. "What happened?" she asked as they hurried toward the cottage.

Naomi sighed as if trying to will everything away. "He was blackmailing me. Each time I saw him, he'd asked for more money. I went to give him the final payment and demanded that he leave."

"But he wanted somethin' else from your momma

before he'd go," Phoebe said. "I knew he would, monster that he is. Just like he been doin' to Coffey. I gave your momma a knife to take with her."

Annabelle visualized the picture they painted. "He had it coming," she said, passing no judgement.

"Coffey came at the end," Naomi said. "She helped me kill him."

"Good," Annabelle said with a morbid satisfaction. "She had the right."

"She went to get stuff to clean the mess up," Phoebe said as the trio approached the cottage.

They climbed the porch steps. Naomi crouched down beside the corpse. Phoebe and Annabelle hesitated, staring at the scene before them.

Zeb Payne lay on his back in a pool of blood. Coffey's rusty blade stuck from his torso; Naomi's stiletto was buried in his right eye. Multiple wounds dotted his body. His shirt was splattered with blood.

Annabelle came closer. When she saw the body, run through and rigid, she gasped, her hand to her mouth. She turned to her mother. "You sure wanted him dead, didn't you?"

Chapter Ninety-Five

"We all gonna have to help," Phoebe said. She eyed the corpse and the puddles of blood beside it

Naomi glanced at Annabelle. Each knew roles were about to reverse, master now servant. "Phoebe, just tell us what you want us to do."

Phoebe paused, looked at the corpse, and shook her head. "We need to get those plants dug up so we can bury him. Do you know where we keep shovels?"

Naomi shrugged. "No, I don't."

Phoebe sighed. "Then I guess I best go get 'em."

"Wait," Annabelle said, lightly touching her arm. "Coffey should be on her way back. I'll find her and tell her what we need."

Phoebe nodded. "That's fine, Miss Annabelle. While you gone, me and your momma can start cleaning, maybe drag the body over to the garden."

Annabelle hurried off the porch, looking for Coffey.

"Miz Naomi, find a sheet or something we can use to put him on," Phoebe said. "Don't take nothin' off the bed. Somebody gonna check."

Naomi went inside, She grabbed the gold coins Zeb had left on the table and shoved them in her pocket. She hurried into the bedroom, finding the bed mussed, the sheets disheveled. A book lay on the nightstand, a small oil lamp beside it. She checked a wardrobe filled with shirts, trousers, and jackets. A bureau near the window held socks and undergarments in the top drawer, towels and sheets in the bottom. As she grabbed a sheet, she saw the rest of the coins she had given Zeb, hidden underneath it. She took them and went back out to the porch.

Phoebe had torn off part of Zeb's shirt and was using it to soak up blood. She had taken the knives from the corpse and wiped them clean. "I found a bucket and some rags," she said as Naomi came out.

"He hadn't planned on leaving," Naomi said as she laid the sheet on the porch. "Nothing was packed."

"He wasn't going nowhere, Miz Naomi," Phoebe declared. "Had a good thing going. Even better if he got what he wanted from you—if you know what I mean."

Naomi soaked a rag and got on her knees, wiping blood and scrubbing the floor. It was a disgusting end to a vile man. It made her sick, and she almost vomited more than once.

Footsteps rustled across the path to the porch. Annabelle and Coffey approached, carrying buckets, shovels, soaps, and rags. Adrian Reed and Billy Giles were with them.

Naomi gasped, her hand on her heart. "But you're dead," she stuttered, staring at Billy Giles.

"Is that really you, Billy Giles!" Phoebe exclaimed.

"Yes, ma'am, it is," Billy said, smiling broadly.

"Oh, my Lord," Phoebe said. She hugged him. "I thought my voodoo queen momma done raised you from the dead."

Billy chuckled. "Quigg told everybody I was gonna hang. But it wasn't true."

Coffey wrapped her arm around him. "He just wanted to scare Billy, told folks he killed somebody. Then Zeb Payne was gonna bring him back, acting like a hero for saving him."

"But I did hurt a man," Billy confessed. "No excusin' that. Zeb Payne had to pay extra money. But then I run off. The sheriff out lookin' for me now. I'm in lots of trouble."

"I'm hoping to intervene on his behalf," Adrian

interjected. "Especially since he's willing to help tonight."

"I told Mr. Reed and Billy what happened," Coffey explained.

Naomi sighed. "I will owe you," she muttered, eyeing Billy. For perhaps the first time, she saw a man instead of property. "Especially if you keep your mouth shut. But I can't give you freedom. Gideon would get suspicious."

"I'll buy him," Adrian offered. "You did say you would sell him if he were caught. We can figure it out later. But Gideon should agree."

Naomi nodded. "Yes, of course, that should work." She turned to the group, looking at each, in turn. "Thank you all so much for helping me."

"Any one of us would have killed him," Coffey said.

Adrian paused. "We need to get started—clean up the mess, bury him, and hide his belongings. I can store them in my barn. And we must all have the same story, should anyone ask. Let's just say he found something better and left with no notice."

"At least he can't hurt nobody again," Phoebe muttered.

Coffey slowly shook her head. "Sometime you can't make a wrong right. You just have to do the best you can."

Epilogue

It was Monday afternoon before anyone realized Zeb Payne was missing. A search of the cottage found no personal belongings—everything else in the house belonged to the plantation. The wardrobe and bureaus were empty; nothing had been left behind.

Sheriff Dodd arrived late on Tuesday, poked around the cottage and immediate area, and asked questions of family, field hands and other slaves. He concluded that Zeb Payne had left covertly, likely for a better opportunity, to avoid a confrontation with Gideon and Naomi over his departure. No one noticed anything unusual in the flower garden.

Annabelle Banks and Adrian Reed were married a month later. The service was conducted on the back lawn, attended by eighty guests. As a wedding gift, her parents gave Annabelle one hundred acres of land that bordered Adrian's property and Coffey Green, who was offered her freedom shortly thereafter. Emma Banks came from New York for the wedding, stayed at Hickory Hill for over a month, and then relocated her family to Washington. Benjamin Banks also attended after arranging a coveted transfer from New Orleans to Fort McHenry near Baltimore. Gideon and Naomi were ecstatic at having their children close by, and father-son chess matches were once again played in person.

Annabelle won her equestrian competition in Annapolis, held shortly after the murder of Zeb Payne. On the land she'd received from her parents, she began raising horses and soon earned a stellar reputation, breeding many winners in both show and sport. She hired Luke, the Hickory Hill field hand, to make custom saddles and tack, starting another enterprise that quickly prospered. Her stables became famous, her horses prized possessions for many of the elite on both sides of the bay.

Adrian Reed bought Billy Giles from Gideon Banks and gave him his freedom. Coffey and Billy were married in a simple ceremony a few months later and were gifted a hundred acres of prime farmland by the Banks family. The Amish, led by Jacob Yoder and Samuel Zook, constructed a sturdy barn and house for them. Billy farmed his land while Coffey remained partners with Adrian Reed, producing a wide variety of household products.

True to Adrian's predictions, Reed & Sons discontinued construction of ocean-going ships, shrinking the family business and limiting production to pleasure craft. They never transitioned to steam-propelled vessels. Adrian developed an extensive distribution network, originally for Coffey's products before adding furniture built by Jacob Yoder and other Amish goods. He left the family business to form his own shipping enterprise, using railroads and steam-powered vessels to transport grains, tobacco, and seafood. In only a few short years, his annual revenue far exceeded that of Reed & Sons.

Artemis Wentworth married Sarah Harrison shortly after Annabelle's wedding and won his race for senator. He became a prominent figure in Washington politics until a financial scandal several years later became his undoing.

Naomi Banks was no longer haunted by the shadow that cloaked a twenty-five-year-old crime. It lay dormant, tucked in the annals of history, along with Zeb Payne's murder, which was never uncovered. She remains mistress of the manor, and the secrets of Hickory Hill will always be kept, passed through generations from her and Phoebe to Annabelle and Coffey Green. The truth will never be known.

BIO:

John Anthony Miller writes all things historical—thrillers, mysteries, and romance. He sets his novels in exotic locations spanning all eras of space and time, with complex characters forced to face inner conflicts, fighting demons both real and imagined. Each of his novels is unique: a Medieval epic, four historical mysteries, two Cold-War thrillers, two 1970's cozy/romances, a Revolutionary War spy novel, five WWII thrillers, and *The Secrets of Hickory Hill*. He lives in southern New Jersey.

Social Media:

Amazon Author Page:
https://www.amazon.com/stores/JOHN-ANTHONY-MILLER/author/B00Q1U0OKO
Facebook: John Anthony Miller | Facebook
Twitter: John Anthony Miller (@authorjamiller) / Twitter
Instagram: John Anthony Miller (@authorjamiller) • Instagram photos and videos
Goodreads: John Anthony Miller (Author of When Darkness Comes) | Goodreads

Made in United States
Orlando, FL
30 November 2024

54707903R00215